THE SILENT SON

BOOK TWO

ALEXIS L. MENARD

Midnight Tide
PUBLISHING

First Edition published April 2023

Editing by Brittany Corley

Copyediting by Stephanie Taylor

Cover and Interior Design by Gabrielle Ragusi

❀ Created with Vellum

For my husband. To Hel and back.

CONTENT WARNINGS

The Last Daughter is an adult fantasy romance that contains strong language and content some readers may find distressing, including violence, death, alcohol use, and graphic depictions of sexual themes.

CHAPTER 1
ERIK

Bodies piled across the deck.

His men, the few brave souls who joined him on this errand to save Ailsa, were all dead. Every last one, gutted or flayed, their open cavities still spilling and adding to the mess on the floor. Empty eyes stared up at a misty sky, nothing left in them to appease his guilt.

Erik stood in the center of them, an axe in one hand, a golden blade in the other. He remembered none of it, only waking to a warm wetness soaking his tunic and the sounds of beating wings. Valkyries flew above and dove to snatch each man from the crowded deck to carry their spirits to the realm of the slain. Each winged maiden eyed him with disdain in her limpid gaze. Their white wings breathed a tangible wind of disapproval as they ascended toward the sky.

Had he done this? Blood covered him, weapons in hand, but his memory blurred any explanation.

When the Valkyrie had taken the final fallen, he was alone on the boat with nothing but the empty vessels of his men. The shock wore off until he trembled so terribly, the weapons slipped from his grasp. The damp air swirling in the Realm Between Realms clogged in his lungs, worsening the tightness crushing his chest.

"Next time, you will do as I say," A voice behind him spoke. Cold and unforgiving, her words more daggers thrust into his heart.

"You..." he whispered, turning around to find the Volva witch. Her glossy hair was a deep ebony that complemented red lips, falling over the one shoulder she shrugged innocently.

"Yes, me again. Remember when I told you to take care of your crew, and you told me *no* all those nights ago?"

"Because they had done no wrong!" he shouted. "For what purpose did you want their lives?"

The witch only smiled. "My reasons do not matter, only your obedience. You made a deal with me. Our blood is covering your skin, inking into runes to bind you to my will. If I tell you to do something, you will do it. If you even think of disobeying me or refusing what I demand of you, I will take matters into my own hands." She spared a glance at the dead clansmen. "Know this, Erik. I was not as merciful as you could have been."

Erik staggered backward, tripping over the lifeless body of the blacksmith, Obretch. The one who had been on his side to rescue Ailsa from the beginning, his biggest supporter and probably the only reason any of the other men had followed.

"You did this to them?"

"That's not entirely true. It was *you* who killed them. I only acted through you."

He was going to be sick. This bargain was proving to hold more stipulations than he realized. "I don't want to do this anymore. You said nothing about controlling me like this.

Take back your power over me and find someone else to possess."

"Are you really giving up that easily?" she said, laughing at his discomfort. "Even when you're so close to your sweet little heathen?" Her bare feet stepped toward him, sinking in the bloody puddles. "Vanaheim is only a few days away at most. And your men are already dead. There is no bringing them back from the afterlife. You might as well keep going, or their deaths will have been for nothing."

But their deaths were already for nothing. They had trusted him, even after nearly facing their doom at the Edge of the World. That trust had never been so wrongly misplaced. This blame would never leave him for as long as he lived. He was grateful he could not remember, or the memory would most likely drive him mad.

Perhaps he already was.

"How am I to retrieve her from this demon's clutches? If he has allies in Vanaheim, how will I get her back? You have left me without a crew and with no protection."

She clicked her tongue, now standing on the opposite side of the dead blacksmith. "Your vengeance will not come easy, I will admit. The elfin, Vali, has brainwashed Ailsa with a spell, you see. He has tricked her into binding their life threads, so if you kill one, you will kill the other."

The spark of Erik's anger struck something in his blood, an accelerant that surged his pulse into a rage. If he couldn't kill the man who took his woman, if he couldn't take her away at all because of this spell, what was the point of coming all this way? How would he ever get her home now?

"Why did you send me all the way here if I cannot do what I came to accomplish? You could have told me that before I traveled across the Nine and killed my kin!" he roared. His voice echoed across the river carving through the Tree of Life, uncaring if the mist curled back as he shouted.

Her hand dipped into the sleeve of her gown and pulled out a glass vial. Inside rolled a clear liquid. "If we want to break this bond between them, we need Ailsa to forget everything that has happened between them since she left your shores. You can place this tonic in her drink. It is tasteless and odorless, so she will never know. It is the only way to unwind the braid of their threads back to their two original, separate strands."

Erik took the vial from the witch's hand and rolled it between his fingers. "I give her this, and it will break the enchantment? And then I can kill him with no consequence to Ailsa?"

"None. It will be like nothing ever happened between them, and you can take her home where she belongs. If you give her this tonic plain, she will forget everything. But if you place a few drops of his blood in it, she will only forget the elfin's strand. Anyone else she crossed along her life's thread will remain."

Pocketing the vial, he looked back at the witch. He couldn't trust her, not after what she had done to his men. But if what she said was true, and that man with yellow eyes and magic fingers truly enchanted Ailsa, then he had no choice but to work with her. To save Ailsa, he would risk anything. Even his morality.

The witch looked down at the dead man between them, turned his face with her toes to assess the wide laceration made across his throat. "I would suggest you come up with a good reason to be in Vanaheim, Erik. Because if she or Vali find out you are working with me, they will kill you."

"Ailsa would not—"

"She isn't the woman you used to coddle back in Drakame," she snapped. "She will protect him with her very life because hers and his are bound. Do not underestimate this spell the elfin has over her. It is strong, and you will not convince her she is enchanted. You'll need to play the long game with Ailsa if you wish to free her from this bond."

But Erik shook his head, unsure about this plan now that he was only days away from seeing her and this *Vali* again after months of vowing revenge. "I don't know if I can do this, witch. I am a fighter, not a schemer. Ailsa knows me better than anyone. She'll know if I'm lying. And surely, she will notice these runes on my arm!"

"No one can see our runes except you and me, pretty boy," she said, eyes slitting as she looked at him. "How many of these men did you lie to? How in Hel's name did you convince them to leave their realm to save one woman?"

Erik's mouth fell open, stuttering on his words. "I... I reminded them of their duty to their former jarl. Of what it meant to be an Otsman—"

She interrupted him with the shake of her head. "You played with their emotions and took advantage of their guilt. You spoke to their hearts to convince their minds. This bond Vali has created with her, it has done nothing to affect the one she has with you. Use your history, Erik. Ailsa is the only weapon you need in Vanaheim. As long as she's on your side, no one will touch you."

"I still don't know—"

"You once vowed you would do anything to save her. Is your love measured by convenience?"

"Of course not!" he said, fisting his empty hands. "I love Ailsa, and I will do anything to protect her. She is *mine*. And I will not let that demon claim her any longer than he already has."

She nodded approvingly before facing him once more. "Glad to hear that. You will dock soon, as the river ends where the Lower Roots begin. Burn the boat and the evidence of what happened here. I do not think Ailsa will want to venture home on the vessel of your dead clansmen."

"How will we get back?" he asked.

She smirked, lifting her chin enough to reveal a long scar spanning the width of her neck. "Do not worry about the journey home yet, Erik, too much lies ahead. I'll check in with you soon."

When he blinked again, the witch was gone.

CHAPTER 2
AILSA

Waves crashed against a distant shore. Ailsa paused her breath, focusing on the direction of the sound. But a pounding beat pulsed beneath her skin, interrupting the quiet lull. A sheen of sweat coated her chest as she finally swallowed a gulp of air. Her legs were sore from running. The sky over Vanaheim had turned from dusky to pitch. The only source of light now were the stars that burned too dimly over the Lower Realm.

After several racing heartbeats of silence, she thought perhaps she had lost her hunter somewhere in the dense woodlands on the outskirts of Njord's territory. The land here was almost completely flat, sparing a few grassy knolls peaking between the breaks in the wilderness. But the trees were many here, blocking the sound of anything—or anyone —until they were too close to hide from.

Just when she thought she was truly alone, shuffling in the underbrush stirred just yards away. A pair of footsteps were coming toward where she hid inside the shadow of a looming palm, their pace showing they were closing in quickly.

Panicked, Ailsa darted to where she believed she heard the ocean. Disregarding stealth to aid her speed, she pushed her tired extremities as hard as she had conditioned them to tolerate, sprinting through the brush as the soft earth shifted beneath her toes. If she could reach the beach, she would be safe. If not—well, she hesitated to think of the consequences.

Gasping through gritted teeth, she dared a stalling glance behind her. The hunter had not yet gained enough ground to reveal his proximity. But she heard him nearing with every step she took closer to the safe zone, the sounds of the sea competed with the hungry paces of the one on her heels.

The tree line thinned, promising her destination within reach. The ground transitioned from sodden earth to sand. Salt greeted her the moment she broke from the woodlands and stumbled upon the shoreline.

Ailsa slowed her strides until her feet came to a stop. Her heart attempted not to burst in its cavity. Burning blood rushed to aid her lungs as she braced her hands on her knees. And yet, despite the trembling in her body, she smiled. The fire in her chest was no longer a weakness, but a victory. Her racing heart did not flutter from the resistance of her breath, but from the strength now worn from a day's hard run. It was the first time she understood why the Otsman had risked the raids—why they felt such a sense of triumph over something so brutal. The battle on her body won, and she chased the reminder of that victory every chance she got.

And tonight, she had finally beaten him.

"What took you so long, *sváss?*"

Ailsa reeled to the side in surprise as a voice lifted above the gentle waves caressing the coast. Vali sat on a beached tree log, his leg propped on his knee like he had been waiting for ages. His wavy hair, only slightly disheveled, brushed behind his pointed ears from the acceleration of his sprint. But other than a few tears in his shirt, he appeared like he hadn't even broken a sweat. His golden gaze traced her body as a smirk cracked his lips.

"How the Hel did you get here before me?" she shrieked. Any satisfaction she felt moments before melted away at the sight of the elfin male. They had been training for weeks, and she had *finally* made it to the beach before he could catch her. But somehow, he had passed her during that last stretch.

He stood from his seat and crossed the sand to where she stood, downcast. Had she anymore energy, she would have put on a tougher front. But feeling as exhausted as she was, her shoulders drooped in disappointment. "Don't look so defeated," he said. "You're getting faster every week. That time, it was actually a little difficult to catch you."

She scoffed. "I'm so glad I could offer you a minor challenge. I'm sure Fenrir and the rest of the gods will appreciate the entertainment before they kill me."

His smirk only stretched into a grin that flashed teeth. "I'm not training you to fight gods, Ailsa."

"Then why have we spent the last several months building my endurance, Vali?" Ailsa planted her hands on her hips. But Vali pulled her tight by the waist, dismantling her fight. His proximity alone was his greatest weapon against her, and she surrendered against his chest.

His lips brushed the shell of her ear. The tone of his voice falling into dangerous territory. "Because your body deserves to be just as strong as your heart. And I've personally been enjoying your extra stamina. Which reminds me..." Hands smoothed down the curve of her spine, fingers digging into her hips. "I still beat you, and you know what that means, *Stiarna*."

"Aye," she sighed. "You get to choose how we spend the rest of the evening. I can only imagine what you will come up with."

Vali smiled, sensing the sarcasm lacing her words. She knew he had one thing on his mind, a heinous motivation to win almost as wicked as the way he was looking at her now.

"I want to go for a swim."

Her brows rose an inch. "A swim?"

Without clarifying, he stepped out of her arms and pulled his shirt over his head. Ailsa only watched his backside as he stripped, tossing his clothes all over the sand as he strode toward the calling waves. Her feet followed, inexplicably drawn to him by a force she had to define.

He slowly lowered himself into the dark waters, turning just as his lower half was submerged. She undressed in the most methodical of ways to draw out his waiting, taking her time to fold her outer garments into a neat pile. Vali hovered lower in the sea, the gentle tide lapping his neck as he watched her like a sea snake, eyes glowing in the silver moonlight as she joined him.

The water was cool. It nipped her warm skin in a way that felt pleasing, soothing the ache in her joints. He tugged her along by the arm into deeper depths until her toes could no longer skim the ocean floor and they were both treading water.

Vali guided her arm around his neck, pulled her nearby the hip with his opposite. "You've worked so hard these past few months, Ailsa. You should be proud of how far you've come. Especially while mastering your new power with Njord and Freya."

Ailsa closed her eyes and dipped her head back, silencing the world as her ears immersed beneath the water's edge and all she could hear was her breath. Each one was clear and full, filling her chest with purpose. She lifted her head to look at him again and smoothed back her wet hair.

"I am proud. I just despise watching you win every time," she admitted, making him smile. "Speaking of my power, I wanted to discuss something with you that Njord mentioned the other day."

His grin fell. "What's that?"

"Mimir's Well," she said. "It is not far from here. His island is just a day's journey off the coast. Njord said that the seeress who told Odin about the end of all things gained this wisdom by drinking from the well. Odin tried to drink from it himself, but the well did not show him his own ending, like it revealed to the witch. When he sought her out, she recited him a prophecy called—"

"The Voluspa. Yes, but what does that have to do with you going to the well?" he asked. The corners of his lips tightened in a frown.

"Have you ever read this prophecy for yourself, Vali?"

He shook his head. "No, but Odin shared it with the rest of the Aesir, quoting the Voluspa when he mentioned Fenrir destroying him and thus beginning a chain of events that will end in the death of all the gods, fae, and mortals alike. The battle to end all battles—the fall of the Nine. It was the reason he had Fenrir tied up in the first place."

Ailsa bit her lip, stalling before she chose her reply. "But what if Odin did not tell the Aesir everything the witch told him? Or what if there is something important the seeress left out? Vali, I want to know the words of the prophecy for myself. We need to know what we're up against."

"And you think the well will show you even when it didn't show Odin?"

"That seeress was none other than Gullveig herself. I am connected to both Heid and Gullveig," she said with a slight lift in her chin. "If the well will show anyone the prophecy, it will be me."

Vali scoffed and tossed a wet strand of hair out of his eye with the flick of his head. "Give a heathen a little power over fate, and she'll think all the Nine answers to her."

Ailsa's smile spread slowly across her cheeks. "Agree with me, and I'll show you a new rune Freya taught me."

His treading kicked him a little closer until their legs skimmed in the salty sea. "This wouldn't be similar in function to the last one, would it?"

"Does the goddess of fertility and sex share anything less than what is advantageous?"

Vali's smile returned with a vengeance—the kind he was known across the realms for. "I knew these lessons with the Vanir were a good idea."

Ailsa threw her head back as her laughter floated to the stars above them. They were almost constant here, only dimming during the brief daytime when the sun fell over the Tree. Slipping from his shoulder, she pushed off his frame and started swimming back to shore. The elfin followed without further debate. His agreement too easily won to feel wholly satisfied, but she counted her wins when she could.

Vali sprawled next to her on the beach, where she curled into his side in the sand. The swells lapped against her bare skin as she traced the rune Freya had showed her earlier that week, practicing the intricate design before she drew it on his chest.

He cleared his throat as she climbed on top of him, feeling

certain she had it memorized. "This rune she showed you, it isn't going to... manipulate the size of anything, is it?"

Ailsa smirked. "Ah, yes, Freya asked if I wanted to learn something like that."

"And?"

"And I informed her it wasn't necessary, because you have no trouble in that area."

He practically deflated with relief beneath her. "Thank the Light. I really didn't need her going back to Asgard with that kind of gossip. You are a gift, *elskan min*."

"And I just keep on giving," she said, letting her fingertips slide down the dusting of dark hair below his navel. The ridges of his abdomen tensed beneath her exploration. Her lessons with Njord and Freya had taught her how to use runes as tools instead of weapons, how to place them on one's skin for gain or weakness. Some runes were binding and permanent, like their *Fraendi* mark. And yet some were binding yet temporary, like blood runes formed from two different bloodlines to create a branding contract.

Ailsa found a shell with a broken edge and lanced her finger, letting a small drop of blood form on the tip. But just as she was about to mark his skin, a coarse rumble split through the sky just to the north. The light of the stars slowly blinked away like a lifted blanket as dry lightning flashed behind the cloud wall. She let the sea wash away the budding magic smeared across her fingertip.

"We should probably go back to our room before I show you what I learned this week." Though it wasn't a helstorm, Ailsa had no desire to let Vali anywhere near lightning ever again.

The first drops of rain fell, hitting him on the nose and making him grimace. Thunder rolled once more, warning them of the impending storm. "What do you think Thor is mad about this time?"

She slanted her head and pretended to think. "It could be anything, I suppose. Perhaps one of his half-brothers stole his hammer again."

Vali sat up. The position made her hips sink lower down his waist. "Unlikely. He only has one of those crazy enough to do such a thing." His eyes fell to her chest, where her wet undergarments were now practically transparent. He wet his lips with a sweep of his tongue. "And that brother is very busy at the moment."

"Busy getting dressed, you mean? I'm not getting caught in this storm, Vali. The rain here is freezing!" She shoved him by his chest back into the sand and stood, starting toward her clothes where she left them just beyond the reaches of the waves.

As she neared the small pile, an isolated swell broke from the surf, surging up the beach to drench her clothes. Ailsa gasped, confused how such poor luck was possible until she whirled around to see Vali, the elfin sitting with an arm propped over his knee casually, failing to fight a smirk.

"How strange," he said. "Looks like you won't be changing anytime soon, *sváss*."

Ailsa huffed a hot breath through her nose. Her frustration peaked when she noticed how pleased he was with himself. Instead of falling into his carefully laid trap, she gave him her most dangerous smile and looked around for the pants he had tossed so carelessly.

"What are you doing?" he asked as she found them. All amusement suddenly barren from his voice. "Don't you dare—"

But Ailsa was already kicking up sand, burying his pants

beneath layers of beach. One kick was enough to ensure he would have a terrible time getting all the grains out, but she kicked a few more times for good measure until she completely submerged them in the sand. Vali's arms were suddenly around her waist, lifting her in the air even as she fought to break from his embrace, before throwing them both to the ground. A surge of laughter floated from her chest.

He leaned over her, messy black hair dripping ocean water and rolling off her cheek as she quelled the remaining giggles. "That wasn't very nice, Ailsa. What do you have to say for yourself?"

With the hand marked with their *Fraendi* rune, she reached up and brushed his hair back to see his golden eyes better. "I'd say you can take the girl from the heathens, but you can't take the heathen out of the girl."

"I suppose I'd have to agree," he murmured, dipping his head to kiss her lips. Just as he pulled away, and she opened her eyes, lightning veined across the dark sky, highlighting the world around them for a fleeting moment with white light. In the distance, the quiet hum of heavy rain approached.

"I'll grab our things. Go to the edge of that cliff over there," Vali jutted his chin toward a rock face. "I believe there is a cave at the base we can stay in to wait out the weather."

Ailsa needed no further convincing, and she grabbed the elfin's dry shirt to throw over herself as she ran for cover. The hem skimmed the middle of her thigh, but the flax was still warm from his heat. Using a reserve of strength, she raced the storm to the shallow cave that sat just on the edge of the shoreline, ducking inside just as the drizzle shifted into a heavy cascade.

Vali appeared moments later, a bundle of wet clothes and a satchel in his arms, still wearing nothing but the briefs he had worn for their swim. Ailsa took in the sight of him as he dropped their things, enjoying the way the wet material clung to his form.

She met him near the mouth of the cavern, draping her arms around his neck. "I promise I'll dust your pants off later, *sváss*. I just wanted to make sure you'd be as disposed as I am until my clothes dry off from that pesky wave."

"Yes, nature seems to be on its worst behavior today," he said with a wink. "How about you show me that rune while we wait for things to calm down outside?"

"You're still going on about that?" she asked, letting a hand skate down his chest. "I'll warn you, it could take a while to wear off."

"We have time. In fact, I'm hoping for that exact situation." His mouth moved to her neck. Ailsa let her head fall back as he sucked the skin of her throat between his teeth, nipping playfully and sending a jolt straight down her spine. The wind howled beyond their sanctuary, whistling against the rocks in agreement.

Ailsa winced as she reopened the tender spot on the pad of her finger, drawing more blood with her nail. A devious smile graced her lips as she traced the rune in the center of his chest, carefully placing it where her hands wouldn't wipe it away accidentally.

"Be careful what you wish for, *Sólskin*."

CHAPTER 3
VALI

" I'm not sure I like that rune."

Now that he could finally take a full breath, Vali's pulse slowed enough he could think again. His vision finally returned as the blood rushed to his head instead of his cock, when he was finally relieved of a monumental amount of pressure built over hours of swelling pleasure started by his blessed *Fraendi*.

Gods below, when she finally wiped the rune away and let him release, he thought his heart would give out from the crash of the climax, short circuiting every nerve in his body and nulling his ability to command his chest to breathe or his heart to beat.

Ailsa tucked herself into his side, her head resting on his shoulder. She was still wearing his shirt. Her finger traced lazy circles where marks once inked across his chest, replacing a power that had once claimed his life with her own soul consuming touch. "Perhaps I let that go on a little longer than necessary."

Vali choked on a dry breath. "You think?"

Her body shook with silent giggles. "I'm sorry. I was enjoying myself too much to let you finish so soon. Was it that bad for you?"

"You can torture me like that whenever you'd like, *sváss*. But I'm going to need a day or two to recover." He sealed his affection with a kiss on top of her head. "Speaking of runes, what's that new one on your hip?"

Ailsa cleared her throat, shifting uncomfortably against his side. "It's a form of contraceptive. It's been difficult to find the right herbs I was using before here in Vanaheim. Freya showed me this one so I wouldn't have to stress about it anymore."

He swallowed, feeling his heartbeat suddenly speed up again. "This rune... is it permanent?"

"No, it isn't. I must reapply it every few weeks before it fades."

Vali wasn't certain why he felt relieved. They had never spoken about the future concerning starting a family of their own. With the threat looming over the Tree of Life and the responsibility Vali knew Ailsa carried to master her gift before it was too late, it did not afford them such luxuries to plan anything outside of saving the realms. And with her history, he didn't want to press the subject before she was ready.

"If that is what you want, Ailsa, then I am happy you found something more convenient than those foul-smelling tonics you were shooting back every night."

She looked up at him, and he met the worry in her gaze with a smile. Reassuring her, he was not the least bit uncomfortable with the idea of... any of this. She said, "Maybe one day I won't have to worry about it at all. After we save the realms, we can think about starting our own legacy."

Vali's smile widened at the thought. "Can you imagine? A

part fae and part heathen child. If the Tree isn't in danger now, it sure will be if we combine our bloodlines."

She pushed off his chest to sit up. Her dark hair fell in tangled waves down her back, but Vali believed she looked even more like a goddess. "Here's to saving the Nine just to end them, *elskan min*."

He grabbed the hand with their *Fraendi* mark and placed it over his racing heart. "My world begins and ends with you, Ailsa. It always has and always will.

The next morning when the sun rose, and the storm had long passed, Vali and Ailsa made the long walk back to Njord's castle, following the coast all the way to the ocean-side kingdom. Njord ruled every sea and tide from the Lower Roots to the High Branches, and his dock was persistently active with creatures of all kinds who came to him seeking favor on their journeys.

Vali pulled her close to his side, taking an inconspicuous route to hide them both from wandering eyes. They had kept Ailsa's location a secret from the witches and the wolves for the past several months since they arrived in this realm, but he saw foes in every unfamiliar face, trusting no one.

Odin and the other Aesir agreed it was best to let Ailsa train with Njord with the goal in mind to eventually raise Baldur before the warnings of Ragnarok were upon them. Baldur's death had been the first sign. The long winter would be the next. And they were currently facing the end of a solstice, with no evidence of summer arriving soon. But if Ailsa could reverse Baldur's death, she could rewrite the events of Ragnarok and stop these events from happening in the first place, because what would follow the long winter would be disastrous.

They crossed over the arch of a bridge made of sea glass, traversing just one of the many waterfalls cascading over the edge of the castle walls and into a small pool in another court-yard below. Each one eventually drained all the way to the Sea of Rán.

Njord's castle was built upon the uneven elevation of the rocky terrain bordering the ocean. They separated each hall on a different hill, the corridors mostly stairwells leading from one level to the next. But the staggered composition of the fortress allowed the natural beauty of the realm to live and breathe both inside the palace and alongside its walls. The towers were many, redundant to count because of the varia-tions in their heights. Whether it was a balcony overlooking the ocean or a private room where arches lined the walls in place of windows, the salty breeze seemed to follow one wherever they strayed.

Before they made it halfway down the corridor leading from the western wing to the dining hall, one of Njord's advi-sors came rushing down to meet them. His shaved head glis-tened against the torches lining the curved wall, perspiring like had just ran clear across the castle.

"Thank the Nine you both are back and in one piece. Where in the gods-forsaken Tree have you two been all night? Njord was about to send search parties out to look for you!"

"Aramis," Vali said calmly, "I informed Njord before we left yesterday that Ailsa and I were going to train for the day. He should have known with the storm we wouldn't be able to return. All is well."

"Is something wrong, Aramis?" Ailsa asked, pushing past

Vali up the stairs to meet him on the landing. "Has Alfheim sent word? Has Seela—"

"The elves have not yet returned, Lady Ailsa, nor have they sent news. I will make you aware as soon as they do." The councilman's gaze softened as it crossed Ailsa, who always seemed to charm everyone she met despite his own first impression of her. "But there is someone else here to see you."

"Me?" she asked, glancing back at the elfin now standing beside her with an inscrutable countenance. "Who would be here to see me?"

Vali felt his stomach drop, his hunger pangs disappearing. No one should know where she was to be visiting her, and if one of the wolven had finally tracked her down—or worse, one of the Volva—then her life was in grave danger.

"Where is this visitor now?" he interrupted Aramis's response to her.

Aramis balked for a breath. "We've kept him heavily guarded in one of the guest rooms—"

"You need to keep him in the dungeons!" Vali growled. "Do you know who she is, Aramis? Do any of you understand how imperative it is to keep her presence here a secret? Whoever this trespasser is did not come by invitation, and they should not be treated like a guest!"

Ailsa slipped her hand around the fist he had clenched at his side. "Vali, relax. Whoever it is cannot harm us here."

"She is right." The councilman shrugged beneath a heavy navy mantle. "And besides, what threat does a single mortal hold in the home of the Vanir?"

The air in the room was suddenly smothering. Vali's head felt like it had just spun off an axis. Ailsa took a step back. The hand that caressed him now hovered over her heart. Her chest rose and fell like the sea in a storm. "What?" she whispered. "Who would... That's not possible."

She looked at the elfin, but Vali had no words to offer wisdom. It wasn't possible—it *shouldn't* be possible—for a mortal to leave Midgard unless under extenuating circumstances such as Ailsa's situation.

"Did this mortal... Did he give you a name?" He could hardly find the words to ask.

Aramis nodded slowly, sensing the tension that had crawled into the space between the three of them. "Yes, Lord Vali. He said his name was—"

But Vali did not hear him say the name, only watched the councilman's lips as it spat the most diabolical words in the elfin's vocabulary. The one he hated almost as much as the wolven they didn't speak of anymore. Vali blocked out his voice, Ailsa's gasp, muted every sound that seemed to commit treason to his composure.

But it did nothing to temper the rage in his blood as he read the name off his lips.

Erik Eurikson.

What in Hel's name was that bastard doing here?

CHAPTER 4
SEELA

The days seemed to stretch longer like a cruel punishment with every week that passed. The waiting game was not one Seela played to her strengths. Alfheim hadn't quite felt like home anymore without the fae who made it so, and with her *Hjartablód* so many worlds away, she struggled to remember how she ever once belonged here. How in a world so filled with Light, she had become a shadow behind those she loved most. Now they were gone, and that shadow remained as permanent as the sun hanging in the sky.

She rubbed away the burning behind her tired eyes as she stared at the map of the elven realm. The Dark Elves had fought back the remaining wolven and Volva the night Vali and Ailsa drew Fenrir out of his hiding place. When news arrived at the Light Palace, Odin and the rest of the Aesir made themselves scarce, leaving the elves with a legion of angry giants, their people exposed to the wrath of the Great Wolf and his descendants, and a massive mess to clean up.

But things had settled in the weeks prior. Vali had

remained with Ailsa in Vanaheim to keep her safe, meanwhile giving her the chance to learn how to master her new power. The Vanir were known for their magic, taught by Gullveig herself when she gave them the knowledge of sedir. And though he had given her the choice to stay or go with them, Seela knew her place was here. Because if Vali knew the true state of his mother was in, he would never forgive her for abandoning her High Lady.

"Commander Seela?" The Head Healer knocked lightly on the ajar office door. "Is this a bad time?"

Without raising her head from the cradle of her hands, Seela said, "As good as any. Come in, but please shut the door behind you." There were very few who knew of Lady Rind's condition, and Seela needed to keep it that way until she got better—or worse.

"I have an update, Commander. Unfortunately, it is not the one we were hoping for."

Seela sighed and sat back in her chair, letting her gaze fall on Greer. Her face could have been made of stone, all hard lines from decades of tough choices.

"How is she?"

Greer pushed up the white sleeves of her smock and sat in a chair across from Seela's desk. "As you know, when the Allfather crushed her airway, it severed her windpipe. While we could heal the bones in her neck, her body just hasn't been able to mend the airway itself. It has prevented her from breathing properly, and I am afraid she has developed a lower lung infection."

Seela shut her eyes again and processed the news. "I've never heard of elves getting infections, Master Greer. Why haven't the healing waters helped? Has anyone tried getting her a batch directly from the well? Is there anything we haven't tried yet?"

"It is true elves and most fae are resilient to sickness, but Lady Rind has been alive for centuries now. Her body cannot heal itself like it used to, nor does it respond as effectively to the water. I have already sent a few of my healers to the well to see if it may buy her some time."

"Time?" Seela reeled, sitting up straight in her chair. "Are you telling me she's... dying?"

Greer offered a sad smile. "No one lives forever, Commander. Not even the fae. Have you been informing Vali of her status? Because I'm afraid she doesn't have long to go before the infection takes its toll on her responsiveness. These next weeks could be her last lucid ones."

But Seela could only shake her head, trying to process the feelings of her own grief as she came to terms with Greer's words. Rind had been a mother she always needed and now suddenly days away from leaving her forever.

She was honest with Vali when she visited Vanaheim a few weeks ago. However, there was still hope for Lady Rind in those days, and the healers had made her think there was nothing to worry about. Especially when her world was practically falling apart at the seams, and the weight of everything else seemed much heavier in comparison. Meanwhile, she had been left to run the realm in secret while the High Lady recovered, but Alfheim was about to have a new ruler, and he was far from the lands that would soon belong to him.

"I need to go to Vanaheim straight away. The Dark Elves can mist me there so I can deliver this update to Vali."

"Seela, you cannot leave," Greer interrupted her. When Seela shot her a curious look, the healer explained. "You have a private meeting with the Well Keepers, who are waiting in the North Wing to update you about Mirrenal. They believe the lands around the Haven should make a full recovery, but they have some suggestions about how to see that through. Vali named *you* as his regent, Seela."

Seela shook her head, a migraine suddenly forming behind her eyes. "Don't remind me," she sighed. As if it did not complicate things enough, Vali had tossed her the responsibility of ruling the realm.

"I need to send *someone* to Vanaheim and tell him," she said beneath her breath. "Master Greer, could you send for Enver? Thank you for the updates. Please let me know if anything changes."

"Of course, Commander."

Seela quickly pulled out a piece of parchment and ink as she left. Sometime later, and after a page and a half of ramblings, the dark elf she had called for finally knocked on her office door before throwing it open.

"Need to let off some steam again, Seela? Or did you just miss my face?"

Seela glared above her letter, barely breaking her signature as she signed the bottom of the parchment. Enver's lanky frame slipped through the doorway, his dark red hair falling long behind his shoulders. Today he pinned it half up, exaggerating the devastating line of his jaw and the jewel green in his eyes.

Tipping her head to see if anyone was in the hall to hear him, she said, "I told you not to speak to me like that—"

"When we're in *public*." He emphasized the last word with the roll of his eyes. Enver's long strides crossed the distance of the office quickly, disregarding the chair and opting to use the top of her desk as a seat instead. "Relax. No one is around to hear me sweet talk their stoic and restrained commander. Our secret is safe... for now."

Sighing, she asked, "Are you quite done?"

He nodded. "What do you need, sweetheart?"

Seela gritted her teeth, fighting the impulse to correct him again. "I need this delivered to Vali, and I cannot go myself. I'm asking you because I don't trust anyone else with this kind of information."

"Back to Vanaheim?" He frowned. "Is it urgent?"

She nodded. "It is a paramount he receives this in the next few days at the latest. Just in case."

The male replied, "I have my own business to tend to this afternoon, but I can leave as soon as tomorrow morning."

She folded the note and placed it inside a black envelope, closing it with a rune seal that would only open for the name she whispered into the wax. She handed it to Enver. "I also have a question for you and could use your insight. Something has been bothering me, and I'm not exactly sure why."

"What's on your mind?"

Seela glanced down at the map sprawled across her desk. "Odin's ravens fly all over the Tree spying. Wraiths linger in the shadows from our realm to the oceans and forests of Midgard. Legions of Dark Elves lived and thrived in the same dead lands where the wolves and witches were hiding. Yet there wasn't a single sighting in all the years they have reclused in our realm. Why? How did they evade us?"

Enver sucked on his teeth, staring into the hearth's fire slowly dying in the corner of the room. "I was thinking about this just the other day. I wonder if they were hiding here at all, or if they had only moved to Alfheim in the last days before the attack."

She reclined back in her chair and thought it over. "How

would they have moved in so quickly? Even sedir cannot move that many wolves and witches in such a short time. Or can it?"

"The witches are much more experienced with sedir than we are, Seela. It is possible, I suppose, but not the only option. There is a forgotten pass the dwarves used to use before they went underground. It is just beyond the Dvegar Mountains."

Her brows furrowed, and she leaned back over the desk. Enver ran a finger over a place on the map that was colored stone grey, fading into the edges of the realm. Nothing to mark the space significantly.

"You won't find it on a map. Not a recent one, anyway. They made it forbidden after the rockslides deemed the path too perilous to travel safely. No one ventures that way anymore."

"Where does this pass lead?"

He shrugged with a heavy jerk of his broad shoulders. "No idea. Like I said, it's been long forgotten."

Seela scoffed. "Not by you, old man."

He grinned. "My lengthy experience is only your gain, Commander. In more ways than one."

She felt her cheeks warm, but said nothing. Since Vali left, she had searched for distraction after distraction—until Enver came along and proved to have enough skill and experience to keep her busy for a *very* long time.

"Is something wrong, Seela?" he asked. His brows kissed, the hard lines of his face now lethally sharp as a knife. "You look like you haven't slept for days—and not in a fun way. You know I enjoy teasing you, but you can talk to me about anything."

The commander shook her head and pushed a forced smile. Enver was one of the few fae who truly understood what she was going through. His *Hjartablóð* died in a battle during the civil war that had plagued this land for decades, and although she hadn't lost her own in such a way, Vali was gone in every way that mattered. He had a stronger bond with someone else, and while she loved Ailsa like the sister she never had, their bond had left something bitter in place of her own. Seela wished she could find her own *Fraendi* if only to fill that rotten hole in her heart with something more fulfilling.

"Vali deserves to know first but thank you. I might take you up on that soon."

"And maybe over some drinks at Greybeard's?" He winked, concealing the letter beneath his green and black tunic.

Her stomach churned at the memory of their most recent visit, but her smile stretched more genuinely this time. "You know what? If you deliver that before the end of the winter solstice in a few days, I'll personally buy our first round." She crossed her arms before adding, "So I suggest you leave my office and get to misting."

"Ahh, sweet Seela." He slipped off the desk and walked backward toward the door, keeping his docile gaze on her the entire way. "You always know just how to motivate me."

"You're not an overtly complicated male, Commander," she replied dryly. "Be careful out there, and safe travels."

He gave her an unnecessary salute before turning to leave. Seela rolled her eyes at his back. They were an indulgence for each other—they both had made that clear the first time she invited him to her room. Their relationship was complicated, having seen him naked far too much to be a friend and yet too overwhelmed with being *regent* to consider going any further.

They stood in a strange place, and she enjoyed being lost in no-man's-land with him for the time being.

Seela waited until his footsteps disappeared down the hall before following him out, locking the door behind her. Before she checked on Lady Rind for the night, there was someone else she desired to see first.

The dungeons were buried beneath the castle. The darkness here was sticky, clinging to every corner until even the Light could not find a way around it. A lone torch burned on the outside of a single cell, illuminating the small space housing a single prisoner. Few stayed here for a significant length of time, but this wolven had been here longer than most.

"Hello, Ivor."

A dark shape curled into a ball shifted on the small cot in the cell's corner. Through the bars, Seela watched her lift her head briefly from the flat mattress. Her black and silver hair was a nest of knots.

"Commander," she only said, before resuming her previous position.

"Still don't feel like talking, I take it?" Seela asked.

Ivor grunted. "I don't need your pardons or your favors. My answer is the same as the day you captured me. I will not betray my family."

"I don't believe that, seeing how they left you for dead." She hoped the wolf felt the ice intended in her words. "When the Dark Elves fought the Volva and the wolven out of our realm, they found you near death with claw marks in your throat and witch blood on your teeth. And let's not even bring Ailsa into this—"

"Everything I did was for Ailsa, to protect her gift—"

"Yes, you did a fine job by handing her to the harbinger of Ragnarok." Seela paced the front of her cell.

"None of that was supposed to happen," Ivor whispered. But Seela had heard this same tired speech every week for the past three months. The witches and the wolves had disappeared from the realm, leaving only a darkness behind that attracted creatures from the void bordering the Tree. But that didn't mean any of them were safe, and the sooner she knew where the Great Wolf had fled, the sooner Vali and Ailsa could return and rule the realm in their rightful places.

"I need more than that, Ivor. I can help you get out of there if you'd just—"

"Leave me alone!" Ivor snapped. "I told you once, and I will not tell you again. I'm not telling you why the witches are working with Fenrir, nor how they hid from you. Figure it out, yourself."

Seela scrubbed her face with her hands and shrugged at the guards patrolling the dungeon hall. "Fine. Have it your way."

She was about to walk away. Instead, she faced the bars once more, resting her hands on the cold metal. "I don't know why I want to help you, after all you've done to me. But I know there is some good in you, Ivor, even if you don't see it yet yourself."

She left the wolven, hoping she wouldn't regret her words.

CHAPTER 5

AILSA

Ailsa paced the width of the dais as they waited in Noatun, Njord's main hall, for the guards to return with Erik. Needles replaced her bones, making it impossible to remain still. A thousand questions had assailed her thoughts since they received word of her visitor, but she tempered her excitement to see him again, if only to abate the elfin standing behind her.

Vali had not said a word the entire time. Even as they entered the hall, he set his golden gaze on the doors where they would soon enter with Erik. His chest hardly moved with his breaths, every muscle in his frame locked there with the stillness of a viper just before it intended to strike.

She crossed the path of his glare, and he finally blinked. His eyes softened as they settled on hers. "It will be fine, Vali," she assured him. "Whatever happens, whatever reason he is here, we will deal with it together."

"And if he demands to bring you home?" he asked. "What then?"

Ailsa reached for his cheek, stroking away the tension firm

in his jaw. "Then I will tell him he came a long way for nothing, *Sólskin*."

The elfin's lips twitched in something akin to a smile before the sound of Noatun's doors sliding open silenced them both.

Ailsa spun, facing the entryway. As sure as if her memory had conjured him from a dream, Erik Eurikson stood on the other side. Every ounce of her willpower kept her feet rooted in the soapstone pavers lining the floor between them.

"Ailsa!" he shouted, his rich voice echoing throughout the room to where the Vanir gods sat on a dais behind them. But Erik hadn't noticed the gods nor the elfin undoubtedly glaring a hole into his skull. Those wide eyes the color of dark mead took in the sight of her, his strides lengthening to get to her quicker. "Thank the gods you're alive!"

Ailsa beamed at him, feeling the warmth of home—a piece of her old life—suddenly wrap his powerful arms around her waist and lifted her in a spinning embrace as he had always greeted her. When he finally placed her back on her feet, Ailsa took a step out of his arms to look him over.

Not much about him had changed since she left her fjord all those solstices ago. His face was chapped from windburn proving a long journey, and his hair was slightly longer, draping over the heavy fur cloak on his shoulders. But his smile was still the same warm invitation that beckoned her ten years ago.

"*Ymir's breath*, Erik, I can't believe it's really you. Why did you... How did you find me here? You must tell me everything that's happened since I've been gone."

His face flushed. "It's a long story, but I swear I'll tell you whatever you wish to know." His hand reached for her face, stroked her cheek with his thumb, but there was something in his touch that didn't feel like it used to. "I didn't think I'd ever see you again, *sváss.*"

"Do *not* call her that," a deep voice spoke behind her, words laced with venom. Ailsa looked to Vali, whose demeanor had not changed, but his hands had fallen open at his sides, ready to intervene if necessary. Njord and the other Vanir sat behind a table on the platform. A few had begun to work on their wine goblets—none of them made a move to interrupt their conversation.

"And what else would I call her, demon?" Erik said, turning to face him. "You are lucky I have not cut your hollow heart from your chest for kidnapping her, and for the rest of your crimes against my kin!"

Ailsa snatched the meaty part of his forearm. "Erik, enough. There is so much you don't know about."

Vali laughed, his lips stretching wide enough to expose sharp canines. "You may call her whatever she wishes, but not your beloved. Those terms of endearment are meant for her mate."

"Mate?" Erik scoffed, his cheeks flaming red. "And who would that be?"

"Vali, don't—"

"Oh, that would be me," the elfin raised his right hand and showed off their *Fraendi* mark.

Erik glanced down at her hand still clutching his forearm, where the matching rune inked her own skin. The warmth in his eyes suddenly chilled over. He yanked his arm from her touch and glared back at Vali. "Bastard! What have you done to her?"

Vali's grin never wavered. "I've done lots of things to my mate, Erik. How specific would you like me to be?"

"Odin's eye," Ailsa muttered. Though neither acknowl-edged her presence at this point.

Erik cursed in the old language and the new. His chest rose and fell with uneven breaths as he reached down to his hip to unsheathe a small sword. The sight of the blade made Ailsa stagger back—the rest of the room reached for their own weapons.

Vali moved the moment he saw Erik reach for his sword, lunging between them to separate the blade and Ailsa with his body. But as he reached for her, his arm crossed paths with the sword, and the tip of the blade sliced him across the forearm, drawing blood. The injury was minor, hardly anything that would weaken him, but Vali stumbled in his shock. His golden glare widened at the evidence of Erik's treacherous weapon.

Across the polished obsidian were markings written in gold, glowing in the presence of a fae, as did all blades from Svartalheim. Erik had come for her, but he had also come for Vali, and his intentions were clear as soon as he threatened her *Fraendi* by revealing his weapon of choice.

"Vali," she gasped. She made to move to him, but Erik extended his arm in front of her, blocking her path with the length of his sword. A familiar provocation pulled awake in her heart, remembering how often and easily the men of her past shielded her with their control, dominated her decisions with their own.

"Erik," she warned, "lower your blade."

His eyes glanced at her for a breath before returning to Vali. "Get behind me, Ailsa. It's all right. I can protect you now, and I will not let him hold you here any longer."

Ailsa stepped closer to Erik's side, slipping a hand through the slit of her skirt to run her finger across her dagger. Vali had custom made the sheath around her thigh to be exposed in one place, protecting her leg while giving her access to a sharp edge. Njord's guards were few, only the ones stationed at the doors, and they had slowly approached Erik the moment he drew his weapon. But Ailsa held up a hand, insisting they hung back.

"I would be very careful where you point that blade, Erik," Vali said. "Threaten me and you threaten my *Fraendi*. I can finish what I started that night in Drakame."

As if to remind him, Erik's coloring turned ruddy, his knuckles blanched in their fists. Steam floated from his lips on a hot breath and Ailsa could feel the heat from his body radiating like a furnace.

"Vali, that is *enough!*" she snapped. Vali looked at her for a beat before uncurling his fists. Slowly, Erik's skin returned to a normal shade.

Njord finally stood from his chair on the dais. "This has gone on long enough," he said. Dark blue robes swept the floor as he stepped around the long table. "This is my home, and I will not have any blood spilled in these halls. Erik, if you do not sheath your weapon at this moment, I will make sure you are dealt with as all criminals in my realm are handled. We made a deal. Now honor your side of the bargain."

Ailsa slipped her hand around the back of his arm, where his sleeve was rolled up high enough she could press the rune on her palm into his skin. Erik's jaw tensed before relaxing, his breaths shifting from shallow and quick to a deeper rhythm. Taking a hesitant step back, he slipped the blade back into the sheath at his hip.

"Thank you, Ailsa. I'm pleased to see you applying your lessons in more practical situations," the god of the sea said to her.

Erik turned, realizing her touch was not one of comfort

but control. He snatched her wrist to inspect the rune, now a bloody smear across her palm. "Is it true then, your family's curse?" he asked. "Are you some kind of witch now?"

"Something like that," she murmured, "and I touched you with a calming rune to clear your hot head, before you did something you would regret." He dropped her arm, recoiling his hand to his chest like she had burned him.

Njord spoke again before she could explain. "I do not need to remind you, Erik Eurikson, you are in the presence of the Vanir. You and your people have asked much of us concerning your voyages and your raids, your marriages and their consummation. From the weather that cultivates your harvest to the wind in your sails, those on this dais have been there when you called on us. But no mortal has ever ventured beyond the boundaries of Midgard. So I ask you now," the sea god descended each step of the stairwell until he was even with them, "what are you doing in my hall?"

Erik faced Njord, but his gaze fell to the god's feet. The stubble on his jaw caught the beads of sweat dripping from his temple. "When we lost Ailsa, the heart of our clan went with her." He spared a look at her directly then. "*My* heart went with her. We did not know what had befallen her after the fae slaughtered our families and kidnapped one of our chieftains. But Drakame's new jarl, Nikros, told us of the Berserker Blessing, and we finally understood why he had taken Ailsa—because of the power she inherited.

"I called upon every force in this universe to help me find her until one day, a strange man appeared out of the Aelder-wood. He claimed he was a traveler passing through, but we all knew who he truly was, as Odin has been rumored to wander Midgard in his blue cloak and grey hat. This man not only dressed the same, but he wore an eye patch as well. He came to me specifically, and I offered him my horn to drink, and in exchange he gave me this golden blade and a map with Vanaheim marked, wishing me safe travels. When the clan awoke the next morning, the old man was gone, but I knew the Allfather himself had blessed my journey. I gathered a crew, and we set sail soon after."

Ailsa watched Vali's reaction to Erik's story, but the elfin's lips only curled as if amused. It wasn't a completely outrageous thought for Odin to send a vengeful mortal to hunt them both down. But the gods knew the repercussions of killing Vali, that she would die with him, and Ailsa was skeptical Odin would risk losing the power over fate when the threat of Ragnarok was still breathing down their necks.

But Odin clearly knew things they did not, and if he no longer needed Ailsa or Vali in his plans to defeat Fenrir, then it was even more necessary to visit Mimir's Well and discover this wisdom for themselves.

"If you left with a crew, then where is everyone else, Erik?" she asked.

His throat convulsed with a hard swallow, a dark look flashed across his eyes. "They did not make it. There were few of us able to leave home because last winter was hard on our supplies. Most of the men were advanced in their years, and we crossed storms and seas unlike any we have ever faced in Midgard."

"It appears he has an answer to everything," Vali spoke to Njord. "He must have rehearsed his tale all the way from the fjord."

"I have answers because it is the truth!"

"Why would my own father want me dead, or did you not realize I am a son of Odin?" The elfin crossed his arms.

Erik's forehead was glistening now. His hairline saturated

with sweat despite wearing a flax tunic of midnight and dark brown leather traveling pants tucked into furless boots. He crossed his arms, reflecting his opponent. "I do not pretend to know the mind or will of Odin. He gave me what I needed to find Ailsa. It is not my fault if the Allfather favors me over his son."

"He favors everyone over Vali. Do not feel special," Frey spoke from the dais. Ailsa hadn't realized he even entered the hall.

Vali shrugged a shoulder. "It is true."

Njord scrubbed a hand over his face and let it fall down the length of his white beard. "So what will you do now, Erik? You have found Ailsa alive and well, but she cannot leave until she completes her training with me and Freya. I owe Gullveig that much. After all she contributed to the Vanir, to make sure her sacrifice means something in the end."

Erik shook his head slowly. "I suppose I am at your mercy, then. I have no crew to manage a ship, no means of returning to Midgard on my own. But if Ailsa would have me, I'd rather stay by her side until I can secure safe passage home." Erik met her gaze once more and spoke to her. "What do you say, Ailsa?"

"Of course—"

"Definitely not."

Ailsa shot Vali a look made of a hundred golden daggers as he spoke over her. Shifting her attention back to Erik, she said, "We can talk about this later. Wait for me in your room. I will come find you when I have time to speak with you."

"Fine. As long as you come alone," he said, glancing once more at Vali for emphasis. "May I be excused then?"

Njord nodded and motioned for the doors leading from the hall to open. Tearing his eyes from the elfin, he turned to leave and disappeared behind the silver doors—a group of guards filled his shadow.

She slowly turned on her toes to look at her *mate*, who was standing there looking entirely too pleased with his performance. "*You*," she said to him. "Outside. Now."

"Perhaps we should move this table to the balcony," Frey mumbled to his neighbor just loud enough for the entire room to overhear.

"What in Hel's name was that about?"

Vali finally joined her on the terrace surrounded by the garden of Nerthus, Njord's first wife. The plants here were mostly night-blooming flowers mixed with the goddess's fertility herbs. But the hedging provided thick enough walls to give Ailsa a sense of privacy from the gossiping group of divines lingering on the balcony above.

"Can you believe that man? Did he really think we would believe that load of *skide*?"

Ailsa crossed her arms and shifted her weight onto one hip. "I wasn't talking about Erik, Vali, I was talking about *you*. You acted like a jealous fool in front of everyone! You've never spoken over me like that before."

"He had no right speaking to you like that!" He jutted a finger toward her chest. "I don't care who he is to you. He will not claim you in the old language, nor will he ever touch you so freely. I swear to you, Ailsa, if I ever see him caress your face like that again or pull a sword within striking distance of you, I *will* boil him to death just to hear his last screams."

She swallowed a large gulp of air, settling the irritation

still heating her bones. "I do not need you to defend me, *Sólskin*. You do not understand the shallow limits of his temper. If we push him past his boundaries, then we will never figure out if he is telling us the truth or not. Vali, to him, you are still the man who killed our families and abducted me all those months ago from my fjord. If you want him to respect our relationship, you need to show him you are not the monster he thinks you are."

But he shook his head in disagreement. "I *am* the monster he thinks me to be, Ailsa, and I don't want him to believe anything different. I do not trust him—"

"Do you trust me?"

He scoffed, waving his hand as if to disperse her question. "That is ridiculous. Of course, I trust you, *sváss*."

She stepped closer to him, threading her hands behind his neck. "Then let me handle this. You already know I have no plans to leave you, and Erik would never hurt me. Whatever is going on here, there is nothing to worry about."

Vali pulled her hips against his, and she felt his need to touch her from the way his fingertips buried into the folds of her dress. "What about the well? I spoke with Njord before the meeting, and he said we could use one of his vessels, but he only has one available these next few days. Otherwise, we'll have to wait another month before his other ships arrive."

Ailsa shrugged. "I guess we'll have to bring Erik with us."

The elfin groaned, throwing his head back like a child. "I loathe that idea."

"You saw the blade he pulled on you. Someone gave him that sword, and until we know who sent him and why, we need to keep him close, if only to watch him. If your father sent him after us, then understanding the prophecy might help us figure out why."

The elfin didn't respond, having no real argument besides his own personal distaste for the man, and Ailsa knew it. He said, "I dislike the idea of you being alone with him, and it is not because I don't trust you. There's something off about him, Ailsa. He's lying. I can *feel* it."

She stroked the concern from his face with a thumb across his jawbone. Erik had been her longest friend even before they had become something more in their young adult years. He would never harm her out of malice, not even if he was jealous.

"Let me fight my own battles, Vali," she said in a tired voice. "You said you trusted me. Now prove it."

He bladed his finger up her chest, reaching for her neck as she arched into his warm palm to feel as much of him on her skin as possible. How easy it was for him to conquer her heart with his touch alone, make her forget all her anger in an effort to control her last thread of willpower.

"I trust you," he said again, with nothing else attached. He dipped his head and kissed her, parting her lips with a whisper of pressure and the sweep of his tongue. She wondered if it would always feel like this, if his mouth would always make her hungry for more, if this deep need in her heart would ever stop craving his touch and his affection. If this wanting was forever, would she ever have enough?

He broke away, sighing against her lips. "You should go now, while there is still some kind of daylight left. Just promise me you will stay within Njord's borders. His protection only stretches so far."

"Of course. I'll see you at dinner, *sváss*."

She watched him walk away, back to the glowing arches lining the castle and illuminating the dusky day. Vali was not the only one who felt unsettled in that hall, not that she would admit it to him just yet. It was Erik's scent, one she had remembered smelling of sea salt and winter but was now replaced by something else that set a tension between her fingers. Being a healer, she knew the smell by heart, had memorized it well enough to avoid it at all costs. Only once had she smelled it on another.

He smelled of belladonna—of the darker spells of sedir and blood magic.

Erik smelled like witches.

CHAPTER 6

ERIK

There wasn't enough wine left in Vanaheim to blur this day from Erik's thoughts. He rushed back to his room after his meeting with Ailsa and scavenged a bottle from a servant's tray along the way, wishing he had packed more mead from Midgard. He hadn't seen a drop of ale in weeks, and the fae wine Njord was partial to keep around was too dry for his tastes.

Ailsa had come for him so quickly after the hearing with the Vanir. He thought she must have been excited to speak with him, that she felt the call in her bones as he did when their eyes found each other from across the hall.

Over the few seasons they had been apart, every piece of her had changed in some way. She was always beautiful to him, but now she carried a flame inside her soul that shined bright through her eyes. Her skin was lighter, glowing and smooth against his touch. The dark green gown she wore was sheer around her shoulders and her legs, revealing a fullness to her chest and thighs where they had once been thin as a doe after a long winter. Her silky hair spun like soft flax between his fingers, longer and thicker than before.

But above all, the most miraculous change was not her beauty, but something on the inside. Healed. *Healthy.* Ailsa was no longer sick. She ran to him without faltering. There was no wheeze in her laugh or blood on her sleeve. He had never seen her so alive and free.

He had never seen her so happy.

"*Skide,*" he cursed, pulling his tunic over his head and throwing it on a leather chair near the hearth. Snatching the bottle again, he paced into the bathing room. The only gods-damned place that didn't have windows.

He lit the small room with candles before slamming the door, letting out his rage with a war cry that echoed back at him from the glossy cerulean tiles lining the floor and the walls. Throat raw from his breaths and his screams, he chugged the rest of the bitter wine and slammed the empty bottle on the white stone countertop, bracing his hands on the sink.

"I take it things didn't go well today," a voice spoke in front of him. Erik drew back with a startle, discovering an image in the mirror just above the porcelain sink.

"What in Hel's name are you doing here?" he whispered to keep his words from wandering to the guards outside. The witch was looking back at him instead of at his reflection. She pinned her black hair up like she was just about to head to bed herself. Her scar hidden beneath a thick knit sweater that wrapped her neck.

"Njord can feel when anyone enters or leaves his domain, so I cannot mist to you until you are ready to leave with Ailsa. I have a few creative ways to contact you without interrupting the veil that protects Vanaheim from threats, however."

"Threats like you?" he muttered.

Her red lips tipped into a smirk. "You know me so well, Erik." Her stare flicked up and down, looking him over. "Were you about to jump in the bath? Don't let me keep you. I can wait."

Erik snarled at the witch. "No, I just got back from speaking with Ailsa. There were quite a few details you left out about this *enchantment.*"

She huffed a breath, blowing a stray lock of hair out of her face. "What did she tell you?"

"That this is not a spell but a choice, one they both made. She is mated, not enchanted. She is connected to him by a fae bond, not a spell. You lied to me, and now I am forced to question what else you have spoken so falsely about!" His fist snatched the wine bottle, shaking it before remembering the damn thing was already empty.

"Did I not warn you about this? The fae do this to mortals. They tell them it's a sweet little bond when really it is their magic that seduces them into this decision, warping their values until they are too far into the enchantment to resist its pull. Then they mark them with that rune to complete the spell. She might call him her *Fraendi,* but he is really her captor, and she is a slave to his devices and his personal pleasure."

Erik wanted to believe her words with all his heart, but when he saw them together, the way she looked at the elfin... never had she looked at him like that. Not even when they were exclusively together those spring months in Drakame before he moved away. His head torn between what he wanted and what he saw with his eyes.

The witch laughed a wicked sound, one that mocked his invisible struggle. "Gods, you are pathetic," she said. "No wonder she forgot about you when Vali came along. You are *weak*, Erik. How many chances will you throw away until you stand up for yourself and claim what you want? Your silly, fat father isn't here any longer to tell you what to do—"

"Do not bring my father into this!" he spat.

"Your father was a swine, using you and your brothers to get money from men more powerful than he ever could have been. Eurkame was destined for failure the moment you left that flooded fjord, and your family will always be second best, no matter what you do." The witch pulled a pin out of her hair, letting the length fall from the top of her head and down her back. "But do what you want. I have more important men to help if you are too afraid—"

"I am *not* afraid, and I am not weak!" He slammed a fist down on the vanity, sending a shudder through the polished stone that traveled up the wall where the mirror hung.

"Then finish this," the witch said, smiling through the shaking reflection. "This is your last chance to do something worthy in your life, Erik. Don't let your enemy steal your victory."

"Why are you helping me so much, witch?" he asked. "What are you gaining from this to make you care so much?"

For the first time, she did not find amusement in his questions. Her lips formed a frown. If he thought she looked dangerous before, her scowl drew her even more terrifying. "You made this deal with *me*, mortal. It is my blood inked into your skin. Question me again, and I will stop your heart before its next beat."

Erik lowered his head until he could no longer see the bane in her stare. Crossing the witch was not an option, and the quicker he killed the elfin and took Ailsa home, the sooner this would all be over. This past year would just be a terrible memory, one she might not even remember if he did this right.

"I don't know how to get his blood for the tonic. He and Ailsa are constantly together and now they're leaving to go to a well—"

But when he looked up again, the witch was gone. His own face stared back at him. All the times before this when he had been too weak to make his own decisions were written beneath his skin, hiding beneath his flesh from sight, but still a part of everything he did. When he looked at himself now, he saw the words of his past paint his profile, defining his fate one pacifying memory at a time.

Erik did not go to bed that night, instead walked out to the balcony lining his room and glowered at the hall across the courtyard just as two shadows chased each other between the arches. He scratched the elfin tonight with the blade—deep enough to spill blood. Not much, but a drop was all he needed. If he could get that shirt, possibly sneak into his room while he was asleep, he could use that blood for the tonic and the hard part would be over.

Blowing out the rest of the candles in his room, he barricaded the bedroom door with the sitting area furniture so no one could come inside while he was gone. Without letting himself second guess his plan, he hopped onto the banister of the balcony and climbed up to the roofline.

With silent footsteps across the slate rooftop, Erik followed the shadows back to their room like an assassin concealed by the night.

CHAPTER 7
VALI

The darkness was impenetrable when the moon floated far from the world at the bottom of the Tree. So far was any source of light beyond the stars that specked the sky in their millions. It was dangerous to travel outside of the palace at this time of night. Vali knew if it weren't for the candlelight spilling from his room, he wouldn't be able to see his hand an inch from his face.

"Vali?" Ailsa called him from inside. Her voice sounded stressed. "Is everything all right?"

He threw back the remaining sips of wine lingering at the bottom of his glass before answering. "Yes, just thinking over some things."

Her hands wrapped around his waist from behind before he felt her head settle on the slope of his back. "What's troubling you, *sváss*?"

"Nothing disconcerting, just thoughts of home, mostly. I've never been parted this long from Seela, and my mother wasn't showing any signs of improvement as of the last report we received. I just wish I knew what was going on up there."

Her arms slipped from him slightly. "No one is forcing you to stay. If you want to go back to Alfheim, then maybe you should return for a little while."

Vali stiffened at her response; her touch suddenly was not as welcoming as it had been a moment ago. "Well, if I'm not needed here, then maybe I will."

"That's not what I—"

"Are you done with the bath? I need to use it thanks to your former lover slicing me open this evening." He stepped out of her embrace and started toward the bathing room to leave her on the balcony, determined to show her the same indifference. Mumbling to himself, "Didn't encourage *him* to leave last I heard."

"Vali, don't you dare walk away from me!"

His traitorous feet stalled at her command, and he cursed under a breath. "What..." he asked, turning to face her finally and simultaneously wished he hadn't. The sight of her over-ruled the implications of his argument. "What are you wearing?"

Her face was set into a scowl, but she wore it with such dedication that Vali felt challenged to remove the frown from her lips—almost as much as her body dared him to remove other things. She wore a long, sheer forest green robe. One embroidered with shimmering appliques that resembled ivy and twisted over her bare arms and legs. A golden shift peeked beneath the green, barely skimming her mid-thigh. The combination of colors complimented her creamy skin—and there was so much of it on display to him. She left him defenseless to a surprise ambush, and he didn't mind surrendering.

"Another gift from Freya," she said, which explained everything he needed to know about her new garment.

"A gift for you or me, *sváss*?" he said, speaking through a suddenly parched throat.

"Depends." She untied the sash around her waist, letting the robe fall to either side of her figure to show off the gold shift, made entirely of a delicate gilded fabric edged with lace. "You seem to have other plans for the evening. A bath that is more important than speaking to me about what is truly on your mind."

Vali swallowed and pinched his eyes shut, pushing the image of her away to recall just what had put him in such a foul mood. "You told him today you didn't mind him staying with you for the time being, and a few hours later, you suggest I should leave. How am I supposed to feel about being sent away when Erik shows up?"

"Vali, you aren't being fair."

"Fair?" he asked, looking at her again. "You are the one who hasn't been fair, Ailsa. I've done everything in my power to please you these past few months. I haven't seen my family or my home after I just returned after half a century of being gone. My mother is probably dying, and I may be inheriting a realm soon. Yet I choose to stay here with you, to help you and make sure no harm befalls you. And suddenly, the man you once claimed to love has appeared out of nowhere and you decide to meet with him in private and decide to keep secrets from me."

"I told you everything he told me this afternoon!" she said sharply. "You think I'm hiding things because you *want* there to be something more incriminating to punish him for, but there isn't, Vali! Why don't you believe me?"

"Because I know what you two talked about," he said through gritted teeth. "The guards are gossips, every one of them. Word spreads quickly when people smell *skide*."

"Oh, so now you're listening to the guards?" Her brows raised, and Vali took a long breath to ease back the frustration rooting itself into his racing heart.

He took a step closer, their faces barely an inch from each other. "Yes. I do not trust Erik, and I will not defend myself any further."

Vali had never taken this tone with her, wasn't sure if they had ever fought like this before they were bonded, and he knew the bite in his words were the reasons for the tears brimming in her eyes. The sight made him uneasy, so he turned his back to her. A poor attempt to shut away the guilt beginning to fester.

"You are not the only one who misses their home," she whispered. "I gave up things for you, too. Some were forcibly taken from me, others I willingly sacrificed to be with you."

His lips spilled an empty laugh. "So that is what I am now? A product of all you have lost?"

"Gods, you fae are hardheaded." Her footsteps quietly approached his back. "I lost everything because of this curse, but I gained it all back and more when I fell in love with you. A family with you and Lady Rind and Seela, a future by your side, a love between us that could change the fate of all the worlds."

The ice smothering his heart melted considerably. "You told him you wanted him to stay. That you missed him—"

"I miss everyone from Drakame, *sváss*. I asked to speak with him privately about his story because I wanted to judge his altruism for myself." She touched the slice in his shirt, skimming the blood stain with her fingertips. "Of course I do not want you to go, but I also don't want you to potentially resent me later for keeping you from your family. Especially with your mother being so ill."

"I would never resent you. I couldn't."

"You might if I never offer you the choice. Resentment is inevitable when you feel trapped by someone—intentional or not. I would know."

Vali nodded slowly, the temper quickly dissolving in his chest. "Ailsa, I promise there is no place in the Nine I would rather be than right here watching you become the woman you were fated to be."

"Then why won't you look at me?" she asked, rubbing her bewitching hands up the broad muscles in his back.

He faced her finally, letting her hands skim his body as he turned slowly. The blood instantly drained from his head to his hips at the sight of her. "Because you're so fucking beautiful in that shift, and it's distracting."

Ailsa slipped her hands beneath his shirt and craned her neck to whisper against his lips. "You say such pretty things, *Sólskin*." She tugged the flax over his head and tossed it somewhere to the side. "Now say them with your hands. Or has all this talk made you soft?"

Vali forgot his frustration completely, forgot Erik and the way he looked at his *Fraendi*, and let himself get lost in her kiss. Her lips spoke the words he needed to hear, pressed against his mouth with a pressure that was just as desperate as the kind in his heart. The gentle tug of his belt pulling free from his pants sent him retreating into the boundaries of their bedroom.

"Soft?" he said without breaking away from their kiss. "Do you forget who captured you all those seasons ago? Do I need to remind you just how cruel I can be?"

"Captured?" she murmured. "Don't fool yourself, elfin. I had you bending to me the day I broke out of your imaginary shackles."

Vali laughed, not only because it was true but because he heard the challenge she dangled between her words. He snatched her wrist with one hand and held it between them, taking a single finger and slicing the tip of her own with his magic. Her arm was limp to his control, letting him guide her finger to the soft skin lining the valley of her breasts.

"What are you doing?" she asked.

"You are not the only one Freya has been teaching. She noticed your trouble with being... obedient."

"Obedient?" she asked, brows raising.

"Docile, submissive, compliant—you don't ever listen, Ailsa." Although, she was letting him draw the rune on her now with little objection, smirking now as it marked her body and took effect. The little heathen was too curious to know what was good for her.

"Maybe you just don't have any good suggestions to listen to."

When the rune was finished, he took her finger in his mouth and licked the blood away, healing the cut he made with his tongue. Slowly, he walked backward until the bend of his knees hit the chaise lounge sitting at the end of the bed. He sat with his legs apart on the dark blue plush, never taking his eyes off her as she stood there frozen in place. "You can be the judge of that after tonight, *sváss*. Come here."

Ailsa's ocean eyes fluttered shut as her body moved under his command. He leaned back on the bed behind him as she stepped between his legs. As tempted as he was to touch her, it would only ruin the suspense. "If I tell you to do something you don't want to do, just erase the rune, agreed?" When she nodded, he motioned to her shift. "Take off the nightdress. Leave the robe."

She made a pouty face but complied, fingering the tiny straps down each arm before letting the entire shift fall to the floor at her feet. Vali moaned, unable to keep the savage sounds inside as he took in the curves of her breasts and hips, the way her wavy hair fell like a waterfall over one shoulder, the robe sheer enough to reveal it all to him. Yet just enough fabric to add a detail to her body that kept his eyes roaming.

Vali shifted in his seat, his pants uncomfortably tight. Her eyes shifted for a beat to the bulge between his legs and that wicked mouth smiled, watching him harden for her.

He asked her then, "Who do you belong to, Ailsa?"

She sighed, settling her quickening breaths. "I belong to no one but myself."

But her body betrayed a different response. He leaned forward, gently coaxing her leg to bend and rest on the chaise near his thigh. With two fingers he stroked her entrance and adored the little sound she made, felt the warm wetness coating her center, brought those same fingers to his mouth and tasted the evidence of her desire—her devotion.

"Liar," he whispered. Vali slid a hand beneath the thin robe and gripped the curve of her ass, the other arm tucked around the thigh propped on the bench. His head dipped until his mouth was near inches from her center, so close he could practically taste her scent. "Tell me the truth."

A command. One she had no choice but to obey. Her fingers flew to his hair, snatched at the roots with a needy grip. "I'm yours, you stubborn, incorrigible, filthy fae—"

But her foul words were forgotten as he spread her with his tongue. Her nails dug into his scalp as she bucked against his face, whimpering as he gave her exactly what she wanted, what she wore that indecent ensemble for in the first place. He swirled her clit and sucked, pulling it gently between his teeth, knowing from memory and experience the pattern she liked. A groan shook from his chest as the taste of her hit the back of his throat.

He worked her with tongue and touch, his hands leaving the curve of her backside just long enough to slip inside her, curling against that spot that made her knee weaken too much to hold up her body. But he was there too, holding her in place against his face, slathering her sensitive skin with the heat of his power.

"Vali, don't stop," she gasped. "I'm almost there." And he knew it too, by the way she writhed and pressed harder into his mouth, begging for him to go deeper. Instead, he broke away.

"No," he said, licking the mess she made off his lips. "You will not come until I tell you to."

It was like a mask had been ripped away. A face once full of bliss twisted into a confused frustration, one that she ignorantly believed she was entitled to avoid. Vali smiled bigger than he had all day.

"What in Hel's name just happened?" she growled.

"Do you remember how unmerciful you were with me last night? Never mess with the god of vengeance, *svåss*. I will do worse and more."

Her teeth gnashed together as she looked down at him. "You really play that god card when it's convenient for you."

"I don't play god, my love, I am one." He tapped the outside of her knee with his wet fingers. "Kneel."

Ailsa leaned forward and gripped both of his thighs, slowly lowering to the floor. Her hands slipped up to where his cock strained against the leather, smoothed her palm up and down the ridge to make him swell a little more. When her own breaths built faster, wrought with hunger, she finally released the ties that bound him from her touch, licked her lips ready.

Without a word from himself, Ailsa pumped his shaft with both hands, using her thumb to spread the desire he half spilled when she moaned for him. It was like she needed this as much as he did, after a day of old wounds resurfacing and new ones marking their scars. A carnal connection to reinforce the testing of their bond, of their choice to be together despite all the reasons they shouldn't.

She slipped him between her lips, tongue stroking the center of his shaft as she took him shallow at first, her hand still moving in tortuous strokes at his base. Vali leaned back against the bed, his head falling slack as she adjusted to his size. Her moans of appreciation were like lightning, charging the darkness with light and lust. The sweet vibrations from her throat unraveled him faster. And as he looked down at her, a storm of blue beneath her lashes meeting his gaze, he was completely undone. His hand found her head, combing her soft hair through his fingers as she took him deep and savoringly slow.

"Fuck, Ailsa, you take it so well. You are so beautiful like this." He breathed through the rising pleasure, taming the urge to spill as she worshiped him on her knees. With a gentle push, he edged her away, not wanting to finish just yet.

"I want to finish inside you," he said when her hands tried to take him down again.

She slipped off. A final flick of her tongue made his legs shudder. Her robe had fallen around her elbows, and she released him to let it fall to the floor with the rest of their things. Ailsa crawled into his lap, the bridge of her nose nestling into his neck as she whispered, "Take me to bed, Vali."

He stood with her legs still wrapped around his waist and flung her back onto the mattress, standing over her and watching her bare breasts, hard and taunting, rise and fall with a starved breath. He was in sync with her, from the beats of their hearts to the race of their breaths, they were one in every way that mattered.

He climbed atop her, settling between her legs as they parted for him, fingers running over the soft skin of the back of her thighs. "Turn around. Lay on your face and lift your hips for me."

A small whimper escaped on the insert of her breath as she listened and obeyed, still keeping that rune on her chest intact, still letting him control her with his words and desires. When she was on her stomach before him, he lifted her with a snatch beneath her hip bones, pressing his cock against the wetness of both his tongue trail and her need.

"*Gods,* Ailsa," he said again, his hands smoothed over her ass, ran down her spine and caught the chill draping her skin. "Every inch of you is so damn beautiful. Do you truly know what you do to me? How frustrated you made me in Noatun? Do you understand what it does to me to see you smile at another?"

"No," she breathed as he coated himself in their mixture, cooling the heat in his blood with a long, howling breath. He guided his cock against her center, running it up and down her apex until Ailsa's back arched and her hips rocked against him.

"It makes me want to bend you over like this, take you in

front of everyone so they know you are mine. To claim you in the most savage, cruel way. Would you like that, *sváss*?"

She didn't answer. Her hands stretched out across the top sheet, filling her palms with bedding as he teased her entrance. "Vali, *please.*"

"I know you would, my perfect little heathen. Tell me you're mine, Ailsa."

"I already told you—"

"Say it again," he said, this time thrusting an inch of his cock inside her. His blood was hot, every muscle in his body tensing as he teased them both. "Say it again and again."

"I'm yours, Vali," she choked, moving her hips to get him deeper. He finally gave in, unable to hold himself back any longer, slowly pushing his way inside her as her walls clamped around him.

A sound broke from his chest, from the wildest, most uncouth part of him. He didn't stop until completely sheathed, and Ailsa cried out with a sweet sound. As slowly as he entered, he retreated, taking his time to pluck at the thinning thread of her willpower.

"I'm yours, always," she said again. He rewarded her with another thrust, then another, each one building strength and speed, until she was moaning into the sheets. Her words were barely audible as he took her from behind.

And Vali was equally unraveled. He needed to feel her shatter around him, but most of all, he wanted to see her as she did so. This position was doing wonders for his build up, but that look in her eyes, that place in her mind she soared to when she came, that was what he chased the most.

He pulled completely out of her, and flipped her by the hips until she was on her back, staring up at him with wide eyes. Vali covered her with his body, quickly thrusting his cock into her at the same brutal, unrestrained pace as before. Ailsa pulled her knees high, taking as much of him as she could. Her fingers burrowed themselves into his back as she arched against him.

"Vali," she could only whisper. "I... I need—"

He couldn't hold back any longer, didn't want to. He pressed his forehead against hers and said, "Come with me, *sváss*."

They both fell over the edge, clutching each other as they tumbled into a starless oblivion. His vision frayed at the borders, eyes locked on her as she screamed his name. The way it sounded from her lips made him spill faster until his heart thundered in his ears, and he could hardly hear her moans of pleasure.

When he was finished drawing out the length of their endings, Vali collapsed on the bed next to her. Ailsa sought him again, weaving her limbs with his until the borders of their bodies were blurred, and Vali couldn't tell where he ended, and she began. So intertwined with her, both body and spirit, he had never felt so whole despite giving her every piece of him he had left to offer.

"No matter what happens, *elskan min*," she whispered into the hollow of his throat. Her fingers skimmed the place above his racing heart. "No one can take this from us. You have stained my soul forever."

Vali tilted her chin to look up at him and kissed her hard, branding her words into his heart as they seared through him with a shudder. There was a rustle on the balcony, the sound of wind tossing leaves that tried to snatch his attention, but he ignored it. Nothing could distract him from the woman in his arms.

Warm and solid in her embrace, Vali slept until the darkness outside their room lifted the next morning.

CHAPTER 8

AILSA

Ailsa sat with her eyes closed, listening to the sounds carried by a breeze rolling off the sea. Distant clamoring from swords and shields rose above the waves crashing against the rocky coast. A brief sunrise peeked behind the castle. The smell of the sun heating the sodden earth and saturating the air with a salty mist greeted her in this place each morning.

She opened her eyes once she felt at one with the world around her. Life ran like threads through a tapestry, twisting and binding everything in place until the land and the air and the beings were all a seamless picture on a single plane. Golden rays of morning light spilled over the spires and stretched long shadows over the rippling terrain. The sun did not shine for long down in the Lowest Root, and so she and the rest of those who lived in Vanaheim soaked it up when they could.

"Where did we leave off the day before yesterday?" Njord spoke behind her. He appeared in the corner of her vision field, one hand around a fruity drink and the other holding a single black rose.

"I believe you were reviewing the template of time?" she said.

Njord nodded in recollection. "And what do you remember of our discussion?"

Ailsa shifted in her seat on the cold tile. "That fate is written and predetermined, but not definite. Everyone has the power over their future, to change the potentials based on the actions of the collective and the individual. The Norns lay out the template for every being, and it is up to us to either overcome our fate or submit to it, to let things come to pass or attempt a higher destiny."

"But if the Norns weave our fates, how do we have free will? How does the tapestry not fall apart when a man changes his fate?" he challenged.

"Free will must be considered when the Norns weave their fates, which is why Gullveig refused to raise Baldur the way Odin wanted her too, because messing with threads that have already been stitched into the tapestry could alter the fabric of our universe. It could have destroyed everything." The answer flowed out of Ailsa from a place of familiarity, like the spirit of the witch who discovered these truths whispered the words into her soul. "But Njord?"

"Yes?"

"How am I to bring Baldur back without facing the same consequences Gullveig was trying to avoid? If he truly is the only way to stop Fenrir, how can I reverse what has happened without subjecting the Nine to an even worse fate?"

Njord paced the length of the balcony, watching the shadows of the palace angle as the sun drifted further from the Lowest Root. "Who says Baldur is the one to defeat the

Great Wolf? There is always more than one way to fight for something, Ailsa." He turned to face her, stroking his long, white beard. "Perhaps the well will give you a better idea. The ship will be ready by noon. I'll make sure the seas are favorable to get you there as soon as possible."

Ailsa stood from the carpet, feeling her joints ache from sitting in the position too long. Her stomach rolled with hunger, eager for breakfast. "Is that all for today?"

"Not quite," he said, extending the rose out to her.

"What do you want me to do with this?" she asked, taking it from his hand. The rose was black as the space between stars, petals perfectly fallen in their bloom to lift their floral scent to her nose.

"I want you to change its fate."

She shot him a look of confusion. "What do you mean?"

"Just humor me," he said, smiling. "Change that rose, however you please."

Ailsa looked back at the flower in her hand. This was certainly a challenge he had never given her before, beyond the usual rune memorization or lecture about the relations between fate and time. This was the first time he had asked her to actually change fate and the first time she would attempt such a thing since she brought Vali back to life on the mountain.

She pricked her finger on one thorn lining the stem, lancing a small hole to form a bead of blood. Smearing it across the petal, she whispered the rune instead of writing it, muttering her command to both the flower and the universe.

Gradually, from the smear of crimson, the darkness washed away. And before her very eyes, Ailsa watched the petals turn from the color of dark ash into a snowy white, the transformation flawless. Its fate changed because of her blood, her power, her command over the strands of life of a mere flower. If she could accomplish something so inherently small yet simultaneously significant, what else could she do to change the fate of the surrounding worlds?

One flower, one soul, one strand at a time.

"All men have the power to challenge their fate, but you have the power to change the fate of all things. The individual and the combined. That is the difference between your power and free will. There are rigid constraints and yet infinite potentials for your power, and when you understand them both, you will save the Nine. I have no doubts."

"Because I have power over everything?" she asked, feeling suddenly winded.

"No." He took the rose from her hand. "Because you will find there is power in all things."

"And all things can be powerful," she said, smiling back at him. For everything, there was a rune. The language of fate tied all beings to their purpose, to an origin. This was was the source of all things. This truth the root of all that thrived.

He nodded with a low bob of his head, twirling the rose between two fingers. "We are done for the morning. Go get some breakfast before your stomach turns more feral. Oh, and I would go check on your elfin down at the beach soon. The guards informed me our new guest was heading down there with his golden sword."

Ailsa's heart dropped somewhere in her toes. "Gods above, why didn't you say something sooner?" She grabbed her satchel and rushed down the balcony stairs leading to the lower levels.

"A little sparring can be beneficial between rivals!" he called behind her. "Especially before putting them together on a ship."

"They cannot sail if they are in pieces, Njord!" she shouted back at him. But the god laughed, finding her predicament amusing.

"Fair travels, Ailsa. May the sea be smoother than your elfin's temper."

CHAPTER 9
ERIK

The clang of gilded metal and steel interrupted the peaceful shoreline for nearly an hour, but Erik would not cease the song noting this dance until the elfin was sprawling beneath his boots and his blade. Vali had challenged him during the morning training session, personally selecting him when it came time for duels. Most of the matches had already begun and finished around them, but Erik and Vali were sparring for something so much more than practice.

"You are nothing without your magic," Erik spat between breaths. "Without the crutch of your power, you are struggling to defeat me."

"How does your head not float off your neck with nothing sitting between your ears?" Vali replied. The elfin's bare chest didn't heave with effort like Erik's was, but he was barely fighting back at all. His blows were weak, unimpressive.

Erik ignored his insults and focused instead on the sword in his hand. He was crafty with a weapon, but there was no one in the Nine Realms as good with a blade as an Otsman.

This fae male had relied on his magic long enough to ignore his technique. He just had to concentrate...

"Vali Rindson and Erik Eurikson, drop your blades *now!*" Ailsa shouted against the wind carried off the sea. His opponent glanced up at her with a small grin lighting up his features, and Erik wanted to punch the filthy way he looked at her from his face.

"*Sváss!*" he called to her. "Have you come to watch me enact my vengeance on your little friend? I promise you, my love—" Vali dodged the arc of his falling blade. "I will not hurt him beyond what he deserves."

"What I deserve?" Erik stammered between breaths. His face heated as beads of sweat rolled from his hairline. "You have taken something of mine, and I will not rest until you feel what I felt waking up that Yule night in Drakame, until I take her back."

"I took nothing that belongs to you," Vali sang through his teeth. "Ailsa is my mate, and she's not going anywhere."

Erik slammed his sword against Vali's in a succession of blows, making the elfin grunt as he blocked each one. He stepped back as Vali regained his footing and his hold on his weapon. A smile pushed across Erik's lips.

He rolled his wrist to swing the golden sword, taunting the fae. "That is what you think, demon. But even your little spell over her is no match against me. I will have her, and you will know pain like never before. Only when I have ripped everything away from you will I finally end your life."

"And how do you plan on doing that? Would you risk killing her in the process?" he asked with raised brows.

"I have my ways," Erik said.

"This is ridiculous," Ailsa muttered under her breath when she finally reached them on the beach. "We are leaving soon, and you both insist on prioritizing your insatiable need to kill the other over everything else."

Vali's eyes narrowed into slits as he stared back at Erik. The real duel was about to begin. The fight pulled out of him at last.

"Fine," Ailsa said when no one acknowledged her, resorting to sitting in the sand to watch. "But I spar the winner."

Vali pounced then. His blows were no longer defensive but aggressive, and he felt the full force of his strength in every strike. Erik's movements loosened, probed by a desperate desire to win, until his technique had all but disintegrated. Back in Midgard, he had been one of the best fighters beneath the shieldmages, Drakame's most promising warrior before he moved across the sea. But that spirit had withered away, leaving a scrappy man whose futile crusade had all but eaten away his skill and his craft.

Vali's gaze on him never wavered, his eyes hardly blinked, speeding up the rate of their dance to a beat Erik could not keep up with. He returned blow for blow, pushing Erik back until he stumbled on his own feet. The uneven terrain shifted beneath his stagger and sent him on his ass into the sand.

Erik tried to sit up, but Vali shoved him back with a heel to the chest. He dragged the tip of his sword to Erik's neck, stilling him where he had landed. Erik knew the look in his eyes, one he was familiar with on the battlefields back home. This elfin was going to bleed him out, here and now. No mercy remained in the brilliance of his empty stare.

"All right, Vali." Ailsa placated him from the sidelines. "That's enough. You beat him, now help him up."

But neither Vali nor Erik moved. Each locked in place by a force he couldn't interpret. Vali's chest rose and fell. His hands gripped the pommel of his sword until his knuckles blanched. Erik swallowed and only waited for what would come next. He couldn't kill the elfin without killing Ailsa as well, and that was the only thing keeping him from sweeping his sword into the male's stomach.

"*Vali!*" Ailsa said his name again to snap him out of whatever he was considering. She was standing now, but too far to intervene. A captain was there with her, holding her back.

"Hear how she defends me?" Erik spoke so only Vali could hear. "Our bond and our history run deeper than a stupid mark. I don't have to draw runes on her skin to make her body do what I want."

The elfin only smirked at him. "I knew I heard someone on the balcony last night. Did you enjoy listening to me fuck my lady, Erik?"

"I've heard all those sounds before," he said with indifference. "Nothing new." The tip of Vali's blade dug into his flesh, piercing a hole into his skin. Erik gritted his teeth, trying not to flinch at the sting.

Vali replied, "Ailsa might get off on others watching her please me, but I will kill anyone that does so without her consent. Stop giving me motives to kill you, Erik, because I'm only one more reason away from bleeding you out."

The elfin took his foot off his chest. But just as he was about to walk away, he slipped the tip of his sword across Erik's cheek, burning a line of fire through his face. He turned on his back heel and walked away, just as Ailsa was rushing to meet them.

"Erik are you all right?" she asked, kneeling in the sand. "What did you say to Vali?" Erik clutched his face, but blood spilled through his fingers and painted the ground dark crimson. She pulled his hand away from his cheek, assessing the split skin that stretched from his jaw to his ear, tearing through the left side of his face.

"Fucking elfin," he groaned, sitting up. "Couldn't even end a fight honorably."

"Well, you deserved it after yesterday. Here, let me heal you." Ailsa pricked a new finger that didn't have scars yet and wrote something above and below his wound. But as soon as her blood touched his skin, it boiled hot with a new burn, rolling down his chin to drip thick, black sludge on his sleeve.

"That's odd," she said, her brows furrowed as she watched her blood dissipate. "It's like your body won't accept my power. I don't think that's ever happened before."

"I'm fine, Ailsa." He swatted her away and replaced a gloved hand to his cheek. "I'll go wash it off in the sea. The salt will clean it and you can stitch it up on the boat."

"Are you sure—"

"I said I'm fine! My body rejects your magic because I do not want it, not even if it is to help me." he snapped. He stood too quickly, tossing sand in a messy display of his irritation.

She said nothing as he walked away, but Erik thought her silence was more condemning than any curse he silently breathed. If the elfin thought a small cut would deter him from his goal, make him fear the male, he was mistaken. Vali would regret the day he crossed him, and Erik would do worse and more before he left Vanaheim.

He just needed to be patient.

CHAPTER 10
AILSA

Ailsa stood apart from the crowd of soldiers on the dock, waiting for their ship to arrive. But even as the crew brought up the remaining supplies, the horizon remained empty. She squinted, searching for a sign of the vessel, worry eating away at the ends of her ribs. "Looking for the ship?" Captain Baelin asked as he approached her side.

She nodded. "It should have arrived by now, don't you think?"

"Yes, but you won't find the Skidbladnir out there, Lady, because it's right here." Ailsa looked at a palm he outstretched to her, a velvet pouch in his wide hand.

She offered him a doubtful look. "You're joking."

A broad smile crept across his cheeks. Baelin was a giant who lived in Vanaheim. He had served Njord since the Aesir-Vanir war to avenge Gullveig, also a Jotun who taught the Vanir her magic before she was burned three separate times by Odin. His skin was such a light shade of lavender, it appeared more bluish in the waning sunlight. But his eyes were bright red, almost as fiery as the mane of hair he wore braided down his back.

"Take it and see for yourself."

Ailsa took the pouch from his hand and pulled the strings to peer inside. Sure enough, there was a small ship, one folded in on itself like a child's toy. She pulled it out of the purse and set it upright in her own hand, marveling at the exquisite detail painted onto such a small surface. "What is this? A replica?"

"That is our actual ship, Lady Ailsa." He beckoned to the end of the dock. "Go, throw it out into the water and watch what happens." When he saw the look she shot him, he added, "Just trust me."

She did as she was told and reluctantly threw the tiny ship into the Sea of Rán, where it floated for a moment before a wave pulled it under. She turned back to Baelin. "Are you messing with—"

A violent sound of disturbed ocean, like a tidal wave clapping on a cliff side. Ailsa turned and her breath was stolen, watching the largest ship she'd ever seen arise from its submergence in the sea. Had she not felt the spray of cold sea against her face from the force of its impetus, she could have convinced herself it was too impossible to be real.

The hull was a golden wash stain over a wood grain she'd never seen before. The body marked with scripted runes that glistened like hot bronze just above the waterline. Her eyes traveled upward, taking in the dark red masts that were still drawn shut, catching on the gold plated railings and the three headed dragon leading the ship's bow.

"Welcome aboard the Skidbladnir, Lady Ailsa. The greatest ship in all the Nine and said to hold every Aesir in Asgard. When those sails open, you'll find there's always a fair wind to guide you along." Baelin motioned for the gangplank to be set up. The rest of the crew lobbied together to tie the vessel in place as they boarded the supplies.

"This is Njord's?" she asked in wonder, feeling quite small against such grandness. "How did he build such a ship?" Ailsa had watched the boat builders in her own village, understood the time and consideration it took to design each longship. Their dependency on sea travel made her people expert ship-builders, but nothing on this level. This was just beauty and craft and what had to be *magic*.

"Technically, it is Frey's, but he lends it to his father if his reasons are good enough." The captain winked. "Long ago, Loki cut off Thor's wife's hair, and if you know anything about Sif, you'd understand she valued her golden locks above all else—as did Thor. To keep his life, Loki was forced to replace it, but in true trickster fashion he gave the dwarves a challenge to complete his task, which fortunately led to the creation of several other magical objects such as Thor's hammer, Odin's ring, and this ship."

"Loki," Ailsa said, shaking her head. "It is a pity there is so much darkness inside him. He could do great things for the Nine if he used his cunning heart for good instead of getting out of trouble."

Baelin's shoulders fell slightly. "There is darkness in all of us. Some are just more transparent than others. But some-times I wonder who's side he will be on... in the end."

The captain left her to assist the men and women boarding the ship. Ailsa turned to find Vali sitting on a crate, eating an apple slice off the tip of his dagger. Just down the dock stood Erik, alone and brooding, the cut on his face now a shocking red from being burned by salt. It must have been painful to scowl with the wound on his face, but he scowled all the same.

Ailsa turned her back to them both, wondering where they would all stand in the end, and who she would face on the opposite side when it came to it.

The journey was a short one, a planned expedition that would only take half a day's time thanks to the Skidbladnir's sails. Ailsa changed into trousers and a linen shirt to climb up to the nest of the ship, so she could witness the space beneath the Tree of Life from all directions. The further they sailed, the darker the sky shaded, until she could hardly make out the frothy black waves or the thin horizon separating an ocean from an entire universe.

"What are you doing up here, *sváss?*"

Ailsa turned to see Vali climbing into the nest, smiling a bit despite her annoyance with him. "How much things have changed since we found ourselves in a similar situation," she said.

He laughed. The sound was a balm to the ache in her heart. He approached her side, leaning against the border. "I remember that day well, and you look just as cross with me now as you did then. The difference is, this time I can't understand why."

She rubbed her tired eyes with the back of her hand and sighed. "I told you to stay away from Erik, then you invite him to spar with you and nearly kill him. I swear to Ymir, Vali, I'm going to draw that obedience rune in a place you cannot reach if you keep going behind my back!"

"I wasn't going to kill him." His voice was barren of feeling.

"The look in your eyes said otherwise," she said, catching his gaze by tipping his face to her. "I know you hate him, *Sólskin*, but he is my friend, whether or not you like it. When he attacked you, it was a misunderstanding. But you made it very clear you can beat him in a fight, and yet you pinned him and injured him when he was already down. "

Vali said nothing, only continued to stare off into the darkness closing in on the ship. Lanterns burned beneath them on the main level, casting shadows over his face that obscured any sign of what he was thinking. "He's still in love with you. You know that, right?"

"That is absurd—"

"A man only goes to the ends of the world for two reasons, Ailsa: revenge and love. In his case, he has motives for both. I only wish you would listen to me for once."

Ailsa reached a hand around his neck to pull his face to hers with a finger beneath his jaw. But he was too tense to turn. She withdrew her hand, feeling a wall between them return. "And I wish you would stop letting him come between us. I already belong to you in every way that matters. What more do you want?"

His upper lip twitched in a brief snarl. "Perhaps I will invite one of my former lovers on our next adventure. How would you like me rubbing my past lives in *your* face?"

The words hit her like a dagger in the chest, and Ailsa shifted her hips off the side of the border. If he was trying to hurt her, he had aimed his words accurately enough. "I'm done speaking about this. You're being ridiculous."

"Ridiculous?" He scoffed, turning to face her at last. "You have defended a man who has done nothing but lie since he arrived. You defend a man against your *mate*. He is hiding something, Ailsa, and if you do not get rid of him as soon as we get back to Vanaheim, then I will."

"You might be my mate, Vali, but you do *not* tell me what to do!"

"Because being your mate means nothing to you, does it?" He was practically shouting now. "Honestly, why did you even become my *Fraendi* if you don't care about anything I have to say?"

Ailsa's chest deflated with a defeated breath. "How could you ask me such a thing? I bound threads with you because I *love* you. But clearly those motivations are not returned if all you care about is control and submission. If I wanted that from a lover, Vali, I would have gone back to Drakame!"

"I feel you are halfway there," he muttered, glaring at the darkness.

Ailsa shut her eyes to seal the tears trying to form behind her eyes. They had never fought so much in such a short time. She knew there would come a time when their bond was tested. She just thought it would be more resilient than this.

"He tried to bring me back to his village that night you took me," she whispered. Vali's eyes shifted to her in interest. "He wanted me as a *mistress*, because he was already promised to someone else. Whatever love he thinks he had for me wasn't love at all. I denied him then when you weren't even a factor, and I will surely deny him now that you are."

"Then why haven't you sent him away yet?" he asked. "You are giving him hope you will go back with him the longer you entertain his advances."

"Because I am fearful someone darker and more cunning than your father has tricked him. I cannot let him leave without knowing he will be safe when he does. But if you cannot trust me, then these marks on our hands mean nothing."

Vali combed his fingers through the length of his hair, tensing his jaw. "Trust goes both ways, Ailsa. If you do not trust my warnings, then it truly means nothing."

She retreated a step, her mouth parted in a visible shock. The tears brimming in her eyes filled with both anger and hurt. There was no sense continuing a conversation where there was no more common ground.

"I'm going to bed. Come find me when you are done acting like a child." She turned to start down the ladder, and her *Fraendi* said nothing to stop her.

CHAPTER II
AILSA

It was the first morning Ailsa had woken up alone. The other side of the bed cold and neat. The quiet was unbearable without the elfin's snore. Vali had not slept by her side for the first time since they had shared a cloak in the Realm Between Realms.

Baelin had offered them the Captain's Cabin for comfort, but she felt only all the empty space around her until it was smothering. Ailsa quickly got up and changed into something suitable for hiking the lands below the Tree, eager to escape the loneliness staring at her from the half made bed. A night's sleep had dissolved the temper in her heart, leaving only a painful memory of their fight behind.

They had docked late last night. The darkness below the tree was so thick, Ailsa hadn't seen land until they had drifted against a shallow edge, scraping the hull. Mimir's Well had been left unguarded since the Vanir had taken the god as a trade deal after the war, knowing Odin relied on him for his wisdom as a direct consultant. But when the Vanir gods felt cheated out of the exchange, they beheaded Mimir and sent his head back to Odin.

Mimir has spoken little since then.

The well he once guarded still existed beneath the Tree, but few knew where to find it, other than the gods themselves. Ailsa wondered if the only ship that could find a favorable wind down here was the same ship they were voyaging.

She strapped her blade to her side and packed a bag of supplies, along with her sketchbook and a pot of ink should she need to scribe anything the well told her—if it told her anything. Just as she turned toward the door to depart, the entrance to the cabin swung open. A man spilled out of the darkness behind it.

"Ailsa," Vali mumbled. His momentum entering the room stopped short as he practically ran into her. She looked him over, taking in his half-dressed state and disheveled hair. He rubbed his eyes, dark circles running long beneath them, and blinked her into focus. His skin reeked of wine.

"Where in Hel have you been?" she asked in neither a tone of interest nor concern.

He shut the door with the back of his heel and glanced around the dimly lit room. "I went below to drink with the mates last night. Ended up sleeping there as well."

"I can smell that." Ailsa wrinkled her nose and started toward their bag of belongings. Tossing him his usual, she kept his cloak for herself. The air was already damp inside her room, it was probable it would be worse when she went outside.

"I'm sorry," he said. When her gaze finally met him again, it was met by someone who appeared too uncertain to be her mate. Vali had sunken into a state that left him unrecognizable.

Ailsa shrugged. "About what?"

"For not being here." He dressed, and she watched him as he stripped, letting the sight of his bare body soften a place in her heart that missed him all night. "I didn't mean to stay out—"

"But you did," she breathed.

A pause stretched. "I did, and I shouldn't have."

"I didn't exactly make it easy for you to return," she said, looking away. "We said horrible things to each other, and we should probably discuss those things. But Baelin said he'd be waiting for me to leave as soon as possible this morning, so I'm afraid we'll have to speak later."

"I understand. But let me at least say this before we go." He stepped closer, his boots heavy across the decking. He took her hand in his own and lifted it to her chest. His fingers twisted the ring she never took off, the same one he gave her when they first came to Vanaheim.

"It is true what you said last night. He is your friend, and I will respect your decision, no matter how much I disagree, to let him stay until you decide to send him away. But I will not let him, nor anyone else, get in between us ever again. This is my oath to you. I will never stop fighting for you and our bond for as long as we live."

His words were a salve to the ache in her chest. No matter how wounded their bond was right now, it was still whole despite its imperfections, still strong enough to withstand the force of everything else pulling them apart. Sensing that strength in him—with him—made her feel like there was nothing in all the Nine that could break them.

She stood on her toes and kissed him hard before whispering, "I vow this too, *Sólskin*. Never leave my bed cold again."

Ailsa thought Vanaheim was dark but beneath the Tree clung a true darkness. One that was alive as the pulse racing beneath her skin, claiming all it touched in this forgotten place beneath the worlds. They took small vessels the rest of the way, blue flames burned in the lanterns leading the way forward, a kind of light that acted as both a tool to illuminate the way and for protection.

"What do we need defending from down here?" Ailsa said quietly as they rowed silent paddles against the black water. Vali sat beside her as they led the way to land, Erik deciding to board the vessel behind them. The ship anchored in the shallows glowed against the backdrop of night. Similar lanterns hung from the masts and the hull for their return.

"There is a dragon who gnaws on the Roots. Nidhogg usually lives in the dark underworld of Helheim, but he flies down here to feast on the Tree, damaging it at the same time. He is sensitive to light, so we use blue flames to avoid his attention."

A shiver crawled up her back, and she pulled Vali's cloak tighter around her shoulders. Njord had left out quite a chilling detail. But no one else appeared concerned about a dragon flying in the darkness above them like a nightmare, so she squinted her eyes and focused on the land coming into view ahead.

There was no sand as they docked, only a shore made up of pale stone and cold earth. The trees lining the edge of this world-less realm were the color of ash and bare of any life. The only thing that moved was the light breeze weaving through the trees, carrying a cool moisture that penetrated her skin and pierced the planes of her face.

Vali slipped a gloved hand into her own, squeezing it gently. Ailsa smirked. "Afraid of the dark, *sváss?*"

His cold lips brushed the shell of her ear as he spoke. "I fear this kind of dark. Stay close to me. Nidhogg is not the only creature Mimir guarded his well from."

Baelin and his second, Daleah, a short giantess with a wide jaw, led the small group. Erik's breath was thick behind her, marking his presence through his own fear.

"Are we sure they know the way?" she asked the elfin.

"It is a bit late to ask that question," he replied. The lantern in his opposite hand revealed an amused smirk. "Njord and his men keep eyes on the well. They have been there before."

"But none have drank from it besides Mimir, Gullveig, and Odin?"

"The knowledge in this well is not the kind most people are after, Ailsa. All wisdom worth gaining comes at a cost. Even the Allfather himself had to pay a price to become all-knowing."

Another detail the god of the sea had left out. Ailsa wondered if she would also pay a price for the wisdom she sought today, and if she would be strong enough to pay it.

Baelin stopped in his tracks, and the rest of their group did the same. He held up a hand, encouraging them to remain quiet as he listened. But for what, Ailsa did not know. There was nothing but silence carried on the biting breeze.

He then turned to face them all, his eyes wide with panic. "Lights out!" he said in a loud whisper, before blowing out the blue flame in his lantern.

Ailsa couldn't contain the small gasp from her lips as Vali

obeyed, watching one by one as every light flickered out and left them swallowed by a void. The elfin at her side moved his hand up her arm, giving her the freedom to grasp the hilt of her blade instead. Weapons scraped their sheath around her.

She wanted to ask what they were up against, but a shudder interrupted her thoughts. A gentle shake through the earth that trembled more violently the closer something *alive* crept closer to their company.

A bright light, the brilliant shade of rubies, briefly disturbed the surrounding void. Raw fire, streaming from the breath of a beast she couldn't quite see in full detail. A deep groan followed a flicker of light, one that echoed throughout the land beneath the Tree and churned Ailsa's stomach with its vibrations.

None of them moved for what felt like hours as they waited for the beast to leave, its retreat noted by the stillness of the earth returning once more. Her party lit their lanterns when they were alone again in the abysmal darkness.

"What was that?" she asked Vali as soon as she saw his face in the blue light.

His hand returned to hers, giving it an encouraging squeeze. "That was a lindwyrm. They are like dragons, but without wings. Several of them roam beneath the Tree, but they are harmless unless provoked. In which case, their soft underbelly is the only vulnerable spot."

"Harmless is a green snake found in a garden. That thing was stepping over the trees and breathing fire, Vali!"

"And it left us alone because we did not draw its attention," Baelin said to her, but his words did nothing to soothe her imagination running wild at this point. This was all too much, the darkness, the dragon, the lyndworms. Njord had mentioned none of this when he sent her to the well.

"I do not wish to risk the lives of anyone here just for a taste of knowledge," she said. "We should go back before that thing returns."

Baelin dismissed her with a wave of his lantern. "Njord did not tell you because you would have never came knowing what was down here, Lady. Trust me when I say this is the safest place in all the Nine. The well is just a little further. Come!"

Doubtful, she listened anyway, following the rest of the crew close behind as they traversed deeper into the web of ash trees. An insignificant path marked the way, padded into the earth unceremoniously as their only tangible guide to the well. Ailsa spared a glance behind her to see Erik holding his own lantern, brown eyes darting around the darkness with equal apprehension. But if he was worried, he kept his mouth shut.

The padded earth became a paved stone beneath their feet. Engraved beneath ash dusting the walkway were runes carved along the edges. Ailsa recognized them as protective spells, watching as they glowed an iridescent white. A faint light, yet just enough to shine the way forward to a dome shaped building.

Baelin walked straight inside, the single archway leading to a short hall filled by his lantern flame. The rest of them followed behind with the glow from the runes beneath their strides reaching the darkness the lanterns could not, leading to a circular room now alive with light.

Ailsa slipped from Vali's grasp when they were inside, looking not at the well at first, but at the dome ceiling. Painted along the stone were moments in time, stories from every world, race, and being. From Ymir, the giant whose body had given life to the Tree, to the gods Sol and Mani driving the sun and moon's chariot, the stories of creation were recorded in this small temple hiding beneath the Nine.

The well stood in the center of the room, its opening so large it appeared more like a pool. Ailsa approached it with hesitant feet, staring into the rippling waters disturbed by nothing but pure forbidden knowledge ready for her to taste.

"Is that..." Erik mumbled behind her. "Is that what I think it is?"

"Odin's fucking eye," she whispered. Floating there, on the surface of the water, was a pale blue eye, plucked straight from its strings of its former skull.

"The Allfather's sacrifice to drink from the well, taken and accepted by Mimir himself." Vali circled the perimeter to stare at her from across the water, watching her hands. "But we do not know what the well will ask of you, nor what it will take. Are you sure about this, *sváss*? No one will fault you if you change your mind."

"It is all I have left to learn," she answered. "Njord and Freya have taught me the runes, but if the well can show me the source of it all, then I may find a way to change the fate of our worlds. Odin tried and failed, but it was not his path to take. It is mine to follow the other witches before me."

"I will not watch this," Erik said in a rough voice. Grabbing a lantern, he started back toward the entrance. "I'll keep watch outside. Finish this quickly, Ailsa."

She braced her hands on the stone lining the border of the opening. Her fingers traced the lines written there, not runes but words, an unknown language forgotten by the ages. Had Mimir made these notes? Did the god of wisdom create his own secret words to record his time here and what he saw? The other gods claimed he drank from these waters daily, yet he sacrificed nothing—the knowledge was rightfully his.

Did the seeress give up something near to her for the truth? Ailsa saw no other eyes in the well.

"Give her the horn," Baelin spoke to Daleah. The captain unhooked from her back the largest gjallarhorn Ailsa had ever seen, which would've been able to hold at least four ales back in Drakame. Whatever beast it was claimed from must have been an impressive kill. Lining the white husk were gold rings inscribed with more cryptic markings. She offered it to Ailsa, who found the handle was smooth black leather, yet tough against her palm as if it had never been used.

Baelin then stepped in line next to her. "When you gather the water from the well, fill the horn all the way to the brim. It is imperative to drink the entire batch, Ailsa. Even if we must force it down your throat, you must finish every drop."

"Why?" she asked.

He shrugged. "Those are Mimir's instructions, ones he gave not only to the seeress who sought him many ages ago, but to the Allfather as well. It is best not to question the wisest of the Aesir."

Ailsa gripped the horn in both hands, the weight of it already cumbersome even without the water. She looked to Vali, eyes communicating her need for him, not to change her mind but to keep it for her. He strode around the well and stood behind her, large hands seated themselves on her hips. With a steadying breath, she dipped the horn into the well water, watching the clear liquid sparkle as it pooled inside her cup.

"*Skol*," she muttered, before lifting the rim to her lips and tipping back the massive horn.

Ailsa burned everywhere.

The water scorched her palate from the first sip and did not relent until the last drop was forced down her throat by the last shred of her determination and her *Fraendi* holding her in place. Even as the horn fell from her lips, fire licked her insides. She suppressed a gag with the back of her hand, stubbornly keeping the water inside her stomach. Ailsa felt her knees give out from the pain, stealing her strength until she was lying flat on the cold stone.

The light dimmed, swallowing the faces hovering around her. Inside, she felt the teeth of the forbidden knowledge, felt it gnaw on her ribs until it licked them clean of flesh and only a hollow form remained in a space that seemed to empty as time passed. She could not judge time, how it came or went, how long each burning moment lasted.

But one thing remained: the paintings on the dome ceiling. Each picture was infinitely brighter, a thousand more shades revealed themselves to her. So many colors now existed she had never known before, bringing the images to life above her.

A chill shook the limbs of the Tree, a great stag appeared and chewed on a Lower Branch, Sol and Mani ran their chariots, pulling the sun and the moon around the Nine as they had since the beginning of creation, and Ailsa watched the universe from a distance. The burning in her bones suddenly gone, her spirit went quiet.

But the serene picture in motion was suddenly disturbed, like a rock breaking still water and sending ripples throughout a pond. Two wolves formed behind the pilasters of the dome, each chased down a chariot, hunting the sun and the moon.

Ailsa could only watch as they closed in on their prey. Sol put up a fight, used the embers of her burning star to slow the beast and char his strides, but the wolf eventually caught up to the goddess, swallowing her whole with its massive jaws. At the same time, the other wolf pounced on Mani, eating the moon in one jaw stretching bite.

Each star blinked out one by one. The light in the room faded as worlds fell into darkness, and Ailsa fell into that same void. Who she was, what existed, all drowned away in the dark depths of the well.

CHAPTER 12
AILSA

The sound of the sea forced her eyes to open. Ailsa was back in their room in Vanaheim, finding a pitcher of water and a plate of food stacked neatly on a bedside table next to a small lantern with a regular, golden flame. Her hands reached to the side of the bed, but it was empty, as cold as the breeze blowing off the Sea of Rán and through her balcony window.

Now lying on her stomach, she pushed off her hands and scrambled to find something—anything—to write with. The scenes she saw from the well were slowly fading like a forgotten dream, and she needed to record what she saw before the memories slipped away for good. Her satchel she packed for the journey was still full, sitting untouched on a leather armchair in the corner of the room. Ailsa darted for the pack, finding her ink and paper exactly where she left it.

The world begins and ends in fire and ice. She scribbled across the stiff parchment. Her writing was messy, hand stiff from sleep.

"Ailsa, you're awake!" A voice ladened with relief snapped

her out of her post waking trance. She looked up to find Erik hopping off the balcony banister to rush through the double doors. Vali always left them open. Feeling the breeze as he slept always reminded him of home, and the notion was becoming familiar to her as well.

She reached for the blanket that had fallen on the floor in her rush toward her bag, covering her shift as he invited himself inside. "Erik! What a surprise." Her voice brushed against a raw throat. Ailsa set her notes down on the table to pour herself a drink. "Did you... sneak in here?"

He stepped closer before stopping near the bench at the foot of the bed. "Aye, but I had to check on you. No one had given me a word since we came back to Vanaheim yesterday, and after you passed out at the well, the elfin forbade anyone from allowing me to visit."

Ailsa's eyes shifted to the bedroom door. "Well, as you can see, I am fine. But Erik, you need to leave before Vali gets back. Your presence here is sufficient for a death sentence to him."

He waved his hand, dismissing her concern. "He was called to a meeting right before you woke up. Something about news from Alfheim—"

"Alfheim? Do you mean Seela is here? I must go see her!" Ailsa's mood perked at the thought. The commander had visited infrequently over the last few months, only sparing enough time away from the High Lady to give Vali brief updates. She started toward the closet to change, but Erik snatched her forearm to stop her.

Her eyes locked on the hand around her arm. "What do you think you're doing?"

He sucked a large breath, licked his lips before replying, "Ailsa, this is our chance. We can leave before he gets back. We can find our own way back to Midgard. The gods guided me here. Surely, they will bless the journey home." His grip turned bruising. "Come with me, *sváss*. Come home."

Ailsa tried to twist out of his hold, but Erik was unrelenting. The look in his brown eyes darkened into hard mud, and she stilled like a doe caught in a meadow, knowing from experience just what that look meant. Before she could react, his face lunged toward her, his opposite hand fisting the back of her head to keep her in place as he slammed his lips onto hers.

Dropping the blanket, she tried to push him off by pounding her fist into his chest, his shoulder, the side of his face. But Erik was solid stone against her, his firm kiss smashing his face against hers until she couldn't see or breathe. She made a sound of panic, wishing now that Vali would come back and kill him on site for assaulting her.

But he swallowed her cry with his mouth, sweeping his tongue against the defiance of her pressed lips. The longer she struggled, the more her lungs burned for air, the harder her pulse slammed with revulsion at the way his tongue tasted her lips.

Ailsa demanded her body to relax, to loosen, to let his hands bend her how he wanted. She willed her mind to calm and take control and think this through. He brushed the seam of her lips once more, and she gave him admittance. Felt a moan shake his throat as his tongue dove deep into her mouth —and bit him.

Erik let out a yelp, and his body flinched in surprise, and Ailsa used the brief distraction to twist her arm out of his grip and punch him with all the strength she had in the center of his face. Her knuckles cracked cartilage as they met his nose, and Erik stumbled away, holding his broken face in his hands as blood spilled between his fingers.

"*Skide*, Ailsa, what the Hel was that for?" he growled,

resorting to use his shirt to plug the bleed.

Ailsa wiped her wet lips and spat into the carpet. "Don't you ever touch me again! How dare you force yourself on me—"

"You enjoyed it for a moment, do not lie!" he growled. "I was trying to break that damn spell he has over you, to get you to remember who I am in your heart. But now I see the truth and what must be done."

"Get out!" she shouted. "Leave before I kill you myself for what you have done today."

He wiped his face with the back of his arm, leaving a blood smear across his cheek. "I gave up everything, Ailsa. The clan, the title of chieftain, all my honor, to come find you!"

"I didn't want to be found," she answered. "And I do not want to be with you in that way. Not now and not ever again." She watched her words slowly break something in his heart, his chest deflating with a sharp exhale.

"Do you feel anything for me still?" he asked.

Ailsa looked away, avoiding the bane in his stare. "I feel sorry for you. That you did not know what you had when you had it, that you only want me because someone else values what you did not. But I am not a land you can take back, nor a title you can win. If you stopped seeing me as a conquest, you would have realized all these things before you left."

A silence stretched that lasted too long. Erik's heavy breaths were the only sound disturbing the quiet. She had to be harsh, was forced to wound his pride so deep he'd never forget it. Vali was right. It was cruel to keep giving him hope where there was none, and she could no longer avoid hurting his feelings, hoping he would see the writing on the wall for himself.

"I lost everything for you. My brothers disowned me, my

clan hates me, Nikros spat on my ship the day I left and cursed my soul to never see Valhalla. If I return without you…" He couldn't finish the thought, but she knew. Coming home empty handed was not something an Otsman could be proud of. There were laws against it. He'd be punished harshly for taking supplies on a fruitless voyage, returning with nothing but a golden sword and the rejection of his once beloved. Her decision to stay sentenced him to exile—possibly worse.

Death.

"I'm sorry you ruined your life for me, Erik. I will write to Nikros and tell the clans everything—"

"I did not ruin my life," he whispered. He turned to leave the way he came, but looked over his shoulder to spit one last remark. "You might have power over fate, Ailsa, but you do not have power over mine. You'll see one day I am worthy of being feared and respected. All of you will."

When he finally disappeared into the darkness draping over the realm, she ran to the double doors to lock them shut. She leaned against the window framed within the door, sinking down the cold glass to sit on the floor where her shaky breaths smoothed into strong ones. The adrenaline in her veins dissolved, leaving her fingers shaking with nothing to do but ball into numb fists.

Vali had been right all along, and she had punished him for it—fought him over it. The anger in her heart ate away into guilt, until all she wanted was to feel him instead of Erik's violent phantom still squeezing her arm and tangling her hair. To replace this defiling taste in her mouth with Vali's sweet discourse, his kind kisses.

Ailsa stood to her feet and smoothed her hair, then searched for something to cover her shift enough to leave her room.

"Njord!"

She rushed down the corridor as soon as his cerulean robes swept into view. The god stopped in his tracks and turned to her, a genuine smile lighting up his face. "Ailsa! It is good to see you awake. We weren't sure how a mortal would stand against the knowledge of the well, but I see you came out just fine in the end."

She caught her breath as she met him in the middle of the hall. "Aye, I managed. Thank you for voicing your concerns ahead of time." He smiled, noting the sarcasm in her words and the hands braced on her hips. "But I learned something— several things, actually. Where is Vali?"

Njord's jaw hovered opened for a beat of hesitation before speaking. "He is in my study. I do not think the news from Alfheim was particularly positive. He asked to be alone, but I think he would be more than pleased to see you."

"Oh," she said, biting at her lower lip. "All right, well thank you for the forewarning. I'll go find him now." He nodded her off, and Ailsa started toward the gods' rooms in the western part of the castle. Where the cliff side dropped off and nothing beyond the wing interrupted the view of the sea.

Ailsa took in the sight as she passed a row of open archways, watching the moonlight gleam off the endless ocean and the stars glow against a dark canvas. The same stars she recognized in the visions given by the well, the same ones that would be burned away after the same moon would be eaten by a wolf. Strange things—impossible things, events so extreme she could hardly hold them together in her mind. She wanted to finish her notes before she lost the words.

Knocking first, a silence followed, and Ailsa pushed back a massive door that led to the god's personal chambers. Njord's study branched from a keeping room, where light streamed from inside the study through an ajar door.

"Vali?" she called.

"I'm out here," he answered somewhere further into the room. Ailsa followed the sound of his voice to find him sitting on the bench of an arching window, one leg propped while the other dangled over the edge. His eyes were distant until they saw her standing there, like he hadn't connected her voice.

"*Sváss.*" Swinging his legs over the side, his boots found the floor and ate the distance between them before wrapping her in a desperate embrace. "Of course, you wake up the moment I'm called away. How are you feeling? Did the well tell you anything?"

"I'm fine, and it told me everything," she said, smiling up at him as he pulled away. "But before we get into that, are you all right? You looked like you were in deep thought before I walked in."

The curve of his lips flattened, falling with his shoulders. "Enver arrived from Alfheim this morning. He brought me a letter from Seela."

"A letter? Why couldn't she come herself?"

Vali's hands dropped from her waist to reach into his back pocket, pulling out a folded piece of parchment. "Read and see for yourself."

She took the letter from his hands and skimmed it over, reading it twice just to give the words time to sink in. "*Sólskin...*"

"I knew it was coming," he murmured. "When she didn't heal at first, I knew then she never would. Fae can heal easily from wounds like hers, but when they age... well, that ability gets weaker." He walked a few steps away, looking toward a window. "I've been waiting for this update since we received the very first."

"You knew then, yet you remained here with me?" Ailsa steeled her voice, taking care not to let her words shake.

"How many times must I say it?" He turned to look back at her. "There is nothing in the Nine Realms that will keep me from you, *elskan min.*"

She swallowed back a stone in her throat, wiped away the tears forming in her eyes before they manifested down her cheeks. "Let's go back. Tomorrow."

"I'll tell you the same thing I told Enver. I am not leaving without you or until you are ready—"

"I have the answers, Vali," she said, hardly above a whisper. The pain in his gaze eased back significantly. "The well told me the Voluspa, but it did more. It gave me the wisdom to understand it." She reached for him, taking his hand. "I know how to defeat Fenrir."

"What do you mean?" he asked.

She pulled out her notes and handed it to him, explaining as he read. "The well recited the Voluspa and how Baldur was destined to be slain. Some things have already come to pass, but so much is still yet to happen. The well claimed a son of Odin would slay Fenrir, but it also said Odin would bury his hope on the funeral pyre." The look in Vali's eyes proved he did not follow, so she continued. "What if Baldur wasn't fated to kill the Great Wolf at all? What if Odin misunderstood the witch?"

"He is the strongest brother I have besides Thor, and even the god of thunder could not beat Fenrir when he challenged him."

Ailsa shook her head. "Odin buried something that would

have ensured his rival's defeat, but the well never mentioned Baldur being raised from the dead. If it is not him, then it must be buried *with* him."

He stared at her for a long time, processing this new theory. "We need to find out what he buried with Baldur, then."

"And we happen to know someone who was actually there all those centuries ago." She smiled. "It's time to go home, Vali."

Vali's jaw shook, then locked, hard as iron. "And what about Erik?"

Her lips fell, remembering their recent encounter. Ailsa shook her head to dismiss his memory, but a tremble ran straight to the fingertips in his hand. "I told him to go home. You were right about him, and I am so sorry, Vali. For all of it. For letting him come between us when I should have trusted you from the beginning."

His eyes studied her, seeing straight through her guard. "Did something happen, Ailsa?"

The gown's sleeves she wore cinched around her wrist, hiding the evidence marking her forearm, but her hands wouldn't stop shaking. Out of anger or the audacity of it all, she didn't know which. "Nothing I couldn't handle. Trust me, I made sure he will never come after me ever again."

He cupped her jaw with his palm, catching a small tear that leaked over with his thumb. "I hope I am never right again, *sváss*, if it means you hurt like this." He pulled her away from the window, toward the door leading from the study. "Let's have a feast tonight, get drunk, forget our worries for a few hours. And tomorrow, we can go home."

Ailsa smiled at the way he said the word.

Home.

CHAPTER 13
ERIK

here was that vial?

Erik tore through the old clothes he wouldn't let the staff take to clean, shaking every pocket to find the tonic the witch had given him. He tried everything to help Ailsa break her spell naturally, but the elfin's magic had too deeply ensnared her spirit. Her heart no longer recognized him and therefore could not want him. But he still had one last chance to make her his own, one last opportunity to kill the demon who had taken everything from him.

And he'd be damned to Hel before he let either of those prospects slip by.

After upturning a foul-smelling shirt, the small, clear ampule fell into the pile of laundry he'd created on the floor. Using the elfin's shirt he snatched that night he sneaked onto Ailsa's balcony, he ripped through the now crusted part of the sleeve, taking care to wet it just enough to wash the old blood from the flax fibers and let it drip into the small vial's opening. He watched the crimson curl into the tonic, twisting in a slow dance until dispersing completely clear once more.

When he capped the ampule, a voice smooth as a stream spoke behind him. "Not having second thoughts, are we?"

He turned, discovering no one there. The fire sputtered, flinging scraps of blazing embers across the marble hearth. Erik drew closer, watching in astonishment as a figure formed in the flames, the face of the witch.

Crouching to see her better, he grinned and held the vial between them. "I've never been more certain of anything in my life."

The witch sighed, blowing smoke into his face. "You've been there for days, Erik. How much longer will you take to finish this?"

"Tonight is all I have, so be ready. They plan to leave for Alfheim tomorrow, and Ailsa has sent me away—"

"Trouble in paradise? I thought she would never do such a thing to you," she mocked. Erik's smile fell, replaced with a scowl.

"You were right about this enchantment. It has completely fogged her memory of what we had together. Our only chance —her only chance—is to be free of the elfin for good."

"Do not forget what else you must do," she said. He noticed her brow arch in the curling ash. "Breaking the spell means their threads will not be bound anymore. It is imperative you kill him, Erik, or he will never stop trying to get her back. No matter where you go, you'll never have peace if he lives."

His fingers skimmed the blade sheathed on his hip. "I know what must be done."

The witch smiled. "Good. Then I will see you tonight."

CHAPTER 14
AILSA

The Vanir needed little to justify a feast, and Aegir required even less to throw a party. The god known for creating the power of the sea brewed a kind of ale he was known across the realms for, and word of his special brew being served tonight flew across the Nine faster than Odin's twin ravens.

Ailsa sat in Vali's lap and watched as gods from each tribe arrived to Noatun. It was a necessary form of distraction, a helpful way to pass the time before they'd have to face reality in the morning. And though she knew he wanted nothing more than to see his mother as soon as possible, they couldn't leave without thanking the Vanir and Njord for their hospitality, especially when just months ago they had been on opposing sides of a battle ground.

One of them snatched her attention with his warm laugh and obnoxious voice. Aegir was a brawny god, who Ailsa noticed seemed to detest traditional clothing, always walking around in nothing but billowing pants with a silver sash tied around his waist. The god never wore a shirt, much less shoes, and Njord claimed he lived in a hall under the sea itself, only surfacing to pull the occasional ship into the deep or when the gods required his realms-renowned services of brewing.

Even some of the Aesir had come to the feast, though they had little care of what they were celebrating, only that there would be enough mead to drown Jormungand. Thor had arrived with his wife, Sif, dragging a massive kettle behind them for Aegir to brew his ale inside. Soon, noise and laughter filled the hall as Aesir and Vanir spoke of past winters influenced by similar circumstances.

"He's going to fill that entire kettle with ale?" Ailsa asked the elfin, who was sipping on something else in the meantime.

Vali nodded. "When the mortals of Midgard decided to make Njord the more prominent god of the sea, Aegir found a new specialty."

"Brewing?"

"Partying, but the ale comes with the territory. He throws extravagant parties in his hall under the sea every winter for all the gods. At least, that's what I've heard."

Her fingers played with the waves of black hair licking the nape of his neck. "Poor Vali, never getting an invitation to all the divine get-togethers."

He sipped loudly from his crystal cup before replying, "Not true. I've just been too busy searching for the redemption of the Nine. She was hard to find."

Loud cheering cut off Ailsa's response as Aegir lit the fire beneath the kettle. Logs of pure gold glowed bright enough to form a blaze beneath the basin. Thor grabbed a large barrel of ale in each hand and assisted the god to speed the process along.

"Funny how good food and an abundance of alcohol can make even gods civil with each other," she said, observing.

"That's because no matter who our rivals are or what tribe they come from, we always have more in common than we do not." Vali held his cup back up to his lips, but did not take a sip. Instead, his gaze caught on something—someone who had just entered the hall. "Unless your rival is *him*."

Ailsa followed his stare until she found Erik sauntering into the room. His straw-colored hair was pulled up high into a bun, his short beard freshly trimmed and a black fur pelt draped across his shoulders. Deep bruises lined the bottom of his eyes from where she struck him, matching the ones he left on her skin with his grip. But from the way he held himself, he appeared to be hosting the feast instead of the cause of it.

A tension stirred between them as man and male locked eyes. The voices in the room suddenly lowered, sensing the change in the air like a shift in the breeze. Erik's steps produced small echoes throughout the hall until he came to the spot across from them both at the long table centering the room. Vali's arm slipped tighter around her waist as Erik sat.

"Evening," Erik said, nodding.

Wary of his friendliness, Ailsa only murmured a greeting. The elfin beneath her shifted in his seat so his boots were flat on the floor. To disperse the tension between them, she broke the silence. "I am surprised to see you here tonight with such a long journey ahead of you in the morning."

"And miss feasting with the gods?" he asked, smiling as he gestured around himself. "This might be the closest I ever get to Valhalla. Besides, how could I rest knowing I would never see you again, Ailsa? Of course, I came."

"If Odin doesn't take you, I sure will," Freya said behind Vali's chair. Ailsa twisted her head to see the goddess draped in white robes. Her dark hair piled high on her head to reveal a slender neck of gold chains. "Remember, mortal, I get the first pick of the slain. And you'd look better in the Folkvang whites."

Erik's face visibly flushed at the compliment. "It would be an honor, Goddess."

Vali's gaze flicked back to him, glaring with an intensity that competed with the blazing gold beneath the kettle. "What happened to your face?" he asked.

Erik's composure broke for a second before reconstructing. "Slipped on a stair. The moisture in this castle doesn't pair well with marble steps and elven wine."

"That must have been a nasty fall," the elfin said. "It almost appears as if someone struck you. But I cannot imagine why anyone would want to do that."

"I was not *struck*," Erik spoke through teeth. "It was an accident."

"Well, I hope you have no more of those *accidents* tonight, Erik. I'll warn you, there are several gods in this room that can make many things look like unfortunate mishaps."

"Is that a threat, elf?"

Vali held up his empty cup to be refilled. One of Aegir's servants rushed to snatch it from his hand. "Yes, it is. Because I find it strange you walked in here and looked at my lady for what should have been the first time in three days, yet you did not ask how she was feeling nor comment about how lovely she looks tonight. Which would lead me to believe you have already seen Ailsa prior to this feast, even though I have been by her side since the moment she found me early today."

"What are you suggesting then? Out with it. Let nothing remain unsaid." Erik leaned on his elbows propped on the table, feigning interest.

"My *Fraendi* has bruises all over her forearm that she has been hiding from me all day. Now, Erik, do you believe she also—what excuse did you give—slipped on the stairs?"

The man across the table glowered at Vali. "I would never hurt Ailsa, if that is what you are insinuating."

Ailsa dragged her fingertips across the width of Vali's back, trying to soothe the tautness coiled in his spine. The attention of every Vanir and Aesir had briefly paused their current conversations, hopeful this would lead to something more physical. Before it did, Ailsa thought of something better.

"You two act like two wolves fighting over the same bone. Why don't you do something more entertaining than this futile back-and-forth banter," she said.

"What did you have in mind, *sváss?*"

Ailsa took a newly filled tankard from the returning servant and handed it to her mate. He would need every drop for what she was about to suggest. "Flyte."

"Excuse me?" he asked with an arched brow.

Ailsa looked at Erik, who seemed to warm to the idea. She explained to the elfin, "Flyting is an old practice of the Otsman, frequently done with drinks and good company. The word comes from the old term *flyta*, which means to provoke. It is a contest of wit instead of strength, a battle of poetic insults. The audience will judge at the end who hurled the best words, and the winner must chug an ale."

"I like this idea," Thor said from the back of the room. His hammer hung on a hip while he cradled his first brew of the night. "It would be fun to watch my thieving *brother* get what he deserves!"

"Count your words, Thor, for your brainpower, you should conserve," Vali muttered over his cup.

Ailsa's smile stretched. "Exactly! You're a natural at this, *elskan min.*"

"And you are a prize I would cheat to win," he said, winking.

"Odin's eye." She sighed. "I've created a monster—"

"The man you hold is only an imposter," Erik spoke, cutting in. "With magic words, he weaves falsehoods and lies. But the only thing bright about him is the gold in his eyes."

Vali threw a cunning smile, then tossed back the goblet, draining every last drop of ale before slamming it on the table. "Speaking of dull, your wit is as sharp as a hammer. There is no honor for a man who cannot take *no* for an answer. Your skull must be as weak as your spine, hollow of substance, the greatest shame in the Nine."

Erik frowned but nodded in appreciation before replying, "I'm an Otsman at heart, and I claim what is mine. I do not need magic to make my woman recline. One day, your spell will break on her heart and her head, and when she is free to choose who's best, she'll come straight to my bed."

"Keep insisting I'll do so, and you'll lose *both* of your heads," Ailsa hissed. Freya spat her drink, choking on a laugh.

Vali's grip around her hip tightened until it was biting into her skin. "You're desperate and sad. I would pity you, but these insults you throw feel more like a threat. I'll warn you once, Otsman, I'm the Norse god of vengeance, though my lady calls me other things when I'm stroking her entrance."

"*Vali!*" Ailsa gasped, shoving a palm over his mouth so he couldn't continue. Freya next to them howled with laughter and clapped her hands with delight. Erik's cheeks burned red, and Thor was currently thrusting the air with his hips and saluting his half-brother with a raised hammer.

She, however, wanted to melt into the floor.

"Flyte him back, Ailsa!" Aegir shouted, currently nursing two mugs while he sat at the table watching the match. He muttered to Freya, "We need to do this more often."

Vali's hand wove deeper beneath her skirt until his entire forearm was hidden beneath the green silky garment, his touch warm from the rush of alcohol. "Do your worst, *svóss*," he said, squeezing the full side of her ass.

Ailsa bit the inside of her cheek, leaning away from him to twist in his arms and view him better. The elfin rested his back against the chair, his smirk infectious, plaguing her with one of her own. Through the haze of her drink, she cupped his face with her palm, smoothed over his lips with a thumb.

With a large breath, she started. "You snore like a bear, you're forgetful and stubborn, sometimes you're as grumpy as a dragon with heartburn. But while you're moody and vain and constantly late, and you speak more than listen and make me irate. You're the god of my heart, my desire in bed, you're my home and my world in one single thread. There are many things in this life I can change regarding fate, but among them will never be choosing you as my mate."

The remaining swells of laughter purged away, replaced with mocking sounds of sickness over her declaration. But Ailsa did not hear their groans or the drunken words of Thor telling them to *find a room*, because Vali had claimed her full attention with his kiss.

She tasted sweet ale on his palate, let herself get drunk off his taste alone, felt her legs part slightly like a reflex to his touch, letting his hand skim around the curve of her leg. His thumb pressed against the inner part, staying high on her thigh but teasingly close to her center where a wet heat was slowly building as his hands triggered flesh memories.

"You win this round," he whispered into her mouth.

"I finally beat you at something," she murmured. His laugh was low, akin to a purr. Realizing there was probably an entire room watching their interaction, Ailsa smoothed her hands over his chest and pushed away. "Stop kissing me like that, or we won't even make it to the room."

"I don't need a room," he said. Gold eyes darkened to brass. "I have a table right there. I could bend you over in front of everyone, make you my own personal feast. Fuck you like we did all those nights ago. Show Freya how that rune makes you a good girl."

"*Vali...*" Ailsa slammed her palm over his mouth for the second time that night, though this time for a different reason. Not to silence his words in front of everyone, but to stop them from burning her blood hotter.

Thankfully, the rest of the hall had already distracted themselves with Aegir's daughters. Three of the eight had crawled out the sea, and Ailsa figured the abhorrence for clothes must have run in the family, seeing the water sprites hardly wearing any.

"Ailsa," Erik said her name across the table. She had almost forgotten he was still sitting there until he called her. "May I speak with you outside for a moment?"

"I don't think that's a good idea, Erik." She eyed him wearily.

His gaze fell to the table. "I would just like to talk to you one last time. Before we go our separate ways tomorrow, I need to apologize for a few things. I do not wish to leave things how they are between us knowing I may never see you again."

Ailsa thought about his offer and eventually nodded in agreement. Erik had been her closest friend for years, her first love, her first... everything. She didn't want these bad memories sitting between them for the rest of her life, and for that reason, she slipped from Vali's lap and started toward the balcony doors.

Vali snatched her hand before she could get very far. "Ailsa, I don't like this. You should take someone outside with you. Preferably me."

She kissed his temple before slipping around his chair. "I won't be long. If I'm not back in ten minutes, come find me. I just want to say goodbye."

The elfin flinched, but his grip loosened, letting her slip from his fingertips. "Ten minutes," he mumbled. "Not a second longer."

⟵╫◇╫⟶

Ailsa stood on the main balcony, away from the wandering eyes of the party guests inside, waiting for Erik to join her. The moon hung high behind the castle, dusting the distant sea with silver. She noticed chariots driven by the Aesir parked in the stretching courtyard, Thor's in particular pulled by two massive goats. The strange steeds were currently being pulled across the grounds by a few of the servants, bleating their defiance.

A flash of green light, so strange and misplaced in this realm, pulled her gaze to the end of the terrace. The glow burned beneath a blur of dark feathers before shifting into the form of a man, and the god Loki smoothed back his golden hair with the pass of a hand. He didn't notice her as he straightened his sleeves and dusted the falcon feathers still sticking to the flare of his coat.

"Forced to wear your own coat this time?" she said.

Loki's body flinched as she startled him, his grassy glare splitting her in half as it crossed her. "Go away. I'm not in the mood, witch."

Ailsa smiled. "What's wrong, Loki? Have you run out of lies to spin? No one left to trick?"

He inhaled a long breath, settling something building in his chest as it fell. He then smiled back with the most unnerving grins in the Nine. "What is that saying you humans love to teach your young? *Where there are a wolf's ears, a wolf's teeth are nearby.* You'd do well to learn how to shut your mouth and listen instead. It might save your life one day."

Footsteps joined them on the balcony, but Erik stopped short, noticing their stare down. Loki tore his gaze from her to Erik. His smile stretched into genuine territory. "Evening, young man. It appears I have arrived just in time for the drink."

"Despite having no one to invite you, it is impeccable timing as always," Ailsa said, turning from the trickster to look beyond the banister instead.

"Always a pleasure, Fate Weaver," he replied, and she listened to his light steps grow quiet as he left them.

Erik joined her at her side, a mug of ale in each hand, but if one of them was for her, he didn't offer it yet. "You feel very comfortable speaking your mind to our gods, Ailsa, but I don't think it's a good idea to piss off the Lord of Mischief."

"He's a snake, nothing more," she replied as she leaned a hip on the marble railing to face him. "What did you want to speak to me about, Erik?"

He stared into the mugs in his hands. "I wanted to apologize for attacking you today, with both my words and my hands. I should have never forced myself upon you, and I am ashamed of myself. Something in me believed if I could just remind you of what we had, you would come back to me and forget this elfin."

"I wish you would stop referring to my bond with Vali like it is a spell you can break." She crossed her arms, his apology hardly melting the ice in her heart. "It is a choice we both made, and because you cannot respect it, I am forced to distance myself from you. You are lucky this is your only punishment, as I assure you Vali would have imposed something much harsher."

"Being apart from you is a fate worse than death, Ailsa." His throat constricted with a hard swallow.

She shoved him playfully by his shoulder. "You are being dramatic. There are Nine Realms out there, Erik. I'm sure you can find a future and a lover for yourself in one of them. We were never meant to be. Just accept it and move on so we both can have peace."

His face forced a small smile, offering a small nod. He then handed her one of his mugs. "Will you have one more ale with me? You won the flyte after all."

Ailsa smiled and accepted his offering with grateful hands. She hadn't yet tried Aegir's famous brew, and her throat was parched from Vali's exploration beneath her skirt. "Of course, you know I'd never pass up a good drink. What shall we toast to?"

His breath dragged with a long sigh. "How about to a past now coming to an end, and new beginnings?"

She gripped the handle and held up her mug to meet his. "To new sagas, Erik, and the paths that led to them."

"*Skol*," he said, clinking his glass with hers. And for the first time in days, she saw a smile on his face that touched his eyes, a glimpse of her former friend as his most genuine self. Ailsa took several long sips of ale, reveling in the sweet burn that pooled in her belly and warmed her body like a full embrace.

"*Skol*," she muttered, before the world around her went dark.

CHAPTER 15
VALI

"You have some nerve showing up here," Freya hissed as Loki sauntered into the room. Vali remained in his seat next to the goddess, waiting for Ailsa to return, when the god slipped into the hall and demanded the entire room's attention.

"What are you talking about? Why wouldn't I come? Even Bragi crawled out of his library for this. Surely someone just forgot to inform me about the celebration." Loki strode around the table, making his way toward the kettle. "But do not worry, Freya darling, I do not hold it against anyone."

The goddess stood suddenly, sending a harsh sound from her chair. "No one invited you because no one wanted you here. You ruin everything you touch, Evil One."

"And you fuck everything you touch, goddess, yet here you are." Loki dipped an empty mug into the brew and drained the entire cup in three sips.

"Don't be an ass, Loki," Thor said, stepping between them before Freya burned him to ash with her glare alone. "The Aesir need time to get over your latest betrayal. You still have not made up for killing my brother, and you failed to bring the Tether to Odin. Now it is too late, and we must rely on a mortal to drag Baldur from the grave," he glanced at Vali, "no offense to your mate, brother. There are repercussions—"

"Repercussions?" Loki's brows rose. "That's a big word for you, Thor. Might I remind you it was *Hod* that killed the golden child. A blind god playing with a bow and arrow is a liability, if you ask me."

"You gave him the arrow and showed him where to aim," Sif spoke drily at Thor's side.

Loki rolled his eyes and filled his cup again. "Nice hair, Sif. About as real as your tits, am I right, Thor?"

"*Loki,*" Thor growled in a warning, one the trickster did not heed. Instead, he seemed delighted by the aggravation he roused in a matter of minutes. Vali looked around the room and found every Aesir standing. Whatever had happened between Loki and the rest of the tribe must have established something with dark roots, one's even the most cunning of the gods could not twist his way out of.

That night outside the hospital wing, when Ailsa rejected his offer to go back to Asgard with him, Vali wondered if that had been Loki's last chance to redeem himself for his mistakes. Perhaps the gods were finally tired of his antics. Judging by Freya's white knuckled grip around her goblet, the elfin was inclined to think so.

"I see the Allfather couldn't make it." Mumbling his words, Loki said, "Must be too busy breaking his oaths and running from fate." Draining another cup, Loki threw the empty glass over his shoulder, just in time for a servant to intercept and catch. "Relax, all of you! I'm only having a bit of fun. I won't be here much longer. I just didn't want to miss it."

"Miss what?" Vali asked.

Loki's eyes narrowed on him, a smirk dominating his right cheek. "The party, of course."

The elfin opened his mouth to ask his meaning, but he was silenced by a great pain in his chest. Vali sucked in a large breath and braced a hand over his racing heart, fighting against the crushing sensation and the air too thick to inhale. With wide eyes, he glanced around the room in a panic, locking on Freya's. With a trembling hand he pointed toward the balcony and noticed something that made his blood turn to ice.

His *Fraendi* mark was fading.

Vali stood on shaky legs and stumbled toward the balcony, lungs burning without necessary sustenance. But the pain was no competition to the one breaking his heart into pieces. Something had happened to Ailsa, and like a poison, it was slowly consuming them both. By the time he stepped outside, the ink on his hand marking their rune had dripped away, erased from his skin.

Like it had never been there. Like it never happened.

Freya was behind him, holding him up by an arm as they looked around the terrace for Ailsa or Erik, but it was empty. "*Find her,*" he choked out as he pushed the goddess away. Since the mark faded completely, it was easier to breathe, to walk, but the fear still encapsulated him until he was drowning. The world seemed to blur until sound was smothered and the surrounding details blurred out of focus.

Njord's voice came from a distant place. "She couldn't have gone far. No one has left the realm since the party began. I've already ordered a lock down on the palace." But Vali was half listening as he ran to the edge of the banister, glancing frantically around the courtyard below. And then he saw him.

Erik carried a limp Ailsa in his arms, her head rolling side to side in the bend of his arm. His steps were slow, unhurried and short, as if he were waiting for Vali to notice him walking in plain sight. Vali shouted his name, but the Otsman didn't look back, only continued into the meshwork of gardens where the walls of the shrubbery concealed them from view. The elfin ran after them, feet barely touching the steps of the pale white staircase that led to the land below.

"Vali, wait!" Freya called after him. "You have no weapon! It could be a trap!" But he didn't need a blade.

Anger, hatred, malice.

Vengeance.

Those were his weapons, the arsenal of power coursing through his veins with such a violence his bones shook beneath his flesh. Any lingering fear melted away, replaced with such raw rage that every sense he had sharpened to aid one single purpose.

Wrath.

"*Erik!*" he roared into the night, to no one, to everything. His strides uprooted the earth as they covered the distance between him and his mate and the man who held her against him.

Breaking through the first rows of hedges, he stopped and listened, hardly breathing to mute his own sounds. He stalked the shadows lingering between the walls, fingers stretched and ready to kill this man at last.

"Show yourself, Otsman!" he shouted. "Stop hiding like a coward, and fight me like a man."

A slide of steel rang from behind him, and Vali had only a racing heartbeat to lunge from the arch of a golden blade. He twisted to find Erik alone, a determination set in his jaw as he swung for the elfin again. But Vali lifted his magic, pushing the heathen against a stone wall of a water sculpture. The pool at its base was shallow, maybe a few inches, but a grown man could drown in less.

"You are weak," Erik groaned against the force slamming him against the wall. "You wield magic against a man who has none—"

"You attack a man from behind who carries no weapon," Vali spat. "There is no greater dishonor than to kill someone from behind. Even an Otsman knows that."

"I will kill you anyway I can, if it means she will be free of you."

"What have you done with her?" Vali asked, stepping closer to the fountain wall. "How did you erase our mark? No mortal has the power to break a fae bond."

Erik laughed a maniacal sound, his gilded blade catching the moonlight as he adjusted his grip. "You have your ways, demon. I have mine. My secrets keep me more powerful than anything you wield against me now."

"We'll see about that," Vali sneered.

He used his opposite hand to make a fist, picturing Erik's throat in his mind, and squeezed the blood and bones and air from his neck until blood spilled from the corners of his eyes as the pressure burst the vessels within. It was a soundless suffering, only the scrape of his boots against the limestone fountain as they struggled for purchase. Crimson dripped into the well below, staining the water pink.

He didn't care if it wasn't a fair fight, only that it would finally come to an end. The man was about to fall into an eternal sleep—until Vali felt cold metal against his throat.

"Put him down," a soft voice said, one he could see in the dark, a sound that changed his life and gave the heart in his chest a reason to beat. She pressed the blade flush against his skin, enough to draw blood and ensure her threat. "I said, *put him down.*"

Vali released Erik, turning his head slowly to look at her despite the blade at his neck, unfeeling its sting. Ailsa stood at an arm's length, holding the dagger she kept sheathed on her thigh, the dagger he gave her the first night they met. The same blade she stabbed him with thrice over. There was a look in her eyes that was familiar to that night, a storm in her misty eyes that was desperate to destroy.

"Ailsa," he breathed. How could she do this? Even without their mark, did she not still see him the same way he saw her?

Her name must have struck something in her memory because her grip on the dagger slipped, and her breaths quickened. "How... how do you know my name?"

"What are you talking about?" he asked. "You're my—"

His words were cut off by a blade. Not Ailsa's, but the man he had forgotten. Golden runes winked up at him, wet with his blood, as Erik shoved the sword through the center of his chest. He looked back at Ailsa, who gasped as she was splattered from the force of the blow, and Vali could do nothing as he surrendered to the fate of the weapon. To that loss of recognition in her eyes.

Erik pulled the blade from his back and Vali fell to his knees, collapsing from the weight of it all. The weakness this hole inside him created, both from the physical blow and the words she left him with.

How do you know my name?

As if he hadn't said her name a thousand times since he learned it.

A slowing pulse beat a drum of war in his ears as he looked up at her one last time, and she looked at him with a look he couldn't quite explain. She was neither satisfied with his fall nor hurt. Indifferent.

"Ailsa," he rasped. "Please, don't... don't leave me." But Erik was behind her now, gripping her shoulders as he laughed. His cheeks were smeared with bloody tears as he watched Vali beg.

Each time he blinked, the world faded a little more around the edges, but Vali fought to stay with her. To stay awake until help arrived. Surely someone would follow them here before Erik kidnapped her across Njord's boundaries. But then he blinked again, and another figure appeared in the garden. A woman he recognized snatched Erik's hand in her own and smiled at Vali.

"I told you having a heart was useless," she said to him.

The one in his chest was starting to feel benign. He fell to his hands, bowing before them, and Nerissa laughed with delight at his meekness. Vali only wanted to reach Ailsa, extending a hand no matter how much it trembled across the grass toward the toe of her flat.

"Erik, what is happening?" he heard her ask.

"Hold me tight, *sváss*. This might feel unpleasant."

"*No!*" Vali used the reserve of strength to lunge for her, trying to skim something she owned to connect with her person. But he was too slow, his reach clumsy. The witch misted them all away, and he caught air as he fell.

With no hope left, no reason for his heart to keep beating, Vali sprawled against the cold earth and watered the gardens with his blood.

CHAPTER 16
SEELA

The Light Palace was alive with activity, rushing to finish the final arrangements to prepare for Ailsa and Vali's arrival. Work to host a grand reunion was currently distracting Seela with enough to keep her mind off her political affairs.

Enver had arrived back from Vanaheim the night before, but one of Njord's personal messengers had sent word that the pair would make an immediate visit home after receiving Lady Rind's health update. Seela felt a weight lifted from her shoulders, a lightness that allowed her to enjoy planning the festivities. For a moment, she could let loose, not worry about the realm and its future. It was the start of a new beginning. A night at Greybeard's and the commander in her bed were a series of poor decisions that followed.

Seela dressed for the day, knowing Vali wouldn't be arriving until tonight since the Lowest Roots were just seeing the beginning of nightfall. She was grateful when she heard Enver pulling on his own boots in the sitting room, hopeful he would leave before she faced him.

She wasn't ashamed of her interest in the dark elf, but their relationship was too strange and undefined for morning cuddles and breakfast in bed. She crossed the bedroom to open the terrace windows and let in the natural Light when she felt *something* that knocked the wind from her lungs. A deep splintering inside her chest.

"*Ahh!*" Seela cried out in pain, doubling over like she had been struck. A pain that felt more like grief, unbearable in its state, twisted an imaginary knife in her heart.

"Seela?" Enver called her name in the room over. When she didn't respond, he poked his head through the doorway. "Seela!"

But she couldn't speak, not through the hurt burrowing into her chest and stealing her voice. She fell to her knees on the floor, seeking the source of the agony, running her hands all over her chest to find evidence of something tangible to explain it away.

"Is it your bond? Is Vali all right?" he asked, his hand firm on her back. Of course, it would be his first thought and her last. When he lost his *Hjartablóð,* Enver told her it had been a pain like no other, a kind that split him in half.

Seela shook her head. "I haven't felt our bond since he left because he's been too far to feel."

"We should get you to Vanaheim... Just to be safe—"

"But the realm, Enver," she spoke through her teeth. "I'm Vali's regent. I cannot leave!"

The commander licked his lips in thought. "And could you live with yourself if you could help him, and you did not?" She squeezed her eyes shut, knowing he was right. "Come on, Seela, take my hand. I'll get us there, no matter what it takes."

"Are you sure you can—" The pain returned, this time sealing her decision. She reached blindly for Enver's hand, squeezing it tight in hers. With only time to take bracing breath, stars and void spun the world of Light into darkness.

The time that passed was immeasurable, though it felt like a lifetime before Njord's palace on the sea conceptualized before her, Enver mumbling something about wards locking him out. When the guards saw them, they ushered her inside, leading her to Noatun. She railed them with question after question, but the soldiers draped in silver mail would not answer her, and it only made Seela even more eager to lay eyes on them both.

Njord paced the opening of the hall when they rounded a corner. He looked up at her as they approached, snapped from a trance, and his eyes lit up with relief.

"Seela, thank the tide," he mumbled, motioning to her to follow him. "We contacted Eir, and she arrived shortly before you did. We've done as much as we can to heal him, but the blood of a *Hjartablód* is probably the only thing that will save him now."

Her worst fears came true as her gaze fell upon the goddess of healing, but it appeared her favor did not extend to gods like it did wounded mortals. Her sleeves were stained red up her elbows as she placed her weight on Vali's chest, a poor attempt to stop the bleeding from the hole beneath her hands. A white light spilled between her fingers as she mumbled a runic incantation to stitch his body back together. Freya was at his head, cheeks smeared with golden tears.

At first glance, Vali looked dead. His coloring a pale grey, a bluish tint ringed his lips, and his eyes were shut as if he were in a deep sleep. Seela ran to where the gods worked on him atop a dining table. Freya moved out of the way to let her near his face.

"Vali," she whispered, stroking the cold skin of his face with a trembling hand. She looked up at Freya. "Where is Ailsa?"

The look she returned was a grim one, and Seela shook her head in disbelief, focusing back on her blood mate and how she could help. "Give me a knife!" She ordered the gods who stood watching on the side. Aegir tossed her a short dagger, and Seela snatched it by the hilt, pressing the sharp end of the blade to her wrist.

She made a line across her skin, only recalling from instruction how to use her very blood to heal her *Hjartablód*. In the near century she'd known Vali, never had she been required to perform a healing rite, had either of them needed it. Enver appeared at her side and helped her tip Vali's head to her wrist, letting the blood pool from the place she sliced and drip between his parted lips.

"Come on, Vali. Don't leave me. Don't leave *us*." Ailsa had to be alive. If she wasn't, there would be nothing Seela could do for him but let him go. But as she glanced down at his hand resting limp on the table, her heart sank a little deeper. Their *Fraendi* mark was gone.

What in Hel's name happened tonight?

"Release me! I have done nothing wrong!" A voice raged on the other side of the hall. Seela looked up to see Thor and Aegir smashing Loki's face into a table, bending him in half as Bragi bound his hands behind his back.

"What should we do with him?" Thor asked the room.

"Bring him to Odin," Freya hissed. "We will take him back to Gladsheim, where Baldur's blood was spilled, and decide his fate there. Sigyn will want to be present when we lock away her pathetic husband for good this time."

"And what are my crimes?" Loki spat as he glared sideways from the tabletop.

Freya stood slowly. Seela caught the tremor that harrowed her fingertips. "You, Trickster, are responsible for this night, however indirectly you might have been involved. This began as soon as you showed your defiling face, and you will answer for the Fate Weaver's abduction."

"You'll twist the truth anyway you like it just to get me out of Asgard, Freya!" Loki shouted.

"Do not speak of truth, Lord of Lies," she replied. "You'll get a trial in Asgard, which is more than you deserve."

They dragged the thrashing god away, his curses falling over every being in the room. Seela returned her focus to Vali, who remained still despite her initial efforts. Eir had closed the wound in the center of his chest, but his agonal breaths were shallow and slow, each one growing further apart from the previous. Until finally, after Seela milked her arm and forced more of her blood into his throat, he choked.

He sputtered and coughed, spraying the air with bloody droplets as Seela rolled him on his side. The fear coiled in her gut loosened so she could take a large breath of relief. They weren't out of the woods yet, but he was coming back from a dark place, and Seela had dragged him back with the shriveling thread of their bond.

"Vali, it's me," she said to him. "It's Seela. You're going to be all right."

But Vali grimaced and swallowed, coughed up more blood. He shook his head without opening his eyes and mumbled, "Just let me die."

Seela felt her face crumble in confusion. "And why would I do that?"

"I don't want to live... It hurts too much."

"What hurts, Vali? Your chest? We can help that."

His mouth pressed into a frown. He flipped to his back on his own, face twisting in discomfort, and looked up at her. He held up his right hand, now bare of a bond. "This... hurts."

The broken mating bond. What she felt tonight that sent her doubling over was not his wound, but his grief. The pain he felt when it was torn from him, one Seela felt Nine Realms away and even from a distance had been so unbearable, she understood why he would have preferred the eternal slumber than enduring that pain for the rest of his life.

She still felt it, the echo of his sorrow, pulse with every beat of her heart. "What happened? Where is she?" she asked him.

His eyes, for the first time in a century, welled with wetness in front of her. Tears brimmed and leaked clear trails down his temples each time he blinked. "The heathen stole her memory of me, and thus must have split our threads into two again. Nerissa misted them somewhere, I don't know," he said. His last words broke into sharp pieces and cut her apart. "Seela, she didn't even recognize me."

The commander held his bare hand tight in her palm and stroked his forearm. "We will find her, Vali. Whatever happened, it was not because she chose this. Someone has taken her, and we will tear apart all the Nine until we get her back. I vow this on our bond and my life. This pain shall pass, and it must—for her sake."

Vali squeezed her hand back and shut his eyes, each breath a fight against the regret sitting heavy on his bloodied chest.

But until he was healed enough to hunt down the bastards that did this, Vali wept. Under the candlelight floating above them in the hall of Noatun, beneath the blanket of stars in the Lowest Root of the Tree, before the divines who watched him with sober eyes and mournful hearts, the god of vengeance wept.

And Seela wept too.

CHAPTER 17
ERIK

There was no place in Midgard that resembled this. No sky he'd ever seen in his travels that burned with ash. His home did not smell of brimstone and melting sulfur, nor did embers spark in the breeze. The place the witch brought them was not Drakame, not even his world.

They were not home like she promised.

Ailsa shoved his arm away the moment the ground beneath their feet turned solid. She gasped for air, choking as smoke filled her chest instead. Her knees sank into the barren earth as she clutched the sides of her head.

"Ailsa, are you—"

"Where the Hel are we, Erik?" she spoke with a sharp hiss.

"I..." He looked around, but the witch was gone, as was anything beside the burnt landscape and smoking mountains in the distance. His tongue felt thick in his mouth as he answered, "I don't know. The witch said—"

"The witch?" She stopped him. "Why in Hel's name were you working with a witch?"

Erik kneeled next to her, taking her head in between his

hands. The mark on her hand was gone, but the runes marking her midline were still permanent, running down her throat like ink on parchment. His gesture did more harm than good, placing an uncertainty in her gaze that bordered on mistrust. His next words had to be calculated, weighed to ensure their appeal. If he were to rebuild this bond they once had, he would need to tell her everything she wanted to hear.

"Trust me when I say it was the only way to get you back," he said. "I would have done anything to save you from that demon's clutches, Ailsa, even sell my soul to the darkness. I know this looks bad, but we are together now. And you are free."

She shook her head, ocean eyes fluttering shut. A single tear streamed down her cheek, dried almost instantly by a hot sulfurous breath. "I feel like I've gone mad. I woke up in a garden, but my last complete thoughts were of Drakame. There are faces and worlds I've never seen before floating in my memories, but I cannot link them, nor do I know how they got there. It's like..." She licked her lips. Her eyes still squeezed shut, internal thoughts hidden from him. "It is like I awakened from a strange dream, one so vivid it felt real. But I woke up too soon, and now I can't recall the moments that stitched all these beautiful scenes together."

Erik sighed and sat on his heels. If the witch lied to him about her memories, none of this would work well for him. The ending he sought would be much more difficult to obtain. At least he knew for a fact she didn't remember the elfin. How sweet it had been to see her hold a blade to his throat, to look at him with such disdain as she came to his aid. That single act made every death on this journey, every doubt, every shameful experience worthwhile.

He asked, "What do you remember exactly, Ailsa? From the day you left Drakame until now?"

Her eyes flew open, staring at him strangely. "I remember—"

But the sound of drums in the distance split her attention. Ailsa rose to her feet, staring toward the steady beat growing louder even as they stood there idle. Erik pulled her close, her body tense against him. They watched as black smoke stirred on the horizon, building as something traveled in their direction.

"We will be fine. The witch brought us here for a reason. Now let's find out why."

She looked around them and scoffed, shrugging helplessly. "Where else would I go?"

A wall of rusty dust formed behind two black riders as they disturbed its settlement, any detail of their silhouette obscured by the rippling heat distorting the distance. The blistering earth ate at his boots, and Erik glanced at Ailsa's flats, a third of the thickness and undoubtedly burning her feet. But she planted them flat, taking a stance of defense as the riders approached.

Two black horses slowed to a stop in front of them. Their eyes were burning coals and snorting smoke as one rider dismounted, flicking a mane that was set on fire with long hair that sizzled orange at the tips. Erik's shoulders fell when he discovered it was the witch.

"Kind of you to show yourself," he muttered as her gaze fell to him. "Care to explain why you dropped us in the middle of nowhere?"

"No, I don't actually," she said through a scarf wrapped around her cowl. "It's none of your business why I do the things I do."

"This isn't what we agreed on!" He beckoned to the wasteland around them.

She pulled down her mask to reveal a grin. "We agreed on this: that I would help you rescue your woman. That when the time came, you would owe me a blood debt." She pulled her black scarf over her nose. "That time is now. So get on the beasts before we make you, and we both know I can."

"I made no oaths to you, Nerissa," Ailsa spoke up behind him. "I should have known you would slither back from whatever hole you retreated to."

Erik flinched. She remembered her well enough to know the witch's name. What history did she possess with Ailsa? Nerissa never told him, not even offered a hint of her own motivations for the woman at his side. And he hadn't even thought twice about it.

A foolish mistake.

Nerissa took several steps closer to them. "Lady Ailsa, or I suppose it's just Ailsa now," she said. "If you still remember me, then I must have made a sizable impression."

"I remember I hate you, though I can't recall why." She crossed her arms and matched the witch's steps. "Why did you take my memories?"

"Ask him." Nerissa jutted her chin in Erik's direction. "He was the one who wanted your memories gone. I just gave him the magic to do what he wanted to accomplish. For a price."

Ailsa's head turned an inch as if she were going to look back at him. Instead, she asked, "What price?"

Nerissa groaned and threw back her head. "Are we really going to catch up in the middle of a burn field? Get on a *bálhross*. We can discuss our arrangement inside." She turned and started back toward the fire horse, speaking over her shoulder. "You will ride with me, Erik."

Ailsa looked at him as he stepped in line with her, her expression disapproving. "We will speak later about what you have done," she whispered, before turning sharply toward the opposite horse. She hardly glanced at the other rider mounted on the massive steed as she pulled her up, needing little motivation beyond the baking of her feet and the miles of barren world around them.

"How much have you told her so far?" Nerissa asked once they were moving. They traveled at a leisurely pace so as not to stir too much dust. But Erik was still forced to pull his cloak in front of his nose, the air burning his face as it brushed his cheeks. He could hardly look ahead to see where they were going, feeling as though he was standing too close to a bonfire.

"Nothing yet," he said. "But I fully intend on telling her the truth concerning the bond she had with the elfin and his enchantment over her."

"Are you sure that is wise?"

"Why would it not be?"

She shrugged a shoulder passively. "It is your choice. But if I were in your shoes, I would control the narrative a bit more sensibly. You do not want her to have second thoughts concerning you or Vali. She might start to wonder... perhaps even feel a longing for someone she cannot remember. Fae bonds are powerful in that way, rooting themselves in both the heart and the mind."

Erik glanced at Ailsa, who was riding behind the other witch, her head ducked behind her backside. He asked

Nerissa, "What would you suggest I tell her then? If we are to make this work, she needs to trust me."

"You give her no reason to doubt you and keep your story as close to the truth as possible. Tell her the elfin kidnapped her for her power, forced a bond on her to use it and free himself from the will of the gods. She hated us because we tried to take her from Vali, and the spell twisted her perspective. You have the opportunity to make him a villain to her again. Don't waste it."

"What does it matter? He is dead. She cannot go back to him even if she tried." But the witch said nothing. Her hesitancy to agree with him unsettled his nerves. "Where are you taking us now?"

"To see the one who needs Ailsa's gift. The only reason I agreed to help you."

"That is not an answer—"

"It is the only one you will get. Patience, Erik. It will be easier to show you all at once." Nerissa pulled her cowl lower and snapped the reins to speed the horse into a trot, preventing further conversation.

They traveled into the smoky mountains, where thick lava pooled in the bends of jagged rock, spilled over steep cliffs into falls of fire. Nerissa led the horses beneath arches marked with a lost language, leading the way to a place of civilization somewhere among this inhospitable terrain. Beads of sweat trickled down Erik's neck as they continued to ascend deeper into the layers of obsidian towers.

Nerissa stopped the horse as they came to the middle of a bridge extending high over a valley splitting the elevations. She looked down the hollow divide, eyes focused on a volcano in the far distance seated at the end of the vale. The peak was actively gushing liquid fire, streams of it rolling down the angular sides. Even from this far, it was difficult to stare at for long. The light emitted from the mountain was bright enough to filter the entire realm in a bloody aurora.

Dissatisfied at what she saw, Nerissa sighed and kicked the horse back in motion, the clatter of its thick hooves against the stone the only sound in the world. The bridge seemed to lead to the last leg of their journey, and as they pressed past the tall pillars standing at the end of the landing, Erik discovered the bridge was simply the start of it all.

More stone arches led to a towering domain carved into a natural curve in the mountain range, each one taller than the previous until it met the mouth of the drawbridge. As they passed beneath the fourth arch, it slowly lowered to allow them passage over a small river of glowing magma, straight into the heart of the fortress. No windows marked the outside, no guards posted in the heat of the night among the jagged face of this kingdom—nothing to gain a hint of what waited inside.

"This is your home? I can see now why you're such a cold-hearted bitch," he said, staring up at the peaks forming castle-like spires on an unworthy kingdom.

His offense made her laugh. "This is not *my* home, but if you think I'm bad, Erik, you have a rude awakening before you."

"What does that mean?"

"It means," she drawled as they entered a darkened tunnel following the drawbridge, "that you should sheath the weapon in your words before you find yourself sparring with the wrong adversary. I can assure you, Surtur will not find you as funny as I do."

Surtur.

The name wasn't familiar.

Shadows swallowed them inside the hall. The horses pressed on, and Erik listened for Ailsa's rider as they traveled, making sure they stayed close behind. But a deeper pulse eventually drowned the sound of hooves through the dark, a quick beat that matched the rate of his pulse.

War drums.

Lining the tunnel were floating torches on either side. As Erik looked closer at the torches, he noticed hands wrapped around the base, and in the dim glow, faces appeared, each one covered with the skull of a beast.

"Gods above," he muttered, watching the strange procession pass him by. "Are they witches as well?"

"No," she whispered. "Eyes ahead. Don't look at them."

But Erik found that to be a challenge when he could feel their gazes following him, even concealed behind bleached bone. The further she led him down this narrow tunnel, the more of them now stood behind his back, trapping them in this place.

They emerged into a large room—a grand hall carved into stone. Pillars of rust colored rock supported the doming ceiling, glowing gold with runes whose purpose he could only guess. Torches multiplied, numbering the bodies holding them in the crowd as Nerissa continued to guide their small party into the center of the room. Drums were pushed to the edges of the room, the creatures striking the skin so loudly in the enclosed space, Erik felt the beat shake his marrow.

They finally came to a stop, and the witch urged them to dismount. He reached for Ailsa as soon as their feet touched the dusty floor, pulling her to his side. This time, she didn't reject his touch, her eyes wide and watching the border of bodies around them, full of the same concern he felt in his gut.

Nerissa and the other witch stepped to the side, disappearing into the crowd as the horses were pulled away to leave them both standing alone before a dais, in front of an empty throne composed of polished obsidian with edges so sharp, one would be impaled if they fell too close. Black fur lined the seat, waiting to be occupied.

"In the memories of your travels," he whispered to her, "do you recognize anything like this place?"

Her lips hardly moved as she spoke. "I've never been here, but I think... I think we are in Muspell. The realm of fire. Which means these creatures could be—"

"Fire giants," he finished. She nodded. There were stories of this realm still told in the mortal world, mostly to paint portraits of the Aesir's power over the giants and how they pushed the brutes back into a realm where they would suffer for eternity or until the Nine fell on top of them. Their motives were ones of pure evil, harboring hatred for goodness and finding pleasure only in destruction.

Erik had taken Ailsa from a demon and straight into a nightmare.

The drums silenced, and a tapestry behind the platform parted to allow three individuals to pass. The first, a small creature dressed in black robes and wearing the skull of what appeared to be a massive stag. Following was a wolf larger than any Erik had ever seen before, a true monster with silver fur and paws the size of his head. Its claws scratched the smooth dais as it stalked to the opposite side of the throne.

Trailing the group was a being born from the flames of Muspelheim himself. With dark crimson skin, his chest was wide and littered with raised scars. His shoulders filled the large entryway, draped in a ceremonial white fur that skimmed the floor behind his thick legs. The giant's face was hideous, with a wide jaw and eyes like hot coals. The only hair on his body was pure white and curtained one side of his head, the other half shaved to the scalp. He took several long steps to reach his seat above every creature present in the room, looking down at them all like they were his objects—his belongings to manipulate, to serve him.

"Nerissa," the giant said. His voice was deep as a groaning ship. The witch stepped out of line and approached the dais with the smallest of steps. "This is the weaver?" His burning gaze swept over Ailsa, disregarding Erik all together.

"Yes, it is her. The one we have searched for since Gullveig was lost to us," she said, bowing her head. "And with her, our collateral, to make sure she will not resist our demands."

"And the elfin?" he asked. "What of the Aesir who guarded her?"

"Dead," Erik spat.

The giant glared at him, as if he had spoken out of turn. He looked back at Nerissa, who confirmed his words with another nod of her head. "We left him bleeding out alone. His blood mate would have been too far to save him."

The giant lord sighed, smoke trailing his breath. "Are you sure about that, witch? Did you see the Light leave his eyes for yourself?"

It was the first time Erik the witch appeared nervous. "I did not confirm his death with my own eyes or hands, if that is what you are asking, Lord Surtur. But there is no way he could have survived the wound Erik left in him."

Surtur squinted his dark eyes at her. "I suggest you make sure the son of Odin is truly slain. Our plans have already been set into motion, and his death will ensure our victory. We cannot afford to be optimistic."

"You killed a son of Odin?" Ailsa gasped next to Erik. He gnashed his teeth together in frustration for their slip of information in her presence. He wanted to be the one to tell her about the elfin, to control what she knew and her perspective on what she learned.

Which was why he said, "The Allfather would not let me kill him if he wanted to protect his son, Ailsa. It was a long journey, and the will of the gods would have prevented me at some point if it was not a part of my fate."

"Not all fates are chosen for us, Erik. One day we all will answer for our choices, will of the gods or not—"

"Do you have something to say, Weaver?" Surtur growled, provoking a jump of her shoulders.

"Aye, I do, actually."

Erik tried to snatch her as she stepped forward before she said something to ruin them both, but the stubborn woman twisted her arm out of his grasp and set her attention on the dais. "My ass hurts from the ride, my feet are charred, and no one here has even acknowledged my presence or Erik's since we got here. Your witch has stolen my memories while Fenrir sits like a pet at your side. Both of whom tried to kill me the last time I remember seeing them. You have dragged us to this waste of a realm for a reason. Now tell us why."

Erik internally cringed at her words, both bold and foolish, but mostly the latter. Surtur smiled when she was finished, the curve of his lips revealing a row of serrated teeth. He stood from his throne and started down the steps of the platform, heading toward Ailsa. He would have jumped between them, but the giant lord did not seem to be one to challenge.

Surtur snatched her forearm in his meaty hand, and Ailsa yelped in pain. Erik lunged for her as her knees gave out, but was stopped by Surtur's cutting glare. His heart was a hammer in his chest as steam spilled between the giant's fingers, burning Ailsa's skin with his touch alone until she collapsed in a heap of silk and sash, still wearing her party gown from earlier that evening.

Surtur finally released her arm, staring down at her as she folded into herself, holding her arm to her chest as small weeps escaped between her breaths. "You do not come into my home and demand anything of me, mortal. I do not care if you are the master of fate. You are not the master of mine. Are we clear concerning our standing?"

Ailsa pushed a sharp breath through her teeth. Her body shook as she slowly looked up at him, still clutching her arm to her middle. "Yes," she hissed.

Laughter from the crowd mocked her as Surtur strode back to his throne. Erik placed a hand on her shoulder to look at her burn, but she jerked away from his touch. Feeling the sting of her rejection, he withdrew, stepping back to find Nerissa watching him. A smile across her blistered lips.

Surtur paced the width of the dais with hungry strides, looking out into the crowd. "The Tree was created from the body of a giant," he spoke as if it were an announcement. "The realms born from fire and ice, from the creation of fire and frost giants. There would not be the Nine without the giants, and yet it is we who are cursed to Muspell and Jotunheim. It is we who are forced to hide until the day we take back what is ours."

Surtur halted his steps and stared down at Ailsa. "You, Weaver, have seen the end. You drank from the well and know how all things will perish. Tell me now how these worlds will die."

Ailsa locked her jaw with a hatred in her scowl. She shook her head and stared at the steps of the platform instead.

"I asked," the giant slowly descended the steps, coming for her again, "how will the worlds end, Weaver? What have you seen?" His hand reached for her again, but Ailsa flung herself away from his reach.

"It ends in fire and ice," she said, voice betraying a tremor.

Surtur spread his arms wide before her. "And what is my fate? You have seen me before. I could tell by the recognition in your eyes when you first saw me. What is my contribution to the Nine?"

"You speak as if you already know," Ailsa said.

He smiled. "Indulge me."

Ailsa stood slowly to her feet, squaring her shoulders with the giant. "You will burn Asgard to ash."

Her words lit a new fire inside the hall. The surrounding crowd erupted with shouts of victory as if it were already theirs. As if Ailsa's tongue wove their future even as she spoke it, could make it certain the creatures around them would not fail. Surtur bowed a low, sweeping gesture to her before rising to look out at his kin.

"When the time arrives and the wolves swallow the sun and the moon, when the realms return to an everlasting winter never to know warmth again, when the heat of Muspelheim ceases enough for us to march beyond the fjords of fire and ash and the curse on us broken, when these signs happen, so then the wall around Asgard—built off the back of a giant—will fall." His terrible grin returned. "And I will burn the dwelling place of the gods to the same pile of powder they condemned us to."

The mountain shook as the cries of victory rose ever higher, shaking the foundation of stone beneath his feet. Erik watched each of them tip up their skulls, revealing the faces of fire giants all around them shouting the sounds of war. They forced him to wonder what his part would be in all this, where else his fate would bring him if it was not his home.

"And you," he said to Erik as if reading his thoughts, "will slay the beast, Fafnir, that guards the flame of Muspell. And when another piece of the Voluspa is fulfilled, then we can fulfill the rest."

Surtur turned his back on them and shouted something to the small figure standing on the other side of his throne. It bowed in response and made its way down the steps, heading toward Ailsa.

"Bring them to their rooms," the giant cocked his head at Erik while looking at Nerissa. She nodded.

"Wait—" he shouted, looking back at Ailsa, who was now shirking off the masked figure trying to escort her. Her gaze fell behind her shoulder, seeking him. But as Erik started toward her, darkness fell like a curtain over his sight.

From the way Ailsa screamed his name, he thought perhaps she had forgiven him for bringing this upon them, and it gave him hope as he succumbed to his dreams. That if she still worried for him, she still cared, and that was all the foothold he would need to see this through.

He would see all of this through, for both of them.

CHAPTER 18
VALI

Anger, hatred, malice.

Vengeance.

Four days he had been stuck in Vanaheim, recovering. Even with an endless source of Freya's tears, as the goddess wouldn't leave his side, the recovery was slow. His body—his blood—lacked any real provocation to heal itself.

And within that time, Vali had lived in a barren darkness. Joy, hope, pain, grief—all of it numb to his being as he dissociated from the sound of his heartbeat—a constant reminder inside his flesh of what he lost, ticking away another second he was without it. But it was all he could do to survive, to live outside of his body and far from the feelings too difficult to tolerate. To watch the world go on as he stood on the outside, wondering how the sun still found a way to rise and the moon still glowed in the sky without his mate to see them there.

Enver and a group of dark elves misted him back to Alfheim when he had finally healed enough to handle the trip. The moment his feet touched his homeland, he was crushed beneath the flood of his longings, all the days he suppressed a desperate desire to come back and sense the Light warm his skin.

He didn't follow them inside right away. The elves left him in the south courtyard where they had arrived. He stood on his feet for the first time in days, staring up at the Light palace as it refracted rays of sunshine into a thousand colors across the greens. His staff would be waiting for him inside, but he started toward the gardens instead.

No one, save for Enver's select few dark soldiers and Seela, knew about Ailsa—it was exactly how he wanted to keep her. A secret. Until he knew if this... separation would be permanent or not. And he would focus only on getting her back, starting with the only clues she left him with.

As the scenery transitioned from glass towers to garden blooms, Vali pulled out a folded piece of parchment from his pocket, reading Ailsa's last words. A few lines she had rushed to scribble down earlier that day before she was taken. Memories from the well. The pieces made little sense on their own, but with another perspective, perhaps it would lead him to an answer. If Erik was working with Nerissa, she wouldn't let Ailsa go until she brought down the Nine. The end of all things began with her, and he had the ticket to where it would start in the palm of his hand.

A fountain of fae memories marked the center of the gardens. A High Lord from a history too ancient for anyone alive now to remember for themselves, the water flowing from his hands supposedly representing the Light he discovered in these lands and vowed to protect for the rest of his generations. He was a distant relative to Vali, but the elfin never cared for his lineage. Being the son of Odin had ruined any pride he once had for who he was and meeting his half-brothers in Asgard had ruined any interest he had in learning the rest.

They hadn't even come to his aid that night. Only Njord and Freya, another goddess he vaguely remembered standing above him at one point. And Seela, his precious commander, the pain in her eyes. The only one in this world and the rest that knew his suffering firsthand and stood through it with him.

A weak whisper tore his attention from the fountain to a bench on the far side. "Vali?"

"Mother!" he said, feeling a rush of wind escape him as he circled the fountain to meet her. She sat alone, hunched and small beneath a quilt. Her black hair was now diluted into silver near the roots, her features finally overtaken with age. Her smile, however, was still strong and full of life, not losing a measure of its warmth.

"What are you doing out here alone?" he asked, wrapping his arms around her shoulders in an embrace. Even in the short time they'd been away, she had withered into a fraction of her former self, and Vali felt his guilt grow with every bone and hollow place his fingers skimmed. Seela informed him she was declining, but his stubborn heart refused to believe it could get this bad, this soon.

She inhaled a slow breath before she spoke, the air wheezing through her crushed windpipe with a sharp sound. "The healers are hiding nearby. I make them take me out here when I'm feeling good. It's peaceful to be alone sometimes," she took another breath, "especially when everyone treats you like you are dying."

"But Seela said—"

"Yes, Vali, I am, but that is beside the point. I can still make my own decisions and go outside when I feel like it."

He sat next to her on the bench and took her hand between both of his. "Indeed, you can. I just want you to be cautious." His gaze fell to where their hands intertwined. "I'm sorry I didn't visit sooner. Things have been complicated in Vanaheim, and I couldn't think of leaving Ailsa's side."

Lady Rind waved a hand in dismissal. "I would have scorned you for leaving her at a time like this. You did what was right, the only thing a mother would want her son to do, no matter my personal feelings. Speaking of Ailsa, where is she? She must have finished her training if you're here now." Her eyes searched beyond the fountain, as if expecting her to appear.

Vali cleared his throat before it closed. "She couldn't come this time, Mother. But trust me when I say she wanted to see you more than anything. It was her idea to make a visit, but fate had different plans."

His mother stared at him for a long moment, and Vali looked away, noticing the scrutiny in her dark eyes and thankful he was wearing gloves to hide his bare skin. If she saw through his excuse, she said nothing, returning her gaze back to the scene before them while squeezing his palm.

"Well, that is unfortunate. I'm not sure how much longer I'll be able to hang on, but I hope I get to see her again. It gives me great peace to know another holds you in the same standard, that she will care for you after I am gone. That you will never walk a single day of your lifetime alone."

A long breath slipped from his lips, shoving down some of the remorse her words brought up. Gods, she was laying it on thick, almost as if she knew. Five hundred years of existing and ruling over Alfheim, and she had never found her *Fraendi*, never experienced the connection he had with Ailsa. It reminded him that, no matter how this ended, he was fortunate enough to know what it felt like to have someone—even if it was just a passing thing.

"Can I ask you something strange?" When she nodded, he said, "You were there when they burned Baldur on the funeral pyre. Did Odin bury anything else besides his son that day?"

Lady Rind didn't answer at first, her mind recalling centuries of memories. "Beings of all kinds came to Baldur's funeral, and many placed objects on the pyre to pass with him into the afterlife in Helheim. I recall Odin placing his arm rings on his son as he said goodbye."

"Rings?" Vali clarified.

She shrugged. "Is there a reason you are so curious about what the Allfather buried? Don't tell me you actually care about his fate now."

He swept his tongue between his lips in deep thought. "As long as Fenrir is alive, he is a threat not only to Odin, but to Ailsa as well. Trust me, I couldn't give an ounce of *skide* for Odin."

Rings were symbols of vows, no matter if the oath was declared before the Nine or whispered over a lover. Whatever Odin swore on those rings, it mattered. Ailsa's notes proved that.

"Do me a favor, Vali," his mother said.

"Anything."

She shut her eyes briefly, her throat convulsed in an awkward swallow. "Never mention that name ever again in my presence."

Vali's room had been stripped bare. All of possessions moved to a different wing to accommodate his bride, but seeing their rooms for the first time without her didn't sit right with him. So he pulled off the dusty sheets covering the furniture in his old chambers and sat in front of the hearth—the same place they consummated their bond and vowed forever. And yet, he was the only one who remembered the sacred words they spoke.

Was he still bound to his oath if the one he gave it to had no memory of his vow?

There are no threads of time where I would not choose you, no matter how they unraveled in the end.

And they had unraveled.

And it *hurt.*

And for the first time in days, he felt the spark of something wild in his beating heart, the sound of it deep and wrathful as a war drum. His hands balled into fist as he stared into the dusty hearth, tasting blood, starting a vengeful fire in the cold logs with nothing but a brutal desire to burn the rest of the Tree down in his mind.

Vali stood and grabbed a razor and a set of blades from his stash of them in a forgotten chest and went into the bathroom, locking the door behind him. He stared at his reflection in the vanity mirror, despising the man he had let himself become, the weakness he identified with as he let himself slip deeper into a well of self-pity. But no longer.

He cut it all off, shaving the sides until there was only a faint dusting of hair over his scalp. A thick band ran over the center of his skull with enough length he could hold it with his fingers, but the sides were exposed to give him more skin for his next endeavor.

Shaking the rest of the trimmings off his clothes, Vali

stepped out onto the balcony with a note in his hand and called one of his messenger ravens with a sharp whistle. When the note was tied securely to its leg, he whispered, "To the Allfather. *Fýsa.*"

Make haste, he told his courier, and the power of the old tongue whisked the bird away on a favorable breeze toward the realm of Asgard.

CHAPTER 19
AILSA

They did not chain her, nor did they put her in a cell like Ailsa expected. Instead, the skull-faced figure on the dais slowly approached her as if nearing a wounded wolf, afraid of its teeth. Ailsa, despite the angry red and blistering skin along her forearm, felt as if she had twice the bite of any beast in this room, including the Great Wolf who sat on the platform.

Those frosty eyes hardly looked at her, remaining focused on something in the distance. Fenrir, the same demigod the well showed her, the images still floating in the back of her memory of the one who would be the catalyst of Ragnarok. And Surtur, the fire giant, one the well also showed her through flames of destruction and catastrophic crossfire.

Two long-simmering evils, both steeping in the same pot. How much longer did any of them have before it spilled over and overtook the rest of them?

There wasn't time to think before the masked giant was shoving her from behind. She glanced back at Erik. But Nerissa had some sort of control over him, and his eyes were a veil of white as she ordered him to cease his struggle against her. Ailsa didn't know what kind of power the being at her back wielded, but if she wanted to remain conscious, she needed to cooperate.

She let the giant push her through the crowds as it parted for them, rows of red-faced creatures on either side hurling slanderous words in a tongue she wasn't familiar with, but the anger behind them was a universal language. She steeled her face, ignoring them all as she set her gaze above their heads, denying them a reaction. Denying them the satisfaction of her fear, though it trembled through her bones and shook her marrow into mush.

They finally broke from the room, disappearing into an empty hall lined with torches of burning tar. Wherever she was being escorted, the route was disorienting. Winding corridors and doors that led to rooms with more doors and more halls on the other side. Ailsa tried to make mental notes about their directions, if only to escape as soon as the opportunity exposed itself.

He opened a door that led to tight quarters, lacking windows or luxuries. There was a small lantern that lit the bedroom with a light, revealing a single bed pushed to one side, a door that led toward a bathing room, and a trunk against the wall.

No bars on the door, no guards posted outside. She wasn't their prisoner, it seemed. Either they knew she had nowhere else to go, or there was nowhere to run beyond this stony stronghold. The sand alone had burned holes in her shoes even as she stood there.

"Cozy," she mumbled, looking around the room. "You can leave now."

Her escort said nothing, instead shut the door behind

them and opened the trunk in silence. The giant pulled out an outfit made of bleached flax and laid it carefully across the bed.

"I told you to get out," she hissed. But again, the masked being ignored her, now moving on to the pitcher of water near her bedside table. It struggled with clasping the handle and aiming the pour, the skull overlapping his head mostly to blame. He set the pitcher down and stepped to the side, beckoning her to drink.

"I'm not doing anything until you leave me alone." She planted her feet to prove her point, crossing her arms. The creature shrugged and leaned against the wall, watching her through the empty sockets.

"Well," she started again, "if you must stay, can you take off that ridiculous skull? It's unnerving."

The mask shook its head.

Ailsa huffed a breath of annoyance. "What's wrong? Are you too ugly? Disfigured perhaps? I promise, I don't care. Take it off, or I'll take it off for you."

She took one step, two steps before he realized her intentions were honest. His composure broke as he stumbled back away from her, but the room was too small to offer him a place to hide from her advance. And after being afraid for so long, it felt good to have a taste of power. To hold the upper hand if only for a moment.

The creature held his hands up in defense, yet made no move to push her off, almost as if he refused to touch her. Ailsa had no problem grasping at the hollow base of the skull, yanking it over the giant's head even as it fought against her, holding the skull in place. Compared to the rest of the creatures back in the hall, this one was small. Possibly a few inches taller than herself if she was being generous, and Ailsa had hardly towered over anyone.

They struggled back and forth, but the giant's clammy hands slipped off the smooth surface of the skull. The sudden loss of an opposing force made Ailsa overcorrect herself, the skull flying off the creature's face and slipping out of her hands. The mask landed somewhere behind her as the sound of splitting enamel connected with the stone floor. But she suddenly wasn't worried about the mask, nor cared if she broke the flawless bone.

Because looking at her now were eyes of pure gold. The creature before her wasn't a giant, but a man—one with smooth, pale skin and long auburn hair pulled back behind his head. He wasn't hideous or disfigured as she assumed, rather he was lovely.

With delicate cheekbones and a neck and shoulder girth that had never seen arduous work, he was so skinny he looked starved. His cheeks were hollow and the rest of his skin sunken between the bones. His chest heaved with quick breaths, gold gaze wide and strange as he watched her study him.

"Your eyes," she whispered. Something familiar in them, a feeling she couldn't place, most likely one lost with the rest of her memories. "Have we met before?"

He shook his head slowly.

"What is your name?" she asked. But he looked away in place of a reply, breaking what little connection had formed between them. She placed a hand on his arm. Every muscle in his shoulder flinched in reaction. "I won't hurt you. You can tell me."

He placed two fingers on his lips and looked back at her, a sadness brimming in his eyes, and shook his head once more.

"You cannot speak," she said. "You have no voice." The man finally nodded at something she said. Ailsa sighed and bit her lip. "Can you write?"

Another disappointed shake of his head.

"How do you communicate with anyone, then?" she asked. His answer came through unspoken words—the hang of his head, the way his gaze avoided the pity in her eyes. No one spoke to this silent man.

She tipped his chin with two fingers, forcing him to look at her. "I don't know why you are with Surtur. I don't know why I am here or what they have planned for me. But I will find a way to speak with you, and when I do, you will tell me your name." There was an urge in her chest to know who he was and why those eyes were so recognizable.

His lips parted in a stunned kind of wonder, dark brows furrowed in confusion. Those golden eyes shined a new light that lit up the room with their hope, and Ailsa knew this man didn't hold the kind of evil she had witnessed in that hall. He was different. Her heart stubbornly believed it beyond the shadow of doubt, clinging to this small thread of familiarity in his eyes.

The door burst open, and Ailsa and the man jumped apart, startled by the sound of wood crashing against the stone wall and rattling the hinges.

"What's going on here?" Erik said with an untampered anger set into the fists balled at his sides. He looked at both of them, eyes darting from one to the other.

"Did you seriously just barge into my room without knocking?" she asked of his intrusion. But Erik looked at her with accusation in his glare.

"I woke up in a room without you. Of course I panicked

and ran straight here to find you! Gods know what these giants could have been doing to you."

"Because *you* brought us here!" she shouted, and she wouldn't let him forget. He still had so much explaining to do.

Erik dragged a long breath and looked at the golden eyed man, who was now cowering to pick up his mask from the floor. "Get out. I'll keep an eye on her. Nerissa left me the keys."

He covered his head once more with the skull, a hairline fracture running through the eye orbit, but the shadows falling inside the deep hole concealed his gilded gaze from sight. As if Erik was above him on some arbitrary board of power, the man actually listened. His head bobbed in the mask before he scurried out of the room. But Ailsa noticed the mask tilt in such a way as if he was looking back at her, just before the door slammed behind him.

"Why were you looking at him like that?" Erik asked her.

"He looked familiar," she said. That answer didn't seem to placate him, but she was too tired to decelerate his internal fire. She had already been burned once this evening thanks to him. No point avoiding the flames now.

"What deal did you make with the witch?" she asked him.

"A deal to save your life at the risk of my own." He strode to the bed, pushed against the curved wall, and sat on a fur lining the feather mattress. "When no one heard from you for months, I went mad. I asked the Volva to find you... and she did."

"What did you give in exchange, Erik?" Ailsa paced the room to stand in front of him.

He looked up at her and gestured around them. "Whatever she wanted, whenever she asked."

153

Ailsa cursed and ran her hands over her face. "You swore an open oath to one of the Volva!"

"And I'd swear it again! You were kidnapped by a ship of fae! What was I supposed to do, let you go? Let that bastard have his way with you? Over my dead body."

"You might just have your wish," Ailsa spat before turning away from him. Her fists shook, clenching to hide their tremble. "And what about my memories? Why did you take them?"

"Because the demon who took you wanted your power for himself. He enchanted you to fall in love with him. He bound your life threads together so no one could kill him without killing you as well. The only way to free you from the spell was to erase your memory of him, and it worked. Everything the witch told me has been true."

But it didn't *feel* true. Ailsa thought Erik truly believed the words he spoke, but she wasn't totally convinced of them herself. "Swear on something," she said, spinning to face him. "Vow to me you are telling the entire truth as you know it, and I will trust you."

With no space for hesitation, Erik stood from the bed and unsheathed his blade, the one lined with golden runes, dried blood from the elfin still caught in the inscriptions. He held the weapon out to her in both hands like an offering, before kneeling before her.

"I vow to you, Ailsa Ledgersdóttir, that everything I have told you is the truth. That everything I tell from this day forward will be nothing but the truth. On my life and my honor, I will protect my word to you until the end of days."

Ailsa listened closely to his simple oath, paying mind to note any discrepancies. There was no greater dishonor than to break an oath, not among her people or the gods themselves. Trust was sacred, and once it was broken, it could never be

mended to be as strong as before. And if one lost trust, one lost everything.

"Okay," she said, plucking the dagger from his hand and turning the handle toward him. He sheathed it again as he rose to his feet.

"Now, can we move on and figure out what these witches want so we can go home?" he asked.

She felt herself nod despite the uncertainty building in her chest. Something about the strangeness of it all made her ask, "Does this mean you love me?"

Erik scoffed. "Of course, I love you. Is it not obvious?" He stepped closer to her, craning her neck to look up at him with a hand beneath her jaw. "Do you not feel this too?"

She cleared her throat and took a deliberate step back. "I am tired, Erik. I need some time to rest after today."

Erik's gaze glanced at the bed before looking back at her. "Of course," he said. "I'll let you get settled then. I'll come find you when you're rested." She heard his footsteps start back to the door. They paused before leaving.

"You know, everything I did was for you. Our place in this mess is just as much your fault as it is mine, but I do not fault you for what transpired with the elf. Only hope you will remember who it was in the end who came for you." He opened the door, and Ailsa heard the jingle of a lock. "Don't open this door for anyone but me, *sváss*."

Her hands didn't cease their tremors when he finally shut the door and left her alone, not until she crawled beneath the furs on top of her bed, wearing the clothes the man had laid out for her. Pressed into her palm was the ring she hid since she arrived in this realm, concealing it inside the empty sheath at her thigh. Something told her Erik would have taken it if he knew she still had it, and it was the last piece she had of her missing life.

The runes marking the ring told a story that had once been hers, a saga of sun and stars. And until she remembered every moment that represented these runes, Ailsa would search for the truth. So she kept it. Like a key to a door she was trying to find.

She slipped the ring back over her finger, and the shakes stilled at last.

CHAPTER 20
SEELA

The witch hunts led to dead ends. Any trail the wolves had left when the Haven fell had long gone cold. Seela ordered every inch of Alfheim searched for a trace of where the Volva and the wolven fled, but nothing turned up. Not even now, when Ailsa's fate may rely on them to find out where the Great Wolf now laid in wait. Now, more than ever, it was imperative to uncover how they slipped away unnoticed.

Seela wrapped her hands around the bars lining Ivor's cage. The wolven had remained well fed, untouched, and taken care of per her instructions to the dungeon guards. She had given her a kindness she did not deserve if only to wait out this stubborn vow of silence of hers that lingered like a bad grudge.

"Ivor," Seela spoke quietly. "Please, if you ever cared for Ailsa, you'll help us find her."

The wolven hadn't moved from her seat on her cot as Seela told her what happened in Vanaheim, her face still as if chiseled from stone. Ivor's secrets were their last hope. Vali's stability was slipping away each day that passed, and Seela knew he was moments away from self-imploding and doing something desperate.

"The pass," Ivor finally mumbled.

Seela pressed her face against the bars to hear her better. "What pass?"

The wolven sighed and scrubbed her face with her hands. "There is an old, forgotten pass behind the Dvager Mountains. It connects to the Ironwood in Jotunheim. It is how the wolven and the witches moved in and out of Alfheim without being seen."

"What's in the Ironwood?" she asked. "Who is protecting the wolven in Jotunheim, frost giants?" But she couldn't imagine the wolves and witches adding the giants to their cause.

Ivor shrugged her bare shoulders. "My family has guarded the lost power in Midgard since the seeress cursed Ailsa's family line. I've only heard rumors of the pass during my reports at the river, but whatever is in the Ironwood is a friend to the wolven."

Seela chewed her lip in thought. Could Ailsa really be that close? It seemed too easy, but it was a lead either way. "Will you come with me?"

For the first time in weeks, Ivor looked at her, and Seela looked straight into her frosted focus. "What did you just ask me?"

"I asked you to come with me," she repeated. "If the Ironwood is a friend to a wolven, then it would be wise to bring one along, don't you think?"

Ivor crossed the small cell toward Seela until her face was framed by metal bars. "What makes you think I won't run the second you open this cage?"

"Because I trust you still have Ailsa's best interest at heart. Don't think I couldn't see the fear in your eyes when I told you about Erik and the witch. You are not the only one with good senses, Ivor."

"You trust me?" she asked, voice lifting with hope.

Seela pushed her face away from the cell. "There is a difference between trusting you as an ally and trusting you with my heart. I can assure you, the only trust between us is in knowing you will do what is right for Ailsa, or I wouldn't have asked you in the first place."

The wolven flinched as if she had struck her in the chest. "If Ailsa is in trouble as you say, then I will do what I can to help. But Seela, you should know—"

"Thank you, Ivor," she blurted. "I will have the guards give you a proper room tonight so you can rest and fuel for the journey ahead. We leave for the pass tomorrow at first Light." The commander turned on her toes and evaded the wolven's gaze like she avoided the rest of her words.

She already got what she came for. Ivor could swallow the rest. Gods knew she had given her more than enough chances to speak up before this. Though inviting her to become an active part in the search for Ailsa had been a spur-of-the-moment decision, one she knew Vali would not approve. The thought of telling him gave her a massive headache, one that only intensified as the evening wore on.

As Seela returned to her office in the eastern wing of the Light Palace, a hall known to be private to the royal family and their advisors, the muffled sound of a scream behind a shut door traveled down the empty corridor.

Seela chased the sound back to an office she knew well. She threw open the heavy door leading to the dark elf's quar-

ters, surprisingly left unlocked. "Enver what in Hel's name
—Vali?"

Vali sat slumped in a chair, Enver standing behind him as
he jabbed the back of Vali's neck with a fine needle. A tray of
silver instruments and black ink laid on a table beside them
both.

"I told you to quit your whining, Lord Vali," Enver said as
he wiped the back of his hand across his forehead. "Someone
was bound to come barging to your aid."

"What are you doing to him, Enver? You aren't a
Runemaster!"

"Close enough," he mumbled.

He held Vali's head in place with a firm grip around the
base of his skull. She noticed his hair was different, cut short
on the sides to show the runes Enver was painting onto his
skin. The ink itself was blended with a bit of sedir so the runes
were active in the flesh, marking the person both internally
and outwardly with an enchanted exposition.

"What are you writing on him? Vali, I never thought I'd see
the day you got more runes after Ail—" she stumbled on the
name. "After what Odin did to you."

"These are different," he only said, motioning to the
parchment on Enver's worktable. Seela crossed the room to
look at the plans, discovering the entire page covered with
runes, intricate and many. She glanced at Vali, realizing why
he found it necessary to cut off his hair.

"This is longer than a saga, Vali. Why are you..."

But then she read it, and it began to make sense. It was
not a saga but a dedication, meticulously worded to give his
life a new purpose. On one side of his head was Vali's own
story, telling of journeys for vengeance and a desperate desire
to prove himself. On the other was a tale of a mortal control-

ling the fate of all that existed, a finite life holding power over the endless. The two met at the base of his skull, converging down his neck and across his shoulders to detail the rest of their story and the tragedy splitting them apart again.

But there was something left over from his old life, resurrected when Seela had brought him back from the brink of death. Vengeance bled into the brushstrokes, one that would not redeem a realm but a woman. It was the rest of his life's work outlined on a page—and now his body.

Vali had finally written his own fate.

"I'm going to Helheim in three days," he said in a taut voice as Enver continued to break the seal of his skin.

"Alone?" she asked.

The fae lord's face flinched. "Hel doesn't allow visitors in her realm. This could likely be a one-way trip, Seela. I won't bring anyone along for such a journey. But I truly believe Baldur has something we need to stop Fenrir. Something Odin made an oath upon and broke without realizing until his son was locked away in the underground realm."

Seela stood there, crestfallen. Enver, sensing a new tension, stepped away for a moment, pretending to clean one of his needles in the moonlight filtering through a stained glass window.

"So that is it, then?" She tossed the parchment of runes back on the table. "You're willing to give up everything, including seeing Ailsa again, just for a *pretty good* chance Baldur will have something that defeats Fenrir."

Vali stood from his chair, closing the distance between them with rushed strides. "I would rather face endless lifetimes in Helheim than let Ailsa live her only one in the arms of *that* man and those witches."

"But, Vali," Seela protested, "she will need you when this is over, however it ends."

He shook his head. "She doesn't even remember me." The loudest silence followed his words, and Seela almost choked on her breath as she felt his pain spill from his essence like a wave.

"I have a lead on the wolven," she replied quickly, swallowing the guilt. "Ivor told me about a pass that connects to a place in Jotunheim. It is how they sneaked around us all these years. And since you will be gone, I'm going to check it out." Her gaze fell beyond him, catching on something else in the room as she said, "I'm bringing Ivor."

"What?" Enver and Vali said in unison.

The dark elf tossed his needle with the rest on the pallet. "I'm going to pretend you didn't say something so foolish, Seela."

"What Enver said," Vali agreed, crossing his thick forearms.

"And I'm going to pretend either of you thinks you can dictate my decisions. I've already put in the orders to have her transferred to a room near mine, and I've sent for Frey to rule in my place and watch over Lady Rind—"

"I cannot believe this," Vali interrupted. He turned to pace the floor, his bare back displaying the incomplete saga. "What are you hoping to gain from this, Seela?"

"Answers, just like you. If I'm lucky, they'll lead me to where they're keeping Ailsa."

Enver stepped in her line of sight. "Then I'm coming, too."

"That's unnecessary—"

"To Hel it isn't!" the dark elf spat, each word a thunderclap. Seela had never seen him so flustered. "If you think I trust that wolven for a second, you're delusional. She might be

telling the truth, but she also might be using this as an opportunity to escape—or worse. That pass is forgotten for a
reason. I'm coming with you, and that is final."

Her chest deflated with a harsh breath set loose. "Fine!
We're leaving in the morning."

"Fine."

"In that case, Enver," Vali said, sitting down, "you'll have
to finish this all tonight."

The commander's shoulders fell, mouthing a curse as he
looked at Seela, but to the demigod in his chair he said, "It
would be an honor, Lord Vali."

She turned on a back heel to leave them, grateful the
conversation was had and done. But Vali called out to her as
soon as her hand reached for the doorknob.

"Seela?" Another surge of emotion from him that made
her bones ache.

"Yes, Vali?"

Another quiet, this one unbearably heavy. She looked back
at him to find him staring at her. His lips parted as if wanting
to say something, but no words to say it. He finally settled on,
"Don't leave without saying goodbye tomorrow. Okay?"

"Of course. You're my *Hjartablód,* Vali. Until the Light
takes us."

"Until the Light takes us, Seela," he mumbled back.

She left the room swiftly after, feeling a panic rise in her
throat, but it was only possible to make it a short way down
the hall and into the sanctity of her office before her chest
heaved with sobs, and she collapsed in a mess on the carpet.

It was a sadness she hadn't felt since her father died, since
the last time she had been left alone in this world by someone
she loved, and Seela was beaten by wave after wave. Each
swell greater than the last, each pulling her deeper into a well

she could see no escape from. She pulled out the necklace she always wore, the one she hid beneath her tunic, stealing a piece of comfort from the metal her father had once touched, as if she could still feel him now.

He had to do this—she had to do this. She knew it. The pull of their fates was too strong to permit them to remain together.

A knock at the door stalled her breath, returning the room to silence in hopes the late visitor would leave. Instead, the door cracked open. Only a few had the ability to let themselves in. Enver had enchanted the locks that way.

"Seela." Vali said her name with an appeal, but she looked away from him, wiping her face dry before he saw the evidence of her grief.

"I can feel your hurt, you know, through our bond. Just as I know you've felt mine this week."

She shook her head and cleared her throat. "What do you want, Vali?"

"Honesty," he said. The air shifted as he sat next to her on the carpet. "Will you hate me for this?"

"If I said yes, would you stay?"

He snorted, wrapping an arm around her shoulder. "You know I can't. I made an oath to Ailsa that I would never stop fighting for her. I must keep it, or I'll end up like my father."

More silence, more waves, it was all she could to hold her head above the surface. "Then promise me you will try everything in your power to get out of Helheim. Vow to *me* you will try to come home."

"I vow it, Seela. Hel will be kicking me out before you know it." He pulled her into the fold of his arm. "Promise me you'll try to find her, but you won't risk yourself. Vow to me you'll be careful."

"I promise, Vali."

His finger tapped the necklace she still clenched in her fist. "You told him about your past."

Seela nodded numbly.

"I'm proud of you. I know it takes a lot for you to open up to someone. That kind of trust is a rare gift, and I know Enver appreciates it for just that."

She rolled her eyes, her tears soaking up. "What are you trying to say, Vali?"

His laugh was quiet as he pulled her even tighter against his side. "That I am happy for you, even if this doesn't lead where I'm inclined to believe it will. You deserve... true happiness. Someone who accepts you for who you are."

She scoffed but could conjure no sharp words to combat his soft ones. She sighed and surrendered her true thoughts. "I just hope I can find what you have with Ailsa one day, Vali. I want that kind of bond, too."

"You'll find it, Seela. And when you do, it will make all these dark day's worth it. Trust me."

The waves of hurt still lapped against her soul, but with her heart's blood beside her, for a time they were easier to withstand.

CHAPTER 21

AILSA

Few things in the Nine could make a mountain tremble, but Ailsa woke to the metal bed frame rattling against the stone wall. Her eyes flew open from a deep sleep to sit up quickly, shifting from rest to ready for battle. Dust sifted from the ceiling as the room shook, covering her sheets with a grey film. Ailsa threw off the furs to start for the chamber door, her heartbeat outpacing her steps.

The handle twisted free as Ailsa threw herself into a dark, empty hall. There was no one on the other side, no masked man waiting or brooding Otsman watching, just darkness stretching in either direction. The burning tar fueling the torches nearly consumed the accelerant, their flames small and dim.

Grabbing the lonely lantern from her chamber, Ailsa started in the direction the man had brought her. She came across another door, left open in a clear rush, the candles inside still burning to reveal a black fur cloak belonging to Erik. Where had he gone? Was he taken and why had she been left behind?

The mountain shook again with a deep rumble, this time with enough force to trip her stride. She followed the direction of the sound down a different path, one that led away from the gathering hall and more familiar tunnels.

Before she could venture further into the mysterious corridors that traced the mountain's base, a hand gripped her hard by the shoulder. Ailsa slipped a gasp of surprise as she came face to face with the stag skull. A chip missing near the long nasal cavity.

"Oh," she said, chest deflating. "It's you. What the Hel is going on? Where is everyone?"

He answered by snatching her wrist and pulling her in the opposite direction of where she had been walking. There was an urgency in his grip, a tensity that hadn't been there before, even when she'd exposed him.

She dug her heels into the rug lining a short portion of the tunnel, twisted her arm trapped in his hand. "Wait! We need to get out of here, the mountain—"

He yanked her hard by the arm with a newfound strength, violently tugging her body forward. "You better not be bringing me back to my room!"

He shook his head, escorting her down a different hall that led to a stairwell ascending to an obscure destination, her lantern light only traveling so far. The silent man pulled her up the stairs, which were more like crudely carved blocks chiseled into a pathway, zigzagging all the way to the landing where another door stood ajar.

She noticed a soot singed sky through the opening. The red filter that stained this realm washed a new color over her perspective, something other than copper rocks and black shadows. The man led her further outside, finally releasing her arm as she stepped out onto a flat sheet of granite. From here, she could see the rocky earth impale the skyline—dark mountains like the one they kept her inside littered the distance everywhere she looked. They were still stuck in a realm of fire, but the fresh air at this altitude was still more welcoming than the drafty chamber they stuffed her into.

There were others here too—witches. Waiting with their eyes turned toward the distance. She wondered what they were doing here until a roar purged the wind in her chest, a thunderous sound that was only equal to a bolt of lightning as it charged the sky. She followed the man's masked gaze to find the beast Surtur had mentioned earlier.

A dragon.

From this far, she could only tell that the beast was golden, with great wings that could push the clouds away with their gusts. It swooped low, breathing a line of fire as it disappeared into the valley.

"Don't worry, Ailsa. Fafnir won't hurt us over here."

Nerissa sauntered from a darkened corner on the mountain's side. Her ever present smile continued to grace her lips in a way Ailsa wanted to claw it from her face. "How can you be so sure? He flies," she said.

The witch replied, "He is a smart creature. He knows Surtur is after his treasure. These attacks on the mountain are frequent but futile. We mostly come up here to watch, not for our own safety."

"Why does Surtur want his treasure?" she asked. "And what use is gold to a dragon?"

"He wasn't always a dragon, Weaver. He was a dwarf, the son of a very wealthy king who lived in a house made of solid gold and glittering jewels. They were shapeshifters in Svartalfheim, and one day Loki killed his brother, Otr, while he was in the form of an otter. The king demanded the gods pay him a storehouse worth of gold for his loss."

Ailsa scoffed. "I'm *sure* Loki did the right thing and paid him back."

Nerissa grinned. "Oh, he paid him back, but at the expense of another dwarf named Andvari. This dwarf had a magic ring called Andvaranaut, which made him extremely wealthy. Loki threatened his life over his treasure and forced him to give up all his gold—and his ring. But this treasure was very special. Swords, chain mail, a helm said to strike fear in the hearts of men when they look upon it, and so brother and father turned on each other. After Fafnir killed his family, he took his new wealth into the wilderness, where no one could find his horde."

Ailsa realized there was greed even in this forgotten place. "Did Fafnir shift into a dragon, then?"

Nerissa nodded, and Ailsa looked back to the beast now soaring through the smoke. Dark clouds rose from the valley he just set on fire. Even from here, she felt the heat carry on a dry breeze, smelled the desolation of fire's fury on a war torn mountain side.

Ailsa blinked with realization, sucked away for too long from the legend of Fafnir. "Where is Erik?" she asked. "I woke up alone and panicked, but no one was in the hall until that one found me." She jutted her thumb at the stag skull.

Nerissa's cool glare looked over at the man before she smiled. "Ah, Sigurd must be taking a liking to you. He rarely interacts with any of us."

"That's his name?"

She shrugged. "It is now." She turned her head slightly to look at him. "He came crawling to Fenrir after his father killed his mother. Sad little thing can't even speak. The Wolf did him a favor by taking him in, but he's utterly worthless."

"Perhaps something could be done about his voice—"

Nerissa's hair flailed around her shoulders as she snapped her head at Ailsa. "I wouldn't go messing with things that don't concern you. You have other things to worry about."

Ailsa narrowed her eyes at the witch. "Like what?"

"Like..." Her eyes drifted to where black smoke columned over the mountain. "Like if your handsome Erik is still wearing his skin."

Her heart dropped somewhere in her stomach. "Do you mean to say Erik is down *there*?" Unreasonable. Judging from the amount of ash swirling in the hot breath of a breeze, nothing could have survived those flames. Especially not...

"Nerissa, we need the weaver immediately." A voice drew both of their attention to the stairwell, where a giant was waiting on the landing, his pink skin stained with soot. "The mortal is alive, but he's been badly burned, and Surtur refuses to let the healers use up their tonics on him."

"Where is he?" Ailsa asked, pushing past the witches in her way.

"We dragged him to his room, he's—"

But Ailsa was already halfway down the staircase leading to the main floor with Nerissa trailing her close behind like a shadow. Her bare feet padded down the stone hall now filled with giants and the scent of singed hair. When she finally made it back to Erik's room, she found him sprawled in his bed, groaning as a woman peeled his half-melted boots from his legs.

"We're in a mountain full of witches and none of you can heal him?" Ailsa spat as she crossed the room to where he laid. His eyes were shut, but the places where his clothes had been burned away revealed red, blistered skin still hot to the touch. She grabbed the knife from his sheath and began tearing his shirt off his chest to keep the fibers from adhering further.

"Sedir is not like regular magic, Ailsa," Nerissa said, coming to her side. "It is used for control and manipulation, not restoration in the natural sense."

Ailsa looked down at the cut on her hand but remembered somewhere in the dream of her memories that she had tried to heal him before. She told the witch, "I cannot heal him with my power. I've already tried before, and his body rejected it for some reason—"

"The blood rune," she said as her eyes shut in realization. "Our vow sealed his fate to belong to me and me alone. You cannot help him then."

"Then find someone who can!" she shouted. "If Surtur wants his precious flame he will need Erik alive, will he not?"

When Nerissa said nothing, Ailsa paused her work to glance up at her, an uncertainty that was unfamiliar on her face. A weight heavy on her brow. "The giant lord's word is law around here. Even Fenrir cannot speak against him, much less a mere witch."

"It sounds more like you are all cowards." Ailsa finished peeling Erik's tunic away after a tedious job of balancing both a quick yet gentle removal. Tossing the clothes somewhere behind her, she spoke to the other witch still standing there with his boots. "We worry first about his hydration and then the possibility of infection. Get lots of wet cloth and soak the burns with cool water to stop the burning process. If you can make a soup with garlic that would be great, but tea with honey also works well to prevent infection. Do you have any herbs like that?"

The witch nodded quickly before discarding the disfigured

leather and running out of the room. Ailsa turned back to Nerissa. "Where is Surtur?"

She sighed and rolled her eyes. "He is probably in the dining hall. He watched the fight from a distance like the rest of us—"

"Show me to him then."

She narrowed her eyes at Ailsa, a silent deliberation behind her dark eyes. "You are going to die."

Ailsa shrugged and sheathed Erik's knife in her belt. "Hate to spoil the ending for you, Nerissa, but we are all going to die. Now take me to the giant lord."

The dining hall was full as the witch escorted her past tables of drunken conversations and laughter, words of Erik's peril quickly becoming legend inside this hollow mountain. The meals they leaned over appeared more like scraps than a post battle feast, and Ailsa wondered where they found what little meat and ale that was obviously rationed carefully between them all.

Surtur sat at a table at the head of the room with the human form of Fenrir, the two speaking quietly before spotting her. Ailsa crossed the hall with hurried strides, her hands bound tight in fist, ready to fight.

"What are you doing here? We did not call on you, Weaver." The giant lord stood from his seat, silencing every stray word in the room. Ailsa swallowed back the intimidation he was trying to rise in her, but when the veins beneath in his skin glowed like lines of molten metal, it was difficult not to feel, to steel her heart from fear. Her arm burned in recollection of his touch.

"Why will you not heal Erik? You need him to retrieve your flame and yet you will let him die instead!" She managed to speak without quivering.

Surtur scoffed. "Because he is a waste of flesh and therefore resources. After watching him fight today, it is clear he will never slay Fafnir. You should do him a favor and let him die while he still has some honor left for Valhalla."

"Then what will you do about the flame?" she asked.

The giant stared her down with hot coals in his gaze. "I'm working on it."

"No, you're not," Ailsa said, trying to laugh. The sound came out hollow. "If you could have slayed the dragon by now, you would have. That explains the scars all over your body, why you're inside the mountain, all of it. You're hiding."

A chorus of growls charged the air behind her, raising the hair on the back of her neck stiff. She cocked a brow at the giant lord, daring him to tell her differently and yet he only said, "You are right."

"I..." she started, thrown off guard. "I know."

Surtur sat down once more and took a sip of his drink. "I cannot slay Fafnir, nor can any of my men. We consulted the Volva, and they explained that the Voluspa explicitly says a mortal will slay the dragon, and we want to make sure the prophecy is fulfilled to the very line. Every prediction needs to come to completion, or the rest will not be certain to follow."

Ailsa shut her eyes briefly and summoned what little resolve remained in her bones, but it felt more like scraping her marrow for something worth substance. How much did she have until it was all gone? Until she became as empty of courage as she was of everything else?

"I'll go after the dragon."

The hall was quiet before, but her offer felled a breathless silence across the room. She waited for their laughter, the taunts and jesting, but the giants said nothing. Surtur studied her with slits for eyes, so focused on her now she thought he could see beneath her skin.

"Why would you risk your life for my flame?"

"Because I have more to gain than you could ever imagine." And because she had nothing left to lose. "Heal Erik in good faith, and after I get your flame, you will make the witches return my memories."

A sharp breath blew at her back, Nerissa's way of showing her distaste for the idea. Surtur did not deny her, however, but thought over the deal as if he were seriously considering her offer.

"I'm the last mortal you have," she said to further her point. "You are fortunate I am even making this offer, seeing as you need me to destroy Asgard."

"And why would you help me burn the realm of the gods?" he asked.

Ailsa took a step closer, feeling victory within reach. "Because if you set fire to the realms, you'll burn down with them. I know how to end you as well, Surtur. Do not mistake my collaboration with support."

They had taken something from her. Something important enough she could sense Nerissa's nerves building as her breath quickened. Whatever they stole, it was in her memories, ones she would need to fight back in the end.

Perhaps she *was* helping Surtur. For now. Better to lose a battle to better the chances at war.

Surtur stood suddenly, crossing his thick arms around his back. "You have a deal, Fate Weaver. What shall we swear this oath upon?"

She quickly shook her head in disagreement. "My word is good on its own. I will not swear on life or limb or treasure. If I break my vow, I do not get what I want."

"And if I break mine?" he asked, black brow arching.

Ailsa smiled. "It is not wise to tempt fate, Surtur, least of all the one that weaves it. I think you know better than that."

The giant lord offered her something like a smile in return, though with thin lips and jagged teeth, it was far from reassuring. "Nerissa, have the healers bring the burn balm to Erik's room. Make sure he gets the tonics he needs to get better. While he heals, Weaver, you will journey to Fafnir's territory in the Mourning Mountains and find my flame."

Fenrir, who hadn't spoken since she arrived, leaned forward across the table to speak at last. "Good to see you again, Ailsa," he said with a wink of an icy blue eye. The color reminded her of a wolven she used to know and love. It hurt twice as much to look at him now. "Funny how fate brought us together again, after all."

Ailsa turned from the head table, starting back down the aisle without giving him the satisfaction of a retaliation. Her memories were finally within reach, and all that stood between them was a dragon.

Fate was a funny thing, she agreed. And right now, she felt the threads of destiny laughing down at her.

"Just cut it off for Hel's sake!"

Erik wailed and squirmed as Ailsa peeled away the dead skin from his wounds, sweat collecting on her brow as she focused. The witches watched her as they held him down against the bed, curious about how she handled the deep burns that scattered his body. They brought her tonics and balms, none of which contained the right herbs to heal his wounds but would at least help the pain.

"If I cut off everything with a burn, Erik, you won't have much of a body left," Ailsa said as she poured a disinfectant over the raw flesh, an angry but healthy red. Satisfied with his lower limbs, she wrapped them in a clean cloth and decided on a break.

"Get some rest," she told him after handing him more broth to sip. "I'll come check on the wrappings later to make sure they stay moist for the next few days until your skin grows back."

Erik's eyes shut as his breaths turned rhythmic, deep, and slow. The process was exhausting, no matter how necessary it had been without her magic to heal him. But Ailsa found it comforting to stretch her healer's mind, even if it was at his expense.

"Thank you, Ailsa," he said finally.

"Of course," she mumbled. "Perhaps you won't go off fighting dragons without me next time."

His face twisted like her words were sour. "I have never known genuine fear until today. Facing that flying serpent..." He swallowed, unable to finish the thought. "It was something I would not wish on my worst enemy, much less you."

She bit her lip, wondering if this was a good time to tell him she'd be doing just that, but Ailsa only gathered the rest of the supplies the witches brought her and tucked them away beneath his bed for safekeeping. If she was lucky, he'd be bedridden until she returned, and he'd be none the wiser until after she slayed the monster. Better to ask forgiveness than Erik's consent—especially when she already knew his answer.

"What do we do now? How do you plan on paying off your debt to the witch so we can be free?" she asked him instead.

He lifted his head off the pillow to look at her. "I'm not giving up. I just need another chance. Now that I know Fafnir's strategy, I can take him down where he's weakest. I still plan on completing what I started."

"Perhaps I can help—"

Her offer was cut off by a laugh, the first sound of amusement she heard from him since they arrived. "No offense, *sváss*, but I don't think there is enough hemlock or nightshade in any healer's apothecary to take down a dragon. Leave the beast to me, Ailsa. I told you I'd get us home, and I will keep my vow to you." He shifted in bed and groaned as she aggravated his wounds. "Even if I must lose the rest of my skin, which seems likely."

Ailsa forced a small smile and nodded, feigning docile. Any bad feeling she had before about going behind his back was smothered away beneath the load of his condescension. Before he baited her into a more precarious conversation, she stood to leave.

As she bid him a good night and cracked the door open, he called her back. "Ailsa, wait!" Mouthing a curse, she slowly turned to face him, sensing what he was going to ask. "Will you stay with me tonight? I know things are uncertain between us, but I would feel better if you stayed. At least just for tonight."

The look in his eyes was one of desperate hope, but she looked away before it dug a foothold in her heart. *No.* He wasn't allowed to do this. To make her feel guilty for something that had befallen him because of his own choices.

"I am very tired, Erik. I'd like to rest in a bed, not a cot on the floor."

"You can rest with me, it's not like we haven't slept in the same bed together before."

Something in her bones told her he was wrong to ask her such a thing, but her logic knew he was right. They were inseparable before fate pulled him away, before their father's split them apart. There was nothing between them that had changed besides time and distance, and yet her heart no longer lurched at the sight of him, no longer broke at his pain nor desired his company.

The problem was, she couldn't explain *why*. Gods, she had been nearly obsessed with this man since he first showed up in her longhouse when they were children, and now he was like a stranger wearing the face of someone she used to know. And she felt nothing for him.

Did that elfin's spell do something to change her heart more permanently? Was this his fault she felt this way? It was one more reason she needed to slay the dragon herself. She needed those memories, or she'd never have peace relying on one person's side of the saga.

"I'll check on you in the morning." Her voice was quiet as it rejected him, and this time he let her escape from the confine of his room to the one in her own.

A lone candle still burned as she entered, shadows dancing across the walls of red rock. She noted something had been placed on her bed, a silver container. Nothing else accompanied the gift, no note or hint of who dropped it off. Someone with a key to her room, apparently.

Opening the small jar, inside was an opaque balm smelling of aloe and the soothing scent of lavender. Exactly what she had requested, but the witches claimed they didn't grow the herbs here, only using what little fertile land remained to grow food for Muspell's sons.

The witches brought a few healing tonics when they came to this land to seek refuge from the gods, claiming it was the last land besides the Shadow Realms they could hide. Burns, however, were a frequent complaint, and their supplies dwindled fast, only motivating them further to break free of this realm.

So where had this little treasure come from?

Ailsa tucked it away in a drawer for later, not desiring to bother Erik again so soon nor revisit their last conversation. He'd been gentle with her when they first arrived, giving her space, hardly touching her. But there was an assignment in his eyes when he looked at her, one she knew he wanted to claim even more than the dragon, and patience had never been one of Erik's finer traits—not that he had many besides his charm and his looks.

Time. The one thing she needed most and lacked more than anything else, and it was slipping away like silk strands through her fingers. But if this jar was any sign, it was that someone was listening to her. Someone was on her side in this realm of fire and misery.

"Thank you," she whispered to the walls, to the ally she had somewhere waiting in the dark. Hope was rare here, but it existed. So she clung to it like the jar in her fist and dared to dream of better days ahead.

CHAPTER 22
VALI

Cold mist covered the morning as the sun peeked just above the horizon, striking the fog floating heavy above the still river. The Gjoll flowed from the original well, Elivágar, one of the eleven rivers that existed at the beginning of the worlds. The only one that ran to the gates of the underworld, separating life from death. Not a ripple stirred the surface nor a sound disturb the quiet. He was alone, for now, simmering in the silence marking the lifeless Realm Between Realms.

The solitude was brief as the sound of eight hooves from a single beast and his rider crossed the countryside. Vali pulled his hood lower over his brow, concealing the fresh ink on his head and his neck from the company arriving behind him. He threw the rest of his belongings he packed for the journey in the longboat and turned to see Odin, his white robes wet from the ride and dismounting his horse, Sleipnir, letting the length of his traveling robes and boots slap the mud lining the river's side.

"You came," Vali said in greeting.

Odin pulled back his own hood, fair hair paler than the last time he saw his father. The lines around his frown were deeper in comparison. Dark circles clung to his eyes, emphasizing his fatigue as Odin's shoulders slumped. No longer the poised king of gods, but a tired man who had everything to lose if Vali failed now.

"I had little choice," he said, blue eye glaring at Vali with a clear bane. "Blackmailing the king of the gods is a new low for you, my son."

"It's about time I played on your level. We need to discuss Loki and the oath you made to him."

Odin took a small step toward him, and Vali matched it. "Is that what you called me here for? My vow to the Lord of Lies?"

"I called you here because I expected you'd want your son back from Hel. Loki mentioned something about broken oaths in Noatun. I need you to be honest with me if I'm to finish this."

But Odin looked away, his chest falling with a monumental sigh. "Loki and I are blood brothers. We made an oath to each other long ago that we would never turn on each other. In return for his loyalty, I gave him the best riches Asgard had to offer. He had a hall of his own, his wife Sigyn, a son Nafri who could shapeshift like him, access to all the realms and my support behind him. Then one day, he killed my son—using Hod, of course."

Vali said, "Loki does nothing without a reason or purpose. What triggered this outburst from him?"

The Allfather winced. "It all started with Gullveig."

"Gullveig? The witch you burned?"

"Yes." Odin paced the shore until his toes skimmed the lapping waters. "Loki wasn't completely satisfied with Sigyn.

She was too good for him, too kind and patient. He's the kind of god who needs more excitement from his bride." He spared him a look. "He was seeking trouble, and he went to bed with it. Behind our backs, Loki snuck around and had not one, but three children with Gullveig. One of them was the wolf that was said to be my undoing."

Vali closed his eyes in realization. "Fenrir."

"When Baldur was born, we all rejoiced, because he was favored to kill the Great Wolf—"

"And then Loki had him killed before he could do such a thing." Vali finished for him, and Odin nodded.

"This forced me to tie up the wolf so he would bring no harm to my family or to me. The way I see it, I took care of the problem with no blood on my hands."

"You still broke your oath," Vali said. He looked back at the elfin, eyes darkening in a shroud of perplexity. "You said you wouldn't betray him. Yet you raised Baldur to slay his son."

"And his son would kill me! Who can you say broke their oath first, then?"

"You did!" Vali was shouting now. "You were so afraid of the empty words of a seeress that you tore apart his family and planted that seed of disdain in Fenrir. The Great Wolf might not want to kill you, Odin, if you had not tricked him and tied him up in chains!"

The Allfather's eye squinted into a slit. "That is the perspective of a vengeful god. Not the truth."

Vali scrubbed his face with his hands, unable to believe what he was hearing. "Where is Loki now?"

"My sons locked him away in a cave with chains cursed to bind him forever, along with a few extra measures to make sure he is too weak to use his powers of illusion. We will not have to worry about his deception for a long time."

Vali laughed out of bewilderment. "It seems that is your answer to everything, Allfather. I wonder when you will run out of chains."

His silence was damning enough, and Vali's irritation had him fall quiet. Until he had to ask, "How do I enter the Shadow Realms without getting stuck there? Hermod is the only god who has done so."

Appearing relieved by the sudden change in subject, Odin reached into his cloak and pulled out a hook attached to a length of rope. "Do not go through the front gate," he said. "Going through Hel's veil will trap you there for eternity. Hermod got around that by jumping the wall."

Vali reluctantly took the hook from his possession, wary of his generosity. "I am surprised you are helping me come back."

The Allfather took a step back toward his horse. "I am helping you for Rind. She didn't deserve what happened to her... what I did to her. She loves you more than anything in this life, and to answer for what I've done, I will at least make sure her son comes back to her safely."

Vali looked down at the hook before he tossed the utility into the boat docked next to him. He turned back to Odin, knowing this could very well be the last time he saw his father if he didn't stop Fenrir's plan for his demise.

"I hope I can bring Baldur back from Hel's realm, Odin."

His father's gaze narrowed on him, stunned into a silence. Vali continued, "I hope your golden son protects you and kills the Great Wolf. I hope we stop the end of the Nine, and I hope you live to see it all come to pass. I hope you live, so I can kill you myself for what you've done to those I love. Your end will come."

He turned from Odin and began pushing the hull of the

longboat nestled into the black sand of the riverbank. When it finally loosened enough, he hopped over the rim and settled inside.

From his horse, the Allfather said, "I titled you well at least. You truly are the god of revenge and redemption, Vali."

The elfin stopped what he was doing to look Odin in the eye. Perhaps for the last time.

"It's no longer redemption I'm after, Allfather. I only bleed for vengeance now."

Vali was about to fill the sail with a south wind when another sound broke the ominous quiet. More hooves, though there were only four beating feet against the earth this time. He squinted his eyes into the mist, wondering who else could possibly know he was here.

"Oh, thank gods," Freya said on the back of a boar. She released a large breath in relief. "You haven't left yet!"

"No, but I'm about to. Why aren't you in Alfheim?"

"Seela's trip was delayed. Something about a troll attack in the northern domain. But she told me about your trip to see Hel, and I wanted to bring you something—some *things*—that might help."

The elfin inhaled a breath to support his patience. Why were gods so generous at the worst possible times? "What is it, Freya?"

"Surprise!" She leaned to the side of her steed to reveal two women behind her. Their faces were strangely familiar... and human.

"Who—" he started, but the one in front interrupted him with a hand and a scowl.

"Well, if it isn't the demon who offed us all just to fuck our sister."

The wind was sucked from Vali's chest. He braced himself on the edge of the boat, suddenly requiring support to stand upright. "Gods below, not you two."

Marrin and Lochare dismounted from Freya's boar and appraised his ship with critical eyes. "Freya said you could use some company going to the realm of the dead. And well, since you already killed us, we figured why not?"

"Because you might never return," Vali said. "You understand the souls who enter the Shadow Realms must remain there for eternity? No more fighting fields in Folkvang."

But the pair of women boarded his boat with little concern over the idea. The elfin looked to Freya, pleading with his eyes for her to stop this, but the goddess shrugged and said, "Seela has told me how much you've been hurting these last weeks. I thought you needed the company, Vali."

He *needed* to save his lady, and yet Freya was more concerned with the state of his sulking than Ailsa's life. Though his meeting with Odin had already wasted enough time, and he wanted to take advantage of the daylight while they were still above ground. Arguing with the goddess would be futile to both his plans and his sanity.

He glared at one sister. "You must promise you will listen. If you want to come with me to the Shadow Realms, you must do everything I say, no hesitation. This is too important to screw up."

The other woman sat next to her sister, blonde hair pulled back in a tight braid down her back. They were practically identical, though the one he was speaking to had a dent in the bridge of her nose, as if it had been broken and never healed properly. "Do you hear that, Marrin?" she said, leaning into her ear. "He expects us to behave."

"We don't like to be told what to do, demon," Marrin said.

"Yes, that seems to run in the family," he murmured. Vali felt his hand ball into a fist as he tried to address them again. "Look, I'm sorry about killing you and all the rest of it, but Ailsa is in trouble now. I think we can both agree to be diplomatic at best in order to help her. If you cannot do that, if you only came to torture me the entire journey, then please do us all a favor and get off this boat."

The pair sat quietly, staring at him. Lochare wore face paint, blacking out her eyes like a blindfold. She shut her eyes briefly before nodding. "We know what is at stake, Vali. Freya has kept us informed about your bond with our sister and the consequences of recent events. We do not wish to be a distraction, only to help."

In a voice too gentle to belong to a warrior, Marrin said, "You are not the only one who misses her, Vali."

A shame like a splinter burrowed its way into his heart. Ailsa always spoke well of her sisters, a relationship he had nothing to empathize with. Perhaps he was underestimating their value in a time like this, where every drop of retribution mattered. If they wanted to help, he had no right to stop them.

"Fine. But there is nothing to say for certain what we will face when we reach Hel. When we leave these shores, I am in charge." The twins said nothing, each looking off into the mist, and he figured they'd probably cut off their fighting hand before ever agreeing with him out loud. Vali sighed and stepped across the bench between them to sit at the back of the boat where it steered.

With a wave of his hand, the bindings snapped, and the sails rolled open, and they began their journey down the Gjoll.

The sisters were quiet as they assisted him, monitoring the boat as he sat in the back of the hull to operate the steer. The river curved against the earth, spiraling deep into the heart of the Tree the further they traveled. Hills rolled into mountains, like they were sailing into a valley, but Vali knew they were really wading deeper beneath the surface of the Tree, where the underground Shadow Realms and all that was forbidden were located.

Thick clouds glazed the sky in a muted grey, darkening the world in a morose filter. A biting breeze filled the sail and pulled them further toward Niflheim, the outer realm bordering the home of Hel. Lochare lit the lanterns as the last rays of the sun were finally blocked, shrouding them in a cold shadow almost impossible to navigate without the light from their boat.

Clumps of ice knocked against the boat as they slipped through the frigid waters. Marrin glanced over the side before speaking for the first time all day. "How do the dead find their way to Helheim if this is the road to Hel? Seems quite a perilous pursuit."

Vali pulled his hood lower around his ears. "Perhaps they don't start as far back as we did. Valkyries may have brought you to Freya, but those who die naturally must find their own way to the underworld. Let us hope this is the most difficult part."

"It sounds as if you do not know how to get there," her sister said, looking at him through the corner of her gaze.

"I told you. No one has gone to the Shadow Realms and came out to tell about them. None but Hermod, Baldur's own brother, and even he had few words to explain the way under. Everyone was too worried about Hel and her demands to release the golden god."

She replied, "Do I sense some resentment for Baldur in your voice? Jealous, they did not love you as the favorite child?"

He snorted, squinting into the distance to focus on something else beside her sneer. "I know what it is to be loved, and it is not what the gods have for anyone but themselves. I think they've all existed too long to remember how to."

"How did our sister, the same girl who would have rather died than be with any man in our village, fall in love with you?" Marrin asked this time, but Vali felt no sting in her question. She was genuinely curious.

While it should have hurt to speak of their bond so fresh after it was split, he felt no grief this time. A weight lifted from his chest as he told them, "I fell for Ailsa like the rain falls for the earth. Slowly, gradually, drop by drop over time, then all at once in a downpour. It was slow and testing at first, then hard and fast and treacherous. As for how or why she fell for me," he shook his head and laughed at the thought, "I was lucky for the first time in a hundred years."

The sisters looked at each other, communicating something in their gaze, before returning to their silent stations at the opposite end of the boat. Vali wondered if he said something that bothered them, then remembered he didn't care. What he had with Ailsa had been real. Real enough, he'd give his life to save her from the witches who stole her, even if she did not know who he was—or ever would.

The bottom of the longboat scraped sand as they drifted into the shallows. The elfin snatched a lantern from the center mast, lifting it above the water to search for signs of land.

"Look!" Lochare whispered. "There are lights ahead!"

He followed her finger toward a dim glow in the distance, outlining the edge of a riverbank. Satisfied, he started gathering his supplies, tucking a few blades beneath his clothes and Odin's hook around his belt. The sisters brought nothing with them beside their resting scowls and the axes clipped to their back. Their motivations here well-defined.

"It looks like there is a bridge ahead," Lochare said as she scouted the way ahead. "Vali, stay behind me and Marrin. Whoever guards the bridge might not let you in if they know you are still alive."

Vali didn't like the idea of letting them take the lead so early on this journey, but the heathen was right. If there was a guard, they'd take one look at his eyes and his ears and send him away.

"Fine. Just be cautious. Don't talk too much."

"You sound like our father," Marrin muttered, and the elfin bristled at the comparison. The pair walked ahead, boots loud in rippling waters that came up to their shins. Icy river water seeped into his own boots, reminding him of just how alive he was to feel the bone gnawing cold.

A silhouette loomed in front of the light on the bridge, a passage wide enough to fit three horses side by side and covered with a roof made of gold tiles. They eventually stepped out of the river and onto a shoreline, a brief piece of land stretching to his left and right, stopping just at the mouth of the bridge, which stretched over the width of the

Gjoll. Vali couldn't see the other side from where they stood, the rest of the bridge disappearing in the darkness.

"Who comes to enter the Shadow Realms?" the figure asked.

"Three mortals seeking their afterlives," Marrin replied, remaining as vague as possible. As they neared the guard, Vali discovered it was a woman, one of Hel's guardians sent here by Odin himself to serve her.

"I am Mord, Keeper of the Gjallerbrú, the bridge that connects the land of the living to the realm of the dead." She looked all three of them over, her stare lingering on Vali for a half a second longer. "Two women and one man arriving at once," she observed. "Let me guess, one of you was married to this waste of flesh and caught the other in your bed?"

"Gods, *no!*" both sisters replied together.

The guard, whose face was framed with a light blue cowl that draped over long, silver hair, smiled at them. She appeared young despite being the only watchman over the ancient bridge.

"It was just an assumption. Don't bite my head off. You'd be surprised how some end up down here." Reaching inside her cloak, she pulled out a handful of what looked like dirt. She rubbed a bit between her fingers, then marked Marrin and Lochare's foreheads. "When you cross the bridge, you will take the road to Hel's gate. If you venture off path, travel down and north. The forest only leads to one place."

She stepped between the sisters and reached out for him. Vali kept his eyes downcast, staring instead at the guard's bare feet to hide his identity. Icy fingers brushed his skin, marking his own face with whatever drawing she made on Hel's patrons, but they didn't stop there. Mord placed her sullied fingers beneath jaw and tilted his face to look at her.

He felt her gaze crawl over him like a spider. "You are not supposed to be here," she whispered in a cold breath against his cheek.

Vali pulled away from her touch, refusing to let the guard see him fully. "No, I should not, but fate has brought me here anyway."

A pause. A held breath. A second of uncertainty before Mord said, "Did you think you could trick me? I could hear your heartbeat echo down the Gjoll." She snatched his jaw in her hands—a vice cold as death—and yanked his face to meet hers before smiling again. "Another son of Odin comes to sneak his way into Helheim. How many will he send before he finally keeps one of his bargains?"

"I do not come on the Allfather's behalf. I have business of my own—"

"Lies! You will not bother the goddess in her home ever again. Tell Odin he can suffer in the afterlife like the rest of us." She reached into her cloak with her opposite hand, the one around his chin sliding to his throat with an unnatural strength. Mord's eyes bled black until their orbits held shadows. Her pale skin sinking into the planes of her skull until a cadaverous face was staring back at him.

"Vali, get low!"

He ducked just as the whir of a blade cut through the air behind the guard. The fist around his throat loosened, slipping entirely as the Keeper's body went limp and fell to the sandy ground. Lochare stood where Mord's shadow once fell, a bloody axe in her hand.

"What the Hel did you do?" he asked, eyes widening as he looked down at the decapitated guard. Her silver head rolled some feet away.

It apparently wasn't the question she was expecting,

appraising the scowl that settled across her painted face. "Saving your ass, and you're welcome, by the way. Now let's go before someone else finds her—or worse."

As if sensing a challenge, Mord's body twitched in the sand. Each jerk of her limbs pushed her closer toward her lost head. Vali quickly kicked it even further from her reach to buy them more time before grabbing the nearest lantern and sprinting after the sisters down the length of the bridge.

They met a bare forest on the other side, the land in the middle of a deep winter. Thick snow pressed beneath his boots as he stepped off the bridge and into the realm of the dead. White fog curled the air in front of their faces as they each tried to catch their breath. A trail marked the way ahead, the snow laying thin over dark pavers leading into the wood.

"Welcome to Niflheim," Vali said, breathless.

Marrin opened her mouth to reply but was cut off by a screeching voice in the darkness far behind them.

"*Garm!*" Mord wailed, the Keeper finding her head at last.

"What's a Garm?" Marrin asked, worry shaking her voice.

A lone howl cried from the forest in front of them, a new monster awoken by the one they had just pissed off. Vali swallowed against the dryness in his throat, desperately needing a drink. He tossed the light into the snow, where it fizzled out with a hiss, hiding them in the dark.

"Run," he rasped. And with little options left, they ventured deeper into the realm of the dead.

CHAPTER 23
SEELA

After a journey across the Tree of Life, one would think they would learn all they needed to know about a person. Seela, however, discovered something new about the wolven she didn't know before.

Ivor was deathly afraid of heights.

"I'm not getting on that thing. I'd rather rot for another four months in my prison." She crossed her arms and stared at the eagle saddled and packed for their departure. Enver was already strapped into his own bird, a black eagle named Ithil.

"We can have that arranged, wolf. I'd rather see you back behind bars myself," he said, glaring at Ivor. The two carried an unspoken tension between them. Palpable enough, Seela could cut through it with her short blade.

Ivor's frosty eyes chilled colder as they shifted from Elísar to Enver. Seela cleared her throat, trying to think of some solution that would appease them both and smolder this spark before it blazed into something bigger. Especially because this journey started approximately twenty minutes ago.

And they had a long way to go.

"Enver could always mist you both to the starting point —" Seela started. As planned, Ivor seethed further with that prospect. "Or you can ride with me, but I'm not wasting more time than necessary riding horseback all the way to the Dvegar Mountains. You promised you would help us find Ailsa, now are you coming or not?"

Ivor growled at her options, but eventually side-stepped her way to Seela, watching the eagle's face the entire way toward her outstretched hand. She helped Ivor behind her in the saddle and gave her the straps to tie herself in place, feeling her fingers tremble with the locks as she assisted her.

"Elísar is the best, I swear it. We'll be there in no time." She tried to reassure her. Though, seeing Ivor nervous awoke something satisfying inside her. A reminder that she had fears and vulnerabilities beyond what she showed through her cold exterior. A reminder there was still a human part of her, no matter how much more dominant the monster side had become.

"Whatever," she mumbled at her back. "Just get on with it before I punch the elven half wit in his obtuse face. Why did you even invite him?"

"Because we needed some muscle in case we met a problem. Enver is skilled in sedir and even better with a bow," she replied. "And he's not a bad view either."

Before the wolven could retort, she kicked off the bird and set him scurrying across the landing, building speed as his great wings stroked the air. Ivor yelped and clasped Seela around the waist, burning her cheeks despite the bite in the breeze. Seela felt her bury her face into her spine as Elísar tossed himself over the side of the Convocation.

They fell for a thin strand of time before the beast of a bird

righted himself and gained altitude, each stroke of his wingspan gathered velocity, pushing them closer to the heavens
and the mountains scraping them in the distance.

Meanwhile, Enver and Ithil enjoyed themselves, twisting
through the air like a corkscrew through a wine bottle, a
motion that made Seela dizzy to watch. He tugged the eagle
into a hard left, cutting off Elisar's flight path and forcing the
bird to jerk out of the way, spooking both of his riders. Ivor
slipped a shrill sound behind her, keeping her face hidden in
the hood of Seela's cloak in unashamed cowardice.

The wind carried Enver's laughter across the space
between them, and Seela rolled her eyes, vowing with a smirk
to pay him back later.

They landed near the mouth of the pass where Seela's old map
and Ivor's memories referred. Past a dense forest of withering
trees and their weeping branches, the land here was stripped
of life where Fenrir roamed and chased away the Light. Even
more stagnant were the foothills of the Dvegar Mountains.
The little that survived here pushed roots through the stone
and rubble to create a border around the mouth of the pass.

Seela stared up at the mountains, whose peaks could not
be seen from the ground they were so tall. These mounts were
impassible, the elevation too steep to climb and the fog ever
present over their bases too thick to fly through—even for an
eagle. There shouldn't have been a way through, according to
the palace records, but the witches had found one. What was
at the end of this trail could make all the difference in saving
Ailsa and the Nine Realms.

Seela approached Enver as the eagles returned to the Convocation, leaving the wolven to settle her stomach behind a thistle bush. "Will you insist on torturing her the entire way?"

He flipped his hood over the slants of his ears and nodded. "After what she did to you, to all the fae, I fully intend to make her life as miserable as possible."

"Enver—"

"No, Seela." He cut her off with a hand. "You don't get to tell me how to treat those who have hurt the fae I care about. Her kind and the witches were the whole reason behind the civil war, why I lost my blood mate. And after what she did to you..." He shook his head dismissively.

Seela's lips turned up in a delicate smile. "You mean I'm one of the fae you care about?"

Enver scoffed, and she noticed a slight flush to his cheeks. "Of course you are. You helped me out of a dark place, even if it was with your—"

"Enver!" she whispered a bit too loud.

He grinned. "I'm just saying. We might be friends who sleep together, but you're still my friend. And I'll kill anyone who hurts you."

Seela slapped him on the arm playfully. "Careful, Commander. You're making me want to keep you around more often."

His brows rose half an inch. "Good. Maybe next time I can stay long enough to buy you breakfast."

A nervous laugh fluttered from her chest at the thought. Had he wanted to stay the mornings after? Because Seela had been plainly unaware. Before she could say something to embarrass herself further, Seela turned to find Ivor standing a few feet away, wiping her mouth with the back of her lips.

"Are you two quite finished? Because if you keep going, I might throw up again."

"We were just leaving," Seela said as she pulled her bag over her shoulder. The way ahead was uncertain, both in what they would face and how long they would endure it.

Ivor glanced around. Her demeanor seemed to shift on the spot. "We're going by foot? No horses or eagles?"

"The mountains are too rough to travel horseback. Even if the pass is clear, the altitude alone is difficult on the horses and the eagles cannot navigate through the mist. It's safest on foot," she replied.

Ivor's confidence didn't appear to sway any further in her direction, but she grabbed a bag Seela had removed from Elísar's pack and followed both the elves toward the beginning of the forbidden mountain passage.

Seela first noticed how quiet it was, the mist and the mountains sealing the air inside these granite walls until only sounds of her party existed. She led the trio while Enver took up the rear, each of them watching for signs of a lingering menace behind the clustered rocks. If this narrow road winding through the foothills was recently used, she didn't see any sign. The wolven and witches had covered their tracks well.

Stairs were cut into the stone where the trail steepened, the quick ascension agonizingly laborious. Soon the quiet was disturbed by heavy breaths and grunts. Beads of sweat trickled down her back despite the air turning damp and cool this far above the world, thinning to make it more difficult to breathe.

"The old maps," Enver spoke after a time, "did they show how long the way is? Half a day has passed and the only direction we've gone is up."

Seela paused where the stairs flattened into a landing of sorts, letting the rest of her party catch their breath as well. "It didn't seem long, maybe a day or two of traveling by foot? I wasn't able to take the terrain into account." She looked around them, but the mist obscured anything beyond a few meters around their stopping place. "You're sure we can't use sedir to travel?"

Enver shook his head. "This is different. Before, I couldn't travel across realms without help because I wasn't skilled enough in sedir. But this? I don't even know where to aim our trajectory. All the places I've misted before have been places I've seen or traveled. We do not know where this pass leads. I'm not sure the Ironwood is even real or a made up place."

"It's real," Ivor said. "The witches might be deceptive, but they aren't liars. Their Mother Witch is someone they take seriously. Besides, we shouldn't use sedir around another who can practice it, especially the Mother Witch. She might sense our coming."

Seela's shoulders slumped. It was worth a try. "I guess we better keep moving, then. Dusk is only a few hours away, and we still haven't found the reason this pass was deemed forbidden. I've got a bad feeling we haven't seen the worst of things yet."

The pair muttered their agreement and treaded further into the misty mountains. Gradually, the staircase flattened, and it granted them a reprieve to the constant climb as the trail wove between the bases of two neighboring peaks. The sun was just setting, indicating they would need to make camp soon. Seela scouted a mostly flat stretch of trail and decided it would do.

"I'll get the fire if you two make the bedrolls," Enver suggested as he started on a pile of rocks. In no time, he had a bright flame burning from what could only be his magic. The lack of wood or any type of accelerant made the feat that much more impressive.

"That magic of yours certainly is convenient," Seela said as she sat on her cot.

"Have I convinced you to come over to the dark, Commander?" he asked.

Seela scoffed. "Vali would kill me if I started using sedir. He still believes Light magic is the only type of power an elf should touch."

"Do you always do what your blood mate says?" Enver asked, rolling his eyes.

"Of course not!"

"Then who cares what Vali thinks? Taste the sedir, Seela, it's as bottomless as the ale at Greybeard's on Thor's Day." He pulled out a piece of dried meat from his pack and winked at her.

Seela laid on her back with a groan, her muscles sore from the day's walk. "I'm afraid I've let you convince me to overindulge in one too many things as it is, Enver. You're a bad influence."

"At least I'm fun."

A frustrated sigh slipped from beneath Ivor's cot. The wolven already shutting her eyes for the evening. Seela grinned at Enver and brought a finger to her lips to shush him. The male responded by throwing an obscene gesture at the unaware wolven.

Seela closed her eyes and listened to the crack of the fire. Rest already seducing her bones into a drowsy pool she was powerless to fight against. She quickly fell asleep to the sounds of Enver's noisy chewing and the silence that draped over them like a heavy blanket. Her guard lowered significantly—too much, believing they were the only souls for miles in these forbidden fields of mountain smog.

⚓

"Where are the packs?"

Enver's panicked voice startled her eyes awake. Seela sat up, blinking until his figure came into clarity. It was still dark; the sun hadn't risen enough to filter its haze through the fog, and the fire had long dwindled out. The commander was shuffling around their campsite, searching high and low for his pack.

Seela reached a stiff arm in the direction she threw her bag before falling asleep, only to feel the cold stone beneath her fingers. "What in Hel's name?" she muttered, looking around but finding her bag mysteriously gone as well. "Make some light, Enver. Unless they grew legs in the middle of the night, they couldn't have gotten far."

Maybe they had just misplaced them. Perhaps the breeze had swept them against the cavernous wall bending to the south of the landing where they camped, or the fog had shifted to conceal them from sight. Any plausible explanation was better than their packs disappearing into thin air.

The longer they searched, the more her questions numbered, and the more her heart pulsed a warning in her ears. "Ivor, do you smell anything?"

The wolven inhaled the air around her and nodded. "Aye, there is a scent that wasn't here when we arrived. It's faint, however, and strange. I've never smelled anything like it."

"Can you follow it? We'll never last out here without those supplies." The wolven nodded. "Aye, but it goes further down the pass. If we lose it, we could be stuck without water or anything—"

"I'll get us back," Enver said with a certainty that eased Seela's apprehensions. "Just follow the trail, wolf. Gods know whoever stole our stuff, he's had plenty of time to put distance between us."

But as they gathered what little supplies they still had left, Enver snatched Ivor by the arm and pulled her close, his face lowering to meet her line of sight. "If this is a trick and you're leading us into a den of your mutts, I swear on the Light I'll gut you first."

Ivor's frosted gaze turned to ice. "I've been locked up for months, you idiot. How could I have conspired against you with my family? Besides, they left me for dead, remember?"

"Just wanted to be clear. Those witch friends of yours can be crafty." He dropped her arm and beckoned forward with his chin, insisting she lead the way.

The wolven scoffed before reluctantly turning on a heel, her silver tipped hair flicking Enver in the chest as she stomped off in the direction of the scent. The elves followed close behind, the heavy tongue behind Seela's parched lips a gnawing motivation to find their packs as soon as possible, the blade at her hip a heavy reminder she would do anything to get them back.

She needed very little of either to kill a witch these days.

Ivor pulled them off the pass for a section to follow the thief's trail and up a loose section of boulders, each step nearly sending Seela rolling into Enver trailing just behind her. The further they diverted from the original path, the louder the warning bells in Seela's mind seemed to blare.

"Are you sure about this, Ivor?"

The wolven picked up her pace, lunging up the gravelly hillside like she was part goat instead. "Certain. The scent is getting stronger, not much—"

A shriek cut her words off. Seela looked up to find Ivor gone, disappearing like their bags. She scrambled to where the wolven was last seen, carefully watching her footing in case there was a sudden drop off, a rockslide, anything to ensnare her under the mountain's skin.

"Seela, wait! It could be—"

But Enver's voice was lost as Seela fell. Not forward or back, not even off the edge of Alfheim, but through space and stone. A thrill burst through her stomach to her heart, spilling out her throat in a cry of disbelief as the hazy sky was obliterated by darkness. Her body was simultaneously weightless and full of lead, unable to move yet transcending to another place entirely.

A sharp crack made her clamped eyes fly open, and Seela discovered it was the sound of her head hitting the stone floor of a dark room. She immediately rolled to her stomach and pushed to all fours, eyes dancing around the perimeter of where she landed. Ivor was there as well. Her claws extended as a throaty growl slipped from her chest—and facing a wall full of bars.

It was then Seela realized where exactly she had fallen. A cage.

Seconds later, Enver appeared next to Seela, repeating the same panicked first impression. Even in the dim lighting, his jade eyes glowed with worry as they connected with hers. "Are you all right?"

She touched the back of her head but felt no blood. Only a throbbing spot where a knot was already forming. "Yes, I'm fine. Where in Ymir are we?"

Enver jumped to his feet and skimmed an ungloved hand over the bronze bars surrounding them. He winced and jerked his hand back as if burned. "This metal was cast in a Svarlteheim forge, the same gold that fills the weapons against our kind. It appears we have fallen into a trap by whoever stole our belongings."

"How? Who could charm a trap to do such a thing?" Though the answer hung on her tongue—witches.

Enver seemed to read the word through her lips, but he shook his head in disagreement. "There's only one kind of fae who could craft something this extraordinary."

"You don't mean..." Ivor said, her voice even beginning to shift into a wolf's raspy bark.

In answer, a door swung open beyond their cage, a room within a room. Four tall figures stood on the other side of each wall, watching them. Their silhouettes draped in soft clothing that moved silently with their steps. Though she couldn't see the details of their faces, Seela didn't need them to realize who they were.

They had fallen straight into another realm, right into the mysterious hands of dwarves.

"Welcome to Svartalfheim," one of them said. His voice was too deep and coarse to be anything but male. "My name is Drasili, King of the Seven Mountains. I didn't think you'd be dumb enough to follow us through an Ungári. But I'm glad my counsel has lower standards of your aptitudes."

"A what?" Seela asked.

His chin lifted. "A kind of portal. Dwarves don't like visitors, so we keep our doors hidden."

She crossed her arms and attempted to turn on her diplomatic charm. Her first meeting with a kin of power wasn't exactly how she expected. "It is nice to meet you, Drasili, even if it is under these circumstances. I am Seela, Lady Regent of Alfheim, and this is Commander Enver and our companion Ivor. We actually weren't intending on stopping by, so if you could return our supplies, we'll be on our way and out of your very busy hands."

But Drasili made no move to unlock their cage. "You were trespassing through forbidden grounds. You are lucky the draug didn't devour you in your sleep."

Enver stepped forward, standing just behind her. "We were investigating. Surely you have noticed activity in these parts with the wolven and witches using the forbidden pass," he said.

The dwarf cocked his head to the side in a small slant. "Yes, we've had unfortunate interactions with some witches a few months ago. They are the ones who awoke the draug."

"The what?" she asked.

"The draug," he repeated for a third time. "They are revenants. Corpses of fallen fae who died during the rockslides over a hundred years ago. It is why the pass was prohibited in the first place, as hundreds died from being crushed while traveling during an annual trade. The mountains are still restless. We still hear violent shifts in the stone from time to time."

"This still doesn't explain why you took our things and led us into a cage!" Ivor spoke, moving to catch Drasili's attention.

Seela thought she heard him mutter a curse. "We were trying to encourage your group to go back where you came from without revealing ourselves, unaware one of you had a nose for tracking." He gestured to the bronze bars. "The cage was to contain you all until we were certain your business in these parts wasn't harmful to our people, but we searched your things and found nothing incriminating."

"Well, now that you know our intentions are virtuous, will you bring us back to the surface?" Seela asked.

There was a pause before his reply that made her stomach clench. "You never stated your intentions. However, I don't entirely care why you're in our mountains. If you keep going down the pass, you will die."

"A risk we will take. Our decisions are not your problem, dwarf." Enver's magic breathed a cold wind behind her as he primed the sedir in his blood. The male on the other side of the bars sensed his hostility and smiled.

"You didn't let me finish." He clasped his hands behind his back in a casual grace. "We have a problem with the draug we'd like your partnership with fixing. Help us, and we will allow you to use the pass to venture wherever you please."

Seela's gaze shifted to Enver, but his face was barren of anything helpful. She looked back at the dwarf. "And if we don't?"

He took a step back from the cage, retreating toward the door where he and his council just entered. "You seem to be in a rush, Lady Regent. I believe I will just wait you out and see what gives in first. Your desperation—" Seela's gut twisted, eliciting a hungry growl. The dwarf smiled, and it was too charming a thing for her to despise. "—or your stomach."

Seela bit her lip until she tasted copper. She had never made a deal with a dwarf, had no experience with one first-hand. They were the only fae who kept to themselves under their mountains of gold and magic, only coming out to trade their wares for more wealth. But her party wasn't exactly in the position to negotiate. The bars entrapping them decided their next move, avoiding it was just wasting time.

"What did you have in mind for the draug?" she asked.

Drasili pulled something out of his pocket. A key.

"How about we discuss things over dinner?"

CHAPTER 24
ERIK

For three solid days, Erik knew only suffering.

Ailsa treated him morning and night, carefully removing the bandages around his burns and rewrapping them. His flesh was raw from where the fire licked him, where it gnawed through his armor and ate at his skin. Fafnir's flames held not only the hottest heat in the Nine but also venom, and it took Erik very little time to realize how much of a challenge taking down the dragon would be. Even with a crew of fire giants behind him.

But he vowed he would get them home, and for that reason alone, he drank the witches' tonics and let Ailsa care for his wounds. Let himself get better every day until he could stand and piss and walk on his own.

He thought of her hands. Ailsa's touch was a phantom every time she left him, which was often. Something still deterred her after even after the bond was severed. Her tending was not that of a caregiver but a healer, methodical and precise, her compassion withdrawn as if the sight of his mangled body had triggered no sympathy for him in her heart.

Numerous times he begged her to stay. To hold him, touch him without an excuse of a bandage or a balm. Each time she refused with another excuse to add to a growing list. It was enough to patronize him, pushing him into a well of pity as he realized how unfair this situation was for them *both*.

He couldn't take it any longer. Ailsa had been gone for hours and hadn't checked on him yet. He stood on shaky legs, lacking strength without the opportunity to keep down anything substantial besides bone broth. With small steps, he painstakingly ventured across the narrow corridor where Ailsa stayed, discovering the door to her quarters open.

He cracked the door an inch to peer inside, finding her standing over her bed, studying something on the sheets. Out of curiosity, he watched her a little longer. Ailsa was making notes about something, planning, plotting into a small notebook with a pen of ink he didn't realize she knew how to use. Another thing those fae creatures must have taught her.

With a gentle nudge, he pushed the door open a little further, but the damn thing groaned on rusted hinges. Ailsa startled at the sound and whipped her head toward the door. Her blue eyes grew wide as they found him.

"Erik!" she gasped, quickly closing the book, and twisted to stand in front of the bed with her hands behind her back. "What are you doing up? Do you need something?"

"What are you doing in here? What were you looking at?" He pushed into her room, closing the door shut behind him. First, she avoided him. Now she was hiding things. If he didn't nip these insignificant acts of defiance in their fruition, it could grow into something truly divisive.

"Nothing," she stammered. "Just looking at the map of

Muspell in case the giants let us go soon. You know, after you get the flame."

Erik forced his jaw to shut instead of speaking. Ailsa had never been a poor liar, but he'd known her long enough to know her tics, the signs that gave her away. The question was, why was she lying to him now?

"Tell me the truth. Why are you tracing paths through the Mourning Mountains?"

Her shoulders fell slightly, eyes shifting to the side where the map sprawled wide over the sheets. "Promise me you won't be angry."

Gods, he was past mad. Perhaps if she had just been honest from the beginning, he could make that vow to her. She had ruined any strand of trust that once threaded between them. But for reasons beyond that, he spit out, "I promise."

Her eyes shut as she inhaled a steadying breath. "I made a deal with Surtur and the witches."

"You *what?*" She shot him a pointed look, and he stepped back, running his fingers through the knots in his bedhead.

"You promised!" She reminded him, placing her hands on her hips. "I told them I would slay Fafnir if you didn't recover soon enough, which is likely given their rushed timeline to destroy the Nine. If they do, I will get my memories back from the witches."

A quiet rage shook his bones until he was trembling all over. There suddenly wasn't a cool feeling in the room, everything hot and heavy and pulsing with an aggravated tension that boiled his blood. "I gave up all I had left to save you from that demon, only for you to now risk everything I have left just to get back the memories of *him?* How fucking dare you!"

It was like he had struck her, the way her face winced. "It isn't like that Erik... You don't understand—"

"I understand enough!" he shouted. If he hadn't been so weak, he'd cross the room and shake some sense into her. "I understand you care more about living in some false reality than in the real world. I see you don't care about anything I've done for you, the fact I lost half my skin three days ago, or the men who died just to save you from his hands!"

A muscle flickered in her jaw. "I didn't ask any of you to save me."

"Because you couldn't," he seethed. "You were manipulated—"

"Shut your mouth!"

"Defiled—"

"Erik, that's enough!"

"Tricked, fooled, beguiled into thinking that demon actually cared about you when all he wanted was what you had on the inside. The power in your blood." He beat his fist across his chest three times. "I am the only man who has ever loved you for who you are, not what you could do for me. Your name, your power, it offers me nothing! And I still stand here begging for your heart like I haven't earned it already!"

Tears leaked down her cheeks, but Ailsa wasn't retreating like he hoped. She wouldn't back down from the whip in his words, ones he wanted to strike her with so hard, her heart would bleed out for him.

"Why are you so afraid of the past, Erik?"

"What are you talking about?"

She licked her lips. "I never said I wanted to remember *him,* the male I am assuming you tried to kill that night you rescued me. The one *you* keep bringing up. If he is so terrible, if you indeed saved me from a life of slavery to this male's

210

control and his pleasures, then why do you care if I remember him or not?"

"Because the bond he put on you warped your perspective—"

"I have no bond now! I can think for myself and decide what I want, and you will not choose for me what you think is best. I'm going after Fafnir and when I retrieve the flame, I *will* remember everything that happened to me."

Erik stepped closer, closing the distance between them. Ailsa planted her feet like she was one with the mountain. "We'll see about that," he whispered, before turning on a charred heel and stalking out of the room.

CHAPTER 25
VALI

Down and north.

The thin moonbeam guiding them through the forest was all that lit the world as they ran from an unseen threat. Ailsa's sisters were fast, even encumbered with axes and knives, and they maintained a healthy distance in front of him as he monitored the shadows.

Another deep howl turned his blood into ice, like the slush beneath his boots and the flakes of frost forming on his hair and his cloak. Now he was cold all over, from the inside out. Each sound of the beast behind them getting closer and closer, but Vali couldn't use the magic in his blood to run ahead and leave Marrin and Lochare behind.

Then something peaked above the skeleton branches. The spires of Hel's hall, the entrance to her kingdom of the dead. The sisters picked up on this and tapped into a reserve of strength to run faster.

They reached the border of the ice realm, finally breaking from the forest. The road opened toward a gate that stood in the center of two stretching walls, spanning the width of this new world in either direction and disappearing from view in the miles that measured them.

Marrin approached the gate first—no, a drawbridge. One that hovered before an abysmal pit separating the entrance to Hel's kingdom from where they stood. Upon closer inspection, Vali noticed it was built from bones, each soldered together to keep the bodies of some unfortunate corpses bending in an unnaturally intricate design. Lochare pulled a lever on the side of the entry, and the ice freezing over the cogs shattered as the wheels lowered the bone bridge.

"I cannot follow you through the gate," Vali said, his eyes falling on the silver veil shimmering in front of Hel's gate.

"You have little of a choice," Marrin said.

The elfin shook his head. "I'll find another way, you two go..."

"We will not leave you behind." Lochare unhooked the axe at her back once more. "That's not how we work, neither in life nor in death."

He pulled two daggers out of the back of his belt and shot her a glare. "Don't pull that Otsman *skide* on me now, Lochare. Get your ass through the veil before you die a final death." He did not know if they could die twice, or if their bodies would regenerate like they did in Folkvang and Valhalla, but he couldn't risk it. Before she could object again, he turned from her scowl and started toward the outside wall, fingers beginning to remove the hook strapped to his belt.

Until he saw it. Emerging from the tree line was the creature that hunted them through the woods. Garm was a wolf. But unlike Fenrir or the wolven, this one was pure beast. Its white fur was stained with blood, a crimson line ran from his jowls and down his chest. But the elfin couldn't look away from its teeth, serrated and on display as Garm snarled at him.

His nose twitched as he caught Vali's scent, marking him like a territory. Claiming him as prey.

"Vali, what are you doing?" Marrin called. "Just use the veil!"

He couldn't change his mind concerning the veil even if he wanted to. Not when a wolf Garm's size could easily lunge and snatch him between his teeth from this distance. Turning his back for a moment only promised death. Instead, he turned to his magic, letting the power in his blood take advantage of the natural world. Drawing cold energy from the air, he made a shield in front of him. A barricade of sharp ice with lethal ends sprawled in a half circle around where he stood just outside the drawbridge.

The wolf slipped a low growl between his bloody teeth as the edges of the ice sharpened into a hundred blades, putting a blockade between them. He spared a glance at Ailsa's sisters, who were retreating toward the gate, still stubbornly watching. Awaiting his fate. Satisfied they were out of harm's way and the wolf's reach, Vali unsheathed the short sword at his hip and focused his magic on the beast himself.

The tendrils of his power reached inside the wolf, slipped beneath his skin to travel his veins all the way to the muscle of his heart where it worked overtime. Garm's pulse was a violent beat, excited by the opportunity of a fresh meal. Vali gripped the throbbing heart, attempting to sweep the ice from the air into his lungs, his veins, slowing the inner workings of his body to a null rhythm.

Garm didn't so much as twitch, though something shifted in his eyes. Sensing what Vali was doing, aware he had a power to manipulate the very air in his chest, the wolf leapt over the barricade and ignored the piercing spears of ice that combed across his underbelly. Vali lunged to the side, rolling across a thin plate of snow and onto his feet just as Garm shifted on his giant claws. Blood spilled into the snow from his chest, coloring his white fur a darker stain of red.

The elfin cursed as he altered his motives for the defensive. If Mord wasn't killed by severing her head clean off her body, then Garm was most likely similarly immortal. How would he get past him now? Wolves were strong, especially the ones of legend. What had Odin done to trap Fenrir from killing the Aesir tribe?

Chains.

Vali's eyes caught on the drawbridge behind the wolf. Large chains, one's thick enough to bind the beast, propelled the bridge from this land to Hel's gate. He couldn't break them until the sisters were safely across, or they'd fall straight into that pit. Before any of that, however, he needed to distract the wolf until they made it across.

The elfin was about to dart into the tree line again to lose Garm in the dark woods like they had done before, but before he could manage a step, a wild cry shrieked behind the beast. Lochare appeared out of nowhere, swinging her heavy axe at the wolf's hind legs.

Garm twisted, snapping at the warrior even as he wailed in pain, whimpering as the wounds stung his flesh and his pride. The wolf's ears folded flat against his head as he chomped at Lochare, who easily swerved from his bite, lashing his face as well while it was within striking range.

"Get to the gate!" Vali shouted. "I need the chains from the bridge."

Marrin, who had followed her sister back across the drawbridge, looked at the thick chains suspending the bridge, then at the wolf, then to Vali. The blue of her eyes—the color so reminding him of Ailsa—were clear as realization struck her.

"You both keep him distracted," she yelled back at him. "I'll take care of the chains."

Without time to disagree, Vali stole a dagger from his belt and lit the tip on fire. The beast couldn't die, but he could still feel pain. And if he hurt, then he could suffer. He let the blade fly true, the knife-edge sinking into the side of his neck.

A wet growl erupted from his bloody throat as the wolf snapped his gaze back to Vali. But Marrin was already using her axe to pound away at the chains. Each fall of her weapon severing a link until he heard a band slink to the earth. Lochare and the elfin volleyed for the wolf's attention as she worked on the other one.

"I've got them!" she said, holding them high above her head.

Vali cursed as Garm snapped his jaws, narrowly missing his face. "When I incapacitate him, tie him up with the chains." He figured they'd bound an animal once or twice in their lives back in Drakame. This shouldn't be too complicated, even if he was five times the size of a regular Midgard wolf.

Lifting his short blade, he charged Garm head on. The last thing Vali saw were his black eyes crinkling as he waited for the elfin to get closer, to lunge so he could catch Vali in his jaws. Vali felt those teeth, how they clamped around his shoulder even as he shoved the blade through the wolf's throat. Each sinking into his flesh until Garm suddenly went limp on top of his sword, great head rolling off his weight.

Vali dropped everything to cradle his shoulder, feeling the venom already mix in his bloodstream and prolong the healing process. Frigid air brushed against the weeping holes left in his skin, burning an already unpleasant injury. It wasn't a fatal wound, just an inconvenient one. Especially when he still had to scale a wall if he wanted to get inside Hel's kingdom.

"Quickly," he rasped to the sisters with their chains. "Before he wakes up like Mord."

They made quick work of him, binding the front of the hind legs separately, weaving the metal to minimize his movement to nothing. When he was sure the wolf wasn't going anywhere, Vali tossed Lochare the grappling hook his father had given him.

"What's this?" she asked with an arched brow.

"A hook?" he deadpanned. "See if you can throw it over the wall so we can scale to the other side." The drawbridge had fallen into the pit after she borrowed its chains, leaving little choice now but to find an alternate way inside the guarded realm.

Marrin inspected the four pronged hook like it was an artifact. "What other weapons are you hiding under there?"

Vali couldn't help himself. A spit of laughter spilled from his chest from her question, and he couldn't recall the last time he'd made the sound. The tension taut in his chest shook away for a bare moment. "Marrin, you'll have to ask your youngest sister for the details later."

"Idiot," Lochare said, shaking her head. "You walked into that one."

Marrin rolled her eyes, and instead of forming a rebuttal, began swinging the hook leisurely at her side to test the weight of it. It took her four tries, but she latched the hook onto the corner of a pilaster, one of the many columns supporting the wall.

Lochare looked at him, assessing his injury. "Can you climb, or do you need one of us to carry your dead weight like we have been this entire journey?"

Vali felt his lips twitch in amusement. He could imagine Ailsa saying something similar, could hear her voice through her sister's words, reminding him how much he missed that foul mouth—how much he missed *her*. "I believe I can manage, Lochare."

Satisfied, she waited beneath Marrin in case her sister slipped on the ice coating the stone wall, following her stealthy climb once she beckoned her clear. Once they were both seated above him on the wall, Vali glanced at Garm, whose body jerked against his new bindings.

Eager to not face the wolf again, he grabbed the rope with both hands and ascended the slick wall, ignoring the lancing pain in his shoulder. His jaw clenched from the aching protest of his joint. It was a small miracle his teeth didn't crack from the pressure.

Easing himself over the top, he took a few placating breaths and waited for the pain to dissolve and for the tears watering his vision to subside. Lochare would never let him live it down if she saw him sniffling from a torn up shoulder.

"I didn't expect it to be so beautiful," one of them said.

Vali looked up at last, but the sisters were focused on the world beyond, their faces kissed with warm sunlight and faint smiles. He followed their gazes, and his breath caught, stolen by the encapsulating view of Helheim.

Sprawling fields of green blanketed the world as far as he could see. Homes dotted the landscape, puffs of smoke floating from warm hearths. Grassy knolls textured the land, disappearing in the distance as Vali squinted to see where this paradise would end and the realm of the dead would start. But it was here, right in front of him. The land of those who died natural deaths, those who did not pass into the afterlife with blood on their brows or swords in their fists. This was

where Hel lived and ruled, and he didn't know why, but this hadn't been what he expected.

They were staring at the best kept secret in all the Nine Realms.

"Do you think we'll find her, Lochare?" Marrin spoke so quietly, he almost missed it.

She draped an arm over her sister and knocked their temples together. "We'll find her, *systir*. Nothing can stop us now."

It took Vali the entire descent down the opposite side of the wall to realize they weren't talking about Ailsa. They had lost another in their family long ago.

As soon as their feet touched the grounds of Helheim, riders appeared in the distance. Almost as if Hel had been waiting on them, knowing they would take the route of the god Hermod before them. Vali had been expecting the goddess of this realm to note their presence, if not by entering her veil, then the chaos they caused on the way in.

"Should we run?" Lochare asked, coming to a stop behind him.

"No, there is little point. Besides, they work for Hel." He shrugged, keeping his gaze on the line of riders thickening as they treaded closer. "With any luck, they'll bring us straight to her."

"I thought you were here for Baldur?"

"I'm here for Ailsa," he corrected her, "and it will be difficult to get to Baldur without Hel's help, much less free him from her realm without her consent. No one leaves this place once they enter her veil."

A lone member of the cavalry approached from the line. The figure was clothed in robes of black and shimmering gold, covering hard black armor that peeked through the break in drapery. Through his helmet, the elfin noticed he was a man with dark skin, with hair like the wings of a raven spilling out from the bottom and down his shoulders. His hand held neither weapon nor shield, but three sacks each the size of a head. The man dismounted close enough Vali could size him accurately, the same height and stature of an averaged size mortal.

"You are trespassing. Why did you not enter through the veil?"

Vali prayed silently to whatever existed above him that the sisters would remain quiet. "I have business with Hel that does not include being stuck here for eternity."

"You're still alive?" he asked, brow arching.

The elfin scoffed. "Thankfully, though the guard dog posted outside did his best to ensure I wasn't."

If Hel's guard was surprised by his entrance, he didn't show it, only lifted the sacks with an outstretched hand. "You are currently in a part of Helheim that belongs to the Peacekeepers. Normally, the veil would have taken you straight to Eljudnir, the hall where Hel resides and rules. You must stand in her court to receive your judgment. Until then, you are not permitted to roam these lands."

"What are those?" Marrin finally spoke, questioning his offering.

"Hoods," he said. "You can either put these on and be transferred there quickly and painlessly or..." His gaze drifted back to the line of guards behind him.

Vali nodded in understanding. He quickly took the hoods from the guard and handed them to the sisters. Lochare nervously snatched it from his hand. "Are you sure about this?" she asked under a breath.

Sensing her hesitation, he said, "I'll put it on first. If it does something strange to me, use the line to get back over the wall. Deal?"

The sister bit her lip, but said, "Fine."

Vali stared into the depths of the black hood, finding nothing obviously suggestive about it. Sucking a bracing breath, he shoved it over his head, and the bright world he once knew was swallowed by a darkness cold as death.

"Awaken."

Vali's eyes opened at the command, finding himself in a dark hall. Stained glass constructed the walls in front of him, filtering the grey moonlight into a hundred shades of blues and purples and golds. Candles suspended from the doming ceiling above sourced the only light, and even those were hardly enough to light the grand space around him. Shadows strategically hung in dark corners, hiding watchful eyes and listening ears as he stood alone—the sisters no longer at his side.

"Where are my companions?" His question clipped out like a demand toward the woman sitting on a dark throne in front of him. She was speaking to someone at her side, her hair a golden curtain hiding her face until she finally looked at him. Vali suppressed his shudder when his gaze fell upon the queen of the dead, the goddess of the Shadow Realms, Hel.

Half her face was a lovely woman, with porcelain skin and a green eye, her blonde hair curled delicately over a black gown dusted in gold shimmer. But the other half was a corpse, the skin on the left side of her face dark grey and pulled back over her bones, exposing her jaw and teeth. An abyss hung where her eye should have been. The hair on that side was stringy and pale white, lacking the luster of the opposite. Her dead side waved a skeleton hand to Vali in a morbid greeting.

Hel's voice came out sharp as a hiss. "I've already spoken to them. They are with their loved ones while they await the outcome of your trial."

"Trial?"

The goddess smiled, one side lifting to form a dimple in her rosy cheek. "Vali Rindson, God of Vengeance. I know when a divine walks through my realm, and I've seen those eyes enough to know an Aesir when they've crossed me." Her chest rose with a sigh. "However, you have caused quite some trouble coming here. Even Hermod did not slaughter my Keeper and my Hound—"

"Technically, I was not responsible for the Keeper," he pointed out.

Hel waved her bony hand to dismiss him. "Semantics. Why have you come here, Vali? I've already told Odin that Baldur may not leave my realm unless everything in creation weeps for his loss. He failed with Hermod. What has he made you come here to do?"

"I am not here for my father," Vali said. Hel sat back on her throne and crossed her arms, apparently not expecting that answer. "I lost someone I love to an evil that can only be slain by the strongest of Odin's sons."

Her green eye rolled. "Baldur."

"Goddess, I only wish to speak with him—"

"You'll stay away from my—" her lips shut tight before the rest slipped out. "You will stay away from the golden god. He cannot leave. If that is the only reason you are here, then I am afraid you have wasted your time."

She stood to leave, the rest of the room shuffling to go

with her. But Vali rushed to the steps leading to the top of her dais, ignoring the rush of guards approaching to stop him. "Wait!" he pleaded. "Just listen to me—"

Her hair fanned around her shoulders as she spun hard to glare at him, and Vali felt every ounce of hatred saturated in her single, bloodshot eye. "I will not help Odin. I will not return his son. It was the Allfather who made sure I could never leave this realm by sealing everyone who entered inside. Odin cannot change the laws of fate just because it conveniences him now."

"I don't give a *skide* about Odin!" he shouted back. "I came here to save the woman I love, because Baldur is the link to destroy the one who keeps her."

Her anger softened with the slow fall of her shoulders. "Even if that is true, I cannot help you, and neither can Baldur. We are *all* trapped here, Vali. And if you do not leave soon, so will you. Life does not endure in Helheim."

"Then there is no harm in letting me speak with him, is there?" he asked. Hel considered him for a moment before stepping down the dais to meet him face to face. Her gaze stripped him bare, until she could see every layer of pain that surrounded his soul, each stitch of vengeance that still held it together.

"What will you ask of him?"

"I want to ask him how to defeat Fenrir, if Odin buried something with him that will help me save Ailsa."

She squinted, seeing something in him that interested her. "And what if he asks for your life? What if he demands you exchange places with him here?"

Vali swallowed. Was that an option, or was she merely feeling him out? He dared to let the goddess see his desperation, leave nothing else unsaid—even if it cost him everything. "If it would save her, then I would gratefully shred myself apart and give him the heart in my chest."

Her broken mouth parted slightly. "You, a god, would do that for a single mortal?"

"Goddess, for Ailsa I would die a thousand deaths if it meant she'd be free."

Hel took a small step back and wrung her hands together in thought. "Very well," she said. "Follow me."

⟵╌╫╌◇╌╫╌⟶

She brought him through the corridors lining the castle, dark as a dungeon no matter how many windows lined the walls. Snow gathered in the corners of the windows as silver flakes beat lightly against the frosted glass, but the cold was sealed away behind the obsidian bricks constructing Hel's hall.

"It wasn't snowing when we arrived," he said.

Hel spoke without looking back at him. "Different sections of Helheim have different climates. But here in Eljudnir, it is either sleeting or snowing."

"Why?"

She didn't answer at first, taking several long strides that made the length of her dress float behind her. "The night the gods took me from my mother, it was snowing. I remember shivering all the way to Asgard. They thought I was afraid, but truly I was just cold."

Vali had never heard Hel's story, only that Odin captured three monsters from a witch and sealed them away to protect the Nine from their potentials. But looking at the goddess, he didn't see the danger the Allfather claimed that clung to her.

Though she was terrifying to look at, she seemed to be more sensitive than her dead side suggested.

He asked, "How did the gods find you and your brothers?"

She halted and turned to him, the look on her half-face unreadable. "My father was one of the Aesir, so naturally my parents disagreed about what to do about having children like us." She motioned to the rotten half of her face. "Fenrir was just a pup. I'm not sure Jormungand could even hear them arguing, but I listened. My father had another wife among the Aesir, and he couldn't lie to her any longer about his other family. He told her about his monster children and his witch wife, and out of jealousy or malice, she went straight to Odin."

"The next thing I knew, the gods followed him back to our home in the woods and ripped me from my mother's arms. She fought for us, screamed for me and my brothers, bargained her life and her heart while my father just stood there. He watched the gods take us away like we were criminals, even though we had done nothing wrong."

"I'm sorry," Vali murmured. "That must have been traumatic for all of you, being just children."

Hel nodded slowly. "I will admit that Odin gave me a significant amount of power over the living realms in consolation. But if he wouldn't have shown such cruelty to my brother, if he hadn't assumed his fate without giving him a chance, he might have gained an ally instead of an enemy."

The elfin thought of Ailsa and the note she left after visiting the well, the one he still kept in his pocket.

By fearing our fate, we let it control us.

"Hel?" he asked. "Your father wouldn't be Loki, would it?"

The goddess turned so her good side faced him. "You can't tell from the resemblance? Blonde hair, green eyes, mischief in my smirk?"

Vali watched her attempt to duplicate Loki's sneer. "I believe your other half bears more likeness, in fact."

Hel scoffed like he had offended her, flipping her golden hair over her shoulder to continue down the hall. "You aren't wrong, sadly. It seems we both have the worst fathers in the history of creation."

"I'm glad we could find some common ground, goddess."

Their conversation fell quiet until Hel stopped at the beginning of a spiral staircase. Vali stretched his neck and discovered it curled into a tower, disappearing some levels above them. She said to him then, "I want to help you, Vali."

The elfin arched a brow at her, skeptically. "Why?"

"Because I know truth when I see it. You have been honest with me since you arrived. Your intentions have been nothing but noble and selfless. I can see the past that follows you has been one of constant trial and tragedy."

"You can tell all of that just by looking at me?" he asked.

"I may only have one good eye, but it sees much." She winked for effect and smiled. "Love is special. Many have come to my realm because of it, so I do not take your mission lightly. I may not be able to help you save her, but I can help you find where she is."

Vali's heart skipped a few beats, his jaw falling slack. "You can do that?"

She pointed upward as her smile broadened across one cheek. "Odin gave me power over *all* the Nine, Vali. That includes the mortal world, the fae realms, the forbidden realms, and everything in between. Sometimes I let souls who have passed unexpectedly visit their loved ones through my looking glass to say a proper goodbye. All you have to do is look for her in your mind, and my glass will do the rest."

But he was still reeling with the possibility of finding Ailsa

—*seeing* her again so soon. For a few seconds, he forgot to take a breath. "Will she see me as well?"

"You will appear like a spirit or a ghost to her, but yes. She will hear you and see you, but she will not feel you. There are boundaries of nature even I cannot cross." Hel was still smiling, like she had guessed what was on his mind. "She will be excited to see you, I'm sure."

"I don't even think she knows I exist," he murmured.

Hel stepped closer and placed a hand on his arm. And it wasn't cold as he expected, but warm and welcoming like her more dominant side. "Does it matter? You are fortunate to have someone worth fighting for, a hope to hold on to. Never let go of that, Vali. It is the only thing that separates you from a life among the living," she turned to leave so her left side faced him, "when the rest of you has died."

She left him to approach the looking glass on the tower's top floor. A single chair was left propped in front of an oblong mirror, the candles lit to flames around the room as he entered. Vali sat in the lone seat, stared at his reflection until he couldn't stand the sight of himself any longer. He shut his eyes and pictured his *sváss*. Let her memory rise to the surface after repressing her picture for so long. An ache in his chest rising with it.

A breeze blew at his back. The walls seemed to sigh as the world around him shifted. When he opened his eyes once more, he was no longer in a tower in Helheim. In front of him was a woman twisted in bed sheets, whose sleeping face was too tense to match the one in his heart's remembrance. Dark hair fanned across a creamy pillow as she tossed and turned on an unstable bed frame, and Vali let loose a held breath seeing Ailsa *alone*.

She was as beautiful as the day she left him. Soft skin

gleaming with a sheen of sweat while her brow furrowed as if she were deep in thought in her dreams. His fist knotted at his sides as he drank up the sight of her, white night dress pushed high around her hips as the blankets were bunched between her knees. A bare leg draped over the thin blankets.

There was no sign of Erik, nor evidence of his companionship in this room. Vali perused the space slowly, noting anything significant that would mark her location. There was only a trunk of clothes and a single candle left burning on the table beside her bed—the light conveniently catching a map that had fallen on the stone floor.

A map of... Muspell?

Vali felt his heart drop and soar all at once. Ailsa was in one of the forbidden realms—and she was trying to find a way out.

A whimper drew his attention from the map to her bed. She shifted, roused out of sleep. The hand curled into her chest skimmed down her front, settled between her legs, and Vali felt his skin flush with a fresh heat as he watched her. Desperate to touch that place where she sought relief. He settled on watching at the foot of her bed and whispered her name.

"Ailsa," he said.

Her eyes flew open.

CHAPTER 26
AILSA

Ailsa.

She had been drifting in that half-suspended space of sleep, held back by a tension coiled inside her core that pleaded for release either by her hand or someone else's. But with Erik being the only one in this realm who wanted to assist her in such a way, Ailsa chose the former.

Sometimes it was all she could think about during the day, and it only worsened at night when she had those *dreams*. The same one every time of a man with golden eyes who whispered her name like a lover, the sound triggering parts of herself that seemed to remember him fondly. Exactly like how that voice just whispered it now...

Ailsa sat up; aware she was no longer alone in this room, and curled her hand back into her chest. A hot flame spread across her cheeks as she gazed upon the man—the elfin— from her lost memories. But it was clear from the way his golden stare lingered across her exposed skin that he remembered her, and was recalling a very specific history between them even now.

"It's you," she gasped.

"Why'd you stop?" he only asked, eyes falling to her hips.

Ailsa almost choked on air, which was suddenly too thick to breathe with him occupying the same space. "You're watching me," she said.

The corners of his lush lips tipped in a half smile. "That's never gotten in your way before."

Ailsa snatched the covers and hid herself from his view, ignoring the way his attention ran a thrill down her spine. "Who are you? And how did you get in here?" she asked in a quiet whisper. He opened his mouth just to shut it again, like he couldn't answer her simply. She spoke again. "Are you the one who took me from my home, the one Erik rescued me from?"

He winced, but nodded.

She glanced toward the door, wondering if she should stay or run. If this man was as dangerous and manipulative as Erik claimed, he could put her under his spell again. Perhaps parts of his enchantment still hung about in the stubborn parts of her heart, and that is why she stayed put.

"I must still be dreaming. You can't really be here." She blinked hard and rubbed her eyes with her palms, but nothing rid the image of his phantom. "You should be dead..."

"It takes more than a blade to kill a god. Remind your lion-heart the next time he tries to stab me in the back." The elfin's words were shards of ice as he spoke, but his voice warmed in the next breath. "Do you dream of me often, *Stiarna?*"

Starlight. What a curious thing to call her. A pet name? "Answer my question, and I will answer yours. Who are you?"

He ran a hand through a band of thick, black hair. The

movement angling his face in such a way she noticed runes marking the shaved sides of his head. He righted himself before she could decode them. "My name is Vali, though you preferred to call me other things."

"Vali," she mumbled. The name fell off her tongue with ease. "Yes, I do dream of you sometimes. Though never in so much detail as now."

Another pause filled with his smirk. "I sleep very little since you were taken, but I think of you often. It is a relief to see you like this. Alone." His eyes trailed over the sheets covering her bare legs. "Have they harmed you? The witches or the wolves?"

"No," she said, wondering why he would care if he was indeed only after her power.

"And Erik? Has he..." The elfin swallowed. "Has he *touched* you?"

The way he said the word, she knew his meaning. "No, but he wants to." Her eyes shifted uneasily toward the bedroom door.

"And you do not." Not a question, but a statement of fact.

Ailsa shifted on the bed until she was on her knees near the end, looking straight into the eyes that were locked on hers. Similar to the man with the stag mask, they were solid gold. Like beams of sunlight had been collected and stored inside his gaze. Sunlight she hadn't seen in weeks since they arrived in Muspell. "How do you know what I want?"

He stepped closer to the bed, their faces a lunge away. "Because the Ailsa I know wouldn't hesitate to claim her desires in bed. If you were with me, you wouldn't be in a separate room, needy and aroused, with your hand between your legs. You'd be... taken care of."

"Is that what you did, Vali?" she asked, cocking her head. "You took care of me?"

Any hint of a smirk fell from those perfect lips. "Sometimes. You are... were very dominant. You took care of both of us, sometimes several times a day."

Odin's eye. The way this male spoke made the throbbing in her core pulse to an unbearable beat until she was sure she could feel something warm lick the inside of her thighs. How he could make her body react like this just with his presence, the things her flesh knew that her mind did not—she needed those memories more than ever.

She reached out to touch his face now that it was so close, but her hand passed straight through like he was made of colored smoke. "This is a dream, then," she said. "You aren't really here, and this is all just happening inside my head."

He stepped out of her reach and walked around her bed, stopping when he reached her side. "Do you want this to be real?"

"Of course, not." Ailsa shook her head defiantly, but even she didn't convince herself. There was a strange appeal to this male, awakening something inside that frightened her. Not because she was afraid of him, but because she wasn't. If what Erik claimed was true about Vali, he was dangerous in more ways than just his power. Everything depended on the truth —the past—and the history that bound together and broke them apart.

"What do you want with me? Why are you here?" she asked, unable to look at him until she swatted down the butterflies in her chest.

"I wanted to make sure you were safe, and I also needed to know where Erik took you."

"You're trying to find me?"

"Yes."

"And why? What do you want with me?"

His phantom fingers floated over the top of her shoulder, following the curve down her arm. He wasn't touching her, not exactly, but there was an intimacy in his graze that raised her skin, reaching back for him anyway. "I want to bring you home, *sváss*."

"I don't even know where that is anymore," she muttered. Too many places competed with Drakame now in her mind, she couldn't be sure what she wanted, not without all the pieces of the past. She turned her face and found him staring back. "Vali?"

"Hmmm?"

She licked her lips, pulling his gilded gaze to her mouth. If he was real, she'd think he might kiss her. "Did you really put a fae spell on me to fall in love with you, so I'd sleep with you and fight for you?"

"Ailsa, listen to me carefully," he whispered. "The only one who did the enchanting was you, and I will forever be under your spell."

The way he looked at her, a tenderness easy in his eyes, it made her wonder if falling for someone like him could ever be a choice. If males like him could harness the ability to steal one's willpower, even in dreams. Because the world seemed to shift as he spoke, tipping her down a path of no return.

Perhaps not all spells were charmed by magic.

"You still wear it."

Ailsa followed his pointed gaze, discovering his eyes were locked on the ring on her left hand. She opened her mouth to inquire more, but the door handle to her room rattled against the lock. Vali's breath slipped a sound of annoyance. "Someone is coming," he whispered. "I have to go."

"Wait!" She reached for him, but he was already retreating. His image began to fade.

"I'm coming for you, Ailsa. Remember, there is nothing in the Nine..." The sound of his voice disappeared, but she finished the vow for him, recalling the words from a deeply rooted place beyond her memory—her heart.

The door burst open, hitting the wall as it swung wide. Erik came rushing in without invitation, his glare darting around the room as she fixed her shift and her sheets.

His head swung back to her, eyes blazing like hot coals. "Who was just in here?" he asked.

"What are you talking about? My door has been locked since I left you! How dare you barge into my room! *Again.*"

"Do not lie to me. I heard voices! A man's voice." He approached her bedside, close enough to see the sheen of sweat glossing her body and the wrinkles pressed into the sheets. Ailsa stood and crossed the room to her trunk, finding something to throw over her thin shift. The elfin looked at her with lust and worshipful adoration. Erik's attention just made her skin crawl.

"Then you are going mad, because no one was in here." And it wasn't completely a lie.

Another figure joined them in the doorway, one wearing a stag mask. Their fight must have been carrying down the hall and attracting an audience. Erik's glare turned murderous. "Was it him?"

She rolled her eyes. "Are you listening to yourself? He doesn't *speak.* How could you have heard his voice behind a locked door?" Her head tipped, realizing just then. "And what were you doing outside my room at this hour, anyway?"

Erik didn't answer at first but continued to pace the length of the small room. Three stomping strides were all it took before he had to turn on a heel and start again. He was obviously beginning to get his strength back, which meant if she wanted to slay Fafnir herself, she'd need to leave soon.

He finally stopped, wobbling a bit as he did so. "I will give you an ultimatum."

"Excuse me?"

"You can either stay with me from now on, so I can keep an eye on you, or I'll use the lock I put on your door. The *outside* of your door, so only I can unlock it. It is the only way I can ensure you are safe, and I can take care of you."

Take care of you. How different this man and that male had ideas on doing just that.

Ailsa's fingers trembled in her fist. Whatever bliss she had found moments ago had been seared away. A lock on the outside of the door would mean she couldn't reach it with her blood. This wasn't about keeping others out; it was about keeping her inside.

"How about a third option? I stay where I am, and you go fuck yourself." She nodded in agreement with herself. "Aye, I like that one best."

His steps devoured the space between them, closing in on her before she had time to react. His hands found her shoulders and shoved her against the curve of the stone wall, cracking her skull against the granite. Ailsa didn't utter more than a grunt of surprise, didn't give him anything to insinuate weakness. That was how prey and predator were determined.

"I am trying so hard to be patient with you," he growled. "You don't care about anyone but yourself, and I'll admit that is my fault. I have been too tolerant with you, too generous with my forgiveness. Perhaps it is time to teach you how to be grateful—"

Ailsa didn't even have time to spit on him before Erik

crumbled at her feet. In front of her was the silent man, his mask removed, his fists raised in a follow through from striking Erik in the side of his thick head. He shook his hand and withdrew as Erik rose to his feet. The man's eyes widened on him.

"How dare you touch me, you *freak,*" Erik said, rubbing the side he struck. He started toward him, ready to strike back, but Ailsa snatched him by the shoulder and sunk her nails into his skin, clawing him to a stop.

"Leave him alone. He was trying to help me because you are being an ass!"

He spun to face her, eyes red where there had once been white. "Make your choice, Ailsa! Or I swear to Odin, I will beat your little friend until he cannot see or hear as well."

Ailsa stared up at him, hoping he felt every ounce of disdain she had for him now in her heart. Erik had been angry with her many times in her life, but the man before her was unrecognizable. Lost in his hatred for the world, he'd never look the same again. "I will *never* stay with you. Lock me up for all I care."

A muscle twitched in his jaw, and he nodded with a jerk of his chin. "Fine."

The silent man was outside the door, still watching from the hall, but as Erik left the room, he bolted. Her once truest friend stood in the doorway for a heartbeat, departing words hanging on his lips. "I'm doing this for your own good. Someday, you will realize this brutal mercy was not a punishment, but an act of love. Everything I did and do is because I love you."

"What did you take from me, Erik?" she asked, feeling her chest shudder as she spoke. "My mind doesn't remember, but my heart does." Ailsa placed a shaking hand over the throbbing pulse in her chest, beats away from breaking against the strain. "And if what I feel is true, then you better watch your back. Because there is nothing in the Nine that will keep him from me."

"No one is coming for you. Your elfin is dead—"

"Vali is *alive.*" And the growing smile on her face set a new tension in the air. A flicker in Erik's eyes was kin to fear. He slammed the door shut, unleashing his anger out on the wood and metal, until the only sound was a lock sliding into place.

Ailsa fell to her knees and let the sting spark sensation through the numbness. How in Hel's name was she supposed to get out of here now?

She sat near the door, dressed in the only trousers and cloak she could find. A thin strip of sheet wrapped around each fist, the quickest weapon she could make from this bare room. Any moment now, Erik would have to open her door, and she'd be ready to jump him with the piece of scrap cloth around his throat.

This was personal now, this revenge. No longer would she let him put his hands on her, shake her into submission. She had been patient, unlike his assessment, but he never learned. He never would until he paid the price for his mistakes.

The lock finally rattled, and she shifted her weight onto her toes. Hiding in the shadow of the door as it opened, she waited until he stepped inside before slowly closing it behind him, taking care not to shut it completely.

Ailsa lunged from behind, about to loop the strip of sheet around his neck until she noticed the auburn hair in the candlelight, the thin shoulders that were several inches closer to her reach than Erik's burly frame.

"*Skide*," she cursed, causing him to startle and spin around. "It's just you." Her hands fell to her side as the strip went slack. He wasn't wearing a mask today, instead appearing like he was going on a journey, obvious from the cowl wrapped around his neck. "What are you doing here? And how did you get the key from Erik?"

The silent man spoke in very subtle ways, with his eyes and the lines around his mouth, often wearing his heart on his sleeve. Today, however, Ailsa saw anger in his golden eyes. An emotion she hadn't yet seen him wear.

He set the tray down and picked up a cup. Jutting a finger toward Erik's room, he then followed the motion with a sleeping face.

"You knocked him out?" Ailsa gasped. The silent man nodded with a solemn smile. Her heart pounded with new possibilities. The door was open. Erik was sedated. She just needed to grab her map and find a way out of the mountain. "Can you show me how to get out of here?"

He held up a single finger and turned back to the tray once more, this time grabbing a knife. His nimble fingers tapped his temple, then hers. With the same hand, he grabbed her palm and dragged the blade lightly across the inside of their hands. There was only one ceremony he could be referring to, bleeding them both.

"You want to make a blood bond with me? Are you sure? This will bind you to me in ways I cannot fully expect."

The man nodded and tapped their temples successively. Ailsa learned about blood runes with Njord all those foggy memories ago, and the one who spoke the rune to life would have submission over the other, a spoken contract written and sealed in blood. If she did this, perhaps they could speak to each other through thought alone. "You trust me to do this?"

The man nodded and flipped the knife so that the handle faced her. She took it from his hands and glanced back at the door. They needed to do this quickly if they were to escape before someone noticed. "Fine," she whispered. "But we must hurry."

Ailsa cut a quick slice across her palm with the butcher knife and handed it to him, who did the same. They joined hands, wet palms connecting them both in a last minute, desperate decision.

"Our minds will be one. My thoughts will be your thoughts, and yours will be mine. We will speak to each other in a place no one else can enter. As long as this blood rune is branded on our skin, our thoughts will connect us. Do you agree?"

He nodded and mouthed the word *yes.*

Her words were simple and specific and quickly took effect. Ailsa felt a crawling sensation burrow into her skin where they were still joined, lines of black ink veined across her arm before fading into red. Runes of blood branded her forearm, matching ones decorated his opposite. When the trickle of power ceased, she looked at him, not sure how this would work exactly.

Can you hear me? She thought the words instead of speaking them.

His smile said everything, but in her mind, there was a resounding answer, a melodious, deep voice she thought suited him despite his meek first impression.

Yes.

Ailsa couldn't help the beaming smile that swept across her face. *Will you finally tell me your name?*

The silent man, no longer muzzled, knelt on a knee and looked up at her. Her hand still in his palm, he kissed the top lightly. Not out of affection or adoration, but a courteous, even gallant gesture. *My name is Vidar. It is a pleasure to finally introduce myself.*

"So polite," Ailsa said, winking. "I hope you mean to help me out of this mountain now?"

I can do that, but if you truly still wish to hunt the dragon, Ailsa, you may require some weapons to take down the beast.

Her palms itched at the thought. Stepping to the side, she motioned to the door. "Lead the way then, Vidar."

CHAPTER 27
SEELA

Smoke from the forges settled into her skin like a perfume. They were countless in this underground realm, where the halls were carved into the flesh of the earth and massive pillars held up the mountain reigning above them. It impressed Seela by how they could make the space so large, dig deep enough into the earth to make rooms and courts larger than the ones she roamed in Alfheim.

Drasili fit them with fine weapons and armor more suitable for the harsh terrain of the pass. Thick leather lined with white fox fur, the chest piece was heavy without feeling smothering yet durable enough to withstand the claws of the draug. They had cast their weapons in a mold of enchanted obsidian, which the dwarves were currently testing against the souls of the undead. A combination that, as they claimed, could cut through anything—including curses.

Seela hoped they had done their due research at the very least. She despised being the test dummy for their weapons, but the reward was too alluring to turn down.

"If I make this arrangement with you, Drasili, no one can

241

know," she said. The glass in front of her overlooked his treasury. The king of the seven mountains had an expansive view of his realm's wealth mounding in piles of gold and silver from his office.

He shifted in his seat, and the chair groaned. "Ashamed to work with dwarves, Lady Seela?"

"Not ashamed, no." She turned around to face him, the king of all the glittering wealth below sitting behind a modest sized desk crafted from a lackluster metal. "You are asking me to slaughter my own kind. If I destroy them in this state... they may never return to the Light. I could be damning hundreds of elves."

"The elves are not the only ones among the draug, Seela." He stood from his chair and met her where she stood. "All kinds of fae were crushed during the rockslides, but if we do not clear the way, then my people cannot forge the weapons and armor you will need in this war to come. We mine from multiple mountains, but with the way things are now, I cannot let my workers utilize the pass to get to them."

"Why not just fight them off yourselves?" she asked.

"Because we are masters of the forge, not the weapons that come from them. Our magic is for creating, not killing." He came to stand in front of her, crossing his arms. "If you want exclusive rights for the fae concerning our blades, if you want weapons at all, you must clear the pass."

Seela tried not to hold her breath at his closeness, but the dwarf was attractive in a strange way. His gray skin had never seen the sun, decorated with raised scars that made intricate patterns across his body. From a crown around his head, lines weaving in and out like a braid around his scalp, to his forearms printed with jagged designs. He was covered in details her eyes couldn't absorb entirely with a single look.

"How many are there?" she asked. "Hundreds? Thousands?"

He shook his head, his white hair shimmered like crystalline water over his shoulders. "Not all who died that day became draug. When the witches came through here, they raised a hundred or so from their graves in the ice. Your party should be able to take care of them."

Seela scoffed at his misplaced confidence. "Such faith you have in us, King Drasili."

His blue lips curled into a grin, revealing a row of sharp teeth. "I've seen how elves fight. You'll be fine."

"Right," she said on the tail of a sigh. "Well, I better go find my companions so we can be on our way. I'd rather not face draug in the dark."

"Where did your friends run off to?" he asked, eyes shifting behind her.

Seela shrugged and grabbed the rest of their gear Drasili had laid out. "Enver is probably where the ale is. Ivor is most likely in a dark room, hoping no one talks to her. And with any luck, they are far, far away from each other."

"I don't understand why we must be the ones to do this," Ivor hissed as they climbed the last stair leading above ground. Seela found her exactly where she left the wolven in the rooms the dwarves had boarded them for the night. Enver, however, had a flush to his cheeks and a scent to his clothes that hinted he hadn't been alone all night, smelling like the smoke from the forges and ale. The male made friends in every realm.

The dwarf leading them back to the forbidden pass

stopped in front of the door bordering Alfheim. A thin whistle cried as the wind slipped between the frame and the locks. Seela turned to face the wolf, already out of breath from the climb. "I already told you once—if we want to use the pass, we must clear it first. That is the deal. Your witch friends made this mess. Now you're going to help clean it up."

"They're not my friends," she mumbled.

Ignoring her, Seela pressed on. As they stepped outside, a violent gust of wind nearly blew her back into the mountain. The king warned her this section of the pass was the most dangerous, highly difficult to navigate through the storms of sleet and snow. His appraisal had been appropriate.

The snow was thickest here, coming up to her shins and still piling on more the longer they stood there. Seela unsheathed the blade at her hip, ready for anything that popped out of the snow, and flipped her hood over her pointed ears. Enver stayed close to her shoulder, his new bow strung and balanced for the most accurate shot. Ivor opted out of the gear and weapons, and Seela wondered what she would do when they faced the undead.

"Why did the witches raise the draug?" Enver asked her above the icy breeze.

"Drasili said they are protecting something in the Iron-wood. The draug make it impossible to get to that part of Jotunheim without taking the obvious route through the frost giant's realm." Journeys through the giant lands were almost as uncertain as their weather, and Seela would rather face a few undead than a winter there.

They pressed on a few miles deeper into a valley between three short mountains, the sun hiding behind their peaks and casting shadows over the pit in the earth. When the pass remained quiet, Seela thought perhaps Drasili had been mistaken, if the draug might have disappeared with the witches when they fled this realm.

Until something snatched her ankle beneath the snow.

"*Skide!*" she shrieked, yanking her leg from its grasp, but the creature had a hold on her. She used her blade to cut the arm from its choking hand, but the severing did nothing to release its grip.

Rising from the snow, the draug sat up, staring at her with dead, empty eyes. It still wore a traveling cloak with ice clinging to the fur draping its shoulders. Its skin peeling from the bones on its face as the bitter cold had eaten away the flesh underneath. But Seela couldn't stop staring at its mouth, too wide for its head, too many teeth behind the snarling lips as it hungered after her.

An arrow struck straight through its throat as it hissed, Enver releasing one of the enchanted arrows he received from the dwarves. The shot was so powerful from this close, it cut straight through, a line of black fire consuming the draug as it did.

"So the enchantments work," Enver noted.

"Seela," Ivor mumbled behind her. She looked at the wolven, but her frosty gaze was wide on something ahead. Seela followed her attention, her knees weakening at the sight.

Hundreds of draug were sitting up from their sleep in the snow, slowly rising to their frozen feet. Enver knocked his bow with another arrow, eyes flicking to each undead, trying to decide which to go after first, then next. A sound like thunder striking sand bolted behind her, Ivor shifting into her wolf form.

"I knew I should have stayed for one more ale," Enver groaned.

245

Seela gripped the pommel of her new sword, the metal practically buzzing with awareness as the undead started toward them. "Get through this, Commander, and I'll buy the next round at Greybeard's for the rest of our lives."

Enver let an arrow fly, striking a draug in the chest. More black flames devoured the body. "I won't make you do that, Seela. How about a kiss instead? A real one on the lips, with tongue, and at least two minutes long."

Ivor growled behind them, and Seela's cheeks burned despite the winter. "You're going to make a move *now*, Enver?"

His arrows suddenly stopped firing. "Oh, darn." He inspected his hand. "A blister. Looks like I'll need some extra motivation if I'm to suffer through this injury and fight an army of undead fae."

"*Gods below*, fine! But you get one minute!" Seela spoke between her teeth as her sword ran through the first draug in her path. Ivor tore between them, lunging up the middle to catch one by the throat. Seela winced as she ripped through its neck, forgoing weapons to take a more personal approach.

"How is she killing them without the dwarf's enchantment?" Enver asked behind her.

"Wolven have poison in their bite, remember? Where do you think the dwarves got the idea from in the first place?"

The valley filled with ravaged draug. Their hollow forms blacking out the white film over the mountainside. Thanks to the personalized blades, they weren't difficult to kill. Their bodies were engulfed in flames the second it pierced their stagnant bloodstreams. But there were so many of them, she began to lose count, forgetting where she'd left the last one after turning to strike another. If she wasn't careful, if she stumbled for a moment or hesitated a single decision, they could overrun her in a second.

Enver sought higher ground, using his archery to thin out the mass migration as the undead sought the life in their bones. Seela couldn't see Ivor anymore, her sight blocked by the piles of bodies beginning to build around her, the smoke from their flesh as it burned and melted the snow into slush beneath her boots.

They had been fighting so long, the sun was setting low behind the mountain peaks. Seela's body was weak. Her moves clumsy and mechanical, lacking passion or fear or anything left that fueled a fight.

Enver had long run out of arrows by now, fighting somewhere beside her as she cut through the remaining draug. Finally, she retreated from her spot in the valley, charging up the cliff face to check on her companions and their progress.

"Gods below," she cursed with a ragged breath. Another wave was coming just over the eastern wall. At this rate, they'd be fighting them off until tomorrow morning. Enver was still going strong, but Ivor's coat was matted with old blood. She attacked more carefully now, less provocatively, and Seela knew the wolven wouldn't last another wave. Neither could Seela.

"Fall back!" she shouted at them. The thin air carried her voice like it had wings. She'd rather go back to Drasili, find another way through the draug, then let her companions perish because she didn't want to submit to failure. Failing left them options. Their deaths would leave her with none.

Just as she turned to start back where they came from, a quiet tremor ran through the stone beneath her feet. Seela stilled, studying the vibrations, sensed they were not coming from the hoard of undead behind her but from the mountain itself. Drasili had told them the rocks still shifted around these parts, but she hadn't taken his word as a warning.

"Seela, get down here!"

She heard Enver's command, but her gaze was too busy watching the mountain above her rattle awake. Rocks broke from their sediment, slipping down the slope where the afternoon sun had warmed the ice into soft slush. The few that broke apart gathered momentum, brought down others with their descension, until Seela was staring up at a rockslide— and she was standing right in its path.

She tried to run toward Enver's voice, but the foundation of the mountain was too unstable, the shake of the earth too violent for her to walk, much less sprint out of the way. Seela dropped her sword and lunged clumsily back towards her companions, clawing on her hands and knees to a safer section in the valley. But Enver's arms were so much further than his voice betrayed. She'd never get to him in time.

A blur of stormy grey blocked her view of the elfin as she was suddenly lifted from the snow. Her wet knees wrapped around Ivor's back as the wolven tossed her on her backside, gripped bloody fur with her frozen hands as Ivor sprinted them back towards safety. She dodged the falling rocks as they tumbled past boulders as large as the wolven herself, and used her claws to dig into the shifting terrain, narrowly helping them escape.

Seela slipped off her back when they reached Enver, out of the way of nature's wrath, but now trapped between a rock wall and a growing number of draug. He helped her to her feet and asked, "Are you all right? What were you thinking going back like that?"

Seela jutted her chin toward the opposite side of the valley behind him. "There's more coming. Too many to hold off."

"Drasili made this sound like target practice. This isn't what we signed up for!" Enver spat.

"Either the king lied, or he didn't know the full extent of the draug problem. Either way, we need to make a choice. We can cut our way out of here or risk going over the rock-slide back to the dwarf realm." And judging by the dark wall of undead forming behind Enver, they needed to decide quickly.

"You know my vote," he said, and handed her a short sword from his belt. "But I've got your back no matter what you decide, Commander, until the Light takes us."

Seela took the weapon from his hand and looked at Ivor, whose chest heaved with effort and beastly face was now black with draug blood. Her eyes, though cold against the frozen landscape, insisted the same.

"The Light," she muttered. The little that was given to her by her father's side. Would it be enough to protect her companions? The male beside her read her thoughts.

He gripped her by the shoulders before wrapping her in his arms, an embrace to hide his words from the wolven. "I know you hide behind the Light, Seela. But that power you hold, the one you ignore because you are too afraid to touch it, let it out. Stop being ashamed of who you are."

"My father made me promise—"

"Your father couldn't protect you from the gods," he pushed her away to look into her eyes, "but I will if it comes to it. We're just a few bad winters away from the end of the Nine anyway, sweetheart."

Ivor barked a warning, and Seela glanced toward the incoming draug, noting the space between them had lessened significantly. This close, she could see the number of bodies was twice as many as she originally calculated. "You're right," she muttered to Enver.

He squeezed her arm. "Who are you, Commander?"

Seela swallowed, but couldn't hold the truth down any longer. "I am the daughter of a Seven."

"What are you, Seela?"

She shut her eyes and looked inward, feeling the Light and the call of her mother's blood mix and bloom beneath her skin. "I am part fae," she said. The next words she said louder, for the first time in decades, "And I am part Valkyrie."

Enver smirked. "Fly high, sweetheart. You were made to touch the stars."

She pushed through Enver and planted her feet into the ice, waiting for the draug to clammer through the thick snow and meet them in the center of the valley. Enver and Ivor came to her side, teeth bared and sword raised. Calling on her Valkyrie would alert the rest of the Seven that she was one of them, and she wanted nothing to do with her maternal family, but she owed it to her friends standing with her now to defend them with everything she had left. Enver deserved that kiss.

And perhaps, not so deep down, she wanted it too.

She recited the words etched into her necklace. *"Valr kjósa."* Chooser of the slain. The rest she recited in the old language, "Grant me your strength and valor winged maidens, to protect the fates of those who bleed beside me, to slay those I deem worthy of sending to their eternal home."

Light pooled around her hands as Seela gripped her dagger and charged into the sea of draug. With each swing of her weapon, it grew brighter, until the surrounding undead were falling to ash at the very sight of her Light. Until her feet were no longer on the ground but suspended above the snow as wings took her soaring above the mass of them.

She plunged and slayed hundreds alone by her sword, and time itself seemed to come to a cessation, allowing her to cut down every undead until there was none left standing. None to oppose them. Not one fae left in this transitory state to be used as feral watch dogs for whoever raised their weathered souls.

When it was finished, she shut her eyes and let the Light wane, felt her feet find the earth again as she sunk to her knees out of exhaustion and the inevitable crash of adrenaline. Her armor, her hands, even her face was sticky from draug residue. Someone stepped in front of her, the crunch of snow beneath their feet.

She figured it was Enver or Ivor in her human form, but when she looked up, it was a woman. Her body draped in tattered black robes around a pale face. The veil of white over her dark pupils purged Seela's peace with a fighter's fear. The warrior inside her demanded she stand with her blade, but her bones were filled with stones. She barely had the strength to lift her head and stare at the blind eyes cast down at her.

A crow perched on her shoulder.

"You destroyed my army," she said.

Seela's eyes only widened in response, her breaths quickening. Where were her companions now and had she flown too far for them to catch up?

"Did it not occur to you by the opposition you faced," she continued, "that I did not want any visitors?"

"Who are you?" Seela asked.

The woman smiled. "I am the one they call the Mother Witch, but you may call me Angrboda."

Seela's sight plunged into darkness.

CHAPTER 28
VALI

Baldur was as handsome as the legends claimed him to be. Every inch of him was gilded, from his dark bronze skin that seemed to have been worshiped by the sun to the same shade in his eyes as Vali's, though they were brighter than the elfin's. Possibly because the god was always smiling, his white teeth flashing every swooning male or maiden that passed him by.

Vali found him in a section of Helheim that was devoted to sunshine and perfect weather, where the only fallen god in this realm sat in a hall with a ceiling open to the sky above. He sat at a long table surrounded by his admirers, who kept his cup full and his lap even fuller.

"You're sure you're a son of Odin?" Baldur asked him after Vali explained the reason for interrupting—what Vali believed to be—a very irritable maiden from finishing her dance for the god. "You don't really look like us. No offense."

"Unfortunately, yes, it would seem so," he clipped. "Did you hear anything I just told you?"

He shrugged and waved a hand. Every move he made

flexed a bulging muscle. "Yes, I'm supposed to leave this realm and slay the beast Fenrir, so he doesn't kill my father first. I know what they fated me for, Vali, but look around. Why would I leave this paradise and go back to the politics of Asgard?"

Vali blinked at him. "Because if you do not kill Fenrir and stop Ragnarok from happening, it won't matter what realm you reside. All the Nine will fall."

"So, you're here to escort me out the front door? Have you spoken with Hel about this?"

"Yes, I did." The elfin leaned across the table, bracing his hands on the sturdy top. "Since she refuses to give you up and you refuse to leave, then I will need something from you. Give me your ring."

"Draupnir?" The god touched the gold band wrapped around his arm. "But my father gave this to me. He buried me with it. It is *mine*."

"And it bears the curse of a broken oath, Baldur. It is a weapon against his fate. Odin should have never given you that ring in the first place."

But Baldur was resistant to the idea, shaking his head. "That makes little sense. You cannot kill him without me. I am the strongest god—"

"You are dead!" Vali found his voice elevating. "You cannot kill anyone until the boundaries of this realm fall and the dishonorably slain can walk the Tree in their afterlife. Will you damn the way to Fenrir's downfall because you are too stubborn to let it go? Or will you give the ring to someone else who can finish this?"

The god leaned forward and squinted until gold spilled through thin slits. "How do I know you do not just want Draupnir for yourself? It was forged by the dwarves to elevate

Odin's wisdom and ambition. He gave it to me to increase my strength, so that nothing in the Nine could harm me. This ring multiplies what it touches, holds more power than you could ever imagine."

Vali was four seconds away from putting the god's dinner knife through his eye. "Because Fenrir has someone I care about."

"That sounds like a personal problem, elfin."

"Vali!"

He turned at the sound of his name being shouted by a familiar voice. Marrin was *skipping* in her knee high boots, a fur cloak floating behind her as she grinned from ear to ear. "We have someone who wants to meet you."

"Now isn't a good time, Marrin."

"Then make it good, elfin." Another voice joined behind her, though Vali couldn't see the source of it yet with Marrin standing in the way. He straddled the bench to look around her, but as she stepped to the side, the elfin nearly fell out of his seat.

An older woman appeared at Marrin's side. Dark brown hair with a white flower pinned behind her ear, she looked nothing like the daughter at her side but resembled another strong enough the elfin didn't have to wonder who this was for a moment.

"Astrid," he muttered.

Ailsa's mother stepped in front of Marrin and jerked her head to the side. "Don't just sit there gawking. Stand up and let me look at you."

Vali glanced at the god still sitting across from him. Baldur's eyes were wide, like he had been caught getting in trouble by mere association. He sipped his mead and pretended to be curious about the shapes in the clouds floating above.

The elfin slipped off the bench and stood as she demanded, feeling suddenly insecure under the critical weight of her inspection. She circled him like a falcon, ready to dive for a kill. He opened his mouth to introduce himself, but she held up a hand to silence him.

"My daughters have told me about you. I know who you are, Vali, God of Vengeance, Lord of Light Elves, *Fraendi* to my youngest daughter."

Vali swallowed. "That about sums it up, yes."

She stopped right in front of him, having to crane her neck to look him in the eyes. "Aye, my daughters told me everything. And I don't know whether I should kill you for murdering my husband and my eldest two..." Her frown softened slightly. "Or embrace you for joining the family."

"In all fairness, Ledger struck first—"

Astrid slapped him lightly on the shoulder. "Hush, I didn't ask for your opinion." He looked to Marrin and Lochare for help, but the pair staggered themselves on the bench and tabletop, smirking like this was a form of payback.

Their mother spoke again. "My husband wasn't the sharpest dagger in the sheath. I have no doubt he struck first and died protecting his family's secret. So no, I will not punish you for killing half my kin. What's done is done, and there is no raising the dead." She gripped him by the collar with one hand and tugged him down, so they were face to face. "Where is my Ailsa?"

"Muspell," he said. "Hel let me use her looking glass, and I was able to find her in the fire giant's realm."

"Muspell," she repeated. She chewed the inside of her cheek in thought. "How do you plan to get to her?"

Vali shifted on his feet, the position hurting his back. "I plan on leaving Helheim the same way I came and following the Gjoll deeper into the forbidden realms. It is said the fire realm is near Niflheim."

"How will you get inside?"

He licked his lips. "I don't know, but I will find a way. I always do."

"You are a fool." She finally released him. "Learn to ask for help when you need it. It will not always come rushing to meet you like it is now."

"Now?" he asked.

Astrid glanced at the god across the table, offering him a small smile, before letting her gaze skim across the rest of their audience. "Come with me. I need to speak with you about this in private." Turning on a heel, she strode down the hall with the sisters trailing close behind.

Vali looked at Baldur one last time. "Please," he said, no longer ashamed of begging. He'd get on his knees before all of them if it meant it would help his cause. "Just think about what I said. Time is not on our side, not even for the dead."

Baldur said nothing as Vali left, chasing after Ailsa's family.

<hr />

Astrid poured him a tea in her small home near the edge of a fjord, the setup similar to Drakame. Vali wondered if everyone who came to Helheim could choose an afterlife like the one they enjoyed on earth.

"You cannot pass this on to Hel," she said quietly, "but there are rumors of some of us trying to escape Helheim."

"Escape?" he asked. "Is that possible?"

She nodded. "There is a ship in Nastrond. Mind you, it's a rough part of the realm where all the murderers and oath breakers are sent. They have been kidnapping people for ages, using their nails and bones to make a ship strong enough to cross the realm's void to Muspell nearby. They want to join the fire giants."

"Why would they want to do such a thing?" Vali asked.

But Astrid shrugged. "Nastrond is a hole of punishment. It is not peaceful like it is here, there exists an afterlife of pain and torture, where the dragon Nidhogg frequently flies and chews on the corpses of those who are sent there."

Her words ran a shudder down his spine. "It is at least worth looking into. How do I get there?"

"How do *we* get there, you mean?" Lochare said with raised brows.

Vali glanced between the sisters. "You still want to come? I figured you'd want to stay here with your mother."

Marrin looked at him like the answer was obvious. "The fate of our little sister rest in your hands, and you've required an awful lot of help just getting to this point."

"For a god of vengeance, you're a bit soft," Lochare said through a mouthful of bread.

The elfin wanted to remind her he had killed them both without lifting a blade, but with Astrid standing beside him, he thought it best to swallow his retort for later. "Very well then," he said instead. "How do *we* get to Nastrond?"

She settled into the seat next to him and took a hot mug between her hands. "There's a man who charters a boat to the hole. As you know, I come from a long line of wicked men, so I've been down there once or twice. Anyone in Helheim can visit the prisoners in Nastrond, but it's incredibly dangerous.

There is no protection. The boat leaves at sunset and comes back at midnight, and if you miss it, you're stuck there until the following night."

Vali's gaze settled on the window, which was open wide to let in the afternoon breeze. "Returning is the least of my concerns. Do you know anything more about this ship to Muspell?"

She shook her head. "No, but I know it is complete and ready to sail."

He gathered what little he brought with him to this realm and stood from the dining table. "That is all I need to know, then. Show me to this boat and we will be on our way."

Astrid finished her drink and stood slowly despite his sense of urgency. "Wait outside for me. I will join you in a moment."

Vali slipped out of her longhouse and wandered the front yard. The sisters opted to wait inside for their mother. Astrid had a small farm on her isolated piece of land near the shores of an inlet, with small animals like goats and chickens as the only company for miles. He paced the edge of a small garden, mostly medicinal plants which were scattered with white buttercups—Ailsa's favorite. He knelt in the damp soil and plucked a few by the base of the stem, whispering words of preservation over the small bundle before slipping them inside his cloak.

With any luck, he could give them to her before they wilted.

"She buried me with one of those," Astrid said. He hadn't even heard her footsteps stalk behind him. Vali turned to find her smiling at the overgrowth of white blooms, touching the one tucked behind her ear. "This was the only thing she sent with me to the afterlife, and it has yet to fade even after all this time. They were my favorite. Grew right outside our long-house in Drakame."

"She is incredibly thoughtful in that way," Vali said, feeling himself begin to smile.

Astrid's lips reflected his grin. "Aye, I am glad she maintained that gentleness she had as a child. I always felt guilty when it came to Ailsa. She was like me—sick. We became too confident with Marrin and Lochare and thought perhaps my sickness would skip our children. Ledger wanted a son, so we tried again. Poor Ailsa came out hardly breathing." Astrid looked away, letting the pain in her gaze strike the horizon. "I only wish I could have more time with her."

He nodded in agreement. "I find myself constantly wishing the same."

Her mother stepped closer to him until her hands could rest on his shoulders. Her eyes were searching him again. Deep pools that could drown him with their pull. "Marrin and Lochare were married to the raids. I knew they didn't need anyone else besides each other and the axes in their hands. I see now that Ailsa chose well for herself. Find my daughter, Vali. Do not let her down."

"Until the Light takes me, Astrid," he said with the jerk of his chin, "I will never stop fighting for her until she is safe."

It was as certain as a law of nature, a fact as permanent as the air in his chest. There was no other potential for his fate than the one he had written across his skin. He'd live in darkness until the starlight was back in his sky.

Astrid blinked a few times, holding back the tears beginning to brim in the creases of her eyes. She patted his shoulders and beckoned for him to follow her. "This way then. No more time to waste."

"Elfin!" They both turned toward the shout, discovering

Baldur sprinting down a thin road cutting the fjord in half. "Wait!"

"I have a name—"

"You were right," he said, finally coming to a stop in front of him. His breath was heavy, like he'd just ran across the realm. "You should take it."

"Take what?" he asked, clarifying.

"Draupnir." The god slipped the ring off his arm and offered it to Vali, his grip hesitating before handing it over to the elfin's possession. "You were right before, about me being dead and useless. I was just being stubborn. Odin should have taken it back when I died, but I think he wanted me to keep a piece of Asgard with me down here. So I would never forget who I was."

Vali slipped the golden ring beneath his sleeve and up his arm, where it settled nicely over his bicep. Where there lacked a substantial change, there was certainly an energy to the ring that made him feel more alive. Like a veil had lifted he didn't know was there, the way ahead clearer than ever before.

"Thank you, Baldur. For the record, I don't think you're useless."

His white teeth flashed with a charming smile. "I know. Do you want to have a drink with me tonight? It's not every day I get to run into one of my half brothers."

Vali looked back at the family already leaving without him. He told the god, "Maybe next time." Before running down the shoreline to catch up with them.

Astrid led them along the rocky edge of a cliff side next to the churning water, barely wide enough for two people to pass at once. The ground was slick with saltwater as the waves slapped the side of the jagged shore, misting them with sea spray. They finally came to a small cave where the channel pooled inside, the end of it obliterated from view where the last rays of sun could not reach.

She stopped them near the mouth of the cave and reached into the choppy waters, feeling around for a moment until she pulled out a chain. Vali assisted her as she tugged on the length, pulling out a small boat hidden beneath the surface.

"Where is this man you spoke of that will bring us?" he asked above the echo of the tide.

"You're looking at him," she said, pulling on her hood. The wide brim concealed her hair and cast a shadow over her face. "I've been the courtier to the hole since the last one didn't come back a decade ago. Figured I might as well since my family was practically the founders of Nastrond. No one gives me trouble down there."

"What happened to him?" Marrin asked.

Astrid stepped into the boat once it was secure and popped off her steering oar. "He's part of the ship now, *dóttir,* weren't you listening before?"

"At least they aren't a wasteful lot," Lochare muttered as she boarded.

Astrid's laugh was too dark to belong to such a small woman. "Just keep an eye on your fingernails. They like those most of all."

Vali's hands balled into fists as he sat in the small vessel, watching as the gradient of pastel pinks and golds in the sunset disappeared from sight.

The way down into Nastrond was quiet. Not a single member of the group uttered a word to the darkness surrounding the vessel. Astrid pushed them deeper into the cave while Marrin held a burning lantern, and they traveled down the throat of a tunnel that seemed to plunge deeper into the heart of the Tree, forgetting the realms of light and life and sound.

"We are almost there," Astrid said quietly. "Before we cross the gates, I should warn you. No one is trustworthy down here, not even family. If you meet Bjorn, he will help you if you can show him how it will benefit himself in the end but avoid him at all costs otherwise. If you change your mind about the ship, I will stay docked until sunrise, but then I must return to Helheim."

No sooner had the words left her lips, the harsh screech of a rusted gate sounded, letting them pass from the tunnel and into the open air once more. As Vali surveyed his surroundings, he realized there was a sky, but not the kind that had ever seen a sun or starlight. Above them was a dome of smoke, curling and spreading from an unseen fire that diffused the air with the scent of burning flesh.

Ashes floated on a warm breeze, greeting them as the boat hit a hard piece of rock that was to substitute for land. The water hissed as it lapped against the porous rock, emitting a foul odor in its steam. Astrid leaned forward and mumbled, "Do not touch the water. Try not to touch anything, really. It's all toxic and meant to burn."

"Noted," Vali said with an uneasy smile.

Astrid then reached down and wrapped him in a tight embrace. The last gesture he was expecting, but her acceptance of him was all he could feel. In his ear, she whispered. "Be careful down here, Vali. Nastrond is not a place for beating hearts."

He patted her back in assurance. "I have both your daughters at my side, Astrid. There's nothing more menacing in all the Nine than those two. We'll be fine."

She muttered a sound of agreement after letting him go. Vali stepped out of the boat and walked some distance across a barren shore of rock and sifting dust as the sisters said their own private goodbyes, keeping them short and sweet and dry of tears. The heathens too stoic to let even each other see them break.

They joined him on top of a rolling bank near the beginnings of a beaten path when they were ready, the trail heading down and North as all roads in the Shadow Realms seemed to lead.

They first came to a bog, avoiding the moist edges of the path that led to bubbling swamp. Thick fog masked anything in the distance, but there were sirens blaring up ahead, a constant ringing that raised the hair on his neck. It wasn't until they treaded closer to the bones of a village that he realized they weren't alarms at all—but screams. One after the other, when one weakened, another would begin. Every element in this world was laced with misery.

"*Skide*," Marrin whispered, rubbing her temples. "Let's get that damn ship and get the Hel out of here."

"Agreed." Lochare fell into step beside him. "Where is everyone?"

The village was built entirely on thin stilts, lifting the hollow homes out of the marsh. But despite the small torches burning on the bridges between each residence and the smokestacks wafting from the chimneys, there was a silence here that shouldn't have been, unsettling his nerves further.

"We're being watched," he mumbled. "Keep your eyes on the windows."

"And the water," one of them remarked.

Following her warning, he glanced below them into the murky waters that veined beneath the groaning deck. Faces, drifting just below the surface, stared up at them. All humanity washed away in their pale expressions as they stared upward with curiously wide eyes.

"Do you hear that?" Marrin spoke. The light sound of her steps fading as she came to a stop behind him.

"The screams?" her sister asked. "Aye, they haven't stopped since we cleared the fog. I'm half tempted to go back just to get some peace."

"No," she said. "A deeper sound, like a drum."

Vali stopped and tried to listen for something beyond the cries of agony. As he focused, he heard what she spoke of, a steady beat against the breeze. A sound both strange, yet familiar. The realization hit him all at once.

Wings.

"We need to hide! Find cover *now*." He spoke with enough urgency. The sisters followed him as he fled through the village. Searching for anything—an empty hut, a deck with an outcropping, something to conceal them from the creature in the sky as that deep, steady sound loomed louder with every beat.

But there was nothing. The homes started to space out, forcing the bridges connecting them to lengthen until they were even more exposed than before. Vali swung his head in every direction, but a white mist prevented him from seeing further than the next hut. The sisters were following on his heels, their breaths heavy from running with the weight of their cloaks and axes.

A roar split the screams, dominating any other sound in this realm with its power. Vali looked to the soot singed sky just in time to see a black dragon falling from an arc, smoke curling around its form as it descended toward the village. Nidhogg, the legendary monster, fell from the sky with his jaws stretched, and Vali snatched both the sisters by their collars to push them in front of him.

"Run!"

A hot wind burned his back as Nidhogg spread his fire upon the bridges behind them. The decking cracked beneath his boots, falling apart as his strides covered them. The dragon passed over as his flames narrowly missed Vali and the sisters, but the wailing behind them proved his fire had not been wasted. New screams joined the others as venomous fire burned through homes and heathens.

Nidhogg angled his wings and turned sharply, heading straight for them again. Marrin and Lochare split ways, forcing Vali to leave one of them as they avoided the spitting flames showering the earth once again.

"Marrin!" Lochare gasped as she turned around and found only Vali, but the way behind them had been reduced to splinters, nothing between the sisters but bog and black smoke from the burning remnants.

"I'll find her," Vali said. "Just get to higher ground, and we'll meet you there." He pointed to a spot near the end of the mist, which was clearing thanks to Nidhogg beating away the fog.

"I'm not going anywhere without my sister!" She shoved him to the side, and dropped into the marsh, her boots sinking into the mud as she searched for Marrin in the direction she left her. The elfin jumped in after her, wary to leave either of them so close to the water's edge.

"Marrin!" she called into the chaos. Bridges and homes collapsed, falling from their stilts and into the marsh. Nidhogg flew much closer to the rooflines, a woman in his jaws as she clawed the air. He gnawed on her legs, hardly noticing her struggle.

"Lochare, wait!" he shouted, but the sister was waist high in the marsh, wading through the murky waters to reach the other side.

Her body suddenly jerked to a stop. She slowly rotated to look at Vali, brown eyes wide with fear. "Something's got me," she shrieked, before a white hand snatched her by the braid and pulled her under.

Without hesitating, Vali shed the cloak around his shoulders and dove in after her, blinking through the toxic waters as they burned his eyes and skin. His hand held a dagger, and with his opposite, he produced a light to illuminate the dark bog, finding a trail of bubbles as Lochare sank from sight.

He swam after her tracks with no idea where or when it would end. White figures blurred past him, shying away from the Light in his palm. He found her near the jagged floor of a sea shelf, a steep slope to an abyss on the other side. Ghostly creatures with webbed hands and scaley figures tore at her clothes and her body, drawing blood with their long fingernails that curled like ribbons from her skin. She thrashed and kicked, but more hands joined the others, stilling her in place, suspended in the water as they feasted on her flesh. Her blood called others from the dark depths, swimming out the abyss with tails as long as Vali's entire body.

Vali strengthened the Light until it blinded the pale demons, and they shrieked with pain. One by one, they unwrapped themselves from her thrashing form, retreating to their darkness in the marsh. He pulled her back to the surface, her movements weak and forcing him to compensate for the drag of her clothes. When they finally reached the surface again, he shoved Lochare on the soggy bank, heaving himself over the edge beside her.

She sputtered, coughing up the water she swallowed. Her cloak was shredded, her skin riddled with deep scratches, most notably the ones across her cheek. When Vali caught his own breath, he asked, "Are you all right?"

She didn't answer, only nodded with a quick jerk of her chin. But her eyes continued to dart around the marsh, searching for her sister.

He gripped her shoulder and shook her until she looked at him. "I'll find Marrin. Just please, do as I ask and head toward the high ground."

She clenched her jaw with disapproval. "What if she fell into the bog?"

He shifted to his feet, surveying the surrounding wreckage. "She didn't. I think I saw her cross the bridge before Nidhogg set it on fire. Go, Lochare. I have magic to defend me here. You do not."

"Fine," she snapped. "But don't get yourself fucking killed. We're too close to finding Ailsa for you to ruin it now."

Under different circumstances, Vali might have made fun of her worry over him. For now, he appreciated it. "Stop trying to get devoured by water demons so I can focus on staying alive."

She was about to say something when the village suffered another attack. This time, Nidhogg tore through one hut and pulled out three others with his talons, a group of people hanging from his jaws already. Without letting Lochare change her mind, he took off through the bog and climbed up the broken remains of the bridge where they last saw Marrin.

The platforms were flooded with bodies trying to flee the village before Nidhogg struck again. Vali darted between them all, calling Marrin's name above the shouts and cries of the crowd pushing the opposite way.

"Vali!" His name was called from a nearby platform—Marrin. But he couldn't get to her from his position. Not with the people running against him, nor with the bridge connecting the two being on fire. He'd take one step across and fall straight back into the water.

He assessed her quickly, noting how the smoke stained her face black and how the tail of her cloak had been burned away. But she was standing on her own feet, which was more than he had expected at this point. "Follow the crowd," he shouted at her, pointing in the direction he knew her sister was heading.

Marrin, being the more agreeable sister, only nodded and started in the direction he commanded. Vali did the same, taking a different route with the remaining connections that still stood in the wreckage of the village. He was just about to step out onto solid ground when a heavy hand jerked him back.

"You will answer for your crimes, elfin!"

Vali looked behind him to see a burly man with a bald head and scraggly red beard. His eyes were lined with kohl and disdain. Before he could react, other men came to join him, holding Vali square by the shoulders and surrounded at all sides.

"He goes to Bjorn for sentencing. He must pay for what he's done to the village."

"What are you talking about?" he asked.

"Everyone knows you must go inside when the Dragon Spire is lit. You led Nidhogg straight here! He wouldn't have attacked us if he hadn't seen you three walking around in the first place. You have brought ruin and suffering upon us all, and you will face the consequences," he growled.

Vali struggled against the grips of the men around him, feigning concern over his situation, not letting them know they were playing right into his plans. "Please, I've only just arrived—" He could have easily swept these men away with the flick of his hand, but he was curious, and the name sparked his interest further. If Bjorn was in charge around here, he was exactly who Vali needed to speak with.

"Where are the other two that were with you?" the man asked, looking around.

"Gone," Vali answered. "Probably perished in the dragon fire."

This seemed to satisfy him. He motioned for Vali's captors to take him away. "Bring him to Bloodblade. That pearly skin of his will be a fine addition to the main sail."

CHAPTER 29
AILSA

They snuck through the mountain, attracting little attention as Ailsa wore the stag mask. The skull was suffocating, smelled of Vidar's breath and sweat, but it kept the giants from looking twice at her, so she was thankful for the convenience of its cover.

As they descended deeper into the lower tunnels, Ailsa tested the new connection of this blood rune. Her right hand was covered in red markings that were only visible if she concentrated hard enough to see them. Every emotion from Vidar, every conscious thought he made traveled down their bond until the fear pulsing from her counterpart was overwhelming.

Odin's eye. Was he always like this? She thought it was his silence that made him timid, but she heard every word in his thoughts now and realized it was just who he was at his core. In the time it took them to reach the stables where the fire horses were tended, Ailsa had practiced how to block his emotions from slipping constantly down the bond, if only to give herself a bit of peace.

We'll need to steal a bálhross if we're to journey to the Mourning Mountains. Vidar spoke, shoving through her boundaries.

I'm an Otsman, Vidar. Stealing is in my blood.

His shoulders rose with a tense breath in front of her. *Don't be fingering that new blade of yours just yet, Ailsa. I have a plan.*

She realized she was touching the pommel of her new weapon, feeling more like herself with a short sword at her hip and a dagger sheathed in the holder around her thigh. Vidar snagged her blade on the way down here, grabbing a lengthy one for himself. Ailsa wondered by the way it hung flimsy around his hips if he had any idea how to use it.

They came to a pair of rolling doors, parted to reveal a type of stable cut into the stone. Beyond the stalls, another pair of similar doors were open, a hot breeze rolling through the opening as they accessed the outside world.

A single worker was tending to the fire horses, the giant wearing thick gloves to protect his skin from hot cinders blown from their noses and flicked off their mane of flames. Vidar motioned for her to stay back, instructing her down the bond to hide herself. Reluctantly, she ducked into an empty stall.

"Sigurd?" the giant spoke as Vidar approached. "What are you doing down here?"

Through the slats of the stall, Ailsa watched as Vidar gestured to the *bálhross* the giant was tending.

"You need a horse?"

Vidar nodded.

The man sighed, rubbing his beard and smearing black ash across his chin. "I'm not sure I can let you take one, Sig. You've been there for me a lot, but Nerissa would enchant my balls to fall off if she learned I was letting you sneak out. They gave us strict orders—"

Vidar pulled something out of his pocket that silenced the giant as he showed him the small container. He took it from the silent man, eyes wide with greed. "On second thought, I was taking a piss when you snuck in. Whatever trouble you get in, Sigurd, it will not involve me. Are we clear?"

Vidar nodded again, and Ailsa felt his relief like a cool river wash down her arm. The giant scurried off, closing the doors to the stable behind him.

"What did you give him?" Ailsa asked out loud now that they were alone.

Burn cream. The giants aren't allowed to use the tonics, so they're a valuable commodity to trade.

She joined him in saddling the *bálhross*. "How do you have access to the supply if it's so rare and valuable?"

I make it.

Ailsa wasn't expecting that answer. Vidar glanced over at her as he tightened the straps around the horse's belly. *When I first came to this mountain, I discovered a spring that led to the outside. I use the space to grow my own stash of herbs for tonics and therapeutic purposes. My mother was a healer.*

Ailsa smiled. "Mine was, too. You'll have to teach me what you put in this cream. I'm assuming it was you then who left the capsule on my pillow?" When he nodded, she added, "It worked well on Erik. Almost too well. I didn't count on him healing so quickly."

I'd be more than happy to show you when we return.

Ailsa didn't even want to think of returning, to give Erik a chance to shame her for leaving without him—or whatever else he could think of to humiliate her further.

Do not worry about Erik. Nerissa will keep him in line.

Caught up in her thoughts, she almost forgot he could hear them. "Will you get in trouble for aiding me?"

A jolt of lightning flickered up their bond. A nervous tingle chased through her nerves.

No. But she tasted something bitter on her tongue as he said it. A lie. *Do not worry about me, Ailsa. I've done much worse and faced far harsher consequences. Let me do this.*

"Why?" she asked. "Why are you helping me in the first place if you work for the witches?"

Vidar came around the horse to look at her, gaze searing through the mask. *Because I didn't know kindness still existed in the Nine until you came to the mountain. And I think you have a better chance of slaying the dragon than Erik. I want to get out of Muspell just as much as you do.* He motioned with his chin for her to mount the *bálhross*.

She settled herself in the saddle, and Vidar sat behind her, taking the reins in his hands as she gripped the horn. "Are they cruel to you?" she asked. Judging by the fear that pulsed from him like a heartbeat, Ailsa could guess they'd given him a reason to be afraid.

Sometimes. He whispered down their bond. *But sometimes I deserve it.*

Without giving her time to think of a response, Vidar slapped the reins to lead them out of the stables and into the fiery lands of Muspell, the failing light leashing some of the heat as they traveled. Fafnir settled in the center of the map, where a volcano gushed rivers of molten fire that had scourged the earth for centuries. It was said that the rest of the Nine were formed from this fire and the ice it melted from Niflheim, the water eventually forming the first giant, Ymir, whose body became the template for everything else.

It was difficult to imagine any kind of life could come from a place so desolate, however. Ailsa pulled up the cowl sitting around her neck to shield her cheeks from the scorching breeze, her skin already stripping away as they traveled closer to the dragon's home.

Any idea how you will slay the dragon, Ailsa? Vidar asked through the bond.

She shrugged, feeling his chest skim her back as he leaned over the saddle. She told him, *I want to put eyes on the area first. Have you learned anything about his approach from his attacks on the mountain?*

His answer came quickly. *Only that he likes to swoop low to the ground as he breathes his fire. I always wondered if perhaps his range was too short, which was why he had to come so close in the first place.*

Ailsa chewed her lip in thought. Fafnir wasn't a true dragon, but a dwarf. It would make sense if he was weak in areas one might think a beast like him was most powerful. He might need to get close to harm them, but so did she. Killing him might not be a battle of strength and valor, but a means of strategy.

Vidar pulled out a canteen of water he had packed on the *bálhross*. They had been traveling for hours, and even as the sun set and the valley cooled, the heat still smoldered from the earth, baking them as they traveled.

How did you come to work for the witches? Ailsa asked him to distract herself from the miserable ride.

He didn't answer at first, but she felt a flurry of thoughts race down the bond before he could catch them. The face of a giantess, broad bloody hands, the teeth of a wolf, the arms of a witch, fire and smoke and the distant sound of screams echoing with the memory. Each image so different from the previous, it was impossible to connect them.

I am surprised you haven't realized who I am by now.

Her brow furrowed. *What do you mean?*

My eyes. They give my lineage away. It is why I usually wear the mask, as my eyes make the fire giants angry, reminding them who trapped them here.

She gasped, suddenly connecting the dots. *You're one of the Aesir! But that would mean...*

I am part god, yes. But I rejected my father's line long ago. Vidar's annoyance prickled her skin as she felt his words. *My mother was a giantess, daughter of a lord. My Aesir father thought she was beautiful despite his hatred for Jotun. She thought she could change his mind toward her kind, that their relationship could heal the animosity between the frost giants and the Aesir.*

By the dread dripping down the bond, Ailsa knew his mother must have been gravely mistaken.

He continued his tale. *Her father was furious when he heard she was pregnant and demanded my father to either wed her or take her back to Asgard to care for us. He refused, of course, as they disregard any Jotun offspring who have no use to them. Worst of all for my mother, the only thing I inherited from the god was the Aesir gold in my eyes. I have no magic, no power, and no skills beyond what she taught me.*

Ailsa felt the wind from her chest sail away as she sighed. She identified with his mother, getting pregnant by a man who did not love her, who abandoned her. This story could have easily been her own. She asked him then, *What happened to her, Vidar?* Although she could guess the answer by the way he spoke of her in the past tense.

They were fighting one day, my mother and the Aesir, and he killed her. She only wanted him to make things right between him and me and her, and he shook her so hard he killed her.

Vidar attempted to throw up his own walls, disconnecting

from the pain filtered from his memories. But her heart broke, still feeling his sorrow pull at the thread of their connection. Though his thoughts were silent, his grief was loud as a gjallarhorn declaring the start of a battle.

Everyone eventually believed my mother's death was an accident, and they thought I had been traumatized into silence, but my father marked me with a rune that night. He took my voice instead of killing me, so I could not speak of what he did. The Aesir were at war with the Vanir at the time, and they couldn't afford the frost giants joining the fight as well.

Ailsa had no words to offer him comfort. She could only shake her head with disbelief and disapproval. *How did you end up serving Fenrir?*

He replied, *There is an old pass that stretches from Jotunheim to Alfheim, where Fenrir was hiding in the decades that followed the war. I heard rumors of the Great Wolf and his plans to swallow Odin, and I sought the witches in the Ironwood. Nerissa was one of them. She took me in and taught me how to serve them and in exchange, allowed me to play a part in taking revenge against the Aesir.*

Ailsa nodded, though the movement was mechanical as she processed the rest of his story. He had been with Fenrir this entire time then—since the fall of Gullveig and the beginning of her family's curse. Whatever loyalty the wolven and witches had to the Great Wolf had been sealed by time and ideals of redemption.

And what then, Vidar? she asked him. *You let Fenrir kill Odin and Surtur destroy Asgard, and there will be no one to protect us from the fire giants when they come after the rest of the realms. The gods might be dishonorable, but the rest of us will pay for their mistakes.*

Ice chilled over their connection, and she sensed she had just nudged a sensitive place in the silent man. *I never said I was on the good side, Ailsa. But last I checked, you are handing Surtur the very flame that will destroy the gods in the end.*

His response was a whip to her words, slicing her with the sting of the truth. Her mission was selfish, her reasons even worse, but it was either she retrieved the flame and get her memories or watch Erik die trying and rot in Muspell. She would not wait for an elfin to come save her like a maiden that needed rescuing. She needed to remember who she was and the journey that brought her here, if only to choose the right path ahead.

The well showed her many fates but avoided telling her own, the knowledge she sacrificed on her end. Ailsa believed this was because it was still being decided on, like a blank page the future hadn't quite decided on writing just yet. A fathomless number of potentials and perhaps only one of them would see them all alive at the end of the worlds.

I didn't mean to upset you. Vidar spoke gently down the bond once more.

She patted his arm and grinned. *I can take a bit of brutal honesty. Never apologize for speaking the truth. Yes, I am hoping to hand Surtur the weapon that will destroy the gods, but I saw the ending the Norns have planned for him. Fire spreads, Vidar, and it burns everything it touches regardless of who starts it. It is the most uncontrollable element in existence.*

He shifted in his seat behind her. *Are we still talking about the flame of Muspell or yourself?*

She laughed and choked at once on the soot in the breeze. Vidar shoved a hand over her mouth, quieting her hacking. She shoved him away and was about to ask what his problem was until her eyes caught something gold against the rusted world. A winged beast descending into the heart of the realm. Fafnir.

It took a great deal of convincing Vidar that climbing into a cooled lava pit was a good idea. The crater in the earth provided necessary coverage, concealing them from the dragon while also giving her time to think of a plan. The terrain leading to the volcano was treacherous by itself, even without a fire breathing dragon watching the world below.

Ailsa could hear his thoughts rambling through the bond. He was frightened in fear's purest form, unable to keep his hands from shaking enough to help wrap her fighting arm with a tight brace.

"Vidar, you need to get yourself together. You're not the one facing the dragon, so I'm not sure why you're so afraid!"

I am worried for you, Ailsa. If you die, Nerissa and Erik will fight over the opportunity to kill me.

She snorted. "How good to know you care about my well-being." Before he could retort, she held up a hand in front of his lips. "I need you to shut off your anxious thoughts for a moment. If I'm to concentrate on the dragon, I need silence on your end to think straight. Hand me that bow."

Vidar handed her a bow he equipped from the archery room on their way to the stables, along with a quiver filled with arrows. The bow itself was made from a material she could only compare to sapwood, both sturdy and flexible that was neither too heavy for her to carry with one arm nor too stiff. The arrows themselves were fletched with black feathers and iron fittings, and she loaded the string with one of them as they waited for Fafnir to approach.

Ailsa briefly explained to him her plan to settle his concerns. She would use the pits to her advantage, jumping to each one to avoid Fafnir's attacks. The old fire beds were easy enough to climb out of quickly, yet close enough she could easily find one to duck inside should the need arise.

And how will you kill him? Vidar's brows rose half an inch.

She hadn't gotten quite that far yet. "Dragons have soft underbellies. Their weak spot is always below the neck. I'll have to strike him there." With no idea how she knew such a fact, Ailsa turned to look for the dragon now scaling the horizon.

Satisfied with her open ended strategy, she sat back against the uneven crater and looked at him. "Vidar, I want to ask you something before I go."

Anything, Ailsa.

She swallowed, feeling the ashes in her throat despite the cowl filtering the air on the ride here. "You are a frost giant, which means you lived in the fae realms for quite some time, right?"

I was a child when my mother died, but yes. I grew up there.

Ailsa bit her lip before asking, "Have you ever heard of fae enchanting another's mind? Either for love or politics?"

But Vidar's face twisted with confusion. *Fae magic does not control or manipulate, that is only done so with sedir. Not even the gods could do such a thing with their power.*

"And bonds?" she asked. "Do they have those?" She held up her hand to imply their blood rune.

They have mates, Ailsa, both blood mates and life mates, but it is not like our bond, I assure you.

She thought she felt something comparable to disappointment in his words, quickly shaking them off when she translated what he meant. Her heart raced, a cold sweat defiling her palms. Vidar was being honest with her—had to be, or she'd feel it.

Mates.

Is that why Vali looked at her with such a light in his eyes? Why he nearly died fighting Erik in the garden that night she was taken? Why her body reacted to him in such a way she felt like he was still controlling her despite Erik breaking the elfin's so called "enchantment?"

Was she Vali's mate? Was that this *spell* everyone kept talking about? Because if that were true, then it changed everything. If their bond had been something she had chosen...

"I'm going to kill them all when I get my memories back," she whispered.

Ailsa gripped her bow with a fresh flame in her chest and faced the dragon, now beginning to fly in her direction. She waited until Fafnir was nearly upon her. These witches had indeed taken from her. Perhaps the greatest treasure of her heart, and she'd become a fire that rivaled that of Muspell's, catching anyone and everything in her path until they were all ash beneath her feet.

The dragon swooped lower, gold wings shining red as the moonlight filtered through the thin skin filling his wingspan. Ailsa heaved herself over the edge and drew her arrow, letting the fetching brush her cheek and soothe her soul into stillness. She looked down the spine and held her breath, setting her aim on the dragon's chest, determined to strike it straight through the heart and make this quick.

Fafnir shrieked, finally noticing her standing there. But he caught sight of her too late. The moment came, and she let the arrow loose, letting it soar toward the dragon's heart as she released her breath.

And it flew true.

CHAPTER 30
VALI

They tied him between two posts on a stage overlooking a black bay. The legendary ship docked at the end of a long pier, the moonlight highlighting the formation of bones and skin, nails and teeth, until it was glowing silver on top of a glossy harbor. Hundreds of people stood between him and the ship, as they laid him out on display to pay for his crimes. Of all the places he believed justice would find him, Nastrond was not high on the list.

They ripped his shirt from his back, exposing his bare torso to the man they called the Carver. Who apparently was the one who provided building material for the ship's integrity, which Vali was both simultaneously appalled and impressed with. But there was no blade that could cut him here. Not that he had seen in their sheaths.

He looked for the sisters but didn't see them amongst the faces staring up at him. A rough looking crowd they were, many of them with scars marring their bodies—teeth and appendages missing. They chanted Bjorn's name until a man joined him on the platform, silencing them with a wave of his muscled arm.

He looked Vali over, eyes settling either on his ears or the markings running down his neck. Vali didn't know which. He circled twice before standing in front of him, blocking his view of the bay with a broad chest covered in ink, detailing his accomplishments during his living years. This heathen had dark red hair that fell to his shoulders, a beard neatly cut around his jaw, and a light brown fur draped over his shoulders, falling behind him like a cape.

He held himself like a king, leaving little room to doubt this was Bjorn Bloodblade, the same man who brought a two hundred year curse upon his family. The reason women like Ailsa had suffered every day of their brief lives. Bjorn was fortunate Vali's hands were tied, or he would have ripped his head from his thick neck and used the holes in his face as a holder for his drinking horn. The ship had become inspiring in the way of his motivations.

Bjorn didn't stall for introductions, but got right to the point of their meeting. "It is said you lured the dragon to one of our villages, elfin. Every home there is destroyed. The venom from Nidhogg's fire ate away everything and everyone it touched. What do you have to say for yourself?"

Vali shrugged against the tension in the ropes. "I don't know what you're talking about. I just arrived in Nastrond and was in the middle of the village when the dragon attacked. There was nowhere to hide."

"And no one offered you shelter?" he asked.

This made the elfin laugh. "Are you joking? Is there anyone in Nastrond who would have assisted me?"

"It is our law, elfin." Bjorn's face remained hard as stone.

"When the Dragon Spire burns," he pointed toward a pale tower piercing the sky just north of where they stood now, "everyone must hurry inside, no matter where you are. Nidhogg will attack if he sees moving bodies. He loves to chew on our corpses, suck on our blood like a leech until he drains us dry and nothing remains. No matter how much we hate each other here, we hate Nidhogg the most. Someone should have offered you shelter."

"Well, there you have it, then. It wasn't my fault."

Bjorn held up a finger. "I did not say you were innocent." He motioned to the Carver. Vali heard the floorboards groan as the mountain of flesh neared him from behind. His heart was racing now, so loud was his pulse he wondered if the crowd could hear it from where they watched.

"I am their king, elfin. Surely you understand that someone must pay for the suffering of my people. What kind of ruler would I be to let you go free without teaching you a lesson?"

"I will not give any part of my body to your boat," Vali spat through his teeth. The rope dug into his wrist, pinching his skin. It would take only a thought to burn this entire platform to the ground, but he remained patient.

Bjorn stepped closer so only Vali could hear his next words. His dark eyes wandered over his bare chest. "What about just for me then? I'm sure, between the two of us, we could work something out. Something that would benefit us both."

The elfin snorted. "How about you hand over your ship, Bjorn, and I will forget this little show *your* people have made of me."

The king considered his threat for a heartbeat before a

wild grin spread across his cheeks. "You came for Naglfar?" He turned sideways to look at the ship draped in moonlight. "One of the largest ships in the Nine, a vessel I designed with the assistance of my most talented boat makers to hold every life-less soul in this realm to the land of Muspell. That is the ship you expect me to give to you?" When Vali nodded, Bjorn's smile fell at last. "You come bringing dragon fire and ruin—"

"I can do much worse than dragon fire, Bjorn Bloodblade," Vali murmured. Little flames slipped from his fingertips, traveling the length of the rope around his forearms until it burned to ash at their feet. Bjorn's eyes widened as he took a step away.

"My name is Vali, and I need your ship to travel to Muspell. You can either join me, Bjorn, or watch me sail away. Because either way, I am taking the Naglfar to the realm of fire, with or without your people."

"It is not time yet," Bjorn stammered, even as he retreated. "She said there will be signs."

"Signs of what?" Vali asked, taking a step closer each time the king withdrew.

"Signs of the end," he answered. "The witch that blessed my family before I died, she said there would be signs to watch out for, ones that suggested Ragnarok would soon begin, and we could sail forth to Muspell where the fire giants would wait for our army."

Vali spat a curse. Of course, the witches had been orchestrating this from the beginning. They would expect the ship then, which was why they were all hiding in Muspell. "Who was this witch?"

Bjorn shrugged. "Her name was Angrboda, or something like that."

The name triggered nothing useful. But that meant little to Vali. "Bjorn, you are making a mistake. Why would you want to help the witches and the ones they serve destroy your gods? Destroy the Nine?"

"Look at us, elfin!" Bjorn spread his arms wide, gesturing to the crowd below. "You have been here for a few hours, but we have been trapped here for hundreds of years. What other choice do we have to get out of here? It is eternal punishment or freedom, and I will support whoever gives me the latter."

Vali wanted to say they didn't deserve to leave this place. If Hel and Astrid had been honest, and only the worst souls in existence came here, then they shouldn't have the opportunity to afflict the worlds once more with their wickedness. If the witches intended to include these heathens in their forces, then he needed to keep them in this realm and far from the front lines of whatever war they were planning.

"I can't let you do that, Bjorn." The elfin rolled his shoulders back, ready for resistance.

He tossed his head back with a barking laugh. "Do you think you can stop me now because you have a little magic in your fingers, elfin?" He scraped his sword from its sheath, a mortal blade he had most likely been buried with. A fine weapon, terrifying to anyone without fae skin.

"I'll see you on your knees, one way or another," Bjorn growled, his head lowering to glare at Vali like a mountain cat about to pounce. But he spoke to the Carver. "Bring out the others."

Vali turned to see Marrin and Lochare being shoved onto the stage. Their thrashing was so violent, it took four burly men to subjugate them, to push them on their knees before Bjorn where he had once been tied. The Carver stepped behind Lochare with a butcher's blade.

"Do not lay a finger on either of them," Vali hissed. His blood roared, power spilling from his pores, fighting to be released at the sight of Ailsa's sisters within chopping distance.

"We might not be able to physically hurt you, elfin," Bjorn continued. "But there is still a debt to be paid for what you made me lose today. And if you want to ride on *my* ship," he tapped his chest with the pommel of his sword, "then you must make your contribution. So choose, elfin. Which sister shall we flay to reinforce the main mast?"

Vali looked at both of the sisters, whose faces did not betray a flinch of fear. But their eyes, the same ones they shared with their youngest sister, filled with an emotion he recognized. One he saw in Ailsa when he was burning at the stake. She didn't let him suffer, and he wouldn't allow her sisters to either. They'd take the ship another way.

"No," he said.

Bjorn rolled his eyes. "I can assure you, we do not let any part of a corpse go to waste. Choose, or I will choose for you."

"I will volunteer," Lochare said. "Spare Marrin and pick me, Vali. If it means you both get to Muspell, then choose me."

"Fuck off, Lochare," Marrin spat at her sister. "I'd rather they use my skull as a toilet than let them harm you."

"And I'd be the first one to shit in you if you did such a thing. Absolutely not," her sister argued.

Vali's lips twitched. As they fought between themselves, he set his attention on the Dragon Spire, fingers curling ever so slightly to spark a flame. It caught, but the fire wasn't big enough to draw anyone's attention just yet, not when something more interesting was happening on the platform.

He sighed a long breath, letting the wind follow his silent command and blow a warm breeze across the land to stoke the flame in the tower. The orange blaze was now tall and consuming.

"Dragon!" a bystander shouted in the crowd, finally catching on. Attention shifted to the Spire, panic ensuing as the massive crowd pushed and trampled their way back to their homes, shoving away whoever was in their path to find shelter as soon as possible. These people were afraid of nothing but Nidhogg. The dragon was the only weapon in the elfin's arsenal, so he threatened the people of Nastrond like he had the monster on a leash.

Using the distraction, he shoved the Carver and his assistants with a forceful wind that knocked them off the platform and into the crowd wrapping behind the stage, where Vali lost sight of them beneath the hundreds of stampeding boots. Marrin and Lochare were already shimmying off their bindings. Bjorn shouted for them all to stay in line, but his warnings fell on deaf ears.

"Throw me a weapon," he called to the sisters, and they tossed the nearest knife the Carver had dropped.

A decent sized carving knife, Vali used his magic to still the heathen king in place on the platform, freezing the bloodless bones in his legs. Flipping the curved blade between his fingers, he pressed the knife's edge to Bjorn's neck, cleaving a thin line below a scar where someone had once bled him out. Vali wondered who had beaten him to it.

"Elfin, wait," he spoke. "Don't do this. This was hundreds of years of work and waiting. Do not take away the last hope these people have of escaping this hole in Helheim. Let's work this out, I'm sure we could come to—"

"Shut the Hel up, Bjorn," Vali said as he snatched the man's hair and exposed his throat. "You've had your turn to speak tonight. Now I will have mine. You deserve this hole and every ounce of suffering that comes from it. For what you made your family go through, for what you made my Ailsa live with, I will make sure you never know joy again. But do not worry, heathen. I plan on bringing you with me to Muspell."

Bjorn swallowed against the knife at his neck. "You do?"

Vali smiled then. "Yes." Weaving the roots of his crimson hair between his fingers, Vali cleaved right through his thick neck with the Carver's knife. He hadn't realized how much he hated the ancestor of his mate until he was on the other side of his blade.

He turned back to the sisters, blood spurting from the head he still held by a chunk of hair. "Shall we board the next ship?" he asked them.

Their eyes were wide as they eyed him carefully, but eventually Marrin and Lochare each nodded and slowly rose to their feet.

Just as he stepped off the platform with Bjorn's severed head, a familiar sound made him pause. The thump of a slow drum growing louder with every beat. Dread filled his heart, turning to ice as he looked at the sky.

Nidhogg had returned.

Without hesitating to wonder if Vali had called him somehow with the flame or if the dragon's presence was merely a coincidence, he shouted for the sisters to run and devoured the distance with his long strides between the platform and the docks. The sisters were nearly on his heels as they dashed toward Naglfar.

"Vali, wait!" Lochare shouted.

Growling, Vali stopped, nearly touching the gangplank. But he looked back to find Marrin had fallen through the boardwalk, and her sister had turned around to help her.

The elfin flung the head into the boat and ran to assist

them, using his magic to assist Marrin before Lochare even reached her. But just as she stood to her feet again on the dock, dripping murky water that steamed her cloak, a blur of black scales separated her from view.

"Marrin!" Lochare screamed. Her voice saturated with agony, as if she had been the one between the dragon's teeth instead of her sister. But she was as helpless as Vali, watching the dragon fly further up the shore with Marrin between his jaws. Her screams echoing over the still water, crying out to her other half.

Lochare turned slowly to look at the elfin, who was already passing her to return to the mainland. She grabbed him by the arm. "What are you doing?"

"What does it look like? We cannot leave Marrin! Someone must know where he brings his victims, a nest or—"

"Vali, stop!" she shouted, her normally tempered voice quivering. "You cannot save everyone if you want to help Ailsa. You'll never make it out of this gods forsaken realm if you try."

"I cannot leave her behind, Lochare. She's Ailsa's sister, she's..."

"Family," she finished for him, her voice softening to a tone he didn't realize she owned. "Aye, Vali. We are family, and I know you do not want to do this. But right now, my youngest sister is still alive and in trouble, and there is only one male in all the Nine looking for her. So you need to continue, or she'll never be free."

"But what about Marrin?" he asked, shaking his head in disagreement as he watched tears smear the black paint across her eyes. "Are you suggesting we go on without her?"

"I didn't say I was coming with you," she muttered. "I will stay and go back for my sister. You will go on and take care of my other one. This is the only way we can protect them both."

Vali glanced at the ship made of heathen parts and back to Lochare. "Are you sure?" he asked. Though there was no debating with a Ledgersdóttir. There was too much certainty in her grip as she held him by the arm. Too much locked away behind that proud jaw that clenched, hiding a tremble. Lochare dug something out of her pocket and handed it to him. He unfolded a piece of cloth to find a rune drawn on the scrap of fabric.

"It is from Freya," she explained. "The goddess didn't tell me what it means, only that it would help Ailsa see your virtue. Freya said once you proved the same to us with your actions, to give you this. And honestly, I should have given it to you sooner. I think..." Lochare grimaced like admitting this was painful. "No, I know Ailsa deserves to remember you, Vali."

He had no words, could only stand there staring at the rune like everything he had lost was given back to him in a single missing piece. He had never seen this lettering before, but from Freya's clues, it was certain to be helpful. This could be the start of it all, the answer to mending their broken bond in the palm of his hand. Lochare did not know of the gift she had given him.

"Thank you," he said. His mind committed the rune to retention before tucking the drawing away for safekeeping. "I am grateful you both agreed to join me on this journey. I wouldn't have made it beyond the front without you."

Lochare nodded in agreement and slapped him hard on the arm to disburse the sentiment growing warm between them. "Go find my sister, Vali," she said before running back down the dock, where the citizens of Nastrond were resurfacing from their homes. He hoped this wasn't the last time he would see the sisters, despite how much he couldn't stand them in the beginning.

Realizing what little time he had until someone would come looking for the rest of Bjorn and the elfin who beheaded him, Vali quickly boarded the boat and began untying the masts with his magic. He did the job of an entire crew, pulling up the anchor, setting the sails in the direction opposite of Nastrond, taking position behind the helm.

The bones soldered together groaned as the ship left the dock, skins sutured together filled with wind the elfin coaxed into a favorable direction. Upper limbs formed spokes in the wheel, turning the ship as he set his destination toward Muspell. The fiery realm that lay just across from this cold, dead world.

Vali found the head he had taken and lifted it, showing Bjorn the shrinking land of Nastrond. The eyes in his head were still wide from the shock of being mutilated. "You see that, heathen king? I am taking your ship and leaving all your wicked friends behind. Do you want to know why I brought you instead of them?"

The elfin tied his head by his hair on the post overlooking the way ahead. He told Bjorn, who Vali knew could still hear him, "I will lay your head at my lady's feet, and when she sees I have taken vengeance for her family, I will throw your head to the same wolves you would have fought beside. And no one will ever remember Bjorn Bloodblade ever again. I will erase you from history and the afterlife for eternity."

Leaving the king behind, Vali found a chair made of stripped clean skeletons and collapsed into the rest waiting there. There should have been something disturbing about captaining a ship such as Naglfar, to steer a vessel of bones, skin, and neatly stacked fingernails. But the elfin had one thing on his mind: the last leg of the journey to his lady.

Anger, hatred, malice. *Vengeance.*

But now... something else to fight for.

Redemption.

CHAPTER 31
AILSA

Her arrow struck the golden dragon in the left side of his chest, avoiding anything vital. It wasn't enough to bring down Fafnir, but it was more than necessary to piss him off.

With a hoarse wail into the night sky, the dragon shifted his wings until he was looking down at her, searching for the one who harmed him enough to spill a small spurt of gray colored blood. Ailsa reloaded before he could inhale a priming breath, let it fly before he could let loose his fire.

As soon as the soft fletchings grazed her cheek like a farewell kiss, Ailsa dashed for cover, slipping down a hard lava pit to avoid the heat of Fafnir's flame without waiting to see if her arrow had struck.

She couldn't linger in the crater too long. Without decent coverage anywhere out here in the wasteland of Muspell, no place was completely safe, but a moving target was more difficult to hit than a sitting one. As soon as the dragon ceased his attack, she was darting for another pit, bow and arrow ready.

Arrow after arrow sunk into the soft flesh of the dragon's

underbelly, but the beast hardly seemed to notice. Ailsa aimed for his wings, but the translucent skin between his bones was too thick for the arrow to cleave through. They bounced right off and fell back to the dusty red earth.

The quiver strapped to her back was lightening as she lost more ammunition to the dragon's flesh, but still Fafnir did not falter. He barely seemed to weaken despite the iron sticking out of him like metal splinters.

This isn't working, Ailsa. Vidar sent the thought down their blood bond.

She took a large gulp of air to settle her racing heart as she answered. *I can see that, Vidar.* Her words were dry. *But I don't exactly have any other option unless you can think of something else?*

Yes. Let's flee and hope the bálhross can outrun a dragon.

Ailsa rolled her eyes at his cowardice, setting another arrow across the string. *I'm not leaving without that flame.*

As if hearing their conversation, Fafnir sent a large breath of fire at the edge of the same pit she hid inside, and Ailsa felt as if her skin would melt away from the proximity alone. Black smoke filled the hole in the earth, forcing her to crawl out on her hands and knees, gasping for a clear breath.

She watched the dragon circle back, eyes on her with earnest. His flame might be short, but it was relentless and hot, and Ailsa didn't know how much longer she could keep up this dance. Especially when he wasn't showing any signs of weakening. She looked down her bond and told Vidar, *I need your help.*

But nothing returned. He went silent, leaving her on her own until the next round. Ailsa stood in time to dodge another line of flames, thankful her endurance had supported her this far.

Vidar, please! I cannot slay a dragon alone!

His words were a whisper. *I'm sorry, Ailsa. I cannot help you.*

A roar of frustration slipped through her teeth as she searched for the original pit. While Fafnir was looping back and couldn't see her, she slipped into the hole where Vidar was curled into himself. His knees tucked into his chest, eyes slammed shut like he could will away the world around him like it was a bad dream.

Ailsa dropped her bow to grip him by the collar, shaking him with every word. "What the Hel is wrong with you? Why are you abandoning me now?"

His eyes flew open, golden gaze trapped in fear. *I told you, I cannot help.*

"Why?" she asked, but shouted like a demand.

He pushed away her hand with a grimace, souring his face. *Because I am a coward. And I am afraid of fire.*

Ailsa scoffed and gestured to herself, now covered in black soot. "Do you think I am not afraid, Vidar? I do not wake up hoping to face dragons, nor do I particularly enjoy the idea of being burned alive. I have too much to live for to die right now, but I still choose to fight."

You are strong and skilled and more powerful than anyone in this realm. I am nothing. His self deprecation was obvious in the way he could not meet her gaze, his shame buried behind a hatred for himself.

She put her hand beneath his jaw and turned his face back to hers, hoping her tenderness embraced his troubled heart, wanting him to feel her confidence in him. "There will always be an enemy who is stronger. Evil that feels too great to challenge will always exist. But that does not mean we should lie down and give up. Power dwells not in strength or magic, but in faith. Believe in yourself for a moment, Vidar, and nothing in the Nine will ever make you weak again."

Using the dagger sheathed around her thigh, Ailsa pricked her finger until a bead of blood formed at the tip and brought it to his forehead.

What are you doing? he asked. Though his tone was cautious, he didn't move away from her touch as she drew a rune across his forehead.

"Someone once told me that there is power in all things," she said. When she was done, she wiped her fingers clean and picked up her bow. "And all things can be powerful. I'm going to bait him over this pit, Vidar, and when I do, I need you to be ready with your sword."

Through the blood bond, she felt the solid wave of courage rise as the rune took effect. Vidar took a shuddering breath before unsheathing the long sword at his hip and awkwardly held it at his side. *This is your fault if things go badly.*

Ailsa smiled and peered over the bed of brittle obsidian, finding Fafnir still searching for her in the multitude of craters defacing the earth. Slipping one of her last arrows from the quiver, the dull pain in her finger sparked an idea. She used the head of the arrow to prick another and drew a rune on its head, this one not for courage, but to slow his acceleration. If she could impair the speed of his powerful wingspan, the dragon would fly lower and within reach of Vidar's blade. She'd give him as much advantage as she could.

Fafnir finally noticed her as she finished the rune, and Ailsa sprinted to the side. Her strides devouring the cracked earth as she held her bow and arrow low, waiting for him to swoop down closer and attack.

Stopping beside a lava pit whose shape and size resembled a river, Ailsa bent a knee to the ground, steadying her aim to lock the arrow on the dragon's chest. Gold skin glowed as fire collected in his throat, a great inhale before the burning, and she let it loose when the embers coiled orange in his belly.

The side of this bed was steeper than the others. The river of lava that once flowed here must have been deep to scourge this far into the earth. Ailsa slipped down the side, stumbling over her feet as she fell down a wall of black rock, the bow flying from her fingers, arrows falling from their roost.

She landed hard, palms scraping the rough bottom. Every bone in her body rattled from the fall. Ailsa blinked her vision clear, searching for the bow she dropped, but it was halfway across the pit. She crawled for it, dragging herself across the rocks with the little strength that remained.

A red shadow covered the hole, filtering the last helpful ray of moonlight. Ailsa looked up to see the dragon descending slowly as her rune activated, drawing close to her, realizing he had her cornered. The sides of the pit were too tall, the angle too sharp to climb quickly. She needed to heal herself, was bleeding in enough places from the cuts across her body to have multiple points of access. But staring face to face with Fafnir, Ailsa could not move.

There was an understanding between them both. This was the end. There were no other places for her to run. She had taken a wrong turn and the decision had cost her everything.

"I'm sorry, Vali," she whispered to the ring still on her finger, the one she couldn't take off like it had vowed to stay on her hand until the end of time. It was all for nothing. She was going to die without her memories—without him. And perhaps it was better to die without knowing how much she'd lost and never get back. To burn to ash like the rest of their days together.

Ailsa!

Fafnir's chest gleamed like molten gold once more as fire gathered deep inside his throat, and her eyes flickered shut, focusing on Vidar's bond. She met his fear with her own, let him see that raw place inside her heart this life had taught her to seal shut. The other side strengthened into something she'd never felt from him before. An anger, harsh and cold, tugging at the thread that connected them until the blood in her own veins stung with ice.

His thoughts cascaded down the bond. Vidar was on the move, and Ailsa opened her eyes just in time to see his lanky body jumping off the top of the pit, sword in hand, each second seemed to slow into a stop-motion pace as he leapt soundlessly over the space between the wall and the dragon —and landed hard on the monster's back.

The glowing embers in Fafnir's throat cooled dormant as his neck thrashed toward the male on his back. He roared in a furious display, bucking his scaly body as Vidar struggled to hang on. But with Ailsa's rune taking effect, his movements were clumsy as if in a stupor, giving the giant a chance to bury his blade between the dragon's armor of scales.

Another wail pierced the night and shook the stars with its agony. Ailsa covered her ears as it splintered her in two. Fafnir's wings beat once, twice, then stilled forever. And the monster and his slayer fell from his hover in the lava pit, shaking the earth with a force that knocked her off her feet.

Vidar was tossed from the dragon by the force of its drop, and Ailsa could only gasp as he fell headfirst from the dragon's back and plummet into the earth next to him.

"Vidar!" she called across the crater, but there was no answer. No rouse in his body, no thought or word or acknowledgement down the bond. Ailsa crawled to him on hands and knees, disregarding practicality in her desperation to reach him.

He was lying on his front, cloak covering his face. She unclasped it from his neck and threw it to the side, worried the fall had broken his spine. With her dagger, she ripped through his shirt to see his back.

His skin was mutilated. Burn scars. Whip marks. Lines of tough, white threads recorded across the broad muscles of his shoulders. Her fingers caught on them all, distracted by the extent of his cruel history. No wonder the male had been afraid. It was no small victory he had survived to see this day —the significance of his actions only furthered by the demons who left their marks on his body.

His breath was shallow and his pulse thready. Ailsa quickly covered his scars with her blood, using every healing rune still available in her memory. They sunk into his skin, changing the fate of the wounds she couldn't see until every rise of his chest drew a deeper breath. She would have healed his scars as well, but they were not hers to erase.

Vidar groaned at the end of a long breath, and Ailsa helped him roll onto his back to look at her. Now that his shirt was loose, she could see a silence rune inked into his chest like a necklace. He'd always had it covered before.

"How are you?" she asked.

I feel like a vase that was shattered and glued back together again.

Ailsa smiled. "That's not too far off from what happened, actually." He blew a sharp breath, a sound between a cough and a laugh. "Thank you, by the way. I would have joined the ash in the breeze if you hadn't come."

You made me brave, Ailsa.

Her brows kissed in perplexity. The rune she had drawn on

his forehead had been wiped away. "What do you mean? There's no rune."

He shook his head, interrupting her with his silent words. *I didn't need a rune.* Gradually, he sat up, grunting from the strain until he was face to face with her. *You had faith in me when I never had it for myself, and for that reason alone, I will always protect our friendship. If you ever need me, no matter how afraid I am, I will be there for you.*

Every ache and bruise in her being was suddenly numb to the warmth that spread through their bond and straight to her heart. Ailsa's smile would have been joined with tears if she had any left in her body. She brought a filthy hand to his cheek and stroked his jaw with her thumb.

"It is good to have a friend in such a harrowing place as this one. Vidar, I can erase those runes made on you so you can speak again. You deserve to have a voice."

But the frost giant only shook his head. *I vowed to myself and my mother's grave that I would not speak until the gods fell, until the one who put these runes on me suffered from all the pain he has caused my family.*

Ailsa used the blood from a grazing wound on her forearm to heal the cuts and bruises littering her body. "My offer will continue to stand, but if that is how you truly feel, I will not get in the way of your vow of vengeance." She stood to her feet, testing the work of the runes carefully before gaining enough confidence to take a step toward the wall of obsidian. "We should get to the *bálhross* and find Fafnir's treasure before the sun rises—"

"Wait," a hoarse voice called behind her.

Ailsa spun toward the sound. The hair on her neck stiffened when she realized the voice had not come from her bond, but from where they had left the dragon to perish. In the place where a monster once laid for his final rest, a male creature she'd never seen before with dark grey skin and long, pointed ears remained.

A dwarf.

Nerissa had told her the truth when she explained Fafnir's story. The fatal wound Vidar left him must have triggered him to shift from the dragon and back to his original form. Ailsa fell to her knees beside the Fafnir, his body spread limp in a pool of dark blood, wetting her knees.

"Fafnir?" she asked.

The dwarf closed his eyes but nodded. "That treasure is cursed, so be careful what you touch. The greed will drive you mad, even make you forget who you are."

"That's what happened to you?" she asked.

"Yes," he said. "I couldn't shift back to my true self even if I could stop thinking about my gold." He brought his hand in front of his face, observing the way his fingers moved as if seeing his body for the first time. "The entrance to my cave is hidden in plain sight. Draw the rune of wealth on the south facing wall and the door will appear, and heed my warning about the gold."

"It is not the gold or wealth I seek from your treasure," she said. "Fafnir, listen to me. I can help you survive this. Let me heal you—"

"No!" he said, choking on the blood in his throat. She waited patiently until he could speak again. "I have killed everyone I care about because of my greed and selfishness. Family, friends, everyone I once loved, they are dead. But... you can help me another way."

"How?" she asked, feeling a sudden stroke of sadness for the dwarf.

He lifted a shaky hand and tapped the pommel of her

short sword. Ailsa nodded in understanding. With the remaining blood on her fingertip, she painted a rune across his forehead, one of peace. His eyes rolled to the stars above them. A slight smile drifted across his thin lips for the first time in probably centuries.

"I haven't looked at the sky in so long. What a lovely night it is," he murmured as she pressed the tip of her blade over his heart. In one easy thrust, she put the dwarf out of his misery, watching as the sparkle in his eyes slowly dulled into nothing more than reflected starlight. Ailsa's hands wobbled slightly as she returned her blade to its sheath.

You did him a kindness you did not owe him. He almost killed you. Vidar was behind her as she stood to her feet.

"He was sick," she said. "Not in body, but in his mind. I've seen enough beings fall to the glutton of greed. He suffered enough, I assure you." As she looked at the hill in front of them, she felt like she was facing a mountain instead. Her bones practically groaned, dreading the task ahead.

Vidar sensed her reluctance, either through the bond or by the way her shoulders fell. *Just a little further. The hard part is over.* His hand patted her shoulder lightly in consolation.

Ailsa thought of all they had left to do, looked back at the dead dwarf who still stared glossy eyed at the star-burned sky, and for the first time felt the weight of her choices and the burden of their consequences.

"No, Vidar," she murmured, looking forward again. "It is only just beginning."

CHAPTER 32
ERIK

Erik stood outside of Ailsa's chambers, a thousand words hanging off the edge of his lips, but none would let go. He knew she was angry with him, had known her long enough to know her forgiveness would take time they didn't have to earn. It was a battle he had prepared all night to fight. To fight for her heart, for their relationship, everything he had left home for in the first place.

"Ailsa," he called through the door. "Are you awake yet?"

There was no answer, but he'd expected as much. She'd ignore him until he demanded her attention. She'd always been stubborn in that way. He reached inside his pocket for the key to her room and said, "Look, I know you're upset with me, but we can work this out. I know we can. I'm going to come in—" The key was missing.

Erik patted his clothes, went back to his room and practically turned the place upside down to find it—and then he realized. The last thing he remembered of the night before was the silent man who served his dinner instead of the usual witch. Erik had fallen asleep without having touched his dinner, as it still sat on his bedside table. The only thing empty was his cup.

He cursed himself for being so gullible, and started back toward Ailsa's room, a new panic racing his heart into a gallop. He should have known the freak would have tried something like this, had seen the way he looked at her when he thought no one was paying attention, but Erik was always watching him. His mouth never betrayed a word, but the look in his eyes spoke loud enough.

Erik banged on her door loud enough to wake a hungover Otsman from a morning nap. "Ailsa, are you all right?" he asked, trying to hide the worry in his voice that came out too sharp. When a sound didn't stir inside her room, he tried the handle—and found it unlocked.

The door swung open to reveal an empty room. His stature blocked the only light filtering from the torches in the hall. Her candle had long burned out, but even in the darkness, he could tell her bed was empty. There was no scowling beauty here to bite off his head. The clothes she was wearing last night were cast in a pile on the floor.

Ailsa was gone.

"Nerissa!" he shouted into the empty hall. He did not know where she stayed in this cursed mountain, but he would call her name until she showed herself. After disturbing several upper levels of witches, she finally poked her head around a corner. His blood-bonded witch dressed in nothing but a robe that skimmed the hot floor around her bare feet.

"Is there a reason you are disturbing me at such an hour?" she asked.

Erik's eyes wandered over her figure before he could control what he was looking at. "Apologies if you were in the middle of something, but we have a big problem."

Nerissa smiled at his reaction and dared another step closer until he was forced to look down at her. He could smell another male on her skin, her normal pretty scent blocked away by something masculine and smoky. "I'm always in the middle of *something*, Erik. What's wrong this time?"

"Ailsa is gone!"

This didn't seem to concern the witch at all. Erik wondered if she knew something he didn't. "That's not surprising, considering she vowed she would retrieve Surtur's flame. She's been studying the maps for days now. I suppose what has you upset is that she didn't inform you. Did you expect her to ask permission, Erik?"

"I didn't think she was serious, Nerissa," he slid the words through tight teeth. "I faced the dragon and was nearly killed. Think of what will happen to her! She could be dead by now thanks to your silent servant who let her out—"

"Let her out?" Nerissa stopped him. "Don't tell me you locked her in her own room?"

Erik rolled his eyes and walked away. She wasn't even listening to him. Did the witch not understand his woman was missing somewhere in the realm of fire? And hunting a dragon on top of it all!

"It was for her own safety, so something like *this* would never happen. She could be burning alive for all we know!"

Another woman joined them in the hall, this one he didn't recognize. But her eyes were a wild green, wide and excited. "Nerissa!" she said, out of breath. "The guards told me to tell you to get to a lookout point over the valley. And to hurry!"

Erik followed her as she turned on a heel and ran through the darkened corridors, somehow recalling the exact stairwell that led to a place outside of the mountain. A landing that overlooked the entire vale, draped in the first rays of morning sunlight and the heat of Muspell as it returned with a fresh vengeance on the day.

But Erik's gaze didn't fall on the sunrise climbing over the horizon, but on the slight disturbance of red dust forming a trailing thread behind a horse. And in the saddle was a woman. Another rider sat behind her. And in her hand was a torch that glowed brighter than the sun in all the realms combined.

Nerissa turned to him with that damn smile already curling on her fair face. "Never underestimate a scorned woman, Erik. She'll make you eat your words faster than you can swallow them."

"Impossible," he muttered. But his eyes did not deceive him.

Ailsa had returned with the Eternal Flame.

CHAPTER 33
SEELA

When Seela awoke, it was not to a cold mountain. The ice in her hair had long thawed in front of a small hearth, her clothes damp from the melt off. The smell of yeast rolls and meat from a warm oven replaced the whipping breeze, and her hunger pangs nudged her tired body awake.

She was not in Svartalfheim, but in a cottage. Her memory successively remembering the witch in the valley, the undead fae she destroyed, the weight in her limbs from using a power she had always been too afraid to acknowledge.

The Valkyrie she called.

Seela ripped off her gloves and discovered white lines threading her palms and forearms. Different from the runes her *Hjartablóds* had inked onto his skin, these were even lighter than her pale skin, as white as her hair and thin as a strand running up and down her arms in a decorative arrangement. Her power had saved them from potentially becoming one of the draug, but what price would she pay now for exposing this side of herself?

The clatter of pans in the next room triggered her attention to her surroundings. She was trapped beneath a cozy detainment of quilts in a single armchair in the center of a sitting room. Seela quietly unwrapped the blankets and carefully nudged from the chair to investigate the cottage while her captor was still marking her presence in the next room with the noise she created.

Night had fallen outside the only window, a shallow brim of snow building on the pane as a light flurry fell. There were no pictures on the walls, just a bookshelf full of old tomes with moth eaten spines, a stool near the fire with knitting supplies.

Three doors led to bare bedrooms on the western wall, this room forming a common area between them. She looked inside, but the beds were stripped. The wardrobes left open to reveal dusty shelves and shadows. There was nothing in any of these rooms to give her a hint of who this witch was or what she was doing out here. Seela eventually snuck into the short hallway leading closer to the noise.

Peering around the corner, she found the same witch from the valley preparing a small meal, navigating around her kitchen from memory. She was younger than she appeared in the valley, with copper hair pulled into a high bun and thin pieces falling out the top. Her eyes were veiled with a thin white film, unfocused as she snatched spices from the cupboard and sniffed each container. The elfin realized she was completely blind as she stepped out into full view and the witch's gaze skimmed over her as if she wasn't there.

Seela took advantage of her captor's impaired sight and stepped stealthily through the kitchen, venturing to the rooms on the other side. Through the crack of one door, she found a bedroom, then a washroom. But when Seela came to the third door, whose entrance was completely shut until she eased it open, she found something worth investigating.

A room of prophecies.

Shelves stacked from floor to ceiling against the far wall, each row with at least a hundred orbs containing a shimmering dust of various dyes. They glowed in the dark room, illuminating their mysteries with pulsing light. Each one a different size, propped on its own individual pedestal. Seela looked back at the witch still busy in the kitchen, before slipping inside the room for a closer look.

Angrboda, she called herself. The Mother Witch. How powerful was this blind woman, and how many lives did she live to write these many futures? Seela found a candle attached to the wall by thick spider webs and let it burn a tiny light.

In a darkened corner sat a table with an empty globe beneath a dusting of grime. She ran the light over the opposite wall, showing three figurines on a single shelf behind their individual prophecies. On the ledge sat a small girl with half a face painted black, a snake tightly coiled into a pile, and a wolf with his teeth bared.

The monsters of the Nine—the children of Ragnarok. Seela knew little about each of them as individuals but heard much concerning their joint repute to destroy the gods and the realms falling with them. She was about to investigate them further when the flutter of tiny wings joined her in the dark room.

She turned to find a crow now perching on the top of the shelf, its glossy black eyes jerking around the room before settling on her. It ruffled its feathers once, then cawed.

A cold rush of unease spread down her back and the elfin darted from the room, expecting she had raised some kind of alarm. As soon as she slipped through the door to return to the main room, the witch stood there, blocking her escape.

"It isn't polite to sneak around a blind woman and look through her things. And to think, I was making you breakfast," Angrboda said, shaking her head in disbelief over Seela's poor manners.

"I'm... sorry," Seela said slowly. "It is not every day I wake up in a witch's house in the woods. I wanted to make sure you weren't planning to sacrifice me to a demon or something."

This made her captor smile, revealing a row of polished teeth and sharp canines. "It is not every day a Valkyrie comes knocking on my door. You have nothing to fear from me. I gave up my powers long ago in exchange for the quiet country life."

Her assurance did nothing to make Seela relax, nor did the uneasy feeling in her gut dissipate.

"Was that the first time?" Angrboda cocked her head in curiosity.

"What do you mean?"

"The first time you raised your Valkyrie. I'll admit, you must be very powerful to destroy all my draug so quickly," the blind woman answered.

"Where are—" Seela shut her mouth, realizing Enver and Ivor were nowhere to be found. The Mother Witch might not even know about them, and it was best to keep them unknown until she knew if this woman was friend or foe. "Where are we?"

"The Ironwood. My crows told me there was a commotion in the pass. I wanted to make sure it wasn't my witches returning, but then I discovered something much more interesting." Her white eyes seemed to look straight into Seela. "What are you doing out here, little Valkyrie?"

"Do not call me that," she said in a low voice. The elfin stepped around the witch to gain some space, and Angrboda turned to the sound of her steps. "My name is Seela, and I am the Regent of Alfheim. I have come all this way because your witches took someone very important. They were using this pass to move the wolven in and out of our realm, and I have been following their trail, hoping to find them and bring her home."

Angrboda glided to the other side of the room as she said, "Well, she is not here. So you have come a long way for nothing."

"Do you know where they went? Or why they are working with Fenrir?"

"Why would I tell you, an agent of Odin, one of his chosen winged battle maidens—"

"Odin did not choose me. I am half-fae. My mother left me with my father to hide me from Odin and the Seven. Please," she took another desperate step toward the woman, "everyone knows the fae are godless. We do not serve the Aesir, nor am I now by asking for your help."

Angrboda considered her words before jutting her chin toward a pair of chairs on the other side of the kitchen. "Sit back down then and have something to eat. I have lived for hundreds of years and have a thousand stories to tell. What you seek to know is not a simple explanation."

"By stories, do you mean prophecies? You have enough of those to write entire lifetimes."

The witch smiled, hand gracefully feeling for a long knife to continue chopping her onion. Seela would have offered to help if she had any skill in cooking. While she could cut a man in half, she couldn't mince him. She couldn't cook, but *gods below* she could eat.

"They are more than just prophecies. I once traveled the realms and read the fates of all beings, sometimes rewrote them for a price."

A cold sweat washed down the elfin's spine. Things were clicking into place. The crows, the strange room, the witch who lived hundreds of years... "Wait," she stammered. "You're not the one they once called Gullveig, are you?"

Angrboda's fingers stumbled as she chopped, muttering a curse as she nicked a knuckle with the sharp edge. She turned from Seela, looking for a dish rag. "How do you know that name?"

The heat from the wood burning stove became increasingly smothering. "The one I am searching for, she inherited Gullveig's power. She was taken by the same witches who claimed to follow the Mother Witch. The same ones who once used *your* pass." Seela felt for her blades but discovered they had been confiscated while she'd been knocked out. She searched the room, searching for the closest thing to defend herself, to subdue the witch if she in fact knew more than she was letting on.

She'd drag the truth from her cold, immortal lips if she had to.

"I have no control over the witches. Ever since we lost the war and I gave up my power, they have looked to a different champion."

"To Fenrir—"

Angrboda faced her again, ageless face barren of expression. "Someone much worse than Fenrir, Seela. If you don't know by now, there is not much else I can do to help you."

"Why not? If you know where they went or who they are serving, then just tell me. Anything at this point could help," she argued.

313

"The gods made many enemies before and after the Aesir-Vanir war, Seela. Explaining each one would take up too much time you don't have." Angrboda threw the bloody cloth to the side and braced her hands on the black iron sink. "Have you ever wondered why Odin split up the monster children? Why he exiled Jormungand, tied up Fenrir with special chains, cast the innocent little girl, Hel, deep into the Shadow Realms?"

Seela stood quietly, but the slight motion made the witch's head jerk in her direction. "So, they could not destroy the Nine?"

"No. So he could destroy me," she replied. Angrboda pushed off the counter and strode purposefully toward the prophecy room, barely using her hands to navigate the entryway and find one of the monster's orbs. Seela waited in the doorway, hesitant to get too close. But the witch held out Fenrir's orb to her expectantly. "Odin made me show him each of their fates when he discovered us."

She took the prophecy into her hands and looked into the sphere, whose shimmer was parting to reveal a scene, one that depicted the wolf swallowing the Allfather nearly whole before a man cloaked in gold shoved a blade through his throat.

"Why are you showing me this?" the elfin asked. "Everyone already knows the fate of the Great Wolf is to kill Odin and die by Baldur's hand at Ragnarok."

"You are not seeing the vision correctly, only through the lens Odin has wanted all of you to look through," she said simply. "Fenrir is killed by the one who seeks restoration. Gold symbolizes the Aesir, but it also symbolizes power and honor. Only the one who seeks to right the wrongs of the Allfather will slay the wolf."

"Then why Baldur?" Seela asked, handing her back the

prophecy. "Why did Odin go to such lengths to bring him back from the dead?"

Angrboda placed the crystal back on its shelf with careful hands. "The man in the vision is swathed in gold. Baldur was so fair and beloved by all of creation, the light would cling to him so that he was constantly shining. Many believed him to be the one who destroys Fenrir, and Odin used that to his advantage, making every living thing swear to not harm him so he was untouchable."

"Odin was trying to write his own fate by molding his son into the chosen one." Seela conjectured out loud. The witch nodded, picking up a different orb. "But he had other sons at that time. Is Thor not just as strong?"

This made Angrboda chuckle under her breath. "When Fenrir was brought back to Asgard, they put him through many tests to assess his strength. Even as a pup, he easily outmatched Thor. None of Odin's full-blooded Aesir sons could beat the Great Wolf."

But as she turned to face Seela, her face had fallen of any amusement, a sobering scene laid in her palms, one she felt instead of seeing. "They feared him because they could not control him, and because of their fear, they made Fenrir into an enemy. I warned the Allfather that his desire to know everything would be his downfall, that the decision to learn his fate would change and singularize his potentials, but he did not listen. The moment he made me show him these visions, the Norns wrote Ragnarok into existence, and there is no changing what is now written into the Tapestry."

"What about Ailsa? She has the power to rewrite fate, *your* power—"

"The Norns weave their threads according to the survival of the Tree. It is never favorable to any being, god or man, only that which helps the realms continue. If she did anything to mess with Ragnarok..." Angrboda's head shook slowly. "That power needs to be destroyed for the good of the Nine.

Seela's head was swimming, the witch speaking in circles that only made her questions number like the ringlets in a still pool. She thought back to the bedrooms she found when she first awoke, counted the monsters on the shelf.

"Angrboda?" she muttered, her heart sinking. "Are these your children?"

She didn't answer right away, just continued to roll the orb between her palms like it was soothing to her. Eventually, she nodded with the smallest dip of her chin. "Loki came to me after I drank from Mimir's Well. He had somehow learned the waters showed me the secrets of sedir, and he wished to learn the dark magic. At first, I refused, but he was so charming. I fell in love with him quickly. I had been traveling alone for decades before he gave me his attention and I drank it up, uncaring he had a wife and child at home. He told me he loved me. Like a fool, I believed every word the Lord of Lies spoke."

Her head bowed in what the elfin assumed was indignity. "There is a reason Odin put Hel in the Shadow Realms—why he made her queen of the dead." She looked up at Seela with milky eyes. "I gave my mortality to the well in exchange for the dark magic. I have been burned to ash and risen each time as a new woman with the same calloused soul, and I will see every torturous age to come without the ones I love most. My sacrifice to the well. It was the worst he could do to me, separating us forever."

Gullveig. Heid. Angrboda. Burned three times by the Allfather to change Baldur's fate, and each time she returned by a different name until she had hidden her power somewhere a god would never look—in the mortal realm.

"Where will you stand, Seela, in the end? What side will you fight for?" Angrboda asked.

The elfin adjusted her posture, feeling a rod of discomfort shoved down her spine. "I will stand with Alfheim—"

"That's not an answer."

"It's the only one I've got," she clipped. "Now, I appreciate all of this information, but it won't help me rescue Ailsa or protect my realm."

Two crows flew into the room, disturbing the quiet with their barking caws before settling. Angrboda shook her head in disapproval and turned back toward a wall of shelved orbs. Her hands skimmed the edges of the wood, letterings engraved just in front of each prophecy. She picked one up and handed it to Seela. "Take this one and be on your way. My crows sensed a disturbance in the woods. The Seven might track you here, and I cannot let Odin find me again."

Seela perked at the news, realizing Enver and Ivor must have finally caught up. "Those are my traveling companions, fae not Valkyrie. They must have tracked me, but I have over-stayed my welcome as it is. Thank you for the prophecy."

"Do not thank me yet. That was my most difficult prophecy to write, elfin. But if you truly want to protect your home, you will fulfill it."

Angrboda did not follow her from the room, instead lingered near the trio of crystal balls in front of their shrines. Seela felt a pang of sadness for the witch, wondering how long she had been alone before Loki tricked her into loving him— how long she had been separated from *that* history. How much longer she'd have to live with herself for putting her faith in the wrong person. Forever was too elusive to be measurable.

Pocketing the sphere in a covered pouch, she heard a

knock rasp a nearby door. "Enver?" she called across the hollow distance. But there was no reply. Seela's skin prickled at the silence. If it were either of her companions on the other side of that door, they'd be breaking it down to get to her, no questions asked. "Ivor?" She tried once more, but nothing.

"Angrboda, are you expecting some—"

Her voice was cut off by not a sound but searing light. A blinding glare contrasting the darkened cottage grew so bright, Seela had to cover her eyes to shield them from the intensity. The house shook, rafters groaning and spilling dust, metal pans clinked together in the kitchen.

"You lead them to me!" the witch shrieked as she stumbled out of her room. "I told you to leave and you wouldn't—so they'd find you here! Agent of Odin!"

All at once, blackness blocked her sight again as crows smashed through the windows and flurried in formation between them, surrounding her, the sound of a hundred beating wings drowning away the witch's curses from the other side of the room.

"I didn't... I wouldn't know how to call them!" Seela shouted above the chaos, hoping she could hear her words. "Please, Angrboda, I don't want them to find me either!"

One by one, the crows peeled away, aiming instead for the outside. Seela rushed to the witch, her steps stumbling over a hundred glass shards. Angrboda wrapped a fist around her throat and snarled, "You have two seconds to convince me why I should believe anything you say."

With the last bit of air she squeezed out of her chest, Seela fought to reply, but through a broken window, a blur of stormy grey burst across her vision. The hand around her throat slipped, and Angrboda fell to the floor, bringing Seela down with her, as a wolven pinned her to the floor with a growl.

"Seela!" Enver climbed through a different window, the glaring light behind him obscuring his details, too painful to look at for long. He was at her side in a blink, helping her to her feet. "We have to get out of here, the Valkyries—"

"How will we hide from them, Enver? We're surrounded. They found me. It is over!"

"No, it isn't," said the reply. But it didn't come from the male holding her up, instead the woman still trapped beneath the wolf on the floor. Her hand was smoothing over Ivor's snarl, a look of peace on her face. "There is a secret route that tunnels under the house and into the Ironwood. A trap door hides beneath an old rug in Fenrir's room."

Seela looked between them, wondering how the witch knew Ivor was one of the wolven, a distant descendant of her own. But there were many things that went beyond explanation, matters of the heart that were deeper than word filled definitions.

"But what about you?" Seela asked. "Angrboda, come with us. Don't let Odin get his hands on you a fourth time."

But she shook her head, rolling it lazily across the stone floor. "I'll be fine. I still have a bit of fire leftover from the last time. Go now, before it's too late."

Enver gave her an encouraging push, and Seela clambered over the wolf and started up the hall toward the bedrooms, where she had awoken. Voices joined the light spilling in from outside, following her through the cottage. Threats in the old language, promising pain if not obeyed. Seela translated the ancient words and understood their demand, to show herself. To give up her long hidden identity.

But the elfin had no plans on joining her estranged mother

or the rest of the Seven. There was no potential in her fate for the control of a god or the eternal service to one. Her mother had almost gotten her father killed for involving him in her little rebellion against the Aesir, seducing him into a one night thrill. Practically ruined his life by throwing a child into his arms with no maternal guidance, no support, no explanation. And Seela escaped from the house like she had escaped that alternate life.

The one and only good thing her mother had ever done for her—leaving and forgetting. Sometimes those were truly the best options.

Angrboda's secret tunnel was barely large enough for Enver to squeeze through, the top so low it forced him to crouch uncomfortably. But the burrow in the earth slowly turned upward, back to the surface where a matching trap door was sealed shut above them.

Seela had to fight to push it open, breaking sprawling roots as they covered the other side of the door from time and lack of use. Her companions filtered from the tight tunnel behind her, positioning themselves behind the draping greenery to look back at the cottage.

"Are you all right?" Enver asked, worry clear in his eyes. His hands skimmed her shoulders with a gentleness that could have been confused with tender affection.

It triggered something vulnerable inside her, brimming her eyes with tears as she looked back at Angrboda's home in the middle of the Ironwood. Seven winged battle maidens circled the homestead, a building made up of little more than stone and wood and straw. The last something she had left in these worlds, and the Valkyries were keen on destroying that too, just to find Seela—find the call of the power inside her.

But the elfin didn't have to worry about the witch for long, not as a burst of flame erupted from the center of the home. An explosion of fire that spread across the roof, its starving fingers crawling over the house until it was completely set ablaze with the witch still inside. And Seela thought she could hear the faint echo of her laugh behind the thunderclap of wings.

"Gods below," the male at her side mumbled, watching the scene unfold. "Crazy witch."

"No," Seela whispered. "Just a woman unafraid to lose what little she has left. Come, before they sense us hiding here. Ivor, can you track the way back?"

The wolven's nose twitched twice before she turned on large claws and slipped beneath the cover of night, away from the light of the Valkyrie and the witch's funeral pyre. But before Seela followed her to safety, she stole one last glance at the beautiful warriors now sheathing their golden swords in disappointment.

And wondered, for a moment, which one she shared blood with—before leaving and forgetting.

"So, that went well," Enver said dryly.

Their group didn't pause for a break until Seela felt the chill of the mountain breeze as they neared the entrance of the old pass. Only then did they pause to collect themselves, regroup, and refocus. Enver offered to mist them back to Alfheim, but the wolven only bared her teeth in response before disappearing behind a tree the size of Angrboda's kitchen. Seela agreed, not thinking it wise to drain him of magic, not when they needed to decide their next move.

"It wasn't completely wasted," Seela said, pulling out the prophecy. "I learned so much about the past, about Loki and the children of Ragnarok. She gave me this off one of her shelves and said it would help us."

"And Ailsa?" Ivor appeared back in her human form, throwing on an extra cloak to cover the torn places in her clothes. "Did she say where we could find her?"

Seela shook her head slowly, avoiding the disappointment likely showing itself on Ivor's face. "They took Ailsa somewhere impossible to find, nor could we do anything about it if we knew where she was."

"So we're back to the beginning?" Enver spoke, running a hand against the loose strands of hair that fell into his face.

Seela stood, rolling the crystal sphere between her palms. "Not quite. We know now that the witches are working for someone who wants the gods to fall." She gulped, forcing this next truth down. "There will be a war, and we will have to decide soon who we will side with. Her life and the rest of the Nine will depend on it."

Enver tilted his head and said, "It is difficult to choose sides when you don't know who you're fighting against, Commander."

Seela sighed and nodded in understanding. "The lines between good and evil, right and wrong, they've always been blurry. But now, I don't think there are lines at all. I think the two mingle with each other, take turns when it is convenient for their masters." She looked down into the prophecy beginning to reveal itself. "Hopefully this will give us a better perspective, if only to prepare us for what we will face in the end."

The shimmer parted, and Seela watched as something unexpected revealed itself. It was Loki, bound in chains. A snake coiled above him with its jaws wide, dripping venom on top of his head. The trickster god writhed with each drop, lips parting in the shape of a scream as the snake's poison ate away at his skin and left it raw and bleeding. The gods had tied him up when he made trouble at the feast in Vanaheim, a time that felt so long ago now. Next to him was a woman who Seela assumed was Sigyn, catching the drops in a bowl to grant him a few moments of reprieve before she disappeared with the shallow dish filled with venom.

But the scene shifted into another, one that sent the blood from her face to her toes. Her fingers trembled slightly around the crystal before she nearly dropped it.

"What do you see, Seela?" Enver asked. His voice sounded like it was coming from a distance as she stared into the vision.

"I see myself standing beside Loki. His chains are in my hands," she answered. Her gaze tore from the orb to her wide-eyed companions. "I am to set him free."

CHAPTER 34
VALI

"We have arrived, Bjorn."

Steam hovered over the water as Vali crossed from one forbidden realm to another. He followed the tide. The breeze from Nastrond pushed him into the hot breath of Muspell, where the fire realm gave evidence of its reputation. Sweat pulled from his skin as he sailed further into the realm, and the dense fog clinging to his ship made him choke with every breath.

Vali used a spyglass he had found in the captain's quarters and searched for land. When he gained a glimpse of red earth through the white condensation, he dropped the anchor, hiding the ship in the ever present haze.

He turned to the head with greying skin hanging from the mainmast. "Sorry you won't have much of a view, Bloodblade, as this will be as far as I bring you. My lady is somewhere close, and I will not keep her waiting. Keep an eye on the ship until we get back."

It might just be their only way out. Bjorn continued to

gape at him silently, unable to respond without the rest of his neck.

Using a dinghy made of yet more fingernails and teeth, Vali squatted in the small vessel and pushed the remaining way to shore, careful not to splash the water hissing with each stroke of his oar. By the time his boat knocked against hard earth, his bare chest was slick with sweat. The ends of his hair stuck to his neck and his mouth was parched even more. He needed to find water, the tepid kind, if he was going to survive this place long enough to find Ailsa.

There was nothing but crimson mountains scaling the horizon in front of him. In the near distance, a volcano burned, rivers of fire spilling from its peak and pushing dark clouds into the sky. A lightning storm flashed behind them, revealing the miles of flat land in front of him and the barren space he would need to cross before finding higher ground.

Vali passed a hand over the runes covering his skull, reminding his flesh of his purpose, of his fate. He gritted his teeth and began what he hoped was the beginning of the end of his search.

The first mountain he scaled detailed the way of the land and the ranges of mountains connecting like a crooked spine toward the center of Muspell, where the rivers of fire were born and sprawled from the heart of the realm. Wherever the witches had taken Ailsa, it would be far from the hottest point, somewhere hidden from the scorching sun and burnt breeze—perhaps a valley or a cave. He was fortunate he had arrived at nightfall, but the day was coming quickly, and he

ALEXIS L. MENARD

needed to find similar accommodations soon or risk drying out into jerky in this heat.

He kept his eyes peeled for such a place. And when he came to the second mountain, the fates were merciful to him, sending a brief shower of rain to coat him in refreshing water. He walked with his mouth open to the sky, catching every drop and letting them slide down his dry throat.

More steam drifted just north of where he trekked, white and thick, fresh from the source. Vali wondered if there could be more water there as the rain collected into the shallow cracks in the earth, where rivers of lava once flowed and had long dried up. But steam of this volume could only mean an equally appreciable amount of water, and if it was as delicious as the kind crying from the broken sky above, he could officially count himself the luckiest male in the Nine.

Whoever was threading his fate on this day must have thought favorably of him, for when he followed the curling steam, he discovered a brook bubbling against the heated stone. Vali didn't care. The water was safe enough for his hands to touch and therefore mild enough for his tongue. He cupped gulp after gulp until his belly was full of water and the thought of another sip made him sick.

Vali sat back on his heels and surveyed his surroundings—which wasn't much at first glance. But upon closer inspection, he noticed something he hadn't seen yet in the smooth, cliff side terrain.

Footprints.

A single pair dotting from the edge of the brook and around the curve of the mountain wall. Vali slipped his last dagger into his palm and stepped across the small stream until he emerged on the other side, following the prints back to their owner. It was the first sign of life he had seen all night,

326

4

4

would have missed it if it weren't for the creeping dawn spilling light over the sharp peaks.

The prints led deep into a cavern that opened again into a wide space. And the elfin had to blink several times to make sure he wasn't imagining what he was seeing as he peered around a rounded edge in the cliff side.

There stood a garden. One of modest size, growing herbs of every kind in wicker baskets filled with compost. Water jugs stacked near the entrance of the garden, half-filled from previously being used. The ground was still wet as the plants dripped the excess along the copper floor.

This space had to belong to Ailsa. There was no one else among witches and wolves who had the mind and thoughtfulness to grow so many varieties of herbs so exquisitely. And yet, if it was Ailsa's garden, it shocked him to find it so well maintained and grown out, having only been trapped here for the past few weeks.

But Vali in his desperation could not rationalize the idea, only that she must have a hand in this, that these herbs would lead him to her—or possibly even her to him. He couldn't think straight when the scent of her lavender skin replaced the stench of burning sulfur in the air. That wild, woodsy taste that caught on his palate, the same one that drove him to do idiotic things—like stumble beyond the concealment of the mountain until he was standing in the middle of a row.

The sound of steel scraping stone prompted Vali back to reality, and the elfin gripped the dagger in his fist, aware he was not alone. Behind him, a soundless presence approached, but he kept his dagger low in case it was indeed his lady.

It was not Ailsa who greeted him. No, his luck had officially expired. Instead, there stood a man an entire head shorter than himself, with auburn hair and *golden eyes*. One of the fae, though clearly not an elfin, possibly a Jotun. Though he'd never seen a fire giant, he appeared nothing like the legends claimed. His outstretched handheld a hand shovel like a sword.

Vali raised a brow at the spade. "Easy there," he said. "Lower your... weapon, and I'll lower mine."

He dropped it mere inches, his gaze cutting toward something behind Vali. The quick rise and fall of his chest betrayed his nerves, and Vali guessed by his frame he wasn't much of a fighter. In good faith, he sheathed his own dagger, watching the tension in the male's shoulders fall.

Vali asked him, "I am looking for someone. A mortal woman who was kidnapped from her family. Her name is Ailsa. Is she here?"

The male shrugged, glancing behind him again.

"You aren't a local here, I can tell. Are you from Jotunheim?" Vali asked. "Whatever the witches are doing or their reasons for keeping you here, I can help you escape. Just tell me where Ailsa is, and I can make sure you both return home safely. Please."

A battle raged quietly inside his head as the male adjusted his grip on the shovel. He eventually nodded slowly, reaching behind him to pocket the shovel in his waistband. Vali looked away for a moment to see for himself what was interesting the giant so much behind him. A door left ajar. Perhaps he still had time to knock out the male and make a run for it...

White powder puffed in his face, and the elfin knew the substance immediately by the scent. Ailsa had once shown him a stash she had affectionately named as Hel's Breath, made from a white herb he could only guess grew in this very garden as well. Bitter, catching all the moist places in his airways, smothering sweet as he tried to cough it from his chest. He only had time to look back at the male who he had gravely underestimated.

There was no satisfaction in his gentle features as the corners of Vali's vision blurred into shadows. He fought against sleep until it was futile.

CHAPTER 35
AILSA

Ailsa stood before Surtur and his giants alone. They had returned from Fafnir's lair the previous day and spent the rest of the night recovering, Vidar bringing her balms and herbs he had promised to show her when they left. Using the directions the dwarf had muttered in his last breaths, the cursed fortune was easy to find. The flame burned exactly how Surtur imagined it did—brighter than all the gold in the piles of the dragon's treasury.

"This is not the flame."

Ailsa stood in the center of the gathering arena where they had brought her the first time she entered this realm. The fire giants a sea of skulls behind her, Surtur back on his podium. In his hands was the flame from the torch she carried into the valley.

"We had a deal," she spoke loud enough for the witches beside her to hear. "If I slayed the dragon, you would restore my memories. I have killed Fafnir and have brought you a piece of the fire. If you want the true flame and its location, you'll have to complete your end of the bargain."

The giant lord didn't seem to appreciate her demands, no matter the merit behind them. "And what then, Fate Weaver?" he asked. "Do you expect me to give you back your memories and let your mortal companion walk free behind my giants as we burn the borders of this realm to ash? Is there nothing more you seek besides the past?"

"Knowledge is a weapon, Surtur. It is the most powerful force in the Nine. Not all battles are fought with iron and steel."

He grunted. "You sound like Odin."

Ailsa shrugged. "I did what you wanted. Now give me what I asked for and nothing will stand in your way from marching on Asgard."

Surtur grinned and motioned for Nerissa to approach his throne on the dais. She did so quickly, leaning forward to hear him mumble something in her ear. She nodded once and disappeared into the crowd behind Ailsa. The giant lord narrowed his gaze at her then.

"You would be in a better position to make demands, Weaver, if you were the only one who knew the location of the flame. Unfortunately for you, I have another who might be more motivated to share this information."

Ailsa's lips parted in objection but shut again as they dragged Vidar from the masses. His stag skull hid his eyes, leaving them at a disconnect. Even through the bond, his emotions were silent. A wall of stone stood between them, and no matter how hard she pushed, it wouldn't budge.

Vidar, what are you doing? She spoke down the bond.

In a whisper, he muttered two words that tested every thread of her judgment.

Trust me.

She grit her teeth as he joined Surtur on the dais, who had

motioned for two other giants to bring out a table and a map. The same one she studied for nearly a week before Vidar broke her out of her confines.

Surtur placed a large hand on Vidar's shoulder, his body shuddering beneath the weight, and its heat. "This one helped you escape, as I understand. He also returned with you on a stolen *bálhross*. Now, little stag, I'm not sure why you left the mountain without permission, nor why you believed you had the right to take one of my prisoners on such a dangerous journey."

"I forced him! He had no part in this besides helping me track down Fafnir," Ailsa shouted. It only took an irritated look from Surtur for two giants to appear at her side. The stage turned sideways as one of them knocked her hard on her left side, the other used her loss of balance to shove her down on her knees, silencing her with their fists alone. Ailsa swallowed the blood pooling in her cheek instead of arguing further.

Surtur spoke to Vidar again. "The punishment for your deeds will be quite severe. But if you show us where the treasure hides, perhaps we can forget all about it and move on to more important matters."

Don't you dare, Vidar. Ailsa begged through the bond. *I need this leverage.*

His mask didn't so much as turn to glance at her as he pointed to the spot on the map where the dwarf had led them to his treasure. To think a heartbeat sooner she had been defending him, and now he was betraying everything she worked so hard to build these last weeks. Whatever history she lost, it was now gone forever—along with her last shred of power.

"So close," Surtur mumbled, shaking his head. "You will

come with us, little stag, to show us exactly where Fafnir's gold is stored. We searched those grounds years ago and found nothing. I suspect there must be a trick to hide it from plain sight."

"What about me?" Ailsa spoke despite the threat of another hit. "We had a deal, Surtur!"

Surtur stood without glancing her way, and it felt as if the entire world forgot she existed, her worth to them worn out. "Throw her in the dungeon until Fenrir decides what he wants to do with her. Her privileges have officially run out. Nerissa, where is the other useless mortal you brought to me?"

"Standing outside, Lord Surtur. Most likely eavesdropping, since he wasn't allowed to attend our meeting. Would you like me to put him in the pit as well?"

The giant lord shook his head. "Give him the option to join us or leave. And if he decides to go, send him off with an arrow in his chest." He snatched Vidar by the arm before he could run off. His crimson eyes glanced at Ailsa. "And you, little stag, will finish cleaning up your mess."

⇠╫◊╫⇢

There weren't enough curses in the old or the new language to send down the bond as Vidar led her deep into the cavernous depths of the mountain, but Ailsa sent them anyway. Her skin shook with shivers, she was so angry. The bindings around her wrist pinched into her flesh as she resisted their restraint.

Ailsa, this is for your own good. I know Surtur. He was never going to honor his side of the deal. He tried to reason with her, but Ailsa threw up proverbial wall after wall each time he came up with another excuse.

She laughed, throwing her head back as he pushed her down an empty corridor. Wherever they were going, it hadn't been used recently. "And this is a better option? If you knew him so well, then perhaps we should have taken the flame ourselves and escaped this wretched realm."

You will understand soon enough.

Go to Hel.

The bond went silent the rest of their walk, and she was thankful for it. They finally stopped at a door, one unguarded and covered in crude locks. Vidar meticulously unlocked each one with a single hand, careful not to let her go the entire time.

The dungeons are rarely used, but there is another down there. He is bound for your protection. Vidar stood in front of the door, moments from sealing her on the other side.

Ailsa blinked back bitter tears, determined not to let them swell and spill down her face. "I don't want to be bonded with you anymore, Vidar. I want you out of my head, so I never have to hear another lie from your mind ever again."

Ailsa, I am still your friend here. His voice was pained in her head, yet it brought her little satisfaction. *Please, don't abandon me yet. I will get you out, I promise.*

"We *were* friends until you betrayed me. But you are no better than Erik, just as self preserving as he is."

His hand fell from her arm. The heavy ache of her rejection pulsing down their bond like an echo, fading a little each time until he accepted it. He took the knife a giant had given him to escort her here and lanced his palm. He took her wrist and dug the blade a bit deeper than before until her hand glistened in the far off torchlight.

They mixed blood for the last time, and Ailsa whispered the words that snapped their connection. Like a plug pulled from a drain, the red ink twisting up her wrist slowly inched back down until the only thing left was the sticky pull of their mixed life source between their hands. Ailsa released him quickly, averting her eyes to the now open cellar door.

"I know why you did it. I saw the scars on your back, all the pain they've caused you," Ailsa muttered. "And I am sorry you had to live through that, Vidar. I truly am. But your fear has ruined our friendship, and I cannot trust you anymore."

He lifted her chin to look at him, golden eyes hard on her without the mask and nodded. Deep down, she wished she could hear his last thoughts before he pushed her gently into the darkness beyond the door, and let it groan shut behind her. She didn't dare breathe until each lock had been set and his footsteps lingered out of hearing range.

The rage boiled back to the surface, sitting in those shadows. There were no cells here, just one large room with chains dangling from the ceiling. A small mercy he had not bound her as well. Ailsa kicked the stone wall, bruised knuckles by pounding her frustration against the grimy foundation.

She had been so gullible, so trusting, so desperate for an ally in this hopeless realm where she had no one left. Even the one man she had known all her life had become someone she could no longer predict. Erik was perhaps more dangerous to her than Surtur, Fenrir, and the witches combined.

"Odin's *fucking* eye," she spat, letting her body slide down the wall to rest on the dusty floor. Her temper was getting her nowhere, especially when she was stuck beneath a mountain in Muspell with no friend, fragmented memories, and no potentials to see herself out of this place.

Chains shifted in the darkness, reminding her she wasn't

alone in this room. What had Vidar said? The other person here was bound to *protect* her. How dangerous could they be to warrant such a thing, to get locked down here with her instead of Surtur's usual punishment? Her heart stammered in her chest as a figure sat up. The single torch burning between them skimmed the prisoner's profile.

"Ailsa?" a voice spoke barely above a whisper.

But not just any voice. *His* voice. The one who had visited her just days ago in her dreams, who whispered filthy things and spoke the language of her heart. There was the same break in her name when he said it in a garden as she held a knife to his throat.

Her heart didn't slow, nor did the air seem thin enough to breathe.

"Vali?"

CHAPTER 36
AILSA

"I found you."

Ailsa lifted the torch from its post on the wall as she neared him. The elfin was indeed chained with his hands bound to the wall behind him. The links were large and locked around his wrists, so he could not stand or do more than sit up straight. The little slack available bared his arms out at his sides, exposing his bare chest.

He said nothing more as she approached, steps slow as she studied him. An urge to reach out and feel him, to make sure he was real this time, prickled beneath her skin. "You're really here?" she asked. The only thing she could think to say.

"I am," he said. Apparently abounding with words, himself.

But how? Surely Fenrir or Nerissa would have had his head on a pike by now. Erik would have beaten her down here to finish what he started in Vanaheim, she was sure of that much. "Who imprisoned you?"

The elfin scoffed. "I discovered an herb garden and thought it might have belonged to you, but I was mistaken.

They used Hel's Breath to knock me out. Gods below, if your sisters ever find out I got picked off by a man with a garden shovel, they'll never let me live it down."

Ailsa nearly stumbled over a loose rock on the floor. "My sisters? You mean the ones you murdered?"

He winced. "Yes. Of course, you'd still remember that."

"Erik doesn't let me forget," she mumbled. "You seem to know them well for someone who met them on a battlefield."

Vali opened his mouth, but nothing came out, like he was trying to choose his words carefully around her. "It is a long story, but they helped me find you. They stayed behind in Helheim so I could steal a ship here to Muspell."

Ailsa didn't know what to think about that. Her sisters were not the forgiving type. Why would they help the man who killed them? What did they know that she did not? And if Vidar put him down here, was that also why he was so eager to do the same to her? He certainly hadn't warned the giants about the elfin. She eyed the shackles around his wrist, wary of the reliability of the bindings. "You cannot break out of those chains? I thought you were a son of Odin."

Vali jerked against the chains, testing their integrity. "Unfortunately, it would seem they were forged by the dwarves, and my magic doesn't work against them. I imagine these could have been Fenrir's chains before they freed him." His golden eyes traced her figure, hardly settling in one place too long. "How are you? What happened to your hand? Why have they put you down here?"

Ailsa set down her torch against a corner to sit beside him. "I'm fine. The slice isn't deep, but it stings a little. I made a deal with Surtur to get my memories back, and he broke his vow. Now he is on his way to retrieve the Eternal Flame to destroy Asgard and the Nine, and I'm still no closer to remembering anything about my past." Her voice shook despite the effort to hide her frustration, and she hated herself for it.

"Hey," he said, shifting her eyes back to his. His lips tipped in a kind smile. "Do not worry about your memories, Ailsa. If the witches do not return them willingly, I will make them. I heard they have a grave dislike of fire. Perhaps we can work with that." Vali winked at the subtle threat.

Ailsa felt herself grin. "And these memories they stole, they are fond ones of you, I'm assuming? Is that why you are so keen on helping me restore them?"

His smirk stretched into a full smile, one that made her heart dip between her ribs. "Not all of them are fond. Our relationship didn't start off well, nor was I easy to get along with thanks to my history with your family. Not to mention, you are the most stubborn woman in the Nine—"

"If that is true, then why are you here?" she asked, arching a brow.

His smile fell then, eyes turned downcast, and she couldn't figure out why the question had turned him off so quickly. "Because I made a vow to you."

"Men break vows all the time. You had every excuse to forget your oath. I certainly did." She crossed her arms and looked him straight in his gilded eyes. "Why did you come all this way just for me, Vali? What do you want with me?"

A muscle in his jaw ticked as he inhaled a long breath. "If I told you the truth, it might scare you."

She scooted closer to him, slipping past the iron boundaries that contained him. "We're in a dungeon. There's nowhere for me to run." Her fingers glided along the bottom of his jaw, relaxing the tension in his bite. "Tell me, Vali."

She thought he would dismiss her question, the way he looked off as if in some deep debate with his thoughts. But he finally said, "In my pocket there is a rune from Freya. She gave it to your sister, who gave it to me. I'm not sure I can quite explain it to you anyway else, other than to show you."

"Show me?" she asked.

Vali nodded and glanced down at his pocket. "Would you mind? Unless you'd rather help with these chains."

"I think we should keep your hands where they are... for now." Ailsa shot back with a baiting smile. She enjoyed seeing him tied up far too much, and it had nothing to do with her own safety.

"Fair enough," he said.

Ailsa reached into the pocket nearest to her, where his gaze indicated, and opened the folded cloth she found there. A marking was scribbled across the broken leather, one her memory recalled like a familiar scent. "I recognize this rune!"

"You do?"

"Yes!" She turned the cloth so he could see it. "I came across it while training with Freya. She would bring books from the library in Asgard when we studied together, and I recognize this one from one of Bragi's favorite sagas. It was a bit of an unusual study for us, so this stands out quite well."

Vali's brow arched. "What kind of books did you two usually read?"

Ailsa felt her cheeks burn again. "Not important." He grunted a sound of disbelief, but she continued before they got off track. "This is a sharing rune. They used it often in the war when they took prisoners from the other side. One could use it on a giant or a god and search their mind for anything they wished."

"That sounds dangerous, having that much access to someone's thoughts." Vali's brows furrowed.

"It was. Which is why it was forbidden after the Aesir-

Vanir war and forgotten from memory." She fingered the shapes with her thumb. "Do you think Freya meant for us to use it on one another?"

Vali shifted in discomfort, clearly unsettled by the idea. "I suppose she thought it would help you remember me if you saw your past in my memories."

Ailsa gripped the rune between her fingers. It wouldn't be quite the same as getting back her own... but it was a start. If he agreed to it. "We don't have to. If you are uncomfortable with this—"

"Of course not," he said. "If it means gaining back your trust or helping you piece together what happened, then do it. The memories will be from my perspective, but they're honest. You'll never have to wonder about my intentions with you ever again."

She searched him for any sign of reservation or reluctance, but found nothing to prove he didn't want to do this for her. There was no bigger invasion of privacy, no greater test of trust. There would be no hiding from her there. "You're sure, Vali?"

He nodded, licking his lips. "*Sváss*, if you wanted me to recite every detail of every moment from the day we met until now, I would do it. Because I remember it all, and it tears me apart to know you do not. Ailsa, I can't go on being the only one who remembers us."

Ailsa blinked, and a tear spilled down her cheek. "That must be difficult for you, being alone in the past."

But he shook his head. "It is worse to know you live in a world I am not a part of."

The way he spoke to her, the agony nailed into every word, it broke her heart. "What will your memories show me, Vali?" she asked.

"Everything. Starting with why I came all this way to get to you." He inhaled a large breath before confessing. "Because I love you."

Ailsa was sure her heart had skipped a few beats, feeling it seize in her chest. She shook her head stubbornly, refusing to believe it. "You are not the first to claim their actions are rooted in love."

"I will be the first to prove it then. Search me, Ailsa. I have nothing to hide from you."

Despite all the reasons she shouldn't, she wanted to believe him, couldn't bear for this to be another scam on her heart. Ailsa accepted his challenge, using the place on her palm still oozing blood like an inkwell to draw the rune exactly how it appeared on the cloth across Vali's forehead. She then leaned forward and pressed their heads together, creating a transient connection between their thoughts through the rune.

Vali's soft breath brushed her lips as their noses touched. She admitted, "I don't know what to do from here."

"I think," he muttered, lashes lowering to stare at her lips. "I think we should give it a moment."

Ailsa resisted the instinctual part of her flesh, reaching for him to close the rest of the distance between their faces. Instead, she shut her eyes and focused on the rune, concentrated on the warmth of his skin against hers. The space around them fell away, the steady sounds of their breath gradually transforming into a pulsing beat. A growing light pierced the blackness, beckoning her forward, and she followed it into his thoughts.

And then Ailsa suddenly saw, without opening her eyes, visions of a life she never lived. They were cold, blurry, a hazy veil covered her sight as she watched images of the elfin's childhood. Training with another fae with white hair and violet eyes. A woman with coal black hair stroking his head as he watched what she somehow knew was the last Alfheim sunset before leaving on a ship.

Ailsa wondered if she was navigating on her own or if he was showing her specific scenes—what he wanted her to see. Trials, hunts, sacrifices, years of searching and disappointment floated by her like a dream she couldn't quite catch until her head ached from the amount of it all. An entire history compressed into a few minutes of images. She decided to take control, focusing on a scene at a time to slow the acceleration, jumping across a timeline to a different place in his mind until she found where she needed to be. The long term saturating into more colorful, recent memories.

These were vivid, incorporating all her senses. Ailsa felt the groan of a ship beneath her feet, the sting of a winter breeze as flakes of frost built on the cloak she was wearing in the memory. In the distance her home was approaching, Drakame as she'd never seen it before—sailing toward it. This memory must have been the one before he found her.

It skimmed to the fjord, where she was looking at herself in a crimson gown, threads pulled all over the elegant sleeves. She looked angry, torn by an impossible decision. Ailsa felt Vali's attraction to her in that very moment, not one of lust but of some strange desire pressing beyond something superficial. His instinct to tear the ring from her shaking hands.

She then felt a great pain in her chest and looked down to discover she was back on the ship, bleeding in three places. Ailsa's image stood over Vali, looking down at him with equal amounts of hatred and hurt, a bloody knife in her hands. Had she stabbed him?

More memories flooded her, stealing all her focus to keep

them settled in the frame so she could experience them as Vali did. Each one more fully developed than the last. She saw flashes of Jormungand and the elfin standing over her as she clawed at him and knew then his panic. The same kind as when he watched her run into a misty forest after being impaled. The relief when she said his name and wrapped her arms around his neck—how a distinct warmth touched those memories, a golden glass lining the edges.

Happy thoughts—his most treasured experiences.

She watched from Vali's perspective as he woke up to her pale face on the shore of a freezing river, the way he enjoyed touching her skin in a bed lined with giant furs, felt an awakening rush that spilled through his heartless chest when she kissed his cheek. And so many more little, quiet moments between them, Ailsa didn't know if it was her heart breaking further with every memory or his own.

From their first kiss in a giant lord's dungeon to the crushing one when they became *Fraendi*, Ailsa learned that none of it had been forced. Through Vali's eyes, she saw their relationship was not one of control but of an overwhelming love and genuine desire on both their parts. There was never a spell. Only her and him and a journey that should have torn them apart but only stitched their threads of life together into a nearly indivisible braid.

And then, finally, Vali took her to their final memory together. The last one that included her. She watched helplessly as he lost her in the garden. The way she looked at him, the light that had once been there was now completely dim. The recognition of every experience she had just witnessed, gone. His grief was almost too much to feel, and she retreated, seeing all she needed to see. Running from a pain that was so visceral she felt as though it would shatter her bones if she remained there much longer.

Ailsa opened her eyes and broke away from his face. Her cheeks wet from tears, she realized she had a hand braced on his shoulder, the other clamped around the back of his neck. He was looking at her with the same golden eyes that intruded every dream since that last memory separated them.

"Please say something," Vali said to break the silence.

She peeled her grip away, his skin damp with sweat. How long had she been in his head? It felt like minutes, but her joints ached from the stasis, knees red and stiff as she shifted her weight.

"Give me a second," she rasped. "Gods above, that was... a lot."

He nodded. "Are you all right?"

"No. No, I am not." Ailsa felt her head shake, but the rest of her body had gone numb. Fresh tears leaked down her face, maintaining the wetness with a steady trickle. "Now I know what I lost, and it is more than I could have ever imagined."

"Ailsa," he made a move to touch her, but the chains stopped him. "I promise, we will make this right—"

"What if we cannot?" she asked, louder than intended. "What if I have lost those memories forever? Vali, if I have learned one thing being the weaver of fate, it is that nothing is certain. You came all this way for someone who might never look at you again the way I did before."

"Look at me," he said. She did, and he was wearing a half smile that eased some of the trouble in her heart. "I came all this way not to claim you, Ailsa, but to make sure you walked free from Fenrir. Whether or not you remember me, I just want to see you safe. That has been my goal from the second you were taken."

Maybe he wanted to mean those words, but he didn't. He couldn't. Ailsa had felt everything he did in those memories. When he lost her, he had lost everything, and it was tearing him apart even as she sat in front of him. How could anyone leave such a thing behind?

"Maybe it is for the best I don't remember my perspective," She squeezed her eyes shut and pushed away his feelings for her, trying to remember herself. Find a way back inside her own head.

"What?"

"We pushed against so much friction just to be together and where has it led? We're in a dungeon in Muspell!" Ailsa wiped her face and drew near to him again. "Why would you keep fighting for us when there is so much pain in our story, Vali? Why didn't you give up when you had the chance?" How could she, a single mortal woman, mean so much to him he would leave his home and risk it all in this forbidden realm?

"*Stiarna,*" he whispered too tenderly, "there are no strands of time where I would not choose us." He jerked against his bindings again, sitting up straighter. "I meant it when I said I came here to bring you home. If we get your memories back, and you do not feel the same for me, then so be it. Don't add more pressure to our situation by thinking you have to restore the realms and our relationship. Let's just get out of Muspelheim, yes?"

She took several slow breaths to soothe the ache in her chest before replying. "Yes, one thing at a time. I just," her eyes flickered to his heaving chest, "I want to try something first. If that is all right with you."

He jerked his head once in a nod, brows kissing in curiosity as Ailsa shifted to her hands and knees and sat close to him. She combed her fingers through his wavy hair, thick with sea salt and dust. They fell across the sharp planes of his face, lingered over his lips as she willed herself to wonder what they felt like in all those intimate memories he showed her.

"It is strange," she whispered, "because my head doesn't remember a thing about you. But my heart" —she spread her palm over her chest— "my flesh, my *soul*, they recognize you in a way I cannot explain."

He was silent, tipping his face into her touch, reveling in the connection of their skin.

"Your mind is a very beautiful place," she told him. "It was a gift to see myself through your eyes and feel what you felt for me." Though it made all of this so much more difficult to understand. Her feelings for him only complicated further.

"You are welcome back anytime, *sváss*." His eyes shut as she brushed his cheek with the back of her hand, exploring his skin, replacing the empty slots in her mind with new memories—learning him all over again.

"Perhaps this is all a gift," she said. A fresh start, a chance to experience all those old feelings for the first time again. "How many people get to have their first kiss twice?"

Vali grinned without opening his eyes. "You're going to kiss me?"

Ailsa climbed on top of him, straddling his waist as she took his head in her hands. Vali's eyes flew open, his smile falling as his gaze traveled from her face down to where their hips knocked together. She tipped his chin up to look at her again as she said, "Are you okay with that?"

His frustration was a hot breath caressing her neck, drying the tears that trailed down her throat. A ridge beneath his belt pressed between her legs, teasing his true wants. "I'd like it better if you would unlock my chains, to give you the full experience, *sváss*."

"Later," she said, smiling. Her fingertips trailed over the muscles of his chest, rode the waves of his breath as she watched him react to her touch.

"What are you doing, Ailsa?" he asked, voice strained. She dipped her head slowly, waiting for him to meet her lips halfway.

"Remembering."

She had watched him travel so many realms to get to her, and yet the distance between their lips felt like the longest journey as he lifted his chin to complete the last stretch. His kiss was grazing at first, but there was a spark that set her off when they connected. Her fingers dug into the back of his neck, spoke a quiet consent to go deeper—and Vali was ready.

Stealing her breath with the current of his tongue, he swept her mouth with little time to acclimate herself to the force of his kiss.

Ailsa's body reacted in a way she could only explain as a reflex to his taste. She tugged at the hair falling down his nape, eliciting a moan from his throat as she climbed higher, her hips joining the motion of her tongue. But her hands didn't stop there—they refused to remain in one place, skating his skin, fingering every tense cord in his body.

It was the smallest form of freedom since she had arrived in Muspell, the safest she'd ever felt exploring. And she found it impossible not to seek more, to not apply a counterpressure to his hardness as he pressed himself against her movements.

Ailsa broke from his lips with a gasp, not realizing at first how quickly this kiss had consumed her entirely. It was a wild chase, her lips following his, a most natural law of nature to which she was forced to submit. Somehow, he was both a stranger and yet knew her better than anyone in the Nine. Her other half in another life. If she could learn to love him once, she could do it again.

This kiss wouldn't smooth out those tattered places on her thread that had been tampered with beyond repair. It wouldn't bring back what she lost. But it gave her something new to have *now*. A connection grounding her in the past he showed her. Gave her something to feel beyond what he alone experienced. And there was not a spell, nor a curse found at the end of his lips.

There was a *life*.

"I missed you," she said as a heaviness sunk her heart between her ribs. "I missed you, and I didn't even know it."

"I missed you too, *sváss*." His mouth moved to her neck, inhaling her scent as he kissed the soft place where her pulse raced for him. "I missed you so damn much. Never leave my side again."

"Okay." She tilted her head back an inch, inviting him in, surrendering to this feeling of reward.

His laugh brushed the hollow column of her throat. "And for once, you don't even argue. That coward of an Otsman didn't break my lady, did he?"

"He tried." She gasped as his teeth raked her skin, gently nipping at her flesh. "I told him to—"

"Fuck off?"

"Aye."

He moaned his approval. "And why would you do that?"

Ailsa's chest rose with a baiting breath as his lips trailed lower down her chest, and she couldn't help but lean back to give him an easier access, inviting her fingers into his hair to keep him close. "Because I don't want Erik."

"Why not?" he asked again, looking for a better answer.

"Because I want... I think I want you, Vali."

His mouth stalled just above her heart, deceptively close to the place she wanted to feel those teeth pinch at her skin again. He traced the way back to her lips with the tip of his nose. "Because you belong to me, *elskan min*. With or without a bond, this will always be our fate, tied together until the end. Nothing in the past, present, or future can keep us apart."

She dug a finger along the slice of her hand, where a small smear of blood still oozed from the slit and wrote the rune to unlock the metal around his wrists. They fell to the dungeon floor with an obnoxious sound, making her flinch. As soon as his hands were free, they were on her, running up and down her waist, clawing at the thin material of her dress.

It was a reunion between her body and his, one her head didn't understand but never questioned. A carnal instinct that wanted to tear anything standing between them, that wanted to feel his rough hands run across her bare skin. Her nerves were on fire, sparking alive with an energy only his touch could awaken.

"I thought you said it was okay if I never loved you again."

He leaned back against the wall, pulling her with him until she was pressed against his chest, his head resting against hers like he was inviting her back into his mind. "And I meant it. You are under no obligation to be my *Fraendi* when we leave here." His fingers threaded themselves into the loose waves laying down her back. "But that doesn't mean you'll be free of me."

Ailsa caught his lips once more in a kiss, this time searching for only the comfort found in his connection. She muttered, "I understand that more than you know." She slipped from his waist, settling next to him on the cold dungeon floor, where he wrapped her in his arm. "What do we do now, Vali?" she asked.

His chest lifted with a long sigh. "Rest, *Stiarna*. Someone will come for us soon, and we need to be ready."

She nodded and pushed off his chest to look him in the eyes. "For the record, I'm glad you chose us. I'm glad you found me... *Sólskin*." The name was a whisper in the back of her mind, but he wore the title so naturally.

Vali's eyes lit up like that first sunrise after a Yule winter night, the arm around her tightened.

"There is nothing in the Nine, Ailsa."

CHAPTER 37
ERIK

Nerissa shoved him into the closest wall, the tiny witch surprisingly strong for her stature. Erik glared at her, feeling the push of her sedir keep him in place. He could do nothing but seethe, watching it all unfold from the other side of the threshold. Did nothing but stand there as Ailsa was dragged from the hall and thrown somewhere in the mountain. Her only crime had been taking his place in front of a dragon.

"Why did you throw her in a dungeon?" he asked. "She was perfectly fine with me—"

"She easily escaped under your watch, Erik." Nerissa snapped. "You couldn't control her even if you were bound by blood. I've never seen a man more incapable of doing something as simple as watching one woman!"

Erik ran a hand through his unbound hair. His braids had fallen from the amount of times he gripped them out of frustration. "What happened in there? Did she get back her memories?"

"Don't be ridiculous," she said, releasing him at last to

pace the width of the corridor. "Surtur doesn't make deals with anyone. He threw her to the side as soon as she lost use to him. Which could have been prevented if you would have just slayed the beast yourself."

"I was healing!" he shouted.

"And now you are stuck," Nerissa said, lifting her hand with their blood rune. "We had a contract, and since you didn't complete your end, you now belong to me permanently. So, I suggest you forget about your precious Ailsa."

His blood boiled beneath his skin. He was done with her control. Erik reached for her throat and slammed her against the same wall she had pushed him, pinning her by the neck as he crushed her airway. His hand covered that hideous scar marring her throat.

"I am done letting you control me, witch. You got what you wanted. Now let me go, or I will kill you and free myself from this cursed bond."

If I die, you will be stuck here without a single ally. They will kill you as soon as they see what you did to me. I am Fenrir's beloved, and that means you cannot touch me.

Her voice rang through his head like a shout, and Erik flinched, drawing back as the sound startled him.

"Idiot," she rasped as she gulped for air. "You are lucky you killed the bastard son of Odin, or Surtur would have no reason to keep you here. If you play things right, Erik, you could be one of the last mortals standing after Ragnarok. Think of the kingdom you could build with no more competition. An entire new world at your fingertips."

Erik almost let it slip that he hadn't killed the elfin, but he guarded the thought as he had learned to cut off their pervasive connection. If Ailsa was correct, he had somehow survived. But Surtur didn't need to know that yet. Nor did she.

Because what the witch dangled in front of him was enough to keep his mouth shut and the cards fall as they may.

"A new world?"

She nodded. "When the old ones are burned away, the Nine will rise again. The Tree will survive, and all will be new. You have a choice, Erik. Go sit in a dungeon with Ailsa and die or be a part of something greater than yourself."

She turned and left him standing there without waiting for his reply, because she knew as well as he did what his answer would be.

Erik returned to his room after his encounter with Nerissa, feeling the weight of his choice drag him down slowly. Whether it was guilt or dishonor, it hung like a carcass across his back, one he would carry for the rest of his life. As the lantern flickered alive from the match he struck, a shadow moved in the corner of his room.

He pulled a dagger from his belt and held it at arm's length toward the intruder. "Show yourself and explain why the Hel you are in my room!"

From the darkness, the silent man stepped forward. The lantern draping him with more light with each step he took. Erik growled, remembering this man as the one who not only knocked him out, but the one who helped Ailsa escaped. Gods only knew what he tried with her. The look he gave her was criminal enough.

"What are you doing here?" He demanded to know again. "Shouldn't you be riding off to retrieve the flame by now?"

The man held out his arm. In his hand, a key.

"Is that..." he trailed. The silent man nodded. Ailsa's key. What was he doing with it and why was he giving it to Erik? Was this some trick?

When Erik made no move to accept it, the man sighed, appearing irritated. He tossed the key on the bed sitting between them and stalked from the room like he was in a rush. Erik followed him out, locking the door shut behind him, but his eyes darted back to the key.

He might never see her again after this. He had wronged her once by leaving her all those years ago, and now he was leaving her again. Neither had been a simple choice, but a necessary one to make for himself. She would understand as she did back then. She always did.

He loved her so much, but she would never be his. He couldn't deny it any longer.

And perhaps he could give her a chance by setting her free. If anyone could survive Muspell and live through the next events of Ragnarok, it was Ailsa. He'd see her again on the other side—of that much he was sure. She had proven time and time again she didn't need him.

Erik snatched the key and went in search of the dungeons.

The halls were empty as the giants vacated the place to join Surtur in retrieving the flame from Fafnir's treasury. Erik drifted to the furthest dwelling in the mountain. The lowest level and the barest one, only a single hall stretching like a spine beneath the crawling maze of corridors above his head.

The dungeon door was marked with several locks, all clustered on top of one another and strapped to seal it shut. Erik methodically unlocked each one, feeling more uncertain as they clicked open. He could only brace himself for her anger and hoped this gesture would be enough to settle the score between them.

In his defense, if she had only listened to him, she wouldn't be down here. They could have founded the new world together, but Ailsa was too impulsive to wait. Just like her father, her ambition had led to her downfall, and he had to jump ship, or she'd pull him down with her.

The door groaned from its own weight as Erik pushed it open, darkness veiling the other side. He took a hesitant step across the threshold, feeling a cold draft meet him instantly. The toe of his boots knocked a torch that had been snuffed out, and it rolled beyond the arcing light from the hallway.

"Ailsa?" he called out to her. There was no response, and he began to worry. "Ailsa, it is me, Erik. I took the key from the witches so you could escape. Please, *sváss*, come to me now before we must part forever. Don't make me leave without saying goodbye."

"Goodbye?" Her voice practically hissed from the shadows. "You are joining Surtur and Fenrir then?"

"I have no other choice, but you do, Ailsa. I brought you a blade and my map to help you escape this realm."

"Place them on the floor, Erik."

He did as she requested, feeling strange as he did so. Why she wouldn't take it from his hands, he had no explanation. He heard her shift in the darkness as she snatched them both from the damp ground.

"Ailsa, I'm sorry this happened to us. I did everything I could to make sure you returned home, but I'm afraid there won't be a home to go back to after this."

"What do the fire giants have planned next?" she asked.

He shrugged. "I have heard them talk over dinner about burning the boundaries of the forbidden realm, saying the Eternal Flame will be enough to break the seal Odin placed around these realms to keep the giants contained. After that, they will march to Asgard."

"And what will you do when the gods burn?"

He sucked a breath, wishing she would step into the light for a moment so he could look her in the eyes as he spoke. "Nerissa said I could lead the new mortal realm after Midgard falls."

She laughed at him, and the sound made his hands ball into fists, despising the sound of being ridiculed. But Ailsa said, "Of course, you chase the power of a proper position, Erik. Your true love was always the next journey, the next raid, the next land to conquest. You will never be happy, and I almost feel sorry for you."

"Stop being so fucking pretentious," he spat. Her games had officially worn him tired. "You are not blameless for your place in this realm, nor in this dungeon. If you're going to insult me, then do it to my face. Show yourself, Ailsa!"

"If you insist," she said, sounding pleased.

A flame burst to life on his left side. But it was not his *sváss* holding the now blazing torch. It was a male he'd hoped was dead despite all of Ailsa's insisting. Erik gaped at the elfin, whose golden glare burned hotter than the torch in his hand.

"Hello, Lionheart." Vali smiled.

Erik reached for his weapon, then remembered he had given it to Ailsa. He had nothing else to defend himself, not thinking he would need a backup knife. He retreated, eyes wide on them both as they stepped closer. Ailsa's profile was kissed with firelight, deepening as the shadows caught around her eyes and haunting her appeal. His knife dangled in one hand.

Her upper lip curled as she said, "You lied to me, Erik."

"*Fuck,*" Erik growled, before turning on a heel and darting toward the prison door. Just as he took a second step, however, something sunk into his back, sending a jolt of pain down his spine so intense he collapsed to the floor, his legs suddenly unable to support his weight.

Just as quickly, the knife in his back was removed by the one who tossed it. Ailsa's bare feet stepped into his line of sight as he lay bleeding on the floor, shakes wracking through his flesh as the wound prevented him from taking a deep breath. One of them flipped him over so he could stare up at them, and he whimpered as the shift agitated his shredded muscles.

"Is this a good enough view, Erik?" Ailsa said. "Is there anything else you demand of me before I end your life?"

"What..." He choked on an inhale, feeling the air leak into his chest cavity. "Why would you..."

"Why would I be the one who ends you?" she finished for him. He nodded, and Ailsa knelt so her face hovered inches above his own. "You vowed to me on your knees you had rescued me from this male, that I was under some spell of his. But the fae do not have enchantments that control the heart, do they, Erik?"

"I... I don't know—"

"You broke a bond between us by unraveling our life threads. Why?"

"Nerissa made me!" he shouted, wincing at the way it disturbed the hole in his chest. "She said Vali had to die, but we couldn't kill him without killing you. I did what I did to protect you!"

"Why did they want to kill me so badly?" Vali hissed over her shoulder. "Nerissa wouldn't have made a deal with you unless she needed something."

"Because they believe you are the bastard son," Erik spoke through his teeth. "The one the Norns claimed would kill Fenrir. If the Great Wolf does not fall as the fates predicted, then—"

"He will survive Ragnarok," Vali said. "Well, it is a pity you won't be able to warn him then that his life is still very much in the hands of fate."

"No! No, please don't kill me. I had no choice with the blood bond!" Erik's muddy eyes were like saucers as he looked to Ailsa for mercy, as if he would find any there.

Her hands trembled as she poised the knife edge above his heart, pinching his skin as the tip dug itself through his shirt. She said, "You tried to steal everything from me, and you almost succeeded. I will not give you the chance to hurt me or the ones I love ever again. This is merciful compared to what you deserve, Erik."

"But Ailsa," he groaned. "I love—"

She shoved the blade into his chest before he could finish his declaration, silencing him as every muscle in his chest clamped around the knife until she yanked it free, blood spilling into his throat, his lungs, until it bathed his insides. Death crawled for him in the corners of his vision.

"I wish it wouldn't have ended this way, but you left me no choice," she whispered. Her eyes brimmed with wetness as she looked down at him. She blinked once, a shiny tear spilled down her cheek. "Goodbye, Erik. I hope you find peace wherever death brings you."

"We need to go, Ailsa," Vali muttered behind her. "If what he said is true, we need to get to Asgard. Surtur could be on his way there by now." She glanced at him and nodded, sparing Erik one last look before standing and leaving with the elfin. Abandoning him to die alone in a dark hole beneath a rock.

"Nerissa," he rasped, using his last breaths to plead down their bond. "Help!"

If she heard him, she didn't reply. Erik placed a hand over his broken heart as he surrendered to his ending.

CHAPTER 38
SEELA

This didn't feel like the right place.

Seela compared the scene in the prophecy to the one before her, but they were identical, right down to the waterfall feeding a river that ran like a ribbon into a thick forest, the one her group had followed to find this place. A small hut sat near the edge of a clear pool where the fall drained itself. The picturesque scene was like something out of a painting.

"Seela, sweetheart, I don't mean to question your judgment, but are you sure we followed that orb to the right place?" Enver confirmed her doubts. They were searching for where the gods had bound Loki after they had arrested him in Vanaheim.

"It has to be," she muttered. "You said yourself you couldn't mist anywhere you hadn't seen before."

"I'm sure there's more than one hut overlooking a waterfall—"

Ivor appeared from behind a tree in her human form, wiping her lips with the back of her hand. "It better be the right place because I am never misting with him ever again. Did you purposefully jerk us around through time and space just to make the trip that much more miserable?"

"I do enjoy a rough ride," Enver drawled, winking at Seela.

Seela shot them both an irritated look to silence them. "The vision shows Loki bound in a cave, but I don't see one from this vantage point. Shall we get a closer look at that cabin?"

They'd been waiting at the border of the forest, watching for any sign of activity for the last hour, but they remained the only souls for miles, it seemed. In this kind of quiet, one could hear for miles, but not even a woodland creature rustled a fallen leaf or disturbed the branches lacing the canopy above.

"I'm not sure." Enver squinted at the cabin. "If the gods did not want anyone helping Loki, they could have laced the place with traps."

"Well, we can't sit here all day." Ivor crouched as if she was about to shift. "I can go sniff out the area."

"That would help greatly. Just be careful," Seela told her. Ivor glanced at her, still surprised each time the commander verbalized concern over her well being, before stepping from the canopy's shade. In a few blinks, she had transformed into her wolf. A gradient of gray painted her fur as she stalked the green space leading to the hut, nose turned up in the west wind.

Enver sat back on his heels, his bow already strung in anticipation for any trouble. He said, "I'm not sure about this, Seela. Why would we free the same god that probably conspired with the witches to take Ailsa?"

She pushed a long breath through her nose, stalling her response. Enver wasn't wrong to have his doubts. Loki was the last god she wanted to help at this point, but she couldn't return home yet without knowing for sure if this was necessary.

"Out of everyone, Angrboda was hurt the most by Loki's actions. The gods might have never found Fenrir and thus began the precursors of Ragnarok had he not betrayed his family."

"She loved him, Seela."

"And?"

He scoffed, plucking the string of his bow absentmindedly. "And people do stupid things when they're in love. Sometimes a perspective can be warped when motivations are fueled by affection."

"Prophecies do not have such motivations," she said. "We vowed to protect Alfheim, Enver. Sometimes that means making allies out of our enemies."

Enver fell quiet, neither agreeing nor opposing her perception on the matter. They watched Ivor wander the bank of the river, appearing no more unusual than any other wolf having a drink from the icy waters.

"Can I ask you something?" he said.

"Sure."

"Why didn't you ever tell Ivor about your past?"

Seela sighed, drinking from her canteen before replying. "Ivor and I were never... intimate. We had things in common that led us to bond with each other, especially when Ailsa and Vali started becoming closer. But she was too busy plotting her betrayal to establish anything with genuine roots with me."

Enver nudged closer, keeping his eyes on the field. "Do you think things would have been different for either of you if you would have both been honest? There were feelings there, surely. I can tell by the way she constantly looks at me like she'd enjoy ripping my throat out."

"She looks at most like that," Seela offered. "I felt for Ivor, knowing what it was like to live among those who differed from me. But shared experiences can only bring people so far together. I cared for her. Part of me still does, but I'd rather be alone with my secrets than with someone I don't trust."

"You trusted me," he pointed out. "What does that mean for me, Seela?"

"You're asking a lot of serious questions suddenly," she said, deviating. Cold sweat collected along her hairline.

His broad shoulders shrugged. "Talk of war does that to a male."

She reached out to him to drum her fingers along the curve of his shoulder. Their relationship had started in a tavern after the civil dispute between the Light and Dark Elves had regulated. Casual at first, yet they had each found what they needed in the other at precisely the right time. Seela didn't know if that made them life mates, but she owed him more than she gave him credit for.

"I trust you, Enver, because when I am with you, I feel heard. You don't know what it's like to be who I am, but you try to understand, anyway. And I think that's what I've always been looking for. Not someone who knows, but someone who listens." She bit the inside of her lip to stop the tears from festering in her eyes, thankful he wasn't looking at her.

Enver lowered his bow and arrow to take her hand in his, kissing the side of her thumb gently. "I know you miss your *Hjartablód*. But I have loved watching how this journey has made you peel back your layers without him. It's been an honor watching you bloom, Seela."

Seela squeezed the hand that held her own, watching as

Ivor looked back at the forest briefly before returning to her scouting. She wondered if the wolven had been listening, if their voices carried on the breeze. But before she could respond to either of those thoughts, a woman appeared behind the fall.

"Who is that?" Enver murmured, catching sight of her at the same time.

Seela had never seen this woman before but knew her from the stories and gossip at home from Asgard. Before them was the goddess of compassion and devoted wife to Loki.

"Sigyn," she whispered. "Where she goes, we follow."

The goddess carried a large bowl with both hands. Her steps methodically descended the side of the fall leading to the pool, careful not to spill its contents. But as she dumped the bowl, a shout roared through the land, so loud and full of agony the ground trembled. The trees groaned as their trunks were inclined to splinter. Seela needed only one guess who the screams belonged to.

"Definitely in the right place," Enver said.

Sigyn's thin shoulders fell as she started back toward the fall. She looked tired, the way her steps dragged and the bowl weakly dangled at her side. Seela wondered how many times she'd taken that route, the same one that trenched into the sand from her frequent trips. Ivor remained in her wolf form as she stalked the goddess, her legs submerged in the river as she crossed the shallow width.

"There must be a cave behind the fall. Ready to confront Loki?" Enver asked.

Seela held up a hand as she stepped in line with him. "Wait for Ivor's clearance." A moment later, they received it. When the wolven cried a deep howl at the base of the pool, they emerged from the shadows of the trees, strides quickly covering the distance to the fall.

Enver offered to go inside first, but Seela quickly cut him off. This was her plan and her life to lose should anything go wrong. Large rocks lined the way behind the waterfall, slick beneath her steps. A small archway became clearly visible as they made it past the pounding cascade, and they quickly evaded the powerful current by ducking inside.

They spilled into a hollow throat of a tunnel. Seela's silent steps crossed the length of it to peer into a large room doming at the ceiling. There she discovered the other half of the vision Angrboda provided her, first noting the giant snake that dangled from a crack in the stone, its jaws wide as it attempted to wrap its fangs around the man tied to four boulders beneath it.

Loki was half dressed with his limbs tied back in heavy chains, each wrapping around its own rock. The venom dripping from the snake's fangs had burned away his skin, leaving the right side of his body red and raw. It was clear he was trying to keep one side from taking any venom, as one half of his body was recognizable while the other was missing the hair on his head and the flesh from his bones. He whimpered as the last drops of venom burned into his shoulder, white steam rising from the spot.

Seela covered her nose and mouth with a gloved hand. The place smelled like burning flesh.

"You have visitors, Loki." Sigyn eyed their group as she returned near the god's head, holding the bowl above him so the fresh drops of venom would not sting him.

But Loki did not answer at first—his pain obvious in the way his vicious tongue was tamed. He slowly lifted his head to look at them. The skin on the right side of his face appeared as if someone had peeled it away.

"Well?" he growled. "What do you want? Can you not see I'm a little busy at the moment being tortured for eternity?"

"Tortured or punished?" Seela asked for clarification. She rested her hands on her belt as she stepped closer. They were in no danger from these two for the time being.

"Same thing," Loki said, setting his head down again.

Seela kicked a chain with the toe of her boot, but it barely budged. Whoever tied these in place must have had the strength of ten gods, or perhaps just Thor himself. "Angrboda sent me."

At the mention of her name, Sigyn slipped, tipping the bowl until some of the venom inside splashed her thumb. She cried out, gasping at the slip, but still kept the bowl held high. Loki laughed a mirthless sound. "Why would that old witch send you here?"

"She told me I needed to free you in order to protect Alfheim. But I know you have no interest in the wellbeing of elves—"

"I have no interest in the wellbeing of *anyone* at this point. I hope they all fucking burn, every last realm."

"You don't mean that, Loki," Sigyn said softly behind him. Gods, she looked exhausted. From this close, Seela could see the tired circles beneath her eyes and the way her arms quivered from holding steady for so long. Seela quickly rounded behind the boulders and joined her where she sat on a boulder.

"Let me hold it for a while, Sigyn. Take a break."

The goddess looked at her with wide eyes but showed no resistance when the elfin took the bowl from her hands and held it over Loki's head. She bowed her head in gratitude before finding a spot on the cavern floor and rested her eyes.

"Why would you free me?" he asked, all smugness burned away from his voice now.

"I don't know," Seela admitted. "What would you do if I did?"

Loki did not answer right away, only glared up at her with his one clear eye. The other had long been eaten away, leaving behind a bleeding orbit. "Did you know my father was a frost giant, elfin?"

"Why does that matter, Loki?"

His wry smile returned to his face. "Bloodlines. They run through the father, do they not? I was not born one of the Aesir, but Odin made a place for me in his hall. Called me a blood brother, and I renounced my loyalty to the Jotnar when I made an allegiance to Odin through our blood pact.

"I have chased the ages away trying to run from who I am, trying to be one of *them*. I vowed my life to Odin, broke my family apart for the Aesir's approval, gave them treasures that made them the gods all warriors fear. When the truth is, I am not one of them, and they will never see me as one."

Sigyn sat up from her rest on the floor. "Loki, you know it's much more complicated than that."

"They have taken all my children away from me!" he roared, and the ground shook with his rage. "They bound me here to be slowly eaten away by a steady dripping venom for the rest of time! Tell me what I did to deserve this, Sigyn, and then name me an Aesir who has not done the same."

His wife stood to her feet, rubbing her aching joints. "I didn't deserve your infidelity either, but here I am! And I am still by your side as I vowed on our wedding day, bound to the same eternal punishment as you, though I have done no wrong."

The trickster god flinched at her words, and Seela thought out of anyone in the Nine, Sigyn's opinion mattered to him. Perhaps Loki did care about someone other than himself. No matter how singular that number may be. "You, my kind bride, are much too compassionate to see the bad in anyone. Gods know you deserved so much better than me."

"You didn't answer my question," Seela said, interrupting them both. "Why did Angrboda say the only way to protect the Nine was to help you? What will you do if we set you free?"

"What I've been doing since the day I was born, elfin." His brow twitched above a jewel green eye. "I'm going to cause chaos."

Seela's arms shook as the bowl filled halfway. She glanced at Enver and Ivor, who were still standing at the mouth of the cavern. He only gave her one of his ambiguous shrugs, like this was her choice to make and he'd support it either way. Sweat tipped down her back, an itch crawled up her spine that only added to the discomfort.

"What's the worst that could happen, elfin?" he asked. "The end is coming whether you help me or not."

"The question is, if I can trust you."

But Loki shook his head, fair hair clinging to the stone, sticky with sweat and moisture from the damp air. "Don't lie to us both. You know who I am. I will help you look out for the jotun and the elves, but I will do it on my own terms. No, Seela, the real question is, can you trust the gods? When the end comes, and it will, who will protect the fae?"

The bowl in her hands suddenly held the weight of the entire realm—perhaps all the Nine. Seela looked at Enver once more and nodded.

He unsheathed the glossy obsidian sword forged by the dwarves, the only substance in the Nine that could cut through flesh, bone, and curse alike. He crossed the small cavern to the first chain near Loki's right ankle, giving her one last chance to change her mind.

"Do it, Enver," she said, the tremble in her body slipping into her voice.

The chains provided little resistance as he let the blade fall across their links, slicing through all four in the time it took to blink. Loki slowly rolled off the boulder, groaning as the raw places covering his right side must have burned from the movement.

Sigyn was at his side in a moment, helping him stand, supporting his good side as he limped farther from the snake and his eternal bed of boulders. Seela carefully placed the bowl where Loki's head had laid, the red venom appearing much like a collection of blood and returned to her companion's side. The tension between her shoulder blades was now replaced with a fresh fear.

Had she made the right choice? Had her decision sealed the fate of the fae or offered them a new one? As Loki's consuming smile returned to his thin lips, his green eyes settled over her. And she knew she wouldn't have to wait much longer to find out the answer to all her questions.

Ragnarok was here.

CHAPTER 39
VALI

"This is it?" Ailsa asked, eyeing the boat with an arched brow.

Vali pushed the small vessel from its docking on the shore and into the lapping sea. His lips twitched in a smile, sensing her lack of enthusiasm to escape in such morbid style. "Oh, do not worry, *sváss*. I have an entire ship waiting for you just beyond that fog."

She stepped closer, squinting at the details lining the hull. "Are those... fingernails?"

Vali feigned ignorance, pretending to study the spot where she was looking. "You know, I'm not sure. Some of these could have once belonged on toes."

"Odin's fucking eye, Vali—"

"It was the best I could do!" He leapt over the side and offered her his hand. "So unless you'd rather stay and enjoy the comforts of Muspell, we must take the heathen hand and foot ship."

She sucked a breath and nodded, eventually finding enough nerve to take his outstretched hand and climb inside.

But the elfin noticed she touched as little as possible, barely sitting on the edge of the bench stretching the center of the vessel.

"Not exactly a white horse into the sunset type of rescue, but it'll do, I suppose," she said as her lips wrestled a grin.

Vali reclined himself across the opposite bench, using his magic to push them into the black sea. "I appreciate you lowering your standards enough to cooperate."

"Well, I'd hate to make you kidnap me again."

"Worked out well enough for me last time," Vali said with a wink. Ailsa rolled her eyes. Her time in the realm of fire had tamed none of the flame inside her spirit—and he silently thanked the Light for it.

A tension resurfaced on her face as she watched the shore distance behind them. Her forehead creased as she squinted. "Vali? Do you think you could maneuver this boat a bit faster?"

"Sure, but why do you ask?"

Ailsa jerked her chin toward Muspell, and Vali turned to find she was looking at a black cloud hovering just above the horizon. The morning sun peeked its harsh rays above the wispy edges. What was stirring the cloud, however, was what made his magic paddle them faster back to the Naglfar.

The realm was catching fire.

Flames licked across the land, covering the crimson earth from the east to the west, until it seemed all of Muspell was burning. Vali had seen nothing like it. The heat from the fire blew a hot gust to nudge their vessel along. The longer he stared, the brighter the light from the blaze, until it was impossible to look at without going blind. Vali blinked the way ahead back into focus, into the fog where the light from

Muspell glowed against the curling dew and illuminated the outline of the ship.

"Surtur must have the flame by now," Ailsa said grimly. "We need to get to Asgard and warn the gods before—" But her words were cut off as a rogue ember fell into her lap. Ailsa stood quickly, lurching the boat as she patted the blazing cinder into dormancy before it caught her dress on fire.

"What in Hel..." Vali's voice trailed as he followed the smoky track the ember left, straight into the sky. Above them brewed a storm, only the lightning flashed like a rod of hot iron, red and scorching, glowing behind the creeping clouds. The land was not the only thing on fire, it appeared the sky had caught as well.

And it was about to rain fire over them both.

Vali snatched Ailsa to his chest to stop her from swaying the tiny boat and thrust as much magic through his body and into the brittle foundations of the hull to race them over the frothing sea, skipping across the waves like a smooth pebble in a still pond.

"Vali, slow down!" Ailsa shrieked, struggling against his grip. She slipped an arm from his hold and pointed to something falling straight in front of them. Not a drop of fire, but a clump of it.

He shifted the trajectory of the boat mere inches to miss the burning ball, but the shift caught a large swell, throwing them sideways with a force the small vessel could not withstand. Vali felt his head hit the water first, slapping him so hard he lost hold on Ailsa.

The tumbling was disorienting. Suspended in the sea, when the elfin's momentum finally stopped, he opened his eyes and looked for Ailsa, thrashing his head in every direction. But it was hopeless, the water's depths too dark to see through, the only light coming from the glowing sky above the crystalline surface.

"Ailsa!" he shouted as his head broke from the tide. The waves were growing more restless, forming mountains in the water he could not see beyond. The remnants of the vessel floated in splinters around him. He called out for her again. Panic thickened the air in his chest each time she didn't answer.

"Vali!" He finally heard her call back. Swimming toward the sound, he found her fighting the waves as they tried to drag her under. Falling fire continued to rain as their fingers skimmed in the water, their connection a lifeline to the other, and Vali gripped her like he was holding onto his very life thread.

"Get to the ship," he blurted between gasps.

"I can't," she said before swallowing a spray of hot saltwater. "I lost it." He pulled her close to his side so she could wrap her hands around his shoulders, and he guided them both toward the Naglfar. The insidious vessel had never looked more appealing as they made it to the ladder woven from hair instead of rope, draping over the stern.

Vali heaved himself over the side when he reached the top, barely taking a needed breath before returning to help Ailsa up the remaining way. Her movements were clumsy and slow, and he noticed the right side of her skull had been sliced open from her eye to her ear, assumingly from the boat debris. The merciless waves had cleaned the wound, but blood still trickled from the wound and tinted the white strap of her dress red.

She climbed over the side, reaching for his neck with the swing of her arms as she tried to twist her legs over the side. Her soaked gown inhibited her range of motion, and Ailsa tripped, her weight throwing itself against his chest with a force that knocked him off his boots. Vali fell on his back while tucking her against himself, taking the brunt of the fall.

"Vali?" she mumbled in his ear. Her lips were cold as they brushed his skin. "Are you all right?"

He held her wet body against his chest for a moment longer before nodding. "Are you?"

"I'm well enough." She slipped from his front, sliding into the bend of his side to look up at the sky. "Do you think that's the seal falling that's kept the giants here for centuries?"

Vali forced himself to disregard the way her curves fit so perfectly against him to consider her statement. "I suppose that would make sense. Pretty foolish of Odin to keep the key to their prison inside their cell, though."

"Technically, they wouldn't have gotten it if I hadn't slayed Fafnir and found his treasure, but we won't mention that to anyone in Asgard."

Vali sat up. "You slayed who?"

She unlaced one of those foreboding smiles. "I'll tell you later. Do you still have the map?"

He leaned forward slightly to pull the soggy map from his back pocket, the one Erik had given Ailsa to help her escape and handed it to her. Her healer hands carefully unfolded the fragile parchment. It was a wonder the map had even stayed in his pocket through all the swimming, but an even greater miracle the ink was still somewhat intact.

Names and borders were blurred, but the thicker lines marking the boundaries of the realm were still legible. Now they just had to figure out where they were in relation to the mainland in order to find the best route back to the River Gjoll. He looked to Ailsa, who had spent far longer in this place and might recognize the landmarks running in diluted streaks across the page.

"Raise the anchor and prep the ship, Vali. I'll figure out the map," she said without looking at him. Her finger hovered over the map as if retracing their journey as the wet parchment flopped in her lap.

He did as he was told, regretting leaving her side so soon. After weeks of being without her, there was a need to constantly touch her in a way that went beyond intimacy. Like she'd fade away if he left her too long, like this was all a dream he'd have to wake up from soon, and he wanted to linger in this place of peace for as long as possible. The giants could have left them both locked in that dungeon until the Nine fell, and he would have been grateful to spend his last days tangled in her hair, lost in her lips.

But fate always pushed them forward despite his feelings on the matter, and Vali knew he was fighting for something much greater than last days and final breaths—he was fighting for their future and all the potentials that remained.

The ship swayed to the motion of the tide as he lifted the anchor. Ailsa joined him on the captain's deck before he even touched the sails. "Here!" she exclaimed, pointing to a corner of the realm so hard, her finger protruding through the parchment. "*Skide*," she cursed, "it's no matter, anyway. Do you remember when I nearly died in the Realm Between Realms? You showed me a memory when we were about to reach Alfheim—"

"Yes, of course," he said. He'd never forget such a day.

"Well, that triggered something in my memory, something I could connect with. I had a vision in those woods from the blind crow, and she brought me to the First Realm, where Muspell and Niflheim joined to give form to the first giant,

Ymir. But there was also a river in that vision, splitting the way between the two worlds, and I think that is the river from my vision. I believe the old text calls it the Elivagar."

"The Elivagar was one of eleven rivers feeding the Tree in the beginning of time," Vali said. His eyes lit up, feeding off her excitement. "As was the Gjoll. If we follow this, we find the Gjoll—"

"And we find a way out of the forbidden realms," Ailsa said, finishing his thoughts. "Odin's seal is burning. If we use the river, perhaps we can get to Asgard faster than Surtur, who will be taking the long way there."

"Brilliant, Ailsa," he said, kissing her quickly on the forehead before moving onto the sails. He'd have to focus on the power of the wind to push them against the tide and toward the river, and being the only fae on the ship, it would take all his concentration.

"Just tell me how I can help," she said, following him as he checked the rig.

His eyes scanned the deck for something she could control without magic. "Settle yourself behind the wheel, *sváss*, and keep us steady. I'll take care of the wind."

"Aye, Captain," she teased. He watched as she flashed her teeth in a smile, fire continuing to fall behind her and burn the distance. And she looked so beautiful with her wet hair framing her face in stringy waves, the orange glow from the sky kissing her honey skin, the way her white dress left little to his imagination as the wetness made it practically transparent. He wanted to tell her right then and there—and maybe he shouldn't. Maybe the moment was all wrong, and he would make her uncomfortable. But it couldn't be helped.

"I love you, Ailsa," he said.

Her smile fell, as expected. And Vali turned from her

gaping mouth and stretching silence to forget his feelings in his work, thankful she returned to the main deck and positioned herself behind the wheel without saying anything to hurt his pride even more.

He meant it when he told her she didn't have to love him back. He'd protect her until the Light faded from his soul no matter what. But *gods below*, he'd never know the end of suffering if that was the case.

Ailsa's scream tore his focus away from the mast.

He darted up the short stairwell to the upper deck, finding her staring with wide eyes at the head tied to the mast. "Who in Hel is that?" she asked through the fingers covering her mouth.

Vali couldn't help but bark a laugh. "That is your ancestor, Bjorn Bloodblade. We didn't exactly see eye to eye on letting me borrow the Naglfar." He untied the heathen, whose face was starting to droop from the heat, and threw his head over the side so he wouldn't be staring at her as she steered. "Better?"

She eyed him warily but took her place behind the helm of bony hands and forearms. "It's a start."

The ship lurched as a wave slapped the hull, like the storm was demanding his attention to return. Vali rushed in the direction of the bow, returning his focus on the foremast that had just torn from the reigning debris.

"A start, indeed," he murmured to himself.

Hours of fighting the wind and sea after his body was starved of both food and water and a well of magic left Vali swaying on his feet as if he were drunk. He leaned against the railing of the ship, ready to toss up the bile in his stomach as his vision doubled. He gripped the edge of the wood, supporting himself up while the unsteady ship threatened to throw him down.

"Vali?" her voice came to him. "You don't look so good. Why don't you lie down—"

"I will not rest until I know we are safe."

"But Vali..."

"No!" He shook his head—which turned out to be a big mistake as he lost his balance and slipped to his knees. He felt her hands on his face, assessing him with adept fingers, combing his hair out of the dampness coating his forehead.

"You're exhausted," she said. "When's the last time you've eaten anything?" Vali didn't answer, because he couldn't recall himself. Ailsa shook her head in disapproval. "You're little good to me in this state. I need you to stop before you drop dead in front of me."

"But the ship—"

"I can control the ship. My father taught me how to sail, remember?" Vali nodded—or made some vague head movement like it. She rubbed his back and said, "Besides, I believe we already passed the seal. It's getting colder, and the fire has finally stopped falling from the sky."

She coaxed him with those same persuasive hands to sit down and pulled him the rest of the way into her lap, where his head rested on the fullness of her thighs. Vali was compelled by her warmth, the scent of her he had almost forgotten in their time apart. Soon he was dragged under by the mesmerizing way the pads of her fingers traced the runes across his skull.

His gaze rolled lazily from the blurred sight of her face looking down on him to the sky above. Ailsa was right—they were no longer in Muspell. Above them now was true dusk, with stars and a sunset sky fading into midnight blue. But there was something else above them, and Vali didn't know if it was a menace or a solace.

Two ravens flew above them, but Vali saw the glassy images of their doubles join the flock. Odin's spies appeared more like a ring of vultures as they circled the ship, waiting for something worthwhile to take back to their master.

Vali reached for Ailsa's arm and squeezed it as hard as his weakened state would allow. "Whatever happens next," he groaned, "do not leave me, *sváss*." The fire giants were dangerous, but they were nothing compared to the Aesir.

"I promise I will still be here when you wake up, Vali. Rest."

He clung to her vow and stared back at the ravens flying above, his last thoughts drifting to Odin and what his father must be thinking at this moment, watching the fire giants march from their exile. Everything he was desperate to prevent now unfolding in front of him. Yet, Vali though it was still less than he deserved.

The day was coming they had all been trying to avoid for centuries, but all roads and fates led to Asgard now.

CHAPTER 40
SEELA

"That's your plan? You're going to let the fire giants break into Asgard using the front door?"

Seela balked at Loki as they met with the Light and Dark Elves' war council back at the Light Palace. The god had shapeshifted into the form of Vali despite her arguments. Unfortunately, the illusion worked well, and no one questioned the disguised god or his decision to demand meetings with the frost giants.

Loki smiled the kind of smirk that did not belong to Vali, a crack in the mask only Seela would notice. "The Bifrost can only be used by the gods—unless there is no watchman to regulate its use. I have a way to deal with Heimdall, and when he is out of the way, all will be able to use the bridge."

"Heimdall can see for a thousand miles in every direction," Oru spoke across the table, one of the five giant lords standing on the other side of a map of the Tree of Life. "Surely he will see an army approaching."

Loki held up a finger, a detail he had apparently already thought through. "Unless it is too dark for him to see anything. And I know someone who can swallow the sun and the moon for us. Temporarily, of course. Just long enough for us to keep Heimdall in the dark—literally.

"The fire giants have officially broken free of Muspell. Fenrir is hunting for Odin, and if fate falls how it should, everything should be in place to break the curses the Allfather has placed upon our lands and our people. In a few days, we could have a new world to create, one that does not include oppression and control from a one-eyed tyrant."

Whispers filled the room, loud in their collectiveness. Even the frost giant lords seemed unsettled by this recent report. Oru spoke for the rest of them when he said, "Few of us are still alive to remember the tales of Surtur. He will not stop at the gods' realm when it comes to his destruction."

"Which is why we keep the fight in Asgard," Loki said. "We begin and finish this there. Between the gods and Odin's and Freya's armies of mortals, many of the giants will fall in Valhalla. But the fae must make sure they do not escape those walls."

"And what of Fenrir and Loki?" Another giant spoke. "What of all the other monsters that will be released in the coming days?"

Loki rolled his shoulders back, exercising a drop of self-restraint Seela didn't know he possessed. "We can only take so much of fate into our own hands. Every man, fae, and god will have a part to play, an influence on the outcome of this war. We can only do our part to make sure the ending favors our people and our worlds."

A finalizing quiet settled over the table. The plan settled with no more questions. Oru said, "I will gather the Jotnar and be at your door at once. We have already sent word to our cousins in the east. They are... much larger than we are." A grin lifted his lips. "Odin won't know what hit him."

"No, Oru," Loki spoke, but Vali's eyes darkened. "He'll know exactly who orchestrated his undoing. I'll make sure of it."

Seela hesitated just outside Lady Rind's room, her heart racing quicker than it had during the meeting. She studied every inch of Loki's disguise, tried to find anything the High Lady would find inconsistent with her own son.

"I don't know what you're so worried out about. I fooled a room full of fae warriors. I'm pretty sure I can trick a half lucid mother," he said.

Rind had been requesting Vali and Seela since word of their return filtered through the castle, and Seela could only put her off so long before she became suspicious. "Not even you are cunning enough to get by my High Lady. Trust me, Loki. This is a bad idea—"

"I'm going in now." He pushed past her to open the door, silencing anything more Seela could say on the matter.

She followed him inside the bedroom, where Loki was making an entrance of himself as usual. Even in Vali's skin, Seela noticed the pride in his steps, the arrogance in his chin, a confidence when entering the room that Vali did not flaunt quite so brazenly. Her *Hjartablód* never demanded attention, and yet now he was drawing the eye of every healer in the room. Loki dismissed them all with a wave of his hand.

Seela stepped inside after the last healer slipped out and lingered a short distance behind as Loki pulled back a draping of sheer curtains that surrounded the High Lady's bed. "Mother?" he said quietly, gently tapping her hand that lay on top of the sheets. Seela swallowed the filthy taste this deception left in her mouth and hoped they would make this quick.

"Vali?" Rind whispered, her voice weaker than ever.

Loki knelt beside her, taking her hand in his to pet it. Seela was just surprised the god had a tender bone in his body. "Yes, it is me."

"Your voice is different. Higher. Are you sick?" But as her fingers slipped into his palm, she flinched, drawing back. "And your hands, they're ice cold."

Loki cleared his throat, pushing his voice down an octave as he said, "It must be the stress. I've had to make many tough decisions lately."

"And Ailsa? She cannot still be in Vanaheim."

Loki glanced at Seela, hesitating his answer. "She... had to stay behind. It is safer for her there. There was no need to bring her into this. Not even Ailsa could change the fate of Odin now."

Lady Rind folded her hands across the heavy blanket. A quiet sigh streamed from her nose. "I see. Is Seela with you then?"

Hearing her name, she spoke, "I am here, Lady."

Her head rolled toward her voice. She patted Loki's hand in dismissal. "Well, do not let me keep you from your duties if you have truly been so busy, Vali. I want to speak to Seela, anyway."

"Of course," Loki said, grateful to get away. "Get some rest, Mother." He kissed the top of her head before he left, leaving the curtain parted for Seela as she entered.

The High Lady opened her mouth as if to speak but remained silent until the door shut behind the god as he left them alone. Rind arched a brow at her. "That was not my son."

Seela lowered her head, unable to meet her eyes. Rind continued, "Where is Vali, Seela? Or would it be better to ask, where is Ailsa?"

She didn't answer his mother at first. The words were lost somewhere between her head and her mouth. "Truly, I do not know where either of them are. But Ragnarok has begun, and I am preparing Alfheim in Vali's place until he returns." She looked back at her then. "He will come back soon. I am sure of it."

"Yes, he will." Rind sighed. Her skin was damp as Seela stroked her hand, some of the warmth there already gone. "The Allfather's purpose for him took Vali from me for most of his life. And now, in my death, he is taken away again."

"I'm sorry," she said, something warm rolling down her cheek.

Rind reached for her hand and caressed it. "How are you, Seela? I see how much your shoulders are carrying."

Seela realized it was the first time anyone had asked her that in a very long time. "I am terrified," she admitted. "What if I trusted someone I shouldn't? What if I made the wrong choice and doomed us all?"

Lady Rind's wise eyes squinted, as if trying to see through her. "Are you speaking of your heart or of Alfheim?"

Seela scoffed, her heart the least of her worries right now. "Alfheim, definitely."

The High Lady shrugged weakly. "Sometimes our heads don't understand our hearts. There are some choices that cannot be justified with logic, some decisions we cannot make with our minds. But when your heart knows some-thing to be right, when reasons for it go beyond all explanation, I like to believe it is fate pulling us where we need to be."

Fate. A word so carelessly used in most conversations, yet the most powerful force in the universe. Greater than logic, power, knowledge, greater than love even. She said, "Then I suppose if this all goes wrong, we can blame it on fate."

Lady Rind laughed a hollow sound. "It'll be our little secret, my sweet girl." She stroked Seela's hand with her thumb until her eyes fluttered, heavy with sleep.

"Your father would be so proud of you," she whispered.

Seela said nothing, but instead smiled to herself, and continued to hold her High Lady's hand until Rind had fallen asleep.

CHAPTER 41
AILSA

She lined the threshold with her blood, shutting the world away on the other side as Ailsa waited for Vali to waken. Her runes sealed the door of their room to the frame, preventing the gods and their servants in the hall from intruding. They were incessant here, trying to pull her away from the elfin who still slept an entire day after he'd shut his eyes.

"I told you I am not leaving until he wakes up. Leave us be!" she shouted through the wall. Their sounds of protest met her back as she walked away, returning to the four poster bed at the end of the long room. Arches to the outside lined the way, but they were so high in a tower above the fields of Valhalla, Ailsa had no inclination anyone would enter from the terrace outside.

A falcon flew in between two marble pillars, landing in the center of the room where the furniture was arranged around a golden chandelier. Ailsa snatched the closest thing next to her, which just so happened to be a tray of food sitting on a brass cart—the leg of some winged animal the most appealing weapon on the plate.

When she turned back to set her aim, she found not a falcon, but a goddess standing there. A coat of feathers draped around her shoulders, golden hair braided into a towering bun on top of her head. Her lovely face sharpened into a scowl as she eyed Ailsa.

"How dare you threaten me with poultry."

Ailsa smiled for the first time since they arrived in Asgard. Her relief loosened her grip on the leg, and it fell to the floor. "Freya!" She ran to the goddess and wrapped her in a tight embrace, one returned with an equal clasp.

"He found you," Freya spoke in her ear. "Thank the fates that elfin is as stubborn as he is tall. I knew he wouldn't return without you."

The goddess pushed her away, raking her gaze over her body. Ailsa had changed into the golden robes prepared for them in this room when the Valkyries brought them both here. She had been grateful when the ravens found them at first. The way up the Gjoll turned cold, and fighting against the tide was a losing battle without Vali controlling the wind. She made a promise to him she wouldn't leave his side until he awakened, but everyone in this realm seemed determined to help her break that vow.

"Where have you been, Ailsa?" Freya asked.

She could only shake her head, not sure of her journey herself. She slipped from Freya's fingers to sit at the end of the bed near Vali, who still slept soundly. If it weren't for his snoring, she'd have thought he was dead. "Muspelheim, it would seem. Why or how remains to be understood since my memories are still gone."

The goddess had a look about her that was both confused

and concerned. "What do you mean? You remember me well enough."

"I remember everyone except *him*," Ailsa said, looking back at Vali. "Any moment his thread touched, it was erased. And I don't think I'll ever get it back."

"But my rune—"

"Was wonderful," she told the goddess. "Seeing the past through Vali's perspective was a gift I never deserved, and it helped bridge some of the gaps needed to trust him again. But they are still his memories. What I *felt* in those moments, I'll never know. I can only guess. It makes it difficult to..." Ailsa's voice wavered. She stopped herself before it broke.

She felt Freya's touch smooth up her arm in condolence. "I understand. But Ailsa?"

"What?"

Her grip around her forearm made Ailsa look at her. "Vali loves you with a passion that is worth giving a fighting chance. If you want to remember what it was like, let him show you."

Ailsa scoffed. "That would be easier if he would wake up."

She backed away from the bed, pulling something out of her coat. "He is a god, Ailsa, more than he is anything else in his bloodline. With rest, he will make a full recovery. But when he does wake, give him these apples from Idun's garden. They'll help."

"Thank you, Freya. As always," she said, taking an apple in each hand. "Did you only stop by for this?"

The goddess shook her head. "Odin sent me in here to get you to talk. He wants to know about Surtur—"

"There is nothing to say. They found the Eternal Flame and are marching now to burn the Nine down."

"The Flame..." she repeated, golden eyes staring at something a world away. "Did Vali mention anything to you about Baldur? It displeased Odin to see he wasn't with you."

"He said something about a ring he took from Baldur when he saw him in Helheim, but it was stolen by a Jotun when he was caught and thrown in their prison."

"A Jotun?" This interested the goddess. "What is a frost giant doing in the realm of fire?"

Ailsa's heart broke thinking about Vidar, wishing she would have trusted him a little more before severing their bond. Whatever his motivations were, even if they were wrong, he had not betrayed her out of malice. He had an endgame in mind she was still trying to figure out, one that included bringing her and Vali together again.

"It seems Odin has made too many enemies to keep track of these days."

Freya shrugged and pulled her coat tighter, stepping toward an archway. "I will let him know all this. The Allfather is still demanding to speak with you both. For your sake, and for all of ours, do not keep him waiting. As it stands, I need to go back to Folkvang and ready my armies."

Before opening her arms to transform back into the falcon, the goddess added, "By the way, should you want to explore your past with the elfin, I left something in the nightstand to help you out."

Ailsa rolled her eyes but smirked. She didn't need to look to know what she left behind. Certainly not another rune. "Thank you, goddess."

"My pleasure," she smiled. "It is good to see you, Ailsa. I mean that." She spread her arms and folded into the image of the falcon once more, taking flight into the sunny afternoon sky.

"Is she finally gone?" a hoarse voice spoke behind Ailsa,

making her startle. She looked back at the elfin, who still lounged on his front, his eyes still shut as he buried his face into the pillow.

Ailsa crawled up the massive bed to sit beside him, resting her shoulder against the gilded bed frame. "Were you faking sleep this whole time?" she asked.

Sensing her weight next to him, he turned to his side, reaching a hand out to skim her knee. "Not the whole time, but her voice was enough to rouse me. You should have woken me sooner, Ailsa."

"You looked terrible. I wanted to make sure you got enough rest before..."

"Before the end of the worlds?"

"Before we meet with Odin."

He scoffed a sound of disapproval before taking an apple from her hand. "Same thing."

Ailsa watched him eat in silence until he was down to the core of the golden fruit. "How do you feel now?"

"Better than ever," he said with sincerity. His hands tossed the apple core to the bedside table, finding themselves sneaking into her lap. "You're still here."

"Of course. I made you a promise." Ailsa leaned forward, grabbing his chin in her grip before gently kissing his lips. "Did you know you snore like a bear?"

He scoffed, shaking his head. "Yes, you have reminded me many times, *sváss*."

Ailsa smiled, enjoying the feeling of being so close to him, but his sour stench was making it a challenge. "You should probably go bathe. You still smell like Muspell." Her nose crinkled as she took in his scent. The evergreen smothered with smoke and sea.

His laugh showed off a flash of white teeth. "You're probably right. I'll get on that, then." He took the other apple from her hands and slid out of the bed, and Ailsa couldn't help but stare at the broad muscles in his back as he walked away, stretching his tight body as he did so. Gods, he was gorgeous in the shadows of the dungeon, breathtaking even soaked to the bone with his skin glazed with a sheen of sea. But here, as the sunlight of Asgard shone approvingly across his Aesir eyes, he was enchanting.

And he pledged he belonged to *her*.

"You can come join me if you want, Ailsa." Vali looked over his shoulder and winked. "The showers in Asgard are big enough for the both of us."

His offer was tempting, but Ailsa was thinking too much on the words the goddess left her with. There was only one potential if she followed him now, and she had other plans in mind for that. Her gaze shifted from the elfin to the bedside table. "Maybe next time," she said in a quiet voice.

She forced herself to look out the archway in front of the bed, focusing on a glittering flag saluting the sun on top of its tower, waving in the warm wind. When she heard the water rain in the Asgardian shower, she took a settling breath and slipped from the top sheet.

She could wait for fate to show her, or she could weave the way herself. With the threat of their future hanging in the hands of Ragnarok, did the past really have any power over her decisions in the present?

Ailsa knew what she felt for him *now*. Was that not enough to take what she wanted?

She pulled back the drawer of the nightstand, gasping as she took in the scraps of fabric Freya insisted would *help*. Her cheeks burned as she pulled it out by the straps, wondering how the lace was even held together with such thin threading.

The garment was solid black, completely see through in all the places that normally required coverage. Tiny gemstones throughout the appliques twinkled a kaleidoscope of colors in the sunlight still pouring in from outside. It was beautiful— not something she would ever find back in her village—but she was far from the woman Vali took from that fjord.

Ailsa shut the drawer. A nervous flutter tumbled through her chest as she made her choice. She needed this. She needed *him*. The past had been erased. The future was waiting to be written. But this hour was theirs to set them all right again.

"Ailsa?" Vali's voice came shortly after she heard the water shut off. She called him out onto the terrace, where the sun was hovering above the horizon. "What are you doing out here?"

She turned to face him, still leaning against the marble edge. Her hands did not greet him when he came to stand beside her, wearing nothing but a towel around his hips. Instead, they pulled the shimmering gold robe around her middle a little tighter, keeping her secret concealed until the time was right.

"Just getting some sun and fresh air. It's been a while since I've had either."

He leaned his forearms against the edge, staring down at the fighting fields, which were empty at this hour. The fallen warriors most likely waiting for word concerning the fire giants. "It's deceivingly beautiful here, I will admit. But there is no better sunlight than the kind in Alfheim."

"Will you go there after this?" she asked.

ALEXIS L. MENARD

He shook his head. "I'll have to stay and defend Odin. I cannot let my personal grudges against him threaten the rest of the Nine. Fenrir is coming, and I must be ready."

"And if you kill the Great Wolf?" Ailsa shifted her weight to the side to study him, finding him looking off across the territories of Asgard.

"Then I will return home and take care of my mother until she passes. There are too many other factors that are uncertain at this point to plan anything more beyond that."

Guilt pinched her heart. "Factors like me, you mean?"

He finally looked at her then, his golden eyes like hot amber in the twilight. "Yes."

"What about me, Vali? How will I change your plans beyond Ragnarok if we both survive it?" Her wonder made her take a step closer until she had to crane her neck to look up at him.

"It was never certain what would happen after I found you," he said, pulling a loose strand of hair off her cheek. "I heard your conversation with Freya, how it is difficult for you to connect with me without your memories—"

"Vali that isn't—"

"It's fine," he said, placing a thumb across her lips. "I get it. But if you choose us when this is all over, everything would be different. I'd have you by my side to rule Alfheim, a life where I didn't just have to worry about myself, but you and your happiness as well." His neck convulsed with a hard swallow. "You'd need only to say it, and I'd give you everything."

She let one of her hands slide up his chest, feeling his damp skin hot from the shower. "I might never remember our past, Vali. Those memories that anchored my feelings for you, I might never get them back." His skin rose beneath her touch, chill bumps littering his chest as she hooked him by the neck.

"But that's okay," she whispered. "Because we can make new ones."

Sensing her intentions like a scent, Vali pushed his hips closer, brushed her hair from her shoulder. "Is there a place you would like to start, *elskan min?*"

Ailsa's lips tipped in a smile. Her other hand fell from the seam of her robe, letting the satin slide from her shoulders and down her body where it landed in a gold pool. Vali sucked a breath in surprise. He retreated, touch and all, to look at her full figure in the short black slip.

He licked his lips, eyes restlessly wandering over what she was offering to him. Ailsa said, "There was a recollection you showed me briefly in the dungeon that looked rather fun. I was hoping we could start there."

The elfin was on her again, hands gripping her hips as he pinned her back against the railing. "And here I thought you were about to stab me again."

"Would you let me?" she asked.

"If it helped." He kissed her hard, his need obvious in his bruising touch, his greedy hands roaming down her back side to snatch her curves. Without moving his face from hers, he asked, "You're sure, Ailsa?"

Ailsa smiled against his lips, adoring the way this fae god against her would fall to his knees if it meant claiming her heart. "I'm sure. Take me to bed, Vali."

He carried her back into the bedroom, gently placing her on top of the sheets, but before she relaxed, Ailsa slipped her hand beneath the pillow, finding the meat knife she had hidden there. She lanced her finger, drawing a thin line of blood. Vali watched her as she reached for his chest and began drawing a rune across his heart.

"What's this for?" he asked.

She grinned. "I noticed you had a problem with obedience." She sat on her knees in front of him as he stood near the side of the bed. "I want to explore you more, but I want to be in control, Vali. At least for the first time." She slipped her fingers beneath the fold of his towel, glancing up at him for permission, biting her bottom lip in a silent beg.

He could have easily wiped her rune away, but instead used his hand to wrap her chin. "I'd never deny you, *sváss.*"

She tugged at the fold, and the towel fell free, exposing all of him to her wide eyes. She drank him in, every inch, and *gods above* there were a lot of inches to take in. Especially when he was completely stiff for her already, prepared to move from exploration to more arduous work.

"You are breathtaking, Vali," she sighed, running her hands up his thighs. A low sound like a growl buzzed from his chest. They finally rose to his cock, slowly letting her hands learn again of his size, of the way he breathed when she touched him in certain places. This power over him, the control of his pleasure, made the desire hot between her legs worsen to an unbearable heat.

"I want you to touch me," she said as she stroked him. She brought her lips to the tip of his length and kissed him. "I want you to mark me, claim me, remind me why I belong to you. Ruin me all over again, Vali."

"*Fuck,* Ailsa," he groaned through gritted teeth, raising a hand to comb her hair with his fingers. His knees jerked a little every time her tongue swirled over his head. "Tell me you're mine, and I'll give you everything you want."

She released him from her mouth and swallowed, his taste rolling down her throat. "I'm yours," she declared. "Always."

Vali bent and snatched her behind the legs, pulling her up and throwing her on her back. He spread her knees apart, still standing on the side of the bed, and took a moment to take in the sight of her. Ailsa's back arched off the sheets as a hand left her knee to stroke her center, slipping over her wet clit. She watched him methodically bring his thumb to his mouth and sample her like the beginning of a feast.

"You taste like paradise, *svass*." He bent his head as he spoke, flicking his tongue where his finger had just trailed, sending a jolt of pleasure through her spine. "Gods, I missed the way you tasted."

"Vali," she gasped.

His snide laugh brushed against her. "I missed the way you said my name. Like your life depends on it, like the air in your chest clings to it." He pushed her knees a little wider and went down on her again, moving rapidly and lightly in a savory pattern, already knowing exactly the way she liked it. Her hips jerked off the bed, hands darted out across the sheets to grip the satin material, clinging to something as he nearly sent her over the edge with his tongue alone.

His other hand smoothed down the inside of her thigh, joining his mouth. With a gentle pressure, he slipped one finger inside her, stretching her before adding another. Ailsa was powerless as she let him defile her. The only sounds she could make came out in soft whimpers as sharp bolts of bliss consumed every thought, every instinct she had left under her control.

"More," she said, when she finally found enough air to form a command. Vali licked her one last time before lifting his head from between her legs.

"Did you say something?" he asked, rising again to his full height, towering over her gasping body. A smirk stretched across wet lips. "I didn't hear you, svass."

"I said *more.*"

He pulled her hard by her thighs until her hips were off the bed. Ailsa wrapped her legs around him to keep them up, inching her way up his hips to feel his cock heavy on her swollen middle. With the sway of his hips, Vali stroked her with his shaft, his smile falling as her wetness coated his length.

"Ailsa," he murmured. "I need to be inside you."

She reached for him. "Come closer, Vali." His hands threaded themselves with hers, and she pulled him on top of her until his face was hovering above her own. She slipped her fingers from his and ran them over his face, taking in the way he looked at her, the hunger in his eyes, the feral way his lips parted as if to devour her at any moment. She'd studied every line and detail, making sure this memory would never be lost.

She shoved him to the side and rolled with him until she was sitting on top of his hips. Vali blinked up at her, a delicious smile returning across his cheeks.

"My turn," she said, spreading her palms across the smooth skin of his chest. "And you will stay there until I wipe that rune away."

"Heathen," he snarled as his fingers dug into the thick of her thighs.

Leaning down, she placed a teasing kiss on his cheek and whispered, "Filthy fae."

"Take what you need from me now, Ailsa," he breathed into her throat. Her hands now woven into his hair, somehow always finding themselves there. "Because when I am free of these binds, I will remind you why you belong to me. I will use your body to convince your mind why we are meant to be together—yesterday, now, and forever."

"I want to steal it all from you," she moaned into his lips, kissing him again. "I want to remember what those memories felt like on my end, how we fit together, what you feel like inside me as you come apart. All the rest of it."

The elfin groaned, his head falling back as his hips lifted in reaction, brushing her center and triggering a tightness from her clit to her toes, curling them against the sheets. "Take it, *svàss. Hel*, remind me how good you feel on my cock."

"I promise." She kissed his neck, feeling his racing pulse with the dart of her tongue. "I will let you go as soon as I'm finished."

He only watched as she lifted the shift up her hips—getting it out of the way. "Just remember, Ailsa, I warned you once a long time ago. The longer you prolong my suffering, the more terrible my wrath."

"And you shouldn't threaten fate, especially when I'm the only one who can help you now." She reached down to find him in her hands again. The size of him, how hard he was, made her heart dance in her chest. She rubbed him down until his breath was heavy and his hips were pressing back against her hands. He watched her work him, and she watched him watch her, both finding pleasure in the other's reaction.

She slowly guided his shaft against herself, letting the wetness of her arousal coat his heat as she pumped him again and again with her hands. Gods, he was a beautiful sight beneath her, the way his starving chest glistened with a mix of sweat and water in the lantern light. His teeth bared like he wanted to take a bite from her throat. Ailsa skated her hands across his tense stomach, bracing herself against his chest, before finally sinking on top of him.

"Oh, *gods*," she gasped as he filled her.

A rumble purred from Vali's chest. His nails dragged across her skin. "Don't stop, *svàss*. You can take it all."

But she was already so full of him and hadn't even settled

completely yet. Ailsa could only focus on her breathing as she let her walls relax and trusted him, slowly letting herself become acclimated to his size as she lowered the rest of herself completely, sheathing him all the way until she was so full of him, he was as much a part of her as her heart or her soul. She gave a few experimental rolls of her hips as she adjusted to his size, pure pleasure splitting her apart with each movement as she clamped around him.

"That's my girl. I told you, we fit together perfectly," Vali spoke, but his voice broke as he experienced the paradise spreading through them both. His praise was all she wanted to hear—needing more. "Take it slow, Ailsa. It's been so long, and I want to savor you."

She nodded, could only communicate with simple gestures as the tension between her legs tightened impossibly more and stole her voice. Her breath came out in frenzied gasps as she lifted slightly on her knees and slammed back into him. Each sound he made in approval sent a new bolt of warmth through her body.

"*Fuck*, Ailsa," he rasped into her chest. "You don't know how many times I've thought of you riding me like this since you were taken away."

"Is this..." she stumbled on the words, unsure if she wanted to know. "Is this as good as before?"

"Better," he breathed. "Every time with you is better than before."

Ailsa could hardly breathe from hearing his truth. The air caught in her throat. "How... how could it get better than this?"

Because now she finally understood why he had tracked her across the Nine. This was nothing like she had ever experienced before—or maybe she had, but she didn't remember until now. It wasn't the pleasure from the sex, it was the glory in their joining.

He muffled a roar with his teeth as she took him faster, her pace deep and frenzied. The muscles in his neck taught as a bowstring. "You are so beautiful like this, but you are even more exquisite on your back."

Curiosity getting the better of her, she smeared the rune from his chest, releasing him from the invisible bonds that held him under her command. When he felt the freedom in his body again, Vali pounced. Suddenly she was on her back— her wrists pinned in one of his hands above her head, his opposite shoving her shift over her waist.

"Are you all right, *sv* ass? I didn't mean to throw you down so hard," he asked.

She responded by wrapping her legs around his waist, digging her heels into his back and shoving herself back onto his stiff shaft. "Harder. More. *Now.*"

And he gave it to her, as much as he threatened. Ailsa felt his vengeance with every stroke, all his anger and frustration pounding into her as he chased his pleasure and his retribution. The male who had everything taken from him, taking it all back, claiming her with his cock. The look in his gaze unhinged, like an animal released from a long spent cage. She could only cry out his name as his hips slammed into her in a brutal, unrestrained rhythm.

This wasn't the way he made love to her in those memories. This was something more passionate, a desperate need for reconnection that replaced the pain with something more pleasing. No, this wasn't their usual sex. This was better because it was defiant and raw and restorative.

Ailsa couldn't hold back any longer. She fell apart around him. Her back arched off the bed, bare breast pressed against his chest as he came with her. His sounds of sweet suffering were loud in her ear as he roared with his release, one that left him trembling on top of her and her legs shuddering from the aftershock.

He collapsed beside her, eyes fluttering shut. "Are you okay? Was that..."

"Perfect," she sighed. "It was perfect. And I am better than okay." Ailsa rolled to the side to look at him, catching her breath.

He stroked her lips with his thumb. "Me too."

"Vali?"

"Yes, *elskan min?*"

"Did it just get unnaturally dark in here?"

He opened his eyes and looked around, brows kissing in perplexity. They both looked to the horizon from their view in bed, but the sun had disappeared. As did the moon and stars from the dusky sky.

"*Skide,*" she cursed.

"One day," he groaned, pulling her into his side for a quick kiss on her temple. "One day we'll have time to enjoy ourselves. But that's probably not a good sign, so we should not keep the Aesir waiting any longer."

Ailsa sighed and made to move out of the bed, but Vali pulled her back onto his chest. "I love you, Ailsa. I don't know if that makes you uncomfortable. But I have to say it. I can't go a day without telling you."

She stroked his face with the back of her hand, unable to feel him enough. Wondering if it would ever be enough, if this thirst could be quenched. "I think my heart is waiting for my head to catch up, to wrap my mind around all this. Because I want to tell you what you mean to me, Vali. I just can't find the words."

He nodded slowly, his gaze clear and focused on her face. "I know you love me. I feel it in your kiss. I see it in the way you look at me. I hear it in your voice when you call me your beloved. Ailsa, I know. You don't have to say a thing."

He loosened his hold on her. Relief and remorse blending in her blood until she felt so undeserving of a male like him. "We are in this together, *sváss*. You do not have to deal with this on your own. I am with you." He helped her stand from the bed, cupping her face with his palm. "To Hel and back again."

Ailsa's grin stretched wider than the twelve territories of Asgard combined. "To Hel and back, Vali."

CHAPTER 42
SEELA

Two wolves stalked the edges of the gate marking the entrance to Alfheim. One black as midnight, the other white as snow. Loki, still disguised as Vali, spoke to them as the fae armies gathered in wait behind her. They camped near the border, where Heimdall could not see past the Light wards, waiting for the darkest night to begin their march.

Ivor stood near in her human form, a helmet masking her identity from those who would rather see her back behind bars. Enver was somewhere in a tent in the Dark Elves encampment, assisting in the weapon distribution delivered that morning by the dwarves. What the reclusive fae lacked in social obligations, they made up for in honor and blades.

"Where did those two come from?" Ivor asked as they watched Loki speak to the wolves. "I've never seen them before, even when Fenrir hid in these lands."

"That is Hati and Skoll," Seela replied. "One hides in the night sky while the other hides in the clouds. They have been hunting the sun and moon since the beginning, causing the sun to set and the moon to rise every night, and so on the next day. But Loki doesn't want them to simply chase the sun and moon chariots this time."

"He wants them to consume them?"

Seela nodded. "It is our only chance to hide an army of this size from Heimdall before Loki can restrain him. If he blows his horn, Asgard will send out their soldiers and shut their walls, and they will lock the fire giants out."

Ivor stepped in front of Seela, demanding her attention shift from the wolves to the wolven beside her. "Are you sure about this, Seela?"

"No," she admitted to both the wolven and herself. "But it's the best chance we've got."

Ivor didn't appear convinced. She looked back at Loki, who had dismissed the wolves and rejoined them at the edge of camp. "I wanted to say I'm sorry, Seela." The wolven looked at her again. "For everything. I was so desperate to join the wolven again, to have a semblance of family again, that I didn't see I already had one right in front of me. And when Ailsa and Vali got close..."

"You felt alone?" she asked. Ivor nodded.

"It's always been me and Ailsa. She called me her sister, and I loved her like one. When she fell in love with someone else... It was like I lost the only family I ever had. And I was so fucking mad at the whole world for it." Ivor looked down at her boots. "Sometimes I still am."

Seela nudged her with her toe. "I knew how you felt, you know. You could have come to me. I lost my *Hjartablód* the day Vali became her *Fraendi*. The life mate is a stronger bond."

"Like I said, I should have done many things differently. Perhaps this could have all been avoided if I would have been honest with you and Ailsa. If I would have warned you both—"

Seela placed a hand on Ivor's chest to stop her rambling. "There's no point thinking about the potentials of yesterday. I forgive you, Ivor. Now forgive yourself." She patted her shoulder and started to walk away—until Ivor snatched her by the arm and tugged her back, her face inches away.

"And I'm sorry I ruined our potential, Seela. I want you to know that specifically."

Through the helmet, Seela noticed her frosty eyes were glossy, and it melted a piece of her heart that had been frozen toward the wolven for too long. "I know, Ivor."

"Enver is an idiot and does not deserve you."

Seela shrugged, "Probably not. But I'll give him a chance, anyway."

Ivor nodded and released her arm. "I wish you well then."

"Commander!"

Loki marched up to them, a large grin painted across Vali's face. "It is time. Inform the giant lords that Hati and Skoll will have the sun and moon very soon. Afterwards, we will march through the darkness and wait near the Bifrost for Fenrir and the fire giants. They should make their appearance first, do you think?"

Seela suppressed a shudder thinking of fighting the demons of Muspell. "Yes, let them lead the way. We can attack from the rear and clean up their mess after. Let the gods have them first." She sighed, looking back at the fae who followed them into an uncertain battle. "And let us hope fate is on our side tonight."

Loki scoffed and threw his arm over her shoulders. "The Allfather refused to tell anyone else their Ragnarok ending after he drank from the well, but I hear he loses. Let's discover what fate has in store for the rest of us, shall we?"

Seela turned to look at Ivor, but the wolven disappeared somewhere amongst the tents. "I'm afraid your curiosity isn't so contagious," she muttered.

Loki barked a laugh, the god unnervingly excited this close to the fated Battle to End All Battles. She made to move from under his arm, but he wrapped a large hand around her shoulder, preventing her escape.

"Not so fast, Commander," he said. "I have a special job for you."

Seela was about to dismiss his proposition until the events of the sky stole her attention and her speech. Muffled conversation from the tents fell quiet around her, not a sound spoken or made in all the lands of Alfheim and beyond as they watched the sun disappear from its place in the sky. There was no moon to replace its orbit, no stars to provide any light left in this realm.

Flames flickered all over the camp as the darkness covered the world in a heavy drape. So deep was this black, Seela felt as if she were stuck in a void. The wolves had done it—completed another sign of Ragnarok by shrouding the Tree in shadows.

"Good girls," Loki whispered to the sky. His grip moved from her shoulders to her forearm. "Well, no time to waste. Shall we go, Commander?"

"Wait... we're *leaving*? But what about—"

She was interrupted by the rush of a great wind that only accompanied sedir when used to mist to another realm. Seela squeezed her eyes shut against the strain, waiting for the pulling of her person to be over. Nearly a full breath later, the wind died, and she opened her eyes to find complete and total darkness.

"Hold this lantern. If Heimdall sees you, he won't be alarmed." A flame appeared in a glass box, and Loki handed it to Seela, still unsure about where they were—until she saw the bridge.

Light from Asgard lit the sky, glowing as its own source of light without the sun to shine down on the iridescent, impenetrable walls surrounding the god realm. The Bifrost was a tangible bridge formed from the light refracting through the walls, glaring a medley of colors across its structure. Formed by nothing but light, and yet the strongest conduit in existence, the walls of Asgard being a close second.

"All right, I'm going to distract the watchman, and you are going to take his horn. He keeps it in his tower near the entrance to Asgard," Loki said with a finite explanation.

"Why on Yggdrasil would I do that?"

Irritation flashed for a beat across Vali's face. Through tight lips, Loki said, "Because Heimdall is on the bridge as we speak. The events tonight have him on high alert, and he is watching for signs of the fire giants. When he sees the army from Muspell, he will sound his horn and shut the gates."

"And you want to delay that preparation?" she asked.

"Correct. Chaos, Seela. That is always the goal."

But she doubted disorder was the most strategic motivation in the case for the end of the worlds. She ventured toward the bridge, leaving the tree line that bordered the realm, knowing he wouldn't let her leave until this was done.

Heimdall practically glowed against the encompassing night. His white and gold armor deflected the light from the bridge. His head was adorned with a helmet, metal wings curling near the sides like horns, and in his hands was a sword of ebony and steel. The blade itself was longer than Seela's body. His gilded horn hung from his hip.

He watched her as she approached, the god of mischief hiding in her shadow. "What are you doing here, elfin?" he called when she was halfway.

"Don't answer," Loki whispered. "Keep walking." She swallowed against a parched feeling in her throat.

Heimdall adjusted the grip on his pommel. "Stop!" he commanded, voice thrumming through Seela like a popped bowstring. "I demand to know your business here before you take another step."

Yet Loki still pushed her. "Faster, Seela."

Seela did not want to face a god, especially one that could wield a weapon of such size. But she was very much stuck between the two of them as one pressed her further and the other demanded she still.

Heimdall met her at the end of the bridge, not letting her get anywhere close to the connection or his tower. "Are you weak of hearing, elfin? Do you not understand—" A shift at her back made him hesitate. His mouth fell open as he muttered, "Vali?"

The gods stared each other down, Heimdall clearly more confused than Seela expected him to be. "How are you here?" he asked.

"Where else would I be, Watchman?" Loki asked.

Heimdall tightened his grip on his sword. The smallest movement of his fingers snatched Seela's attention. "But if you're here," he said, "then who did they bring back from the Gjoll?"

"Vali's in Asgard? He's here?" Seela spoke in a hushed voice. The prospect of seeing him again swept away any fear. "What about Ailsa?"

The watchman opened his mouth to speak, but Loki gave him no time to answer. In a blink, he shifted back into his Loki form, a trickster god draped in black and silver robes, a dark cape sweeping his back. Heimdall had no time to raise his weapon as Loki used his power to knock him back, barely even lifting his arm to do so.

The watchman tumbled a short way across the bridge, skidding to a stop. His sword still in his hand as his head reared back at Loki, golden eyes a fire of rage. "Who in the Nine set you free, Betrayer?"

But as Seela looked to Loki, she found his gaze had gone black. A white staff was in his right hand, smooth and bleached as bone. Silver lines veined through the sedir staff, moving like blood, laced with unrestricted power. He tapped the rod once and vanished, appearing a second later behind the watchman.

"Fate," Loki answered. Heimdall swung the sword without looking, but the blade went straight through the trickster's neck. His figure was nothing more than an illusion as the real Loki appeared at Heimdall's back again, this time placing a hand on his golden helmet.

He cried out and fell to his knees. Loki swung his staff and crushed the side of his head. Heimdall sprawled against the bridge. Seela saw her opportunity and ran, diving for the horn as it dangled freely from his belt. But her fingers skimmed nothing but air as he rolled in the opposite direction, out of her reach.

"It wasn't enough to kill Baldur," Heimdall shouted as he regained his footing. "You won't stop until we're all bleeding at your feet!"

"It's nothing personal, Watchman." Loki flipped his staff

adeptly in one hand. "I just can't let you warn Odin his end is coming. It would spoil the surprise."

Heimdall flipped his sword in his hand, causing a bolt of light to flash up the pommel and transform the weapon into a staff similar to Loki's. But this rod was solid gold, a testament to the watchman's namesake. He spoke something in the old language under his breath just as Loki lifted his own staff in another attack.

The world around them slowed to a near stop, time bowing to Heimdall's voice. He moved swiftly despite the seconds stretching into minutes, but Seela couldn't force herself to move faster than a sluggish pace as his power spun her in a twister of time. Loki gritted his teeth against the resistance of his movements, the sedir in his rod releasing too late.

Heimdall moved out of the way of his attack, and in the same motion summoned a burst of powerful light that slammed into both Seela and the god, pushing them both off the bridge and back toward Alfheim.

The golden god wiped his lip where a gilded tooth had bit through his skin. "Be gone with you both. I will give you this last chance to walk away."

"Loki!" Seela scrambled to the god now rising to his knees, dark eyes void of feeling. "Loki, turn around. Look at the sunrise!"

Somewhere behind the blank mask of his power, he heard her. The god turned his head and looked into the forest, where an orange glow had snuck over the horizon. "That's not a sunrise, Commander," he said in a gravelly voice. "That's fire."

"No," she whispered, as if denying it could erase the scene of a burning forest, of the fire following the giants who marched for doom and desolation.

"Get the horn, Seela. I'll distract him."

Without waiting to plan how, the elfin charged the bridge. Behind her, Loki muttered the words to an incantation, creating a ring of fire that encompassed all three of them. The sedir flames were silver and black, flickering shadows that rose taller than the trees. Seela felt the heat, felt her palms sweat against the hilt of her dagger as she pulled it from its sheath.

Heimdall held his great sword once more, ready for her. But as he swung, Seela dropped to her knees, sliding under the blade angled to butcher her. She twisted on her knee, swatting the link that clipped his gjallarhorn. Her dwarven dagger sliced clean through the metal, and she snatched up the horn before it hit the earth.

Heimdall spun, but the weight of the sword dragged him down, and by the time the momentum of the weapon slowed enough for him to face her, she was already on the other side of the circle, gold horn in her hand.

"Fae scum!" the watchman roared. "Give that back!"

Loki pulled the god closer to him with his staff, demanding their fight resume. "No," he told the god with a grin.

Seela could only clutch the horn in her arm and watch as Loki and Heimdall fought a bloody duel, each using their powers in ways that outsmarted the other, only to be subdued in the next move. Meanwhile, the fire in the forest was growing brighter until the light from the blaze gleamed against the voided sky from the east to the west.

Loki thrust his staff into the watchman's side, and the god hurled over in pain. "What did you lace the end of your staff with?" he grunted, stumbling away from Loki.

But the trickster smiled, maintaining the distance between them with leisure steps. "Venom, Heimdall. The same kind that dripped on my face as I was chained to a rock."

"Damn you to Hel—"

"That's my daughter, you golden piece of *skide*."

Holding his side, Heimdall thrust his sword out one last desperate time, catching Loki across the middle. The trickster dropped to his knees, holding the laceration together with his arm before he looked to Seela and tossed his staff to her.

"Touch *Laevatein*," he gasped. "It will take you back to camp. Hurry, before the giants come."

Seela shook her head, unsure why he had given up so easily, so quickly. Once the watchman's death was sure, he hadn't even defended himself. "But Loki, you'll die if I leave you now."

A sly smirk curled his cheek, fair skin sullied with blood. "I will die, and I will watch Asgard burn as I fade. Take the staff. Go home, save your kin."

She nodded, unable to think of the right words to part with the god. He was a horrible creature, not wholly evil but not even close to good. He had caused so much strife in the Nine and yet somehow always turned the chaos into splendor. Cunning, deceitful, master of manipulation, and stubborn as a boulder—unwilling to move or break. What was left to say to a god like that?

"Thank you, Loki." For his chaos in the fight for order, for his lack of control, for everything he did that made life unpredictable and challenging. For teaching the Nine good and evil were not opposite, but two sides of the same coin.

He winked at her, falling on his heels as his blood spilled over the grass. His face watching over Asgard, waiting to see it burn.

Seela touched the staff and misted back to Alfheim.

CHAPTER 43
AILSA

"Thank you for finally gracing us with your presence."

Odin's words were clipped as he sat at the head of a long table. They weren't brought to a grand hall but an intimate room bare of anything on the walls. It wasn't used very much, whatever purpose this place held.

Every Aesir was in attendance, minus the watchman guarding the gate. Vali felt Ailsa draw close to him, her hand slipping around his arm as the number of bodies in this room pushed them close.

"I apologize if my poor health was an inconvenience to you, Allfather."

"Not *that* poor, judging by the sounds I heard across the fighting fields."

Freya cleared her throat to catch his attention, and when he looked at her, she grinned impishly. Ailsa cursed beneath her breath, but he only shrugged at his father. "What is it you would like to know from my journey to the forbidden realms?"

Odin's knuckles cracked as he fisted them. "You can start with why you came back alone. Where is Baldur?"

"Helheim. Where he will stay."

Odin took a deep breath. "And why did you not bring him back?"

Vali huffed a heartless laugh. "I couldn't. He is dead and cannot leave the Shadow Realms. A law *you* created, might I add. This isn't new information to you, and I don't understand why you are wasting time asking questions when you could be preparing for Ragnarok, for the giants that come as we speak!"

"You brought her back. Why didn't you bring back my son?" he seethed.

"Ailsa was not sent to Hel. The witches took her and brought to Muspell. Much different. And we wouldn't have been able to leave if Surtur had not burned down your seal with the Eternal Flame."

"He has the flame?" Tyr, the god of war, interrupted.

"Yes," Vali answered, grateful one of them cared about something relevant. "And Fenrir is with him. We were lucky to beat them here, but they cannot be far behind."

"What does it matter?" Odin said wistfully. "Vali did not bring back the one who can slay the wolf. His negligence will cost us the Nine—"

"Baldur was not destined to kill Fenrir," Ailsa spoke at his side. "Stop lying to them, Odin. Admit it, Vali was the one you should have groomed this entire time instead of wasting it trying to get Baldur back."

"You do not know what the well spoke—"

"I know because I drank from it, same as you!" She stepped forward and Vali couldn't help but smirk at the small heathen putting the king of gods in his place. "If you do not believe in Vali, then you have already sealed your fate, as well as the Nine. No one can save you from yourself."

The Allfather glared at her. His breath was heavy with hatred. "I should have drained you of your little gift when I could. Look at you, the sick little heathen suddenly all healed and powerful and now you think you can speak to me like that. Get out of my war room! You have no purpose here."

"Do not speak to her like that. Never speak to her like that again," Vali hissed. His warning obvious without voicing a threat.

Ailsa spoke, her voice breathy, "Vali—"

"No, *sváss*, there is no excuse for taking his anger out on you—"

"Vali, I see fire," she said, louder this time. She pointed toward an archway, where the distant line of the horizon was burnished with orange. The rest of the Aesir stood from the seats and gathered on the terrace outside, murmurs and gasps muffling the collective conversation.

"Why isn't Heimdall alerting us?" Thor asked. "Isn't this his sole purpose, to blow the horn at Ragnarok? They could already be through the gate!"

But Odin did not think more about the watchman. A raven flew in from the archway, settling on his shoulder to caw a message in his ear. He muttered a single name, "*Loki*."

When he saw the flames of Surtur himself, he barked orders at anyone who listened. "Gather the *Einherjar*! Make sure the fallen mortals are lined in front of Valhalla. Freya, get back to Folkvang and do the same with your men. Alert the Valkyrie and the rest of the halls! And Vali—" he slapped a large hand over his shoulder "—you will stay here with me."

The elfin pushed his hand away. "I will go prepare for battle with my lady, and when we are fit, I will return. Make no mistake Odin, if Fenrir gives me the chance, I will slay him. But you will beg for mercy and forgiveness at my feet so I will not do the same to you."

He pulled Ailsa away from his father. As he left, he heard him call to him, "You would protect a single mortal over your own father? The king of the gods?"

Vali laughed for the second time that evening. "I have a long list of beings I would protect over my own father. I will see you on the fields, Odin."

Ailsa clung to him as they ran down the hall and out to the courtyard. Darkness from the starless sky obscured anything further than the next wall torch. Before he could step foot across the pavers back to their tower in Valhalla, a white horse trotted in front of him, rearing back as its rider hauled it to a breaking stop.

Freya.

"Vali, Ailsa, get on, and I will take you to Folkvang. We can get you both armor there."

"Ready, Ailsa?" he asked, turning to her with a hand outstretched. She glanced at it nervously.

"You mean you're bringing me into battle?" she asked.

Vali's arm dropped an inch, confused. "Of course. You're an incredible fighter. There is no one else I'd want at my side at the end of everything."

She smiled with her eyes. "My family never let me join the fight." She accepted his hand and squeezed it. "But I suppose that changes today."

He helped her mount behind Freya, seating himself behind her as he said, "Everything changes today, *elskan min*." He grabbed her waist as Freya slapped the reins, riding back to her hall through the dark realm.

"That won't be necessary," Ailsa said as one of the armory fitters measured her neck for a helm. The woman looked at her doubtfully. She explained to the woman. "Otsman do not wear helms. We want our foes to see our faces when they perish."

Vali grinned from the wall he was leaning against, watching as they finished dressing her in Folkvang whites as they clad him. Their armor was similar, with a gold breastplate engraved with Freya's protective runes and a white draping cascading over her shoulder. She had a belt sheathed with daggers and knives of all sizes, matching ones around each of her lean thighs, and a single-handed sword with a gilded pommel at her hip.

"What are you staring at over there?" she asked, eyeing him.

Vali pushed off the wall and offered her a glass of wine he had snatched in the disorder of Freya's hall. "I'm trying to decide if you look better in that shift or covered in blades."

She took a sip of the elven draught, hiding a smirk. "And?"

"It's an impossible decision."

Ailsa shook her head, setting the drink aside so she could assess the armor herself. "What do you think?" she asked. "Any vulnerable spots?"

"Besides your neck? I think you look ready, *sváss*. Just one more thing." Vali reached inside a leather pocket and pulled out a small tin, inside a supply of kohl. The way she smiled at the paint in his hand made the search for it worth it. "Would you to do it yourself or—"

"You must do it, Vali." She stepped close to him and tilted

her face up at him. Her hair was braided tight on both sides and flowed free down her back, out of her face.

"All right, though I don't know what I'm doing. I'll just copy what I've seen on the other heathens." He traced three crossing lines down her forehead, like Marrin had worn. He lined her eyes with the band Lochare often glared at him through and struck her bottom lip with a thin line of black that fell down her chin.

"How do I look?" she asked.

Vali smiled despite the drums of war calling them to the fighting fields. "Like a tiny yet terrifying heathen."

She inhaled a shaky breath, a crack betraying in her bold pretense. He tipped her chin to look at him once more, eyes focused on her like a raven. "No harm will befall you out there, Ailsa. I vow it."

"We have faced Fenrir before and could not beat him. How will we best Surtur and the Great Wolf and the armies they drag behind them?"

"One at a time, my love. And if I fall, I will find you in whatever afterlife awaits us after this." He stroked her braid with his palm, the design tight like ropes against her skull.

Ailsa nodded, offering him a broken smile. "You always find me, Vali. I am not afraid."

Vali borrowed some of that steel courage in her eyes and faced the fighting fields once more. With his *Fraendi* at his side —and hopefully fate as well.

419

CHAPTER 44
ERIK

Erik rode his *bálhross* behind the fire giant lord as he paved their trail with fire. Everywhere he turned, flames licked the scene, spreading from the Eternal Flame stored in Surtur's massive sword. The giant seemed to triple in size, his steps singeing the ground as he brought up the rear of his army.

Thousands of fire giants marched behind into the mouth of Asgard. Erik lost himself in the magnificence of the walls surrounding the god realm, of the Bifrost beneath his horse as they crossed the final link into Odin's home. Days they had been traveling, burning everything in their shadow.

Fenrir was already in his wolf form, stalking the front lines. But Erik was happy to linger behind the witches in their formation. The hole in his chest hadn't quite healed, even after Nerissa restored his health with her sedir. It was the only time he appreciated their bond, but now he was in her debt. A life debt with a blood bond—he would never be free of her.

Unless something happened to her during the battle...

His thoughts of her manifested as Nerissa pulled her steed near his to speak with him. "You will stay with me and protect Fenrir as he hunts for the Allfather. You aren't strong enough to fight on your own right now."

"Nerissa—"

"Shut it, Erik," she hissed. "You should have told me the elfin was still alive *before* he showed up and stole Ailsa from the prison. Now everything we have worked for could be at risk!"

Erik swallowed as they crossed the gate into Asgard, staring up at the god's palace that stood in the center of all the territories. "What does the bastard matter? We have Surtur and Fenrir. Nothing can stop them as a force together."

"It shouldn't matter," she said, "but fate has told us otherwise. And I have a plan in mind that should make up for your pitfalls in the past."

Erik grumbled beneath his breath. Hardly excited to face him again. Though, this time, he would have a weapon. "Fine."

Asgard fell quiet as the army ahead settled in their formation, waiting for Surtur's command. The fire giant behind them stomped across the dull rainbow bridge, clutching the sides of the gate to throttle a roar. Smoke curled around his body, fire glowed beneath his skin and out of the horns on his head. He raised his flaming sword once and struck either side of the entrance to Asgard, each strike a thunderclap.

The walls, built from the hands of a giant before him, quickly caught fire despite their impenetrable reputation. A circle of flames reached the sky, burning the realm from the ground—up.

"Friends of fire," Surtur thundered across his army,

speaking to the heart of every giant. He hissed one foul word to set the Battle to End All Battles in motion.

"Destroy."

And like a quake, the giants charged through Asgard.

CHAPTER 45
AILSA

They waited in the last circle of Valhalla. Odin's Einherjar were thick in battle with Surtur's army. Asgard was already burning around them, scalding the other eleven territories, each settled on a different branch on the Tree.

The Allfather was seated in the highest place in the realm, watching it unfold in the place they had once bound Fenrir with the original chains. His ravens circled the desolation and returned with more news. The Valkyrie soared over the destruction to pull broken men from the lines, doing their best to heal them and keep as many as possible in fighting condition.

Surtur was easy enough to find with plain eyes. The giant towered over his army, slicing through the honorably slain with a fiery sword that challenged the sun with its brilliance. Fenrir, however, had yet to be seen.

"My father is down there," Ailsa muttered to the elfin at her side. "I can't imagine what he's facing right now."

"His destiny," Vali said. "What did he always tell you? Fight like you are already dead, *sváss*. Now he gets to live those words."

"Where do they go after this death?" she asked, voice breaking. If the afterlife was reduced to ash, where would the dead go then? To Hel? Or did their ashes dust the Tree of Life, forever floating in eternity?

It was a question he could not answer, nor did he lie to spare her feelings. This fight would be brutal. The second deaths of these men and women was just another chance to grieve them.

Freya's soldiers shouted a collective cry as the second wave rushed forth.

"There's too many of them," he muttered. Vali unsheathed his sword, ready to join them. He turned to face his father, who was now pacing the dueling hall—a stone floor bordered with gray pillars. The smoke from the fire around them curled above the open roofed arena, reflecting the golden glow of the flames burning the realm. Screams of the dying carried on the bloody breeze hot across her skin.

"Will you just hide up here while your family burns below?" he shouted at him. "Will you let everyone fight and die for you before you pick up your sword?"

"My sons are coming to help. Thor and Tyr will arrive soon and when the time is right, Fenrir will come to *me*," he spat through his teeth. "And you must be ready when he does, or we will lose the Nine! There is nothing more important than this moment, right now."

"The Nine are already lost." Tyr suddenly appeared as if hearing his name, calling from Thor's chariot he was driving. His face sullied, armor charred. "The oceans flooded the borders of Midgard, setting Jormungand free. Thor went to stop the serpent before he damaged the Tree. This fire is spreading along the branches. The realms are falling, Odin. There will be nothing left for whoever survives this."

Odin was silent for several heartbeats, the eerie calm on his face never faltered. He said, "I created the Nine with my brothers nearly a millennium ago. I can do it again." He looked at Vali. "But I will have to endure this."

"What sound logic. To Hel with the rest of us then." Ailsa turned from the god, unable to hide her disgust.

The ground trembled beneath their feet to a beat, a pace, like a beast on the run. Ailsa turned to the sounds of battle in time to see a massive wolf charging up the hill to the duel hall. It wasn't Fenrir, but a monster of a wolf all the same. A chain dangled from its thick neck, like it had just broken free of his bindings.

"Garm!" Vali shouted.

Without time to draw her blade, Ailsa lunged to the side, falling behind a pillar just as his jowls smacked in her peripheral. She spun to face the wolf again, now with a sword in one hand and a lengthy dagger in the opposite. But Tyr had already leashed the animal by its chain, using his one arm to pull himself onto its back. He pulled the leash around his throat to strangle the wolf, but Garm swung his massive head from side to side, trying to buck the god off.

Tyr dug in harder, pulling the chain until his face was red and the veins in his arms were threatening to burst. The wolf faltered without air, stumbling toward the edge of the platform, and fell off the cliff face lining the opposite side.

"Tyr!" Odin ran for his son, blue robes floating behind him as he crossed the width of the hall and peered over the steep edge. He fell to his knees, bracing his hands on the stone floor.

"My sons," he wept. And Ailsa felt his agony from the

break of his voice. "All my sons are falling in front of me. First Baldur and then Heimdall. I see Thor in my Sight, thrashing with venom from the serpent. Now Tyr has followed his brothers to a dire fate."

Vali rushed to her side, pressing his hand against her chest as he said, "I need to find Freya and send for reinforcements. Where one beast goes, more will follow. If Garm has been freed, there's no telling what else will crawl out of hiding."

"Vali, no! You said you wouldn't leave my side!" she argued, snatching him by the arm.

"I will be right back, I promise." He slipped from her hand. "Stay here and do not risk yourself protecting that waste of divinity. If Fenrir shows, you run."

Despite all the reasons she disagreed with this, she nodded, not wanting him to see her afraid. She could fight, protect herself. She wasn't defenseless, nor did she need a man to protect her. But she was hesitant to let him go after finally getting him back.

"If you do not return here in ten minutes, I'm coming to find you," she said.

"Deal. While you are waiting, try putting up some wards, but do not use too much blood. Just enough to shield you from the giants should some stragglers break through." Vali nicked her finger with his nail, his magic gently splitting the skin.

She watched him disappear down the hill, smoke embracing him and hiding his form. Ailsa set her mind to the wards, marking the pillars with runes in her blood, shielding the area from unfriendly company.

"It'll take more than that to keep us out, Weaver."

Ailsa spun to find a witch smiling at her, peering around a marble column. Her face painted with blood. She dropped her hands to her belt, finding her weapons again.

"Nerissa."

CHAPTER 46
VALI

For the first time since Ailsa crossed his thread, he had done something he claimed he would never do.

Vali lied.

He wasn't going back to the platform. He was going to find Fenrir in this cesspool of a battlefield, where beings of all races littered the scorched earth, and the heat made every breath a fight of its own. He would find him and finish this here, where the monsters of Ragnarok could not touch her. A last minute decision he had enough confidence in to make peace with his impulsivity.

A fire giant charged him, molten face hissing as it swung a battle axe for his head. Vali swiftly ducked and snatched the giant by its collar, pressing the tip of his blade into the small of its back. "Where is the wolf?" he demanded in his ear.

The miserable creature only laughed. Vali shoved his sword through its spine to silence it forever and moved on to the next giant. One by one, they each seemed less inclined to tell him what he wanted, until his forearms were sticky with boiling blood. But none of them would betray the Great Wolf's strategy—until Vali caught sight of *him.*

Erik wandered within the chaos, each side believing he belonged with them, and therefore no one attacked him. The slain mortals were too busy to notice the colors he wore were not aligned with his own kind. His eyes were searching. For what, Vali didn't know. He didn't care.

Anger. Hatred. Malice.

Vengeance.

Each one was another beat to the drum of war in his heart as he approached the man responsible for stealing everything good in his life. Erik didn't even see him, nor did he notice when his skin began to steam. Not until the heat reached his bones. The fear that widened his eyes as Erik dropped his weapons and looked around, searching for the source of his agony, it almost brought Vali enough satisfaction to move on from his grudge.

But not completely.

He raised his sword to the heathen's neck, and Erik froze. "How many times must we kill you before you die?"

Erik turned to face his opponent slowly, arms wide at his sides in surrender. When his eyes fell on Vali, his fear fell away into something more hopeless. "At least once more, demon." His words were choked as the blood clotted in his chest—Vali felt the beat of his heart race to fight against the resistance.

"Where is the wolf now?"

Erik's lip tipped in a smirk. "She tricked you."

Vali swallowed, pulling back the heat in Erik's marrow to let him explain. "What are you talking about?"

"Nerissa used me as bait to take your attention away from Odin. She knew vengeance was too important to you. She's probably with Ailsa now. Fenrir won't be far behind his beloved witch," he rasped.

Fear clenched Vali's throat this time, and Erik saw it. It made the heathen smile, his gums bleeding as the elfin continued to roast him alive. Vali didn't lower his sword, nor did he walk away until the male fell to his knees before him, his chest rising with a final, gasping breath before hitting the earth and perishing at his feet.

Only when he was sure his suffering was prolonged to the fullest extent did Vali run his sword into his back, killing the heathen definitively. He soaked in the sensation of his blade sinking into his flesh, the sound of his pulse pausing forever, until finally pulling his magic from the man and his blade with it.

He turned to go back and check on his *sváss*, but someone stood in his way.

"Hello, last son of Odin," the towering figure said. A shirt-less man with silver hair and frosty eyes. Claws lining his hands—bare hands—that needed no weapon to kill.

"Fenrir," Vali muttered.

The Great Wolf growled once in warning, then lunged, shifting as he pounced midair. Vali felt his sword sink into something soft, just as his insides were pulled apart, shredding as he fell back. The moist earth that was saturated from the blood of the fallen leaked into his armor, stained the white to red.

Pain seared through his body until it was all he knew.

CHAPTER 47
AILSA

A thousand glass pieces. That's what her bones felt like as Ailsa struck another stone pillar. Nerissa was relentless, tossing her around the hall like a drinking horn. Still, she clutched the hilt of her sword and rose to her feet, each time meeting the witch's glare with a look as if to say, *do your worst.*

"I will admit, what you heathens lack in magic, you make up for in hardiness, but I will break you, Ailsa." Nerissa raised her palms in front of her, whispering runes that floated from her fingertips and dissipated into smoke. Ailsa noted the incantations and gathered the blood oozing from a split on her forehead before marking the air with the counter to her attack.

She lined her blade with more blood. "*Fysa,*" she whispered to the steel, before sending it flying toward the witch. It flew true—and fast, thanks to her spell. She lost sight of the blade until Nerissa's right shoulder stopped its momentum. Ailsa cursed, knowing she had aimed too high, only wounding the witch.

Nerissa gasped as it sunk into her flesh. Her eyes were wide on Ailsa as she pulled it from her body, blood spilling freely from the hole in her chest. "I can do that too," she hissed, drawing back.

Ailsa had taken the opportunity of her distraction to toe a spot on the floor where her blood had spilled, and with the sharp point of her boot, she had drawn a rune that sent the stone beneath her feet cracking, a great wave rolled through the floor of the platform and knocked the witch off her feet. Ailsa was there then with her sword going for her throat. The scar across her neck a convenient line to trace.

Nerissa rolled away at the last second, before she could settle over her. Her palms slapped the pavers and a jolt of lightning shot through her like a rod. Ailsa landed hard on her back, her view shifting to the black sky and the burnt smoke. Embers danced on the tail of a hot breeze that so reminded her of a Muspell night.

She tried to move, but the air had been knocked from her chest. She writhed against the floor, trying to find friction against the polished stone. Her hips dug into the floor as Nerissa sat on top of her, seating herself comfortably on Ailsa's stomach.

She smiled down at her. "I want to tell you something, and I want you to listen."

Ailsa only glared at her as her breaths wheezed, her airway struggling to open. Another reminder of a painful past, one she could never forget. Nerissa placed a hand on her chest, and Ailsa's arms were pinned against the ground, forbidding her from lashing her face with the sword in her hand.

"Vali is facing Fenrir as we speak. And he will die alone on the battlefield of Valhalla. As did your father and your Aesir friends. As will anyone who resists the new order of things," she whispered sweetly.

Ailsa shook her head. It wasn't true. She was trying to distract her, to give her a reason to concede. She wanted her to feel hopeless—and Ailsa did. She couldn't see a happy ending beyond this night, but that wouldn't stop her from gaining the retribution she deserved. Her own piece of vengeance.

"At least I have people to grieve. At least I have someone who loves me enough to risk himself for me. You have no one who will miss you, Nerissa. And when you burn, you will be forgotten like the rest of your kin, disappearing from memory and time like dust from the ashes of Asgard."

"Here comes Fenrir," she said, grinning. "And he has something in his teeth. An elfin from the smell of it."

Ailsa shook her head, tears leaking from the corners of her eyes. But Vali's ten minutes had come and gone, and still he hadn't returned. "He's not dead," she stammered. "He always comes back for me."

"Not this time, Weaver."

Fenrir stepped near them in the form of the Great Wolf, just close enough she could see crimson staining the matted fur down his neck. A body in his mouth, the head hanging limp near a piercing canine, covered with runes she had traced only an hour earlier.

No... No. He wasn't dead. Their past had been stolen, their future unraveling before her eyes. A thread of potential, stripping thinner every second he hung between the Great Wolf's teeth.

"*Vali!*" she screamed. No, whimpered. The pain snatched the breath from her throat. An anguish so visceral, every inch of herself was drowning. Sagas such as theirs didn't end like this. Evil never triumphed in the legends. The heroes didn't die without claiming their victory. Where was Vali's redemption? Where was his victory? Where was her revenge?

A fierce anger burned inside her heart, building higher, up and up until fire was all she could see—all she desired. Ailsa spat in the witch's face, a mixture of spit and the blood that leaked from a slice in her cheek. Before the witch could wipe it away, Ailsa hissed, "*Logi!*"

Nerissa swatted at her cheek as a flame sparked. She shrieked as it spread across her skin like it was soaked in accelerant, her hair catching next, unable to tame the wildfire Ailsa spoke to life with the very heat that rolled beneath her skin. She wanted the witch to burn. She wanted to tear the wolf apart with her bare hands. And if Vali could not, she'd finish it for him.

Ailsa shoved Nerissa off her hips, flipping their position. Fenrir snarled in warning, but she ignored him. She found her favorite knife the next second and sent it straight through her throat, letting the fire lick her arm as she made sure the blade was sent completely through her airway. The pain a reward.

Nerissa stilled beneath her. The only movement from the witch was her skin as it blackened and peeled, fire burning through flesh and vessels and hollow organs.

"Ailsa!" Odin called from the end of the platform. She looked back to see the Great Wolf had completely abandoned Nerissa, hardly caring to intervene on her behalf. Instead, he set his eyes on what he came for, what he'd been waiting centuries to finish. The wolf tossed his last victim to the side, where Vali's body tumbled limp across the smooth floor.

But she could have sworn she heard a sound escape from him. A grunt. A sigh. Whether it was her heart tricking her mind, it gave her some small sliver of hope to cling to.

The Allfather pulled a sword from the fold of his lavender

blue robes, pointed it half heartedly toward Fenrir. Ailsa would never reach them in time, but she pushed off the burning corpse of the witch anyway, digging a finger into one of the many places she was bleeding, priming her power.

Fenrir circled Odin, his eyes shifting to her every now and again as she approached, her strides cautious and quiet. She gripped the hilt of her blade, steeling her heart to do this. To try. Because if Vali could not, then who else would? If she was the last one standing between the end of the Nine and its redemption, fate hadn't given her any choice on the matter.

A hand clasped her shoulder, holding her back.

She whirled, turning to find Vidar. His mask gone, auburn hair flapping wildly in the sultry breeze. His skin was clean, clear he hadn't lifted the blade at his hip nor stained his armor with the blood of his foes.

"Vidar, what are you doing here?" she asked.

He brought a finger to his lips before taking the sword from her hands, and Ailsa was too perplexed to refuse. She could only watch as he crossed the remaining distance between Fenrir and Odin, as silent and composed as he always was, the pair as intrigued as she.

The Allfather's face fell from fear to curiosity. His pale blue eye suddenly blowing, the recognition a flicker of hope across his face. Ailsa sucked a stale breath, pieces of the past he had shared with her suddenly falling into place. That story, of being the bastard of a god who killed his mother, who silenced him for lifetimes. His Aesir father was not just any god—Vidar was a son of Odin.

"Vidar!" Odin smiled. "I remember you, my son! And now you come at the very hour your father and the Nine need you most. I knew you were destined for great things."

A deep, throaty rumble slipped from Fenrir's throat as he

swung his head at Vidar, who had hidden his identity not just from Ailsa, but from them all.

But Vidar stopped short between them, made no move to challenge the Great Wolf. He looked at Odin and threw down Ailsa's sword. The weapon clattering sharply through the night that had gone silent as the man himself. The realms shushing, the battle stalling, waiting to see what would happen next.

"He's not going to save you," Ailsa said when the Allfather did nothing but gape. "You ruined his life, Odin. You destroyed everything on your path of self preservation."

Any fleeting joy on the god's face had floated away as quickly as it came. "I did what I had to do to maintain the realms."

Ailsa shook her head. "You did what you did to save yourself, not the Nine." She gestured at the burning world around them. "Look, Odin! Did any of the horrible crimes you committed, the oaths you broke, the lies you told, did any of them stop this?"

He shook his head, refusing to take the blame. "It is not my fault fate brought this upon my realms. I never wanted this to happen."

"But it did," she said. Her gaze shifted to Vali's still body on the floor. The ache in her chest had eaten away at her heart until she felt nothing. Numb, hollow bones the only thing keeping her in place.

He shut his eye. "It did. And I wished it hadn't."

The way he said it, Ailsa knew he truly believed his words. He didn't want to watch his sons die, no matter how much he viewed them as mere weapons in his arsenal for power. A god who wanted to change his fate as much as she wanted to change her own. She recognized that selfish need inside herself, in Vali, in all of them.

Light and darkness, good and evil, right and wrong, life was but a constant fight to find the balance between them both. What separated them was the purpose in their path.

"You have endless wisdom besides this, Allfather," Ailsa said, taking a step back. "Our fate is not important. It is what we do with our fate that matters, the honor in which we face it and seize it, knowing there will be a day when it all comes to an end, and yet we face that day courageously. The Otsman who died for you in those fields knew that, prepared every day of their living and afterlife, understanding they would perish come Ragnarok. They knew it, Odin. How did you not?"

Odin did not answer. The tremble of his blade as his hands wobbled spoke for him, falling to the floor. Surrendering at last to his written ending. And Fenrir, having no last words for the king of the gods, kicked off his back legs to sweep him up in his jaws. Ailsa turned her face as Odin's screams mixed with the snapping of bone, the sickly crunch of his spine as it was severed between the massive teeth of a canine, no more ceremonial than an animal who had caught its prey in the Aelderwood. The wet spill of his blood sloshed over the pavers, tinged the air with a metallic scent.

When Odin's sounds of agony had finally cut to a sharp ending, Vidar unsheathed the blade at his hip. A simple sword. It wasn't near as grand as the one he had tossed on the floor at Odin's feet. Fenrir gnawed a few more times on the Allfather, like a dog seeking the last flavor on a bone. But when the Great Wolf heard the scrape of metal against sheath, he thrashed his blood stained muzzle to the side, staring down Vidar while the remains of a god hung between his teeth.

"You can do this, Vidar," Ailsa whispered behind him. "There is power in all things." And after crossing the Nine, she had found the greatest power lied in those that were believed to be inherently powerless. The tender hearts who sought the good despite knowing only darkness, the meek and quiet parts of existing, in love and honor and friendship. All things had the potential to be powerful—even a sick heathen who should have never survived her curse.

Or a silent son who had lost everything but his name.

Fenrir tossed Odin's body to the side and snapped at the man, whose body flinched, fighting the urge to run. The wolf slipped a bark that simulated his laugh. His head drooped low in front of carefully placed steps. Vidar held up his weapon. The loose fabric around his arm fell away to reveal a single ring wrapped around his upper arm, the one Vali spoke of.

Draupnir.

The wolf lunged for him, but Vidar thrust his sword at the incoming jaws, sinking the blade into the back of his throat. Fenrir whimpered, jaws slamming around the sword to shake it from Vidar's hands.

But the silent son slid the blade from his teeth with a strength none of them could have known he would harness, and just as Fenrir opened his jaws once more to devour Vidar where he stood, he thrust the blade deep into the wolf's cavity. Fenrir's body twitched; a weakening whine gurgled from his throat as blood filled his insides.

Blood from the beast pooled over the pavers, soaked Vidar from wrist to boot, washed away the threat of Fenrir's reign and reestablished the call of fate that had unknowingly marked his life since the day he was born. What Odin had forgotten, what he tried to hide away in the shadows of his shame, it was a bridge to his redemption he had thoughtlessly burned. And how easy it had been for Vidar to step into his calling, to do what no other in the Nine could do simply because he had the courage to face it.

Vidar impaled the beast once more, this time arcing the blade over and under to bury the weapon deep in his chest, in the range of where his heart should be. He was inexperienced but obviously had been watching—possibly in preparation for this day as he followed the Great Wolf for lifetimes. Right into the corner he backed himself into.

Fenrir staggered on his heavy paws, weight shifting back and forth until he finally fell to his side, sinking to the floor with a shudder that rolled through the realm. The force of his fallen deadweight cracked a thick line through the pavers, cutting the width of the platform in half. Vidar turned slowly, stiffly, to look at her. A wetness brimming in his eyes and diluting the crimson smeared across his cheeks. Ailsa felt her feet move, drawn to him. The blood on her fingers charged with a need to brand his skin one more time.

Somehow, even without their bond, he had read her thoughts, pulling at the collar of his poor fitting armor so she could see Odin's runes. He let Ailsa lift them from his skin, his soul, his tongue, knowing he had fulfilled the vow he made to himself.

"Ailsa." His first word uttered in gods knew how long, and it made a smile touch her eyes. His voice was deep and hearty, the kind that could sing epics and no one would tire of listening. "I killed him," he said. She wondered if he was speaking of the wolf or his father. Perhaps it didn't matter.

"You did," she said. "Vidar, I am so sorry I didn't give you the chance to explain before—"

"There is no need for apologies. Go to your elfin. We need to get out of the city while we still can. I'll go find some horses," he said. His eyes scanned the distance before returning to hers. "If you aren't here when I return, I'll meet you beyond the wall."

"Be careful, Vidar," she said, before watching him run off into the smoke now hovering over the fighting fields.

"Vali," she breathed, calling to him. Hoping with a spare piece of her faith he'd answer this time.

Ailsa ran and collapsed to her knees beside him. Barely alive, his breaths were empty against the back of her hand, his chest hardly moving to prove he was breathing. She used her coated fingers already tainted with power to heal each wound as she found them, wasting no time.

"Ailsa," he moaned too quietly.

"You lied to me," she cried. "You didn't come back, Vali."

He had been gutted, his abdomen a mess beneath the cover of his armor. A gash was taken from the thick of his neck, blood still rushing from the vascular area. The healer trapped within her heart suddenly rushed forth, demanding a surreal calm to wash over her so she could think straight, stilling the shakes in her hands.

"I'm sorry, *sváss*." His words were raspy. But she wished he would shut his mouth if only to preserve what was left.

Pressing a palm to his heart, she muttered words of weaving, healing, restoration, and replenishment. His heart was beating, slow but stubbornly. Her power over fate changed his body one invisible suture at a time to bind him back together.

Time lapsed in a monotonous blur. Ages seemed to pass as she hovered over him. Their blood mixed against her palm, and a memory—his memory she had now borrowed—flickered an idea into her thoughts.

Gathering a scrape of blood across his chest, she mixed a little more of her own in her palm, then used both of their life sources to draw a rune across his hand, one that spiraled up his wrist. It was longer than the one in his memory, but it needed to be for this.

She drew the same on her opposite.

"Vali," she whispered, shaking him slightly. His eyes fluttered, fighting to stay awake. "Vali, I choose you to be my *Fraendi*. I choose to join our life threads together. I choose to share my life with yours, every part of it, from my heart to my very strand. To walk every day of this life and the next with you, forever."

"Ailsa, you can't—"

"I love you, Vali." She stroked her thumb across his lips, silencing him. "I love you in every past and present and future. I love you not because I remember everything about you or what we went through before I lost my memory, but because it is in my very being to love you. We were always meant to be bound. By fate, by choice, by every power in the Nine."

Vali's eyes shut briefly, drinking her words. Everything he wanted and needed to hear at the worst possible time. "I am dying, Ailsa. Your power cannot change that. Why link yourself to my fate?"

"Did you not do the same?" she asked. "I'll give you the very life still spinning my thread if it means saving you. This is my choice. Do not take it from me."

His jaw clenched before relaxing, an entire war raging behind the shield of bronze in his eyes. Vali's hand skimmed the inner part of her forearm, caressing the gold gauntlets covering her skin.

"Ailsa, there is no thread of time I would not choose to be your *Fraendi*, that I would not love you. Even when the worlds burn to dust and all memory of this life fades, when everything that happened to us and the rest is a forgotten whisper in time, I will still love you."

He clasped his hand in hers, his fingers cold, grip weak. "I take you Ailsa Ledgersdóttir, to be my *Fraendi*." Vali's lips flashed a smile. "Again."

She ignored the approach of a horse to kiss his cold lips, copper filming his taste. He was fading, and they were dying. Ailsa could feel the ice in her fingertips even now. The rune on her hand hadn't even stained her skin yet.

"Ailsa! Vali!" Freya called from across the field. Her dark horse nearing them. Ailsa looked around, but Vidar had disappeared. No sign of him anywhere in the barren distance. The goddess dismounted in a rush, gold tears smeared down her cheeks. "Thank Ymir, you both are still alive. Where is Odin?"

"Dead," Ailsa said in a chilled voice.

Freya's eyes shut with unease. "And Fenrir?"

"Dead as well. Vidar, a son who Odin had kept hidden from the gods, slayed him after he watched his father be torn apart."

Freya cursed, scrubbing her face with a gloved hand. "For a god who knew everything about everyone else, he certainly had his secrets. We must wait to mourn the loss of the Aesir. Surtur is still on the march, and if he isn't stopped, he will burn the entire Tree down."

"Any ideas on how to do that?" Ailsa asked.

Her golden eyes looked off into the flames consuming the great city. Something shifting in them, a grimness not flattering on her face. "One. But I will need your help. Take my horse and get to the gates, then use your power to seal them shut."

"Seal them?" Ailsa asked to clarify. "But that would—"

"I know what it will mean for me," she said, still not meeting her gaze.

Ailsa swallowed the knot in her throat, reaching for her as she spoke, beckoning for her to come near once more. "Goddess."

Freya took her hand and knelt beside them both, wrapping her solid arms around Aila's trembling shoulders. "Do not weep for me, Weaver. Your tears will do you no good." She pushed away to look at her. "Get out as quickly as you can. The fire giants have already started to break down the wall, and if they finish, they can spread the Flame to every branch, and every part of the Tree. When those gates are sealed, I will make sure Surtur burns instead." She looked down at Vali and pulled a small vial from her pocket, her tears collected inside. "And give this to him. I'm not sure if it will help now, but it's worth a try."

Ailsa wiped her face and nodded, taking the tears. "Thank you for everything, Freya. I'll make sure they'll build you the largest altar when this is over."

She rose to her feet and smiled. "Just as long as it's bigger than Thor's."

Freya assisted her in getting Vali's body onto her horse, who had fallen back into his stupor. But sensing the horse beneath him, the elfin roused and gripped the reins. He found a new reserve of strength now that his core was whole again, and they had poured the tears of the goddess down his throat.

Freya stopped her with a hand on her shin, looking up as she said, "You know, I rarely use sedir to see into the future, but I have a strong feeling you and Vali will rewrite the stars tonight, Ailsa. Good luck."

She'd never cried in front of her sisters when they left for their raids. Ailsa always saved those tears for private. But saying goodbye to a divine who had filled the hole her own family left, the same rules she once lived by did not apply.

"You too, Freya. I will miss you."

Freya let go and slapped the horse on his backside to send them away.

⊹

The gate was in sight. Ailsa sat in front of Vali to let him lean against her back, his heart still thumping erratically as her pulse danced to the same tune. Freya's mare clamored down cobblestone roads that once paved the way through the god city. The buildings were reduced to ash and rubble. All that was once gold and glittering now black and charred.

But through the smoke and crimson haze, the wall of fire came to a breach. They would be through the gate in moments. Ailsa fought against the weakness creeping through her marrow as the rune bound their threads. She gripped Vali's arm tight around her waist; the strength left in his embrace encouraging.

"Ailsa." His voice like gravel in her ear. "Wolves. Behind us." Peeking over her shoulder, she discovered an entire pack of wolven on their trail, beginning to close in on them on either side. Vali said, "Lead them over the bridge. They'll tear us apart if we stop now. We'll have to come back for the gates."

"And what about the rest of them?" she asked, still staring down their pursuers.

Surtur was still destroying the center temple of Asgard, waving the Flame like a banner against the black sky. They were running out of time to escape the realm before he burned it down. Surtur's followers sensed this as well.

Rows of fire giants were fleeing the city, a crimson wave storming behind them.

Vali turned her head with his icy fingers to look ahead instead. "I will keep them back while you seal the gates. But we must close them, Ailsa. Even if it's the last thing we do together."

She could hardly see the burning walls holding up the scalded gates as tears blurred her vision. How she had any left in her heart was a wonder of its own. She squeezed his arm around her waist even tighter. "Together, then."

A wolf at her heel suddenly dropped. Another whimpered, crying out as something struck it, before falling behind with its kin. The high tune of an arrow cut the air to her left, sinking into another wolf until the pack number had diminished significantly. Ailsa followed the smoky trail of the arrow to a man standing on the remains of a scorched building. His lithe frame leaping from banister to balcony as he shot at the wolven on their heels.

"Who is that?" Ailsa asked, unable to make out his face through the smoke. His red hair the only discernible part of him as it floated upon the hot breeze with every swiftly loaded arrow on his bow.

The elfin behind her let loose a breath that shuddered like an incredulous laugh. "That's Enver, the Dark Elves Commander. Which means..."

He could hardly finish before the smoke thinned enough to reveal the gold and green chest plates of the Light Elves. An entire wall of them, wielding glossy onyx blades Ailsa had never seen before. She slowed their horse to a stop as the final wolf fled or perished—she didn't turn around to check which.

"Hold!" a voice shouted from the sidelines. A familiar face charging down the line to meet them in the sliver of space between fae and fire giants.

Seela.

Vali's relief couldn't be contained. His astonishment slipped from his chest on a choked cry out. "Seela!" he shouted, reaching for her as she approached them on horseback. Ailsa was relieved to see her as well, but even more so that they could see each other.

The commander's eyes were already shining with tears as she embraced him back. "You did it, Vali! You found her," she laughed, glancing at the incoming giants. "And you even brought down the Nine in the process, just as you vowed to do."

"Yes," he breathed. "But Seela, as glad as I am to see you, you must get your army out. We must seal the gates to contain Surtur's fire when Freya destroys him—"

"Then you will need us to hold back these beasts." She jutted a chin toward the red wave. "Go on, both of you. Between my legion and the frost giant lords, we will give you time to close the gates."

"Seela, you cannot stay—"

"My fae will not run, Vali." Her tone had dropped from playful to somewhere darker. Spoken like a true commander, and every bit as confident as one. "I know who I am now and why I am here. Do not be afraid for me or any of our people. We will fight until the Light takes us, or fate demands us to keep going."

Vali turned in the saddle, the giants nearly upon them now. His breath was fast at Ailsa's back, reluctant to leave her. "But," he stammered. "Seela, *no*."

The commander looked away, blinking quickly. Ailsa took

Vali's hand in her own and rubbed it knowingly. "Thank you, Seela," she told her. "Show them what wrath feels like."

She looked at her *Hjartablóds* one last time. "Take care of him, Ailsa," Seela said softly, before kicking off her horse and demanding her soldiers part for them.

A wolf appeared in the fold, icy blue eyes locked on Ailsa, wide with interest. Ailsa could only whisper the name to herself, *"Ivor,"* as the horse galloped past too quickly for anything more attentive.

"Stubborn fucking fae," Vali growled behind her as they moved on. "Why wouldn't she just retreat?"

Ailsa didn't answer him because it was futile. He knew why. She didn't have to explain Seela's reasoning behind her decision. But he was angry about it all the same. She smoothed a hand down his thigh and squeezed his knee, hoping it served some sort of comfort. Seeing Ivor there among the dedicated martyrs, she knew firsthand his heartache.

"Focus, Vali. Let's not let Freya's or Seela's sacrifice be in vain. If we do this right, we could save thousands more. That is why she is staying behind—so we don't have to."

He was quiet as they passed through a legion of elves standing side by side with frost giants. Some of the Jotun nearly four times the size of their own kind, sacks on their hips filled with boulders instead of blades.

When they finally made it to the front gates, Ailsa called on two of the massive Jotun to pull them shut for her, as Surtur had done good work on smashing the hinges into shambles. They did as she requested, pulling shut the groaning stone as it slid across the bridge leading into Asgard.

Silence fell. That same eerie quiet which soothed the world just before a storm. The same soundless warning as strong as any vow, settling over Ailsa and Vali as they caught their breaths. Neither speaking, words stolen in the calm.

Maintaining that quiet, Ailsa dismounted and approached the gates. She'd cut her hand on her blade, her palm smeared with power. But she was numb to the sting of the cut.

She was tired of this. Tired of this responsibility, the weight of what she was about to do, as it crushed her. A heaviness on her shoulders until she couldn't breathe. Her body shook with quiet sobs, hand braced on the stone door, unable to make the runes it took to seal them shut. Seal their friends, their family, *Hjartablóds* and *systirs*. Lock them all away to be burned.

And why did she get to stand on the outside? Because she was the master of fate? This power in her blood, it didn't make her special. She had done nothing to deserve it but survive a curse.

Vali pressed himself behind her. "I do not know the rune, *sváss*. I cannot draw it for you."

"I can't, Vali," Ailsa cried. "I can't seal their fates."

"You can," he said, threading his fingers behind her bloody ones. "You can, Ailsa. There is nothing I'm more certain about than this, that you were meant for this moment, and this moment is only yours to decide. You're about to write the fate of not just those inside these walls, but of all those who stand outside of it."

"I'm sorry," she spoke through a choked breath. "I wish I could have stopped this sooner, before it came to this."

Vali kissed her temple. "Every being that has ever existed is responsible for the events leading to this one. Hurry, Ailsa, before Surtur makes your decision for you."

She nodded, sucking a long breath, and began tracing the

rune to seal the doors shut forever. So no being, friend, or fire giant could escape.

The stone rumbled beneath her palm.

CHAPTER 48
SEELA

"Enver!"

As soon as the line between armies thinned to nothing and the battle engaged, Seela looked for the dark elf everywhere, searching for him before it was too late. She pushed her forces against the fire giants until the doors to Asgard sealed shut behind them.

Only then did she drop her fight, did she silently thank her people, *her* people, for trusting her enough to follow her here. To their end. Somewhere along the journey from being named regent to standing here, as High Commander of the Elves, did she actually believe she could do it. Did she finally believe in herself.

And she had—*damn* the audacity—a male to thank for that.

Ivor appeared at her side as she scaled a charred light pole. She asked the wolf, "Can you find him for me? I know the scents are many here, but can you find Enver?"

The wolf twitched her nose to the sky and whimpered. Seela's shoulders fell, her head pressed against the hot metal.

Of course, she couldn't. There were hundreds around her, clashing metal smothering her voice, scents blurring Enver's trail. She'd never find him in time.

Unless...

Seela reached down in her being once more, breaking her vow to never set that secret part of her free again. Especially not in Asgard. But the gods were probably dead by now, and so would she in a matter of moments. Did any of that really matter anymore?

A familiar light spilled from her core, where her pulse bounded as something poured into her blood. Light veined her arms, the skin across her back tightening and itching mercilessly as her wings unfurled. Though they weren't the white, sleeked, feathered kind the true Valkyrie donned. Hers were made of Light, reminding her she was not just one or the other, but she was both elven and Valkyrie.

There was power in finding acceptance from another, that much she learned from Enver. But to accept oneself, every pretty, damaged, and perhaps confusing part, that was how to become truly fearless.

There were whispers and mutters that drifted beneath the sounds of battle as she stood there, completely transformed and transparent. A circle formed around her, giving her space to glow. Only Ivor dared to remain where she was, large canine eyes reflecting Seela's bright image.

"Only one thing left to do, then. Face our foes and our fate with a blade in one hand," she looked at the wolf to her left, "and with a friend at my side."

Ivor slipped a low growl of approval.

Seela looked up to where Surtur and Freya were fighting on a bridge, the Flame in his hand thrashing at the goddess as she fought him with the dark magic of sedir and a sword of

ALEXIS L. MENARD

what appeared to be made of ice. His antithesis, her last challenger, the goddess sliced through his arm holding the Flame. And the world fell quiet as every being watched the Eternal Flame fall from his hand and toward the earth.

The ground shook as Asgard caught fire.

Seela snatched Ivor by the hide. "I know you hate flying, but you'll have to deal with it for a moment." The wolf whimpered but did not fight her as she lifted them both from the ground and to a higher point, where the bones of some old temple had not burned in the first assault stood in the center of a city square.

Fire spread like a breeze sweeping through. In an instant, the world was covered in a thick blaze. And even from several stories high, Seela felt her skin dry from the heat alone. Smoke rose in billowing columns, ashes of her enemies and her kin floated together and up into the dark heavens. She clung to Ivor as the fire spread beneath them, consuming the temple's foundation.

"I think..." Seela gasped on the heavy air. "I think I can get us over the wall."

"Seela!"

The elfin whirled her head toward her name, the only sound left in the world besides the brief cries of the beings below before it consumed them. And that's when she found him, Enver, dangling from a rafter that was just about to break. He couldn't have been over twenty yards away, and she saw every ounce of regret in his jewel eyes. Every word he wanted to say, that she had also left unsaid, hanging there like his very life.

That pain in his gaze would haunt her into whatever afterlife followed this.

Ivor whimpered in her grip. Seela looked at the wolf she

452

was still holding onto. She didn't have time to get to him. They all three knew it. Enver shouted through the smoke, "Fly high, sweetheart. Have a pint for me when you get back to Alfheim."

Tears pricked her sight, and Seela blinked them away so his face wouldn't blur. Ivor struggled in her grasp, fighting her now.

"Ivor, what are you doing? You're going to make me drop you!" she said. Seela would stay with Enver until the fire took him. She couldn't leave him alone to perish. But Ivor continued to fight her, thrashing her heavy body until she was slipping from Seela's sweaty fingers.

"Ivor, no!" Seela cried.

But the wolf bucked once more, and the elfin inevitably dropped her. Those frosty eyes never left her face until the flames embraced her, and Seela lost sight of the wolf, lost her friend forever.

A sound like lightning snapping from Enver's direction tore her gaze away from her empty hands. She had maybe heartbeats of time to get to him now, to make good on Ivor's sacrifice. The rafter he was hanging from cracked from the rising heat.

Seela spread her wings and dove, holding her breath as she cut through black smoke and the smell of burning flesh. The banister snapped, and Enver fell quiet, accepting his ending as he fell toward the all consuming Eternal Flame.

She collided with his body before the fire could so much as scorch him.

"Seela?" he mumbled into her neck as she held him tight against her. She gritted her teeth and pulled him close, fighting to fly upward against the heavy smoke clouds.

"*Gods below*, you are heavy," she slipped through her teeth.

ALEXIS I. MENARD

"And those walls are a lot taller than they look from down there."

Enver laughed, warm breath skimming the dampness coating her skin. "Touch the stars, Seela. You glow brighter than all of them now."

She couldn't say anything more until they ascended above the eastern wall, resting for a moment on a pillar to look down on the desolation below. Enver sat beside her to wipe her tears away, their legs dangling over the edge as she caught her breath between weak sobs.

"She knew I couldn't save you both," Seela said. "She sacrificed herself so I could get to you in time."

He pulled her against his chest, sparring her a strength she required. "And we owe her everything, sweetheart, but you do not owe her any guilt. She was a good friend to the very end."

Seela shook her head, not wanting to accept it. "Why do some people hide their good, Enver? Loki practically saved the fae realms from *this*, Angrboda stood for what was right even when it burned her in the end, and Ivor—" She couldn't finish, but Enver smoothed a hand down her spine, insisting he understood what she couldn't say.

"Some people don't need the glory that comes with goodness, Seela. That's what makes them the very best of beings."

The elfin shut her eyes on the burning world. It was over. Ragnarok had played out exactly how the fates had written, if not how the rest of them had imagined it to happen. The old worlds had fallen, but there was something new that had risen as well. And she believed it now lived in each of them, having witnessed the very best of beings forge the way ahead.

"I owe you a kiss," she whispered against his shoulder. "One minute, with tongue."

He tipped her chin to look him in the eyes, skimming her lips as he spoke, "You owe me nothing, sweetheart."

She hooked him by the neck anyway and gave him more than what was due. She was a star, the brightest and most brilliant in the sky. And she'd never stop burning. For Ivor, for the male against her lips, for her friends who had become true family, for the worlds she would help make anew.

Until the Light took her.

CHAPTER 49
AILSA

Winter had slipped away with the subtle nudge of Spring. Mani and Skoll had returned the sun and the moon to their places in the sky. Ailsa stretched her legs on a morning walk in the gardens weaving beside the Light Palace, desperate for the sunlight and the solitude. She had been sitting in meetings all morning, ones she mostly attended out of support for the new High Lady.

Seela and Enver had survived the fires of Asgard, the only ones. And seeing as neither Ailsa nor Vali could accept the throne now after what happened, the regent had dolefully accepted the title officially. It wasn't a position she had sought, but it was one she deserved more than anyone. Her actions and leadership at Ragnarok had defended her well enough that no fae questioned her ascension.

Asgard was gone, but from the ashes a new world had risen. One green and flourishing and ready to be tended into something of equal greatness by the gods who had survived. Vidar, who was no longer silenced thanks to the removal of Odin's runes, had somehow slipped from the fight and survived to see today. Baldur was set free by Hel, whose boundaries had finally lifted now that the one who cursed them was dead. The Vanir who protected Vanaheim had also endured. Hod, Thor's sons, Sigyn, and a few other goddesses had avoided the fire. This new Tree would still have gods, but ones with much different perspectives. Different ideals. And Ailsa thought the Nine could only be benefitted in this way.

"Ailsa, is that you?"

She turned to find a Jotun approaching her from the opposite side of a rushing fountain. A beautiful frost giant lord's wife, one of many that had come to discuss the future of the fae now that their husbands had perished. The curse on Jotunheim had died with Odin, the seals he created in every realm falling with them, and now the giants were free to roam and live like the rest of creation.

"Skiord," Ailsa said. A genuine smile lit her face as she strode to meet her embrace. "Were you in the hall before? I'm afraid I didn't see you."

She slipped from their hug but kept her fingers tenderly gripping Ailsa's shoulders. "It was quite crowded in there, and you had so many Jotun to speak with. I followed you out here, hoping to catch you before I returned home to my daughters."

"And I am so glad you did! It's wonderful to see you again. I hope your daughters are doing well after... after all that has happened." Ailsa's gaze dropped slightly in regret.

Skiord nodded. "Yes, they miss their father, but we know he died protecting our realm and our kind. All our kind. Might I ask you something?"

"Of course."

The giantess's eyes fell to Ailsa's stomach. A memory she remembered well now burned a new shame in her heart. She had been so kind and doting to her, and she had told the Jotun a vicious lie. "Oh, Skiord, I must apologize. When we needed shelter in your hall…"

She interrupted her apology by placing a hand on her lower belly, and Ailsa flinched, knowing she'd find her empty of any life beyond her own. But Ailsa wasn't prepared for the small smile that grew into a grin on her face, and suddenly she was no longer apologetic, but concerned by that intentional smile.

"I know you and Vali lied to us, Ailsa. Jotun like me, healers in your terms, have a sense about these things."

"And yet you still helped us?" she asked.

The giantess shrugged and folded her hands behind her back. "It takes fae magic to sense a babe, but none to know when two people are in love."

"We were hardly in love then." Ailsa laughed, remembering it all. She looked down at their new *Fraendi* mark, where the joining of their life threads had restored every lost moment between them—both good and bad.

"Perhaps not knowingly," Skiord said. "But when a man would do anything for a woman, including one desperate as Vali was to keep you safe, how could I turn you away?"

Ailsa broke eye contact with the giantess to stare at the fountain of the elven lord. "You're kind, Skiord. But we shouldn't have betrayed your trust."

The giantess grabbed her hand and stroked it with a thumb. "It all worked out in the end. Imagine where the Nine would be right now if you two hadn't found each other." Skiord dropped her hands and lifted her skirts to depart. "Or the life that would not be if I had turned you away like my husband would have preferred. Goodbye, Ailsa. Come use my hot spring anytime. It's quite safe for you."

Ailsa mumbled a goodbye but was hung on her words.

Before she left the gardens, she called out, "Skiord?" When the giantess turned her face, she asked, "Did you... Did you sense something when you touched me just now?"

Another quiet smile drifted across her profile. "You'll know soon enough. Good luck, Ailsa. It was a pleasure to see you again."

Ailsa demanded her heart to slow before she entered the former High Lady's chambers, taking large breaths to calm her nerves as she approached Rind's bedside. Vali was seated next to the bed, holding his mother's hand. The pair had drifted off to sleep after she left.

She assessed Rind's breathing, watching her breaths turn apneic, each further apart than the last. Ailsa placed another pillow below her head to help with the fluid in her throat, looking up to find Vali watching her.

"How much longer do you think?" he asked. His golden eyes were exhausted, dark circles stretching beneath them like shadows.

Ailsa sighed. "There's no telling exactly, but hours to days at the most."

Vali nodded, as if he had figured that much. "She woke up for a few minutes earlier. She was happy to see me, of course, but she said I looked different. Do I really look that strange with these ears?"

Ailsa grinned, pulling the blanket from his lap to seat herself there instead. She fingered the round edge of his ear where a sharp point used to peek through his hair. "You look different, but not in a bad way. You'll get used to your mortal appearance. The lack of magic, however, will be a little more difficult to manage."

He bit his lip, looking back at his sleeping mother. "Am I a bad person for not telling her?"

"What? That you were dying, and we bound our life threads for a second time? And since your thread was shriveling, your life latched onto my thread and now you are a mortal with no fae or god magic? Or the part where you cannot be High Lord because I ruined—"

His hand covered her mouth. "Don't you dare say you ruined anything for me, Ailsa. I am only alive right now because of your love for me. I don't regret losing a single thing. It is but another grand adventure I get to experience with you."

She sighed a breath of relief, glad to hear him say so. She wondered if perhaps he wasn't happy with the way things turned out. Standing from the chair, she asked, "Come with me on the balcony for a moment?"

He followed her out, heading straight to the railing to take in the full view of Alfheim. The lands he grew up expecting to rule one day, and now never would. "There hasn't been a day since I loved you that I wouldn't have traded all of this in a heartbeat for your hand, Ailsa."

He snatched her into his side and said, "When my mother passes, we will give her a proper funeral and see that Seela is set up nicely before we leave. Then we can travel to the mortal realm and live out the rest of our days together. I'll build you a longhouse on a foggy fjord, and you'll be my lady until my mortal heart stops beating and these human lungs fail."

"That sounds perfect, *Sólskin*. You just might need to add one little detail." She turned in his arms, holding his face in her hands as she watched it frown in confusion.

"What else do you want from me? Name it and I'll see it happen."

Mimir's Well had told the Nine that at the end of Ragnarok, two mortals would survive and replenish the human realm of all that was destroyed. Ailsa never thought fate would lead her back home, but it was funny in that way, always twisting in ways she least expected—even as its master, if there could ever be such a thing.

"Just make sure you add enough bedrooms. My sisters had to share one and they nearly burned our longhouse down three times. And..." she stumbled on the next words, unsure of how to say them, "and you might want to start on them sooner than you think."

Vali blinked several times, as if trying to decode the meaning dangling between her words. But then his eyes widened, suddenly understanding. Those gold eyes—thank the fates he had kept from his former thread—lit up like the first sunrise after Ragnarok. The same sun that would shine upon her every day for the rest of their fleeting lives.

"You're sure?" he asked.

Ailsa nodded. "Skiord mentioned it when I saw her earlier. I went to Greer right after to confirm." With everything that was happening in Muspell and Ragnarok, she completely forgot her contraceptive rune had faded. But Vali didn't seem displeased by the slip in the slightest. He pulled her tight into his chest, and she listened to his heartbeat fly—with fear or nerves or joy, she felt them all speed her own as well.

"I love you, Ailsa. I don't know what fate has in store for us tomorrow, but I trust the ones who hold our life thread."

"Aye, Vali, they seem to know what they are doing."

Laughter from his chest shook her cheek. Or was he hiding his tears? Ailsa didn't remove herself from his arms to find out.

461

"Vali!" Seela joined them on the balcony. Ailsa hadn't even heard her enter the bedroom. "Not to disturb you, but Lady Rind is awake, and she is asking for you both."

He kissed the top of her head and took her hand, leading her into the High Lady's chambers as Seela ducked back inside.

"Well?" he asked. "Shall we go tell them?"

Ailsa beamed at him. "Lead the way, *elskan min.*"

THE END

GLOSSARY

This story contains many names and places from Norse Mythology, most of which I chose to Anglicize for easier readability. With that being said, some of these terms may appear differently in other works and retellings. Below I have listed a glossary of people and places included in this story. For my research I used the *Prose Edda* by Snorri Sturluson, translated by Jesse Byock by Penguin 2006. I also used the *Poetic Edda*, translated by Benjamin Thorpe by Corundum Classics.

Aesir- One of the two tribes of Norse Gods. They reside in Asgard and are associated with war and knowledge.
Balder- son of Odin. Known to be the strongest and best of the Aesir. Loki became jealous and tricked the blind god, Hoder, into killing him.
Bifrost- the rainbow bridge leading to Asgard

Fenrir- the giant wolf, son of Loki and Angrboda. Fated to devour Odin at Ragnarok

Frey/Freya- brother and sister in Norse Mythology, come from the Vanir tribe. Associated with fertility.

Frigg- wife of Odin. Goddess of fertility

Gullveig- a mysterious witch, also known as the "gold witch." According to the Völuspá, is known to be the source of conflict between the Aesir and the Vanir

Heimdall- the watchman who guards the Bifrost. Son of Odin.

Hel- the goddess who rules the underworld, Helheim, where those who died of sickness or old age reside. She is the daughter of Loki and Angrboda. Half her body is rotten flesh.

Jormungand- the Serpent of Midgard. Circles the world and is fated to be freed during Ragnarok. Son of Loki and Angrboda

Jotun- the race of giants, enemies of the Aesir.

Loki- a trickster figure, father of Fenrir, Jormungand, and Hel. Can shape-shift and often uses his ability to cause mischief.

Norns- most powerful entities in the universe. Weave the tapestry of fate beneath the World Tree. They create and control fate for all beings, including the gods.

Odin- Also known as the Allfather, he is the highest of the Norse gods and has two ravens that circle the worlds.

Ragnarok- the final battle between the gods. Many of the Aesir gods are predicted to fall, but out of the ending of the old world, a new one will be born.

Skuld- Norn who weaves the fates of the future

Thor- god of sky and thunder

Tyr- god of war whose hand was bitten off by Fenrir.

Valhalla- a literal translation of "hall of the slain" where warriors who died in battle reside. Watched over by Odin.

Each day begins with a battle in preparation for Ragnarok and ends with a great feast.

Vali- son of Odin and (in Norse Mythology) the giantess, Rind. Was said to have been created to seek revenge for Balder's death.

Vanir- one of the two tribes of gods. Reside in Vanaheim and known for their association with wealth and fertility

Volva- a seeress. Usually female practitioners of magic and foretell events.

ACKNOWLEDGMENTS

Thank you to each and every reader who picks up this book. It is an honor to have my story in your hands and I hope you enjoyed it as much as I enjoyed writing it. Writing a retelling based off of mythology is something I took very seriously, because I wanted to make sure the core parts of the stories belonging to Norse Mythology remained true while also giving the reader a fresh adventure and fun experience.

I finished writing The Last Daughter when I found out I was pregnant with my second child. I finished writing The Silent Son two weeks before I delivered. So many of my fears, insecurities, and life lessons from those nine months were poured into this story. This saga ends in a way a chapter of my own life closed, and I think you'll understand what I mean when you read the ending! It was completely intentional to end this duopoly with the start of Ailsa and Vali's new adventure, and something that was very important to my journey as a mother.

To my children, you won't get to read this until your much, much older. But thank you so much for being my motivation and part of my team. You're both too young to realize that you are the reason I stay up past your bedtime to write these stories, why I wake up before you to edit. Writing stories in the beginning was just for me, but when I realized you were watching, I wanted to pursue my dream with everything I had. I hope you grow up to discover that dreams can come true if we have the courage to pursue them (my favorite quote from Walt Disney).

To my family, thank you for reading these books. To my husband, thank you for giving me the time out of our very busy lives to pursue this dream. To my friends, thanks for meeting me in coffee shops to discuss plot holes, spicy books, and morally grey men. (I'm looking at you Brittany.)

To my bookstagram community, the booktok friends, and everyone I've met through socially media across the globe, know that your support is heard, seen, and appreciated. I wouldn't be here today without you, and I am humbled you took a chance on this indie writer and gave this saga the life it needed.

This is the end of this saga, but it has been a beautiful adventure.

Til Valhal
Alexis L. Menard

ABOUT THE AUTHOR

Alexis Menard is a fantasy romance author and happily ever after enthusiast. She lives in Hammond, Louisiana with her husband, toddler, and two dogs. She graduated from Southeastern Louisiana University in nursing. She enjoys long walks through the Renaissance Fair, reading smutty romance into the dark hours of the night, and wine nights with her "Finer Things Club." She hopes to enrich the lives of her readers with worlds they can both escape in and take with them long after the final chapter.

MORE BOOKS YOU'LL LOVE

If you enjoyed this story, please consider leaving a review.
Then, check out more books by Midnight Tide Publishing

WOLVES OF ADALORE
BY MORGAN GAUTHIER

Niabi killed for it once and is prepared to kill again.

Crispin wants it and is determined to have his revenge.

Salome wants nothing to do with it, but has to fight for it.

After years of people insisting she must be cursed due to her discolored left eye, Salome starts to believe they might be right. But when Harbona the Seer unexpectedly visits her, he reveals not only has the Year of the Hunter begun, but Salome's distorted eye is in actuality the Mark of the Hunter, and she is charged to avenge the blood of the innocent.

With the Immortal Seer, their axe-wielding guardian, and a dangerous bounty hunter known as the Wanderer in their company, Salome and her brother, Crispin, embark on a journey to defeat their sister and reclaim the White Throne.

Made in United States
Orlando, FL
22 June 2023

34434281R00288